SHATTERSTEEL

BENJANUN SRIDUANGKAEW

ISBN 978-1937009-97-7 (TPB)

Also available as a DRM-free eBook.

Apex Publications, PO Box 24323, Lexington, KY 40524

Visit us at www.apexbookcompany.com.

To my huntress, who's watched these books grow from a small thing to an entire trilogy.

THREE TO PART

THE PROSTHETIC ARM NEVER SEATS QUITE RIGHT, DESPITE countless adjustments. The court chiurgeon has insisted that it is as flush as it can be, as well-connected to the rest of Nuawa as any prosthesis possibly can, but she still finds it strange, discomfiting. She looks down at it now. In appearance, it is nearly impossible to distinguish from flesh, and the seam where it joins her elbow is slim and smooth, easy to hide under clothes. Its tactility is another matter: when she touches it with her good hand—her normal hand—the surface of it is like silk on ceramic. Far too frictionless to be true.

She inhales and concentrates. The fingers twitch, insect-like. There is an instant of revulsion, visceral and nauseating, where the movement does not match what she feels—which is nothing at all at the best of times, a lancing ache at the worst—and the motion does not seem like it belongs to her. And it does not, after all. The chiurgeon told her that to move this false limb takes the same act of will that allows her to engage with the thaumaturgic force of her sword or even her calling-glass. But those things are effortless, have always been. This is agonizing, like moving underwater or trying to run in a nightmare. The pit of her stomach pulls and her breath quickens. Little by little the fingers clench into a fist.

It is marginally easier after that. She raises the arm, and it goes halfway up; progress. Exhaling, she flexes the fingers, then uses them to pick up a block of wood she's procured for such exercises. She does not trust the prosthesis yet with anything more delicate, anything that requires finer control. No pens, barely utensils, and no weapons. The most she can eat with that hand is flatbread. Her shoulder throbs.

A knock on her door. Guryin enters without waiting for her to answer.

Nuawa schools her face, her composure, her voice. She lets the prosthesis fall to her side. "What would you have done if I'd been indecent, Major?"

"Cover my eyes and beg forgiveness, naturally. It would not do to tarnish the modesty of a bride." The major is in dress uniform—a first for xer that Nuawa has seen—freshly laundered, crisp as paper; xe wears a generous helping of gold and black pearls at xer earlobes and xer throat. Expensive, given how far Kemiraj is from the source of their harvest. "Fortunately you're perfectly covered. About all ready?"

She is not. Dressing herself has been a trial, but she came to an arrangement with the tailor to make every lacing and button accessible from the front, and more importantly, possible to do up one-handed. Jewelry is easy, as she wears only the hyacinth and a bracelet on her flesh wrist, and a servant has been in to brush her hair into sleekness and pin it. But cosmetics have been chancier. "I can't paint my eyes." Even admitting this exposes her more than she would like, so much so she did not say it to the servant.

"Ah! My favorite. These are the colors you've picked?" Xe motions at the pots of pigment on the dresser. "Fantastic."

Whatever else the major's other faults—like barging in—xe is deft with the brush: pewter pigment on Nuawa's eyelids then black along the line of her upper lashes, drawn slightly upward and ending in a sharp point. A touch of stardust white on her philtrum and then the midpoint of her bare lips. Guryin stands back and grins. "Very striking. You look like Raam the hunter god, girded to best a wild and peerless beast."

Nuawa glances at her reflection, but no more than a glance. She doubts most hunter gods are one-armed. "I'm appreciative, Major. I don't think you came just to make sure I look presentable, though. I was hardly going to run away from my own wedding."

Xe tuts. "Of course not, though I *am* miffed you're getting wedded before I do, but who am I to resent young love?"

She doesn't point out that the major is, at most, two or three years her senior, and Lussadh is considerably older than them both. Instead, she eyes the clock. It is nearly time and with Guryin here, she is, indeed, unable to escape. Her composure used to be second nature, faultless steel. Now all there is are fault lines. One more time she makes her false hand move: it spasms a little, but it does approximate what she wants it to do—she should be able to handle cups without embarrassing herself. Her temple pulsates with the effort.

It is informal, especially compared to what is customary for Kemiraj royalty. Guryin stands in as Nuawa's kin, escorting her into one of the palace's smaller feast halls. The corridor has been decorated for the occasion, jasmines and rice grains painted gold strewn on the ground, symbols of good auspices in Sirapirat weddings. Yellow tapestries cover the walls, the Kemiraj color for matrimony.

Guryin precedes Nuawa into the hall, brandishing a bronze goblet. "I am the keeper of jasmines! I demand my tribute."

Ulamat strides forward, filling the cup with cactus claret— pungent with desert flowers, the rich red of lynx blood. Guryin hands the goblet to Nuawa; she holds it in both hands with more care than she's ever held any cup. On the other side of the room, Colonel Imsou calls out, "I am the keeper of rice! I demand my tribute." Their cup is filled with rice wine the gold of sunlight on topaz and then passed to Lussadh.

Nuawa's breath judders and for a moment she forgets the strain of the prosthesis. It is not as though she has never seen Lussadh in full glory, dressed for a feast. Yet this exceeds even that sight. The general is in a dress of citrine threads worked in starburst lattices, clinging to her chest tattoo-close, and flares into a skirt like spun candle flame. Her face is nearly unadorned save for the whorl of gold on one cheekbone and the sheen of precious metals on her eyelashes. She glides into the hall in splendor and Nuawa can see why the al-Kattan dynasty was said to be of the sun: incandescent, deific.

"The tribute has been given," Guryin declares. "I entrust Nuawa Dasaret to her intended, Lussadh al-Kattan."

"The tribute has been given—" This from Imsou. "I entrust Lussadh al-Kattan to her promised, Nuawa Dasaret."

They move toward each other, meeting in the center of the hall. Nuawa's heart drums madly as she tips her cup against the general's lips. Lussadh drinks then presses the rice wine to Nuawa's mouth.

Someone is singing. All Nuawa can hear is the roar of her own pulse. The wine tastes of burnt copper and vertigo and limbic dissolution.

From the alcove that must have once been the domain of a priest, the Winter Queen strides, a monster in white that owns all she looks upon and is pleased about the fact. She is smiling and the glint of her teeth is nightmare-bright. She closes her fingers over Nuawa's and Lussadh's. When her hand leaves, there is a thread of red frost joining their wrists, impossibly fragile and perfect as rubies.

"You are hereby pronounced lord and consort," the queen says in a voice that carries to the hall entire. Muted applause from the other glass-bearers. "I entrust you now to one another."

ONE

IN THE BED, NUAWA CRIES OUT. SHE ARCHES, SHUDDERING, all of her drawn taut to the cusp of *snap*.

Her vision clears, though the wine—more than the pledge wine, the wine she drank after and lost count of—still simmers in her, marching through her blood to a drumbeat all its own. She exhales. Beneath her, Lussadh lies spread like an offering, eyes gleaming and skin like metal: the sheen of fever, or lust, or both. The general is still firm inside her, and Nuawa holds herself there a little longer while the last pulses of release subside.

Another inhalation and she pulls herself off—a soft wet noise —and rolls to her side, holding out one arm. "Come to me, General."

And Lussadh does, eyes never leaving Nuawa. The distance closes. The general pushes inside her and Nuawa curls her leg around Lussadh's waist, locking her in place. She moves, guiding the pace. Even so, each motion is a shock; she's raw still, all engorged nerves, and the general fills her deep.

"Nuawa," Lussadh whispers. Her climax is seismic and Nuawa holds on as the general buckles, pouring into her like an avalanche.

They pant into the sheets, into each other's skin. Lussadh reaches down, strumming between Nuawa's thighs, drawing a noise out of her. "No more," Nuawa says, hoarse, though she is tempted. "I'd take you again and again if I could. Though now we have a proper conjugal bed—we've anointed it as such."

The general slips out of Nuawa and laughs. "Ah, that means we must anoint everything else too, for a complete set. A conjugal chair, a conjugal dining table, a conjugal wall."

"I've never seen you so happy, my commander. It makes me want to capture your joy and wear it in a vial over my heart."

Lussadh touches the silver anthurium at her breast that Nuawa commissioned for her not so long ago. Like everything else it is sweat-damp. "I have every reason to be happy. I'm surrounded by friends, I married a woman I adore, the day is full of blessings, and we've just fucked gloriously. When you walked into that hall, all I could think of was the silk and velvet falling off you. I'd seize what it unsheathes, and you would fill my hands like a dangerous, exquisite light. But the reality of you always exceeds my imagination."

Nuawa glances at the crumpled clothing—Lussadh's in a puddle, hers disassembled and scattered on the sheets and the floor and the backs of chairs. Her disrobing was done in steps, pulled off one by one, partly by herself, partly by Lussadh. The structured bodice in indigo, the close-cut trousers brightened at the hip and waist with silver coils, the shirt in alabaster silk. Then she turns back to the general. Where she has gripped Lussadh with her false hand, a vivid mark has formed. Hip, shoulder. "I've bruised you."

"Nothing I won't survive, and you've left more on me before. You owe me some ointment."

"I'll personally nurse every blemish I've left. With my mouth, if necessary; I hear wounds can be kissed into healing." She reaches to part the curtains: there is still some afternoon left, incongruous next to what they've been doing, all these visceral acts meant for the dark. It feels like a full evening ago since they left the wedding feast, Lussadh carrying her part of the way and Nuawa keeping her face turned inward so she could pretend the Winter Queen was not there. Guryin sang at the top of xer lungs as the procession moved to the bedroom Nuawa and Lussadh share. An islander marriage ditty, though no one else understood it except Guryin's betrothed Imsou—judging by them turning crimson, the lyrics were especially lascivious.

It has merely been hours, two or three. Nuawa's sense of time has run away from her. But she is sober now, and it is no longer possible to pretend she is in thrall to the wine, to the headiness, to the escape represented by the hidden places of Lussadh's body. Carnal indulgence can only go so far, for all that they are both in possession of exceptional stamina. She feels the general's gaze on her, imagines what Lussadh sees. A person not quite whole, a silhouette not quite right. Still, there was no disgust, no flinching from the part of Nuawa that's no longer flesh.

Her shoulder twitches. The prosthesis moves with it, but in the way of deadweight, limp now that she's no longer focusing on it. She looks for a robe and throws it on, to cover the false limb more than for modesty.

"The chiurgeon is optimistic that you'll be able to use it as naturally as your other hand." Lussadh sits up, cross-legged. "And they're honest with their prognosis, I can tell you that, actually brutally blunt. I've seen them tell a dying man he had no hope and he'd best get his will and testament in order. Not a minced word."

Nuawa lets out a chuckle, involuntary. "They do seem the type. I'll trust in their wisdom." She approximates what it would be like if all this is true—the marital bliss, the completion. All she requires is to perform the part, match the motions to the image. She will do it well. This entire time she's been able to; why not longer, one day at a time. "Do we have anything else to see to? Beyond registering as spouses on the census. I admit these things have never crossed my mind, and so—"

"A few legalistic matters. I'll have clerks sent for, but we should come to an agreement as to our personal property."

"I own very little." Her thought bends homeward, to Sirapirat, to what she left behind. "A countryside house of unimpressive size and the land it's on. I've been thinking of selling it, but haven't had the time to contract any broker to manage or even appraise the matter. Or I could keep it—who knows, it might appreciate in value one day—but I don't intend to live there."

No question from Lussadh as to why. The fiction that Indrahi was Nuawa's aunt rather than mother has held, and not a particularly kind aunt. "What's yours will remain yours; by Kemiraj terms, these things are not automatically joined. By my preference, you're entitled to a good deal of my resources. Settlement of assets and so forth is determined at separation to account for each partner's financial circumstances."

"Romantic," Nuawa says blandly. "But practical. I can't believe you studied law too, though I shouldn't be surprised. Was there a subject your education didn't cover?"

"Agriculture, acrobatics, how to be married. It was thought too frivolous a subject since Kemiraj kings didn't necessarily take consorts and could rule alone if they wished. I don't know how to paint. Ah, and I didn't learn engineering."

Something has caught the general's eye. Nuawa follows the direction of Lussadh's gaze. In the courtyard, a contraption has been wheeled out: a bright metal base mounted by a replica of the god-engine Vahatma. Colonel Imsou oversees—they are one of the queen's court mathematicians and has a more intimate knowledge of the project than any other glass-bearer. The contraption is fed a few ghosts. It lights up and levitates a meter off the ground, though not for long. A test, though she can't begin to guess what.

Nuawa watches and feels, again, that unreality—the impression that she is falling, that the ground beneath her has heaved and upended her with it. She is no closer to discovering what the queen means to do with Vahatma. Much of the proceeding has been redirected to Imsou, and she hasn't been able to meet Penjarej for months. The queen may own Nuawa's soul but evidently does not trust that Nuawa might not turn traitorous, given a little information.

Ferreting out the true point of this and finding a way to thwart it, is one of the few things that keep Nuawa from putting a bullet in her own head.

The general steps behind her and wraps an arm around Nuawa. All igneous nakedness, scented by what they've been doing together. Nuawa lets herself soften, settling into Lussadh's hold. This too, she will concede, stands between her and that bullet. Not just the queen's secrets alone. Like all else it is conditional; Lussadh is conditional. But here, for now. Her anchor.

When Lussadh finds her, the Winter Queen is sitting with two snow-maids curled up at her feet like cats. She is eating souls frozen into cubes, nibbling and licking them as though they are fruits she does not relish, but which she must consume out of necessity.

"My queen. I've never seen you bring so many handmaidens here." Normally the queen is spare when she comes to Kemiraj, careful with expenditure of power.

The queen absently strokes the head of one handmaiden and swallows down the last of the ghost. She does not take them the way machines do—engines aspirate ghosts in the form of smoke —but in a manner of her own, solids and occasionally liquids to be sipped from small cups. "To this day this land rejects me, remains the one territory of mine that seems bent to unseat what I am. But I prove ascendant yet. Congratulations on your nuptials, my treasure."

She is sensitive to her queen's moods and there is something secret to the queen's smile, something hidden. "You're happy for me."

"I am, entirely; did I not officiate? Your bride intoxicates you, and if she commands the lion's share of your affections that is only to be expected, her being so novel."

"You intoxicate me as much as she. I'm fortunate to have the joy of you both." Lussadh seats herself by the queen, at the small, tidy desk. The queen doesn't often take a room of her own—she doesn't need to sleep—but this visit to Kemiraj is a longer one for her, and Lussadh's suite is otherwise occupied. One of the hand-maidens shifts aside to make room. Lussadh lifts the queen's hand and scrapes her teeth across pale, perfect knuckles.

The queen shuts her eyes and cranes her neck back, smiling. "It is not simply her personal appeal. The shard of my mirror inside her is exceptional and, what's more, exceptionally drawn to yours. Those two must've been of a piece, laid close to the core. You're compelled toward her more than any other glass-bearer, yes? More than any of your human lovers? You must have pressed her face down into the mattress countless times, not letting her up until she's full of your seed and her skin is a study of your teeth."

"I—yes."

"Splendid." The queen opens her eyes. A patch of frost has budded on the chair and floor, spreading where they touch her skin, a sheen finer and crisper than any jeweler can impart. "I would have you myself this very instant—the thought of it, the wicked music I could pluck out of you. But our great labor calls. Look at this." She lifts her hand from the desk, unveiling an ice miniature.

The model is no larger than Lussadh's hand. Flawless, down to the smallest detail. The god Vahatma sits cradled in gleaming petals. In its lap, a tall cage rests, the bars set close together and the roof tapered like the head of a shark—feral elegance. "You've still not told me what it is."

"It's something I have wanted to make for a long time, but there was always the question of power. Vahatma is an immaculate apparatus. It requires few ghosts and little outside fuel now that it's been brought back to life. This cage is decoration; the true cage is Vahatma itself, and what it will contain shall be a thing of wild puissance. What do you know of Yatpun?"

That is not a turn Lussadh anticipated. In the years they've known each other, Yatpun hasn't come up. The queen has been reticent about her homeland, and Lussadh has been content not to pry. She understands the virtue of leaving the past where it belongs. "I know what you have told me. Otherwise, I know that it's an island, impossible to reach." Many expeditions have attempted; none have returned.

"Yes, and Yatpun isn't truly its name—that is what a scholar in Qingyuan came up with, not that it matters. What surrounds my homeland is a stretch of frozen time. All that passes through it slows, then slows again. Perhaps the first explorers from this side of the world are still in there, and in a thousand-thousand years they'll breach Yatpun's shores at last." The queen gestures as though to dismiss the eventuality as preposterous. "The god-engine is capable of miracles. One needs only to give the correct command, arrive at the right formula. Vahatma can fold distances. It can become a gate through which I pluck a fruit I've long coveted."

She stares at the miniature, at what it promises. All this time the queen has kept her purposes close to her chest. "You mean you want to…?"

A cool finger on her lips. "Let us not speak of it yet; saying something aloud imbues it with a certain substance. I will say only that my methods have altered due to complicating factors, but my final objective remains the same. To become equal to those who made me. To ensure my siblings, what's left of them, become free. That was my promise to them long ago. Ah. I nearly forgot." From the folds of her robes, she draws a torque of white gold. The band is wide, engraved with a feather motif, and at the center is a single fire opal. Immense and sanguinary, its flame incandescent. "My wedding gift for Nuawa."

Lussadh takes the torque and smiles, teasing. "And for me, my queen?"

"Patience." The queen cups Lussadh's chin, curving her palm around it as if it is precious glass. "Yours will be far more special, far more excellent, the dearest gift I've ever fashioned. It just takes a little longer to perfect."

TWO

THE SIGHT OF A HOUND BOUNDING TOWARD HER IS NOT QUITE what Nuawa expected when she comes to the palace gate. The animal lopes with such vigor and strength that it drags along its master, a broad-chested person in uniform with limbs like trees. He is older, gray-haired, a fact that comes as a surprise—she assumed all glass-bearers would be like Lussadh, well-preserved, nearly ageless. But perhaps Captain Durgesh was discovered late in life, or else the mirror shard doesn't necessarily hold mortality at bay in all bearers. He is laughing, good-natured, jogging to keep up with the dog.

He reaches her. Unclips the hound's leash and motions it to run, before saluting Nuawa. The laughter has disappeared. "Lieutenant Nuawa. I've heard much about you. We haven't met."

"The pleasure's all mine, Captain Durgesh." Not a governor but commander of the garrison in Jalsasskar, modest in title and status among senior glass-bearers: by choice, she hears. "It looks like we're all here." Of those that have been summoned—she knows a few bearers have been left out, for reasons discernable only to the queen.

"Imsou and Guryin were some of the first, I take it—ever

punctual, those two, and inseparable. And you, you're the general's consort, I understand." He appraises her, not quite looking up and down, but he does not hide that he's taking her measure. Piece by piece, slotting each attribute into calculation: the way she bears herself, the breadth of her shoulders, the physical space she occupies. Perhaps even her name is under scrutiny, the way it rises and falls on the tongue, the muscles one needs to engage to pronounce it. Like anyone in winter, he has certain notions about Sirapirat and all who hail from it. "I apologize I wasn't able to attend the joyous event."

Nuawa has the clear impression that he intentionally did not attend. "A beautiful dog." She nods at the beast running laps about the courtyard, no doubt having pent-up energy for days on the train. "I've never seen its like."

And she hasn't. In shape, it resembles a wolf, but no wolf is quite this massive—its head might come up to her stomach or even her chest—and its coat is pure, like the skin of a glacier. Charcoal muzzle, amber eyes, legs built for endless distances, and sudden pounces. Where the light strikes its coat, opalescent glimmer answers, faint blue. Unbidden, her sight shifts to glassy vision she now suspects is linked to the shard; through that filter, Tisui is a living, blue-white pyre.

"Her name is Tisui. A gift from the queen." He puts his fingers to his mouth and lets out a whistle.

The hound returns to his side. Now it is calm, crouching low, panting slightly and alert. Nuawa knows the queen does not breed or keep animals of any kind. From its coloring—no natural crossbreed can possibly be this color—it must be artificial somehow, muscles and coat and teeth spun from ice like the queen's snow-maids. Or else it was a normal beast once, transformed by the queen's touch. Impossible to guess either way. It meets her gaze, placid.

Nuawa looks up from the dog. "Shall I show you to your room?"

"No need, Lieutenant. I've been here before."

Despite herself, this dismissal gets under Nuawa's skin. People have tried to kill her, sometimes on sight, but she has never been so thoroughly snubbed by a complete stranger. "Nevertheless. There have been some changes to the general's wing of the palace, and her aide is otherwise preoccupied. You must let me show you hospitality."

"If you wish," he says. A slight tensing of his jaw. "I have some idea of what happened here. Much might have gone differently if the general had had more people to protect her."

The implication that Nuawa failed Lussadh against the Heron. Which she did, and at the time she did not care until she saw the general hemorrhaging on the ground. "She does not, by and large, require protection. In fact, she would find the thought insulting."

"Yet she was in extreme peril. She is mighty, not invincible, and one of our duties is to defend her. With our lives, if needs must. But congratulations, Lieutenant, on your matrimonial accomplishment."

She keeps her smile on, stiff, not rising to the bait. For the rest of the way, they do not speak.

Once she's seen the back of Durgesh, she retreats to Lussadh's sparring room, a place accessible only to her and the general. Private and unfurnished save for racks of weapons and a row of practice mannequins quiescent in the corner. She finds a likely one, a stocky model with thick limbs and a passing resemblance to Durgesh, and turns the key on its back. It convulses and twitches into motion.

She plucks a wooden sword from the rack. The mannequin comes at her, swinging with a blunted iron blade. Easy to deflect even with her false hand, and soon she finds her balance, her rhythm. It feels good to be exerting herself again, to make use of her body, to feel the pull of her muscles and the stretch of her limbs. In this routine even the prosthesis feels right, weightless, an extension of her finally. The mannequin steps up and she matches its pace. Thought stops; she is motion, parrying, answering strike with strike. Her feet are unmoored, on air, her movements effortless. All of her coordinates.

A muscle twitches and jumps—her elbow, where flesh ends and artifice begins. She stumbles and the mannequin swipes, the tip of its mock weapon raking hard across her stomach. Nuawa is on the floor, from the shock more than the pain. The mannequin steps back, goes still now that its opponent has fallen.

Slow applause from behind her. She gets up quickly—she will face this on her feet.

The queen sits in a throne of her own making, solid ice the color of clear steel, high-backed and immaculate. Frost brush-strokes run across her body, water frozen mid-cascade covers her hips and frazils glitter in the black river of her hair. It is ostentatious, a statement that even in Kemiraj, she may manifest this, squander power as the mood strikes her.

"That's going to turn into a small lake once it melts. The servants will have a difficult time cleaning this up." Nuawa does not extend an honorific. The queen knows where she stands; in private, all dissembling is moot.

"You've grown insolent." This is not said as though she takes genuine offense. If anything, she sounds indulgent, as she would when humoring a child's rebellious temper. "But there's honesty to you. What was once hidden is now worn plain and bared. You don't have to put up with this clumsy device, you realize? I can craft for you a new limb or—if you'd be still for a minute—force your body to grow a new one. Flesh and bone, all yours, just like the one you were born with. My mirror's completely enmeshed in your muscles and marrow. It will be simplicity itself to heal such a trivial injury."

Nuawa returns the wooden sword to its place. She stands there, considering the rest of the rack—long, blunt staves; spears without hafts; clubs; short blades. Nearly anything imaginable has been included here, just as the mannequins available come in every build. Diminutive or statuesque, thin or wide. Any permutation of combat can be recreated, albeit in a safer, more flattened form. Lussadh told her this was where she practiced as a child. "I regretfully decline." The thought of lying on a slab, her body open to the queen's surgical ministrations. Her stomach does not heave up her breakfast, but it gets close.

"I'm not going to do to your arm what the Heron did." A slight pause, sly. "I have no need to, and you do make Lussadh very happy—that commands its own price, and for the time being I'll pay. No doubt she would enjoy you better if you weren't wallowing in this ridiculous mortal misery."

"I appreciate the thought. Nevertheless, I must say no."

The queen leans forward, and her neck seems a little too long, a little too flexible. The way a bird's might be. "What is it that you fear? That I would reach all the way inside you, stroke a nerve here, readjust a chamber there, and spin the pivots of your heart? Do you imagine I could make a captive of your mind overnight so that you wake from your dreams and believe I'm the rightful altar at which you must kneel after all? Even the gods cannot accomplish such a tall order. Memory and belief are complex things."

The weapon rack, absurdly, makes Nuawa feel safer. They are symbols. In practical terms, they're all useless, but they represent what she is, what she has been made for when that ghost-kiln forged her. What she could still do. "Was there anything else you wanted of me?"

"I want you to swear that you will protect my general."

This catches her off guard. She studies the queen, the sculpted face, the eyes like lightning gouging the dark. It is not idle words the queen is looking for: this is more and the queen has been negotiating for it, offering her this and that, the promise of making her whole. "In both words and action, I have strived to do so."

"That was not always the case, isn't that so? She is the fetters by which you may be bound now, but when you set out to destroy me, no doubt you thought of her as a bridge to cross.

One to annihilate, if you believed that might hurt me." Factual, not gloating. "It stands to reason I would want reassurance. And I do want it with some urgency, considering what has recently transpired."

No threat delivered, though it is never absent — by merely being here the queen implies it, that she can expose Nuawa any time and order Lussadh to execute her. She bargains from a position of strength. Will it be easy for the general, Nuawa wonders; do the fetters bind both ways — but she cannot test out that hypothesis and is pressed for time. "If you wish." She says it as if it doesn't mean anything. "I pledge to keep General Lussadh safe from harm to the best of my ability."

"And to preserve her life?"

"And to preserve her life," she says. "To the best of my ability." Not *at all costs.*

The queen runs her hand across the armrest of her throne. "That will do." The frost blisters, turning blue where she has touched it and Nuawa hears a distant sound, as of beating wings. "My offer stands — I am fair in my dealings."

All gifts from this creature come with hidden thorns. "No," Nuawa says one more time.

Long after the queen has gone, the throne remains there, unmelting.

The weather shifts and for the first time in a month, Lussadh sees the sun. Crepuscular and slow-moving, it parts the sky in stages and pools in the courtyard. She has never been religious, but the faith of Kemiraj affixes itself to the sun, regards that as the whole and total of divinity — all that is holy radiates from it — and some of that has stayed with her. Too many lessons in theology and too many prayers for it not to. She keeps the window open, moves her chair to where the light concentrates. It does not take away the dullness of her work — administrative, routine, voluminous despite Ulamat having filtered out the inessential—but it does lift her mood. Of the pile, there is only one item that demands urgent attention, and it's a note in Ulamat's hand rather than something from the bureaucrats.

"Come in," she says before Durgesh knocks.

He is preceded by his hound. Tisui comes straight for her and rubs its head against her knee, tail wagging. Durgesh shakes his head. "I swear she likes you better than me."

"It's only that she hasn't seen me for months." Lussadh scratches behind the dog's ears. It exudes little musk and never has that damp, wet dog smell no matter the weather. "A good child as ever, Tisui. How have you been, Durgesh? Jalsasskar still treating you well?"

"Excellently in the barracks. I'm about as well-liked as usual by the politicians. I left my second-in-command there, to sit in meetings, to be a thorn in the governor's side. So it goes." He salutes. "By all accounts, you've been busy."

"It has been a tumultuous year." She pats Tisui and nudges the dog toward its master and gestures at the small mountain of wedding gifts Ulamat has left on one of her side tables. She still needs to sort through them and more are due to arrive. "Some of it turned out rather well, so one must count one's blessings."

"General, you nearly *died*." Durgesh's voice climbs. He scowls and leans back, visibly composing himself. "I don't want to overstep my bounds, it's only that this could have been very different and whatever company you had at the time was not … up to the task. And we cannot weather the loss of you. Ulamat will overwork himself to death signing papers in your stead."

Lussadh laughs. "We come to my real value—signing papers. I'm sure everyone will manage to keep on with the governing and commanding, one way or another. What happened was out of the ordinary and, for the most part, my fault." Chasing Nuawa out of the palace, over that corpse, that dead monk. In retrospect it *was* foolish: she exposed herself to the Heron. "By the queen's grace, I survived and my recovery was swift. Have you reported to her?"

"I have met with one of her handmaidens; apparently she's preoccupied with another matter. She should make you something like Tisui."

She supposes the queen could—a pale leopard with ready teeth, a long-backed lion with a sastruga mane. The idea is not without appeal. "She's a magnificent beast, no doubt about that. But I would make a poor master, I suspect, all the running and hunting such a beauty would require. In any case, the danger is past." She does not ask him if he's met Nuawa; he has carefully not named her, but *whatever company you had at the time* does not paint a rosy picture of his opinion on her bride. "This many of us in one place is a rare occasion, we ought to celebrate. You've had your accommodation seen to?"

"I have." He hesitates. "General, I've looked into the lieutenant's background."

"Yes." Lussadh tamps down her impatience. "So has Ulamat. I know about her aunt and her monk cousin." Both corpses.

"There's more than that. Lieutenant Nuawa shouldn't be alive." Durgesh holds up his hands. "I know how that sounds. I mean this—when I heard of what happened in Kemiraj, it made me curious. I tracked down a retired soldier, he's ancient and probably will die of liver disease in a few years. But he was there to oversee the execution of an insurgent cell in Sirapirat, and despite his age, he has a particular memory for faces. He was certain he put a mother and a child into the kiln, back then. The child being the lieutenant."

That gives her pause. "Assuming that is right, then she survived because she bore the queen's glass." Not something she knows for certain but it is as educated a guess as any.

"General, this means her mother was put into the kiln *while she watched*. From the inside. I have a hard time believing she would be sanguine about serving the queen or wearing the hyacinth."

Lussadh does not point out that she killed her own family in the queen's name, even if ultimately the queen never quite asked for it: she did it for her own reasons, with the knowledge that any bearer of al-Kattan lineage — other than her — would be used to disrupt Kemiraj's peace, a puppet usurper. "People survive. Nuawa survives more deftly than most. I'll hear you out if you have anything concrete, Captain."

His face pinches. He schools it. "I received an order from the queen, delivered by one of her handmaidens, that I should prepare an atelier and make anything Imsou deems necessary. So far that's a void solvent, a century tincture, some aqueous diamantine."

The Vahatma project, though at this stage Lussadh expects the queen keeps the details compartmentalized. Imsou knows more than others, Guryin likely very little, and Durgesh will be informed only insofar as he needs to perform his alchemy. "I'll procure any raw ingredients you need. Do try to get along with Imsou."

"We always get along," he says gravely and slides a piece of paper across her desk. "I've taken the liberty — these are the things I'll need."

Lussadh folds the paper into her pocket. She will have to do it personally; the court hasn't had an alchemist for some time, not since Ihsayn's fall. It hasn't been something Lussadh has concerned herself with — she tends to associate court alchemy with dynastic tailoring, the sort that went into her own genesis. "Make what you can with what you have, and I'll deliver these to you as soon as possible."

She sees him off to his atelier and then rereads Ulamat's note. Old business, an unsettled score. She will need to deal with it later. For now, she heads to where Imsou works.

They have taken over what used to be the birthing chamber, a windowless space of polished mosaics and cavernous ceiling, and wrought iron brackets that once held the wombs. Two rows of them, perhaps half active at any time, built of finer materials and thaumaturgy than any extant in the empire—what used to be the empire. In these machines, the court alchemist fed precisely tuned compounds that would mold the developing fetus, ensuring the best result the throne could purchase through gold and status. A fierce will, strength of body and mind, an enchanting face: every advantage possible granted *in utero*, so that each al-Kattan would be born ready to meet the king's exacting standards. On the dawn Lussadh ended her dynasty, she paid this place a visit; it was gurgling with new lives. The alchemist held an infant wet with amniotic fluids toward her, begging for mercy.

Now the wombs are gone—as well as the stains commemorating that day—and what dominates the floor is a piece of what the queen has shown her. None of the cage structure yet, only its base: Vahatma reassembled to full glory, its chest stirring as though alive, its body cupped in wide lotus petals hammered from copper and brass.

"We're making good progress," Imsou tells her, without preamble, "for what little personnel I have."

Which is to say only one person other than Imsou themselves—Professor Penjarej. Lussadh eyes the Sirapirat engineer, who keeps her head down and her mouth shut. "Impressive work, given that. It's not easy—I appreciate that ideally you would have a large team." More engineers, more mathematicians, at least a couple thaumaturgists with the correct interdisciplinary specialty. "Durgesh will come through with what you need soon."

"Yes, the rest will be a matter of some ... unorthodox transmutation, I understand, that the queen will take over. Ah, look at the time. Penjarej, you've been skipping meals, that won't do—we need you healthy and well-fed. Find some fresh air and food, why don't you? Treat yourself, send me the bill."

The woman knows dismissal when she sees it. She bows and leaves the hall, where she will be escorted wherever she goes. For her safety, per the pretext.

Imsou watches her exit. "She's been slowing her work down. Very little things, tiny errors. I wouldn't have noticed them if it weren't just the two of us. One sloppy calculation here and there, a few fragments missing. I wouldn't say it rises to the level of sabotage, but I'm concerned, General."

"Can she be replaced?"

"With how classified everything is? And I hate to admit it— usually this is really not the case—but her knowledge and skill set are unique. I suppose one could scare up another academic obsessed with god-engines if one's willing to turn every institutional stone in Sirapirat for the next five years or so. Her Majesty, I get the feeling, will not countenance that delay."

Lussadh eyes the god-engine, for now quiescent, not yet meeting its purposes or destiny. As much in the dark as any of them, but indifferent to the fact, above mortal concerns. "We can't afford quite that generous a postponement. Keep an eye on her."

———

On the morning Nuawa is assigned to oversee an execution, she issues an order that no children will go into the kiln. All convicts younger than fifteen are to be sent to prison.

Softness on her part, but the children are such a minority that their absence will not affect the final tally much. Two ghost-kilns have been brought out, black hulks the size of small houses, smooth all over. She has never discovered what they are made of, this material half like iron and half like volcanic glass. All she's been able to deduce is that they are made in specialized factories, and the queen personally imbues them—without her touch, they are only deadweight.

A hundred and fifty prisoners have been collected from territories closest to Kemiraj. Some have already been processed; she was there to oversee, along with Guryin, a shipment bound for provinces in need of ghosts. Two scores sent out, the remaining ninety kept here for the queen. She used to think ghosts were as insubstantial as wind, but recently she's discovered that—fresh out of the kiln—they command their own mass and weight. They compress well, much better than human bodies, into cubes of wicker and paper no larger than Nuawa's hand.

From a window above, a shape haunts her view, a visual nuisance. Nuawa lifts her head so that Captain Durgesh, watching from the second floor like a voyeur for mass executions, would know she has seen him.

She paces the courtyard, around the condemned. Criminals, some felonious, others guilty of no more than petty theft or insulting the wrong governor. Others are foreigners who have overstayed their welcome in winter and whose consulates offered no help. She spots a few occidental heads, the rusty orange and the straw yellow. All are bowed in sedated submission. None of them will think, or feel, or fear. She notes a handful of Sirapirat faces, their expressions as slack as the rest, mouths parted, strings of drool down their chin. The state of abjection robs a person of so much humanity. One is tempted to think these creatures deserve what they are getting.

A cloudless day. The sun high, the courtyard broad. It is not public, walled as it is from outside view, but neither is it a secret. Each participant of the execution—soldier or technician—can stand proud as they perform this duty and go home to sleep soundly at night. It is work, like any other. No wear and tear on the conscience.

For one last time, she scans the mass. No children. "Send them in," she says to a corporal.

The kilns' maws open in unison.

Afterward, she does one more circuit of the courtyard to check the dead drops she's placed in unobtrusive locations and then leaves to meet Guryin for lunch.

Anonymity provides an aegis of its own and only a month ago Nuawa enjoyed its full extent—another face in the crowd, no more distinguished than any other save perhaps for her nationality and her hyacinth if she discloses it. Now she is a public object, eminently recognizable as she walks down the boulevard with Guryin. The wedding was not broadcast, but neither was it secret; the palace staff knows who she is and news travels fast. Whatever public opinion of Lussadh in winter at large, at home she is popular; the philanthropy has paid off—opening the palace's food stores, sponsoring hospitals, distributing assets belonging formerly to corrupt officials. The regicide must not have counted, somehow, or that too is now regarded as correct and righteous. She is not familiar enough with Kemiraj history or its people to guess at what they truly think of the regime shift. But at the surface all is well, considering the recent revolt and subsequent executions. Considering what Nuawa has just done, herself.

At a teahouse, the proprietor comes to personally seat her. "Lieutenant-Consort! You honor this establishment. What would you like today? We have a fresh import from Sirapirat—spiced mangoes, sugared tamarinds, sesame pearls in coconut milk."

There was a time when Sirapirat food was rarely served outside Sirapirat; Nuawa did not expect her new position to elevate her to taste-making. But then, when Lussadh first rose to prominence, there was a rush of eateries all over winter filling their menus with Kemiraj cuisine. "The sesame pearls and some of your fried date pastries, please."

"Of course, Lieutenant-Consort. On the house."

"He barely paid attention to me!" Guryin whispers, scandalized. "What about *my* order? This is terrible hospitality."

"I thought you weren't hungry, Major."

"It's the principle of the thing. I'll steal some of your pastries, he's going to bring a massive portion anyway and whatever extras he'll be throwing in. Oh, you should tell him you've a craving for oysters and squid, I love those. He'll bring himself to financial ruin if he thinks that'll please the Lieutenant-Consort."

Nuawa sits back against the wall; they have been given a table behind a screen, shutting out prying eyes if not prying ears.

Even the furniture is prettier than the rest of the property's, redwood with inlaid nacre, brought over from Johramu or Qingyuan. She peers at the rest of the diners through tiny gaps in the screen's latticework. "Is that a real title?"

"Probably not." Guryin pours xerself a cup of Ceylon. "Back in the day, they'd just call you Consort, or Your Excellency, or something. But the general isn't prince anymore; you're setting new traditions. So—Your Excellency? Your Radiance? Your Very Gracious Incandescence?"

She makes a face. "None of them. You're making me queasy, Major. Speaking of that, I received Captain Durgesh the other day."

The food arrives and, as Guryin predicted, much more is set on the table than she ordered. The date pastries and sesame pearls are larger portions than usual, and there are side bowls piled high with sugary yam, sultanas, crystallized pitayas. An absurd excess. Xe tucks in immediately and, between mouthfuls, drawls, "Cheery person, isn't he?"

"He has a lovely dog."

Guryin swallows a slice of pitaya, washes it down with tea, and guffaws. "Oh, you have a way with words. He's very kind to that dog and we all love the thing. So you want to know why Durgesh didn't exactly take a shine to you, is that it?"

"Plenty of people don't take a shine to me." Nuawa refills the major's cup. "Sometimes for good reasons. I just can't figure out what the captain's are, seeing that I'd never met him before and can't imagine what I've done to give him offense." Beyond the obvious, being her failure to take that spear for the general.

"Do you *really* want to know?" Xe grins and spoons one of the sesame pearls out of Nuawa's bowl. "I should make you bribe me for it or trade me a favor. But I'm feeling magnanimous. When he was new, Durgesh was smitten with the general. Absolutely head over heels, puppy pining, all that."

"Was the problem that she doesn't find men pleasing?"

"What? No, no." Guryin raises an eyebrow. "Durgesh is

masculine, not a man—he'd be annoyed to be called one, *you should know better*. It's more that he follows a religion that frowns upon polygamy, and since the general doesn't exclusively commit … What really entertained me is, once he realized it could not be, he decided to keep it to himself so he could feel especially tragic. He then swore to devote the rest of his days to the general's well-being. Quadruple the sorrow."

Nuawa helps herself to the yam. Still steaming; the sweetness comes from palm sugar—another nod to Sirapirat cuisine. "I'm not the general's sole partner."

"Sure, but you are her only wife and that's not prone to change any time soon."

It's only a formality, she wants to say, but it is more than that. It signifies that she is honored, she is elevated, and status is inevitably attached to it. A bride, a wife, she's never thought of herself as either. She has never thought of herself in a later stage of life; all begins and ends with the Winter Queen's downfall, an act she was never going to survive whether in failure or success. Marriage is for lasting, for old age, and she has not gravitated to either concept. "We already shared our living space before that, and little has changed with—"

Guryin pinches her in the arm. "Come now. I saw what you were like when Lussadh was mortally wounded, remember? This stoic act will not work on me. Aren't you a little bit happy? Surely you must've dreamed of this sometimes when you were tiny? A glorious ceremony, a delightful spouse."

Nuawa cannot remember her dreams from when she was a child. They must have existed. But she can't recall any beyond the practical: wishing to master a weapon faster, to perfect her marksmanship, to cleanly skin a wolf. They were stark fantasies, though they were also very attainable. "I'm not unhappy." The general in gold, the wine, the ache behind her sternum when Lussadh says her name. Evidence of madness, by now inescapable.

"Oh, you dour woman. Let me try to help you loosen up.

There's a bistro across the street that serves decent seafood. Then there's this gambling house that just opened, and there's a fighting pit—though I appreciate *you* won't be interested in that."

She is not. "Was gladiatorial sport always present in Kemiraj?"

"Pretty recent, pretty recent. Revival in interest. You can guess why, you are an economic force. So gambling house then, it's a couple levels above. Let's finish this feast—I hate wasting food—and I'll show you the latest delights Kemiraj has to offer."

THREE

THE GAMBLING HOUSE'S AIR IS HEAVY AND A FEW PACES IN
Nuawa discovers why: past the antechamber, the establishment
splits into the games proper and an oneiric drug den, separated
by a corridor. She knows the smell well, the cloying sweetness,
flowers bled and distilled to disguise the bitterness of the hallu-
cinogens that induce shared visions—anything can be had in
them, however fantastical, however visceral. Guryin leads her to
the games.

The gambling hall is enormous, the high ceiling festooned
with glass fruits and glass talismans, a nod to or mockery of
Sirapirat temple prayers. Each is delicately blown, tinted in
psychedelic shades, and illumination undulates between them
like northern lights. A peculiar orrery. Gambling tables line the
area, several partitioned off into booths. Machines rattle against
the wall, swallowing and spitting up coins. Mostly swallowing,
Nuawa notes, and she thinks—very briefly—of people who died
to power these contraptions, who died for no better reason than
to animate these brass-and-copper grotesqueries. Coins and
levers and gilt. For a moment her stomach turns, even though
she's already participated in all this and given the orders for the
kilns, even though her hands are now inextricable from the great

machine that takes and takes. Somehow this tips the balance and revulsion gathers in her stomach, acidic.

Guryin joins a card game; xe cheerfully cheats, using familiars the size of shadowed slivers to sneak about the table and look at xer opponents' hands, and then gives xer chips away by the fistful. Alcohol fumes and scented breaths. A crowd gathers around xer table, making bets and fighting to catch the chips xe flings in the air. Nuawa watches for some time, observing the arc of the lacquered chips—to her they appear to slow, their trajectory clean and calligraphic. She snatches a few out of the air, handful after handful; soon realizes she becomes part of the performance and concludes it by handing the chips to the nearest onlooker.

She wanders off to seek her own amusement. It is a raucous place, packed with addicts to chance and probability, addicts to a fruitless fight. She wonders at it. When she fought in Sirapirat arenas it was never a matter of chance: she fought to win, and she ensured she would achieve this result. To let the cast of the dice or the rattle of a bone cup decide one's fortune, to let such things hold one's dreams hostage, she does not understand it.

To the far end of the hall is a stage, and on it is poised a tall, clean-limbed person who stands on one leg. Their arms are spread wide, their stance like a dancer's. Along their biceps and shoulders, and on one lifted leg, are arranged pieces from the game River's Hands, which is being played on a board set before the stage, in the middle of an execution phase: three players pass the bone cup between them, rattling and casting each other's pawn moves. As far as Nuawa can make out, the cast determines where and which game piece will be placed on the figure onstage. Each piece is witched to radiate intense cold or scalding heat. Whoever succeeds in toppling the dancer wins. It is not an iteration of River's Pawns she has seen before but she watches with mild interest—there are thirty-six game pieces in all and a time limit. If by fifteen minutes, the performer still hasn't fallen over, all players will lose and forfeit their chips to the house.

"This one's amusing," a voice says from behind her. "Who do you think is going to win, the dancer or the players?"

Nuawa glances at a person about her height dressed in loose cloudsilk belted at the waist with platinum and larimar. Sharp-faced, with avian cheekbones and prominent nose, a thin mouth. A scalp shaved clean and unadorned; two earrings dangle from their earlobes, pristine blue, topaz or aquamarine. "The house. This game looks fairer than most, less luck-based, but River's Hands is adversarial by nature. Without any premeditation, they'll play to make sure the rest *don't* win rather than to seize their own victory." She nods at the performer. "Of course that one could be bribed, but I imagine the house has strict rules against such collusion. Maybe they keel over every once in a while to show that the house plays fair, but otherwise, they can probably stay one-legged for an hour. Can't be comfortable though, with the witched pieces burning and freezing them both."

"You're very cynical, soldier," the stranger says, approving. "Name's Ghazal."

Ey, not they. She doesn't oblige by disclosing her name — either ey already knows or she can enjoy her anonymity a little longer. "You sound well-traveled. Where might you come from?"

"You mean to say my pronunciation of Mehrut is terrible." Eir laugh is rounded and warm. "Care to join me for a game? River's Hands but properly. There's some strategy to it at least rather than blind luck."

Nuawa holds up her empty hands. "I don't actually have any chips, I'm just here to accompany a friend."

"The one cheating at cards? They must be very important, your fellow officer, or the house would've thrown them out long ago."

By now Guryin has conceded two games and won, by Nuawa's estimate, twelve. "Who says xe's cheating? Perhaps xe is a master at cards. Perhaps xe has ensnared luck and commanded it to dance at xer bidding."

"No one is that lucky," Ghazal says, handing her a dozen chips, "or that good."

They find a booth and a prepared board: the River's Hands stage is often basic but here it is a gracious circle of mosaics, inlaid and beveled, jade and carnelian arranged in lines of greenery and boundless bloom. A summer landscape, Nuawa realizes. Some artisan's imagination escaped the chains of winter, either by accident or in rebellion, the smallest act of sedition. She appreciates it, running her fingertips over the cool surface, the greens, the reds, the russet.

They position their pawns. In this version of the game there are only eighteen in total, nine for each player. The pieces are deployed, made to traverse the circular board; whichever reaches the center first wins. Most of the tiles between are traps and various pitfalls that would take the pawns out of the game. Nuawa chooses to deploy only two in the first turn. Too many and she runs the risk of losing. Too few and her opponent will outrace her. Ghazal deploys three.

Ey holds up the bone cup, begins rattling it. "Since the house hasn't thrown *you* out, either, despite you not having bought a single chip, I must assume you're someone of importance as well. So, soldier's privilege or aristocracy? Are you a duke, perhaps?"

"I'm not a duke. You could ask around."

"Where'd the fun be? I like to solve mysteries, I enjoy figuring out puzzles." Ghazal upends the cup. "Most likely it is just that you're a high-ranking officer, but isn't it interesting to imagine you are more? Something powerful and daring and exotic. Like that adventurer in those books, Sushmita or so?"

She looks at the bone tokens and counts. Then she moves her pawns forward, both at once, per the rules. One tile lights up and chimes, indicating that it is a trap tile. She removes that pawn from the board. "Technically she's a detective. Very itinerant, very unattached. A free agent in every definition of the word."

"Ah, you read those books! I picked them up when I was passing through Qingyuan and I've been obsessed since. I met a bookseller who theorizes that Sushmita is employed by an island hierophant, maybe from Pamalidos, and that's going to play out in a grand plot twist."

Nuawa shakes the cup. "You've read all thirty-six volumes?"

"Oh yes, I devoured them in a week, a thirty-seventh is coming out soon. The writer must be truly industrious." Ey advances eir pawns, winces when two tiles glow, and plaintively sets aside the defeated pieces.

"I understand there are multiple writers, working under the same pseudonym, on account of how lucrative it is. Still, I do read every volume, one can hardly live solely on *The Dialectics of Cosmoses* or *A Lateral Theory of Birds*."

"Yes, yes. Every shelf must make room for *The Detective and the Woman in the Gown of Fire*! I don't trust anyone who only puts *Dialectics* or *Theory* on theirs, anyway, it's clear they do it to impress guests and don't actually read the things."

In the end, Nuawa wins by a hair, her pawn having reached the center one tile ahead of Ghazal's. Ey lifts an imaginary glass to her victory. "And me being a thaumic mathematician," ey says, laughing as ey pushes eir chips over to Nuawa. "Clearly my grasp on this particular board isn't as good as I thought, even accounting for this being the first time I've played River's Hands. Let's have a rematch another time, mysterious soldier. I'm staying at the Ruby Moth."

Nuawa doesn't think she will be seeking em out; this was a halfway amusing diversion but she has more pressing business. As she adjourns to fetch Guryin, her calling-glass pulses. Colonel Imsou. Who informs her that they are all being summoned to attend the queen's project. She tenses as she listens to the colonel.

"I'll be there at once," she says. All this time wondering what exactly the queen means to do with Vahatma. "I wouldn't miss it for the life of me."

The hall is well-constructed, like the rest of the palace, but unadorned: nowhere else in the general's home looks so bare. No furniture, no murals, space cleared out for the queen's project. It makes Nuawa wonder what this place used to be for, what portentous function it served. Lussadh's expression, seamless and remote, is not informative.

At first, Nuawa hardly recognizes what she sees: the cage is so large, so tall, outsizing the god-engine itself. It is crafted of metal paler than palladium or platinum, the bars nearly hairs-breadth-thin and set close together. There is no lock or door apparent. Behind it Vahatma sits nearly dwarfed, its deep colors looking blanched as though its vitality has been bled and lent to the cage contraption. Its chest moves in slow rhythm, its eyelids twitching now and again like a sleeper plagued by strange dreams.

She is not one for national pride. She has never felt deep attachment to an object that represents Sirapirat. Yet this churns her stomach, the sight of a weapon made for her homeland's defense suborned and turned to enemy purposes. Vahatma was the pride of Sirapirat once and, these days, the only relic that testifies a past exists outside the Winter Queen's control. A past that predates subjugation, a past that predates the kilns.

"I have," the queen is saying as she circles the god-engine and the cage like a prowling cat, "an ancient oath that I made. For a long time, I have moved toward it, worked the world itself, braiding forces great and small. My path was to voyage to Yatpun and penetrate its shield, force it open wide so that I may fulfill that promise. But much has changed." She puts her hand on Vahatma's carved knee, strokes it, almost erotic in her atten-tions. Her gaze meets Nuawa's. "Why bring the fight to them when I can *force* them here? This device will serve as a locus to which I shall call and bind certain entities."

No, Nuawa realizes, she has *already* called and bound one— whatever it is. She sees a wisp thinner than smoke, eddying within the cage in slow pavane, the nacreous gray of Sirapirat dawns. Almost certainly she's the only one who can see it, apart from the queen: no other glass-bearer reacts. She schools her gaze and expression and acts as though she's seen nothing. She meets the queen's gaze, those nightmare supernovae, those starbursts buried deep within the queen's skull. Perhaps that is her true substance, a great pillar of shining frost whose incandescence bleeds through the apertures of her pupils. "Like ghosts, Your Majesty?"

The queen's mouth curves, a sliver of an expression. "The principles are not dissimilar. During my great work, this place must remain undisturbed at all costs and I don't trust any but glass-bearers to guard it. You will defend this room, and this engine, in pairs."

"It will be our highest honor, Your Majesty." This from Durgesh. He says it so earnestly Nuawa briefly imagines what his skull would look like beaded with bullets, a work of art in mixed media: cranium and lead.

"And you, Lieutenant Nuawa." The queen continues to caress the god-engine. Now she lifts her hand to the cage's bars, lightly plucking them as though they are harp strings. "General Lussadh has located a disturbance in the city. You've demonstrated supreme talent at rooting out such things, and I've deemed it the task best suited to you."

A trivial task to keep her occupied and away from guarding this chamber, this repurposed god-engine. "It'll be a pleasure, my queen," she says without inflection.

"Then I will leave the rest of you to arrange your shifts. Imsou and Durgesh, you'll also have more specialized matters to tend to—the god-engine will still require minor adjustments and maintenance, is that not so?"

Imsou nods at Vahatma. "I expect no complications. The engineer, Penjarej, does her part well enough."

Meaning, Nuawa surmises, that Penjarej is still needed but not performing to expectations; *well enough* is no compliment. Knowing the woman, she expects that is intentional—Penjarej has done what she can to delay the project. There's time yet. Now if Penjarej would notice and pick up any of Nuawa's dead drops. "Then I'll be off to fulfill my duty. With your leave, Your Majesty."

The queen gives a gracious nod. Nuawa exits the hall, breathing a little easier once she's in the corridor—proximity to the queen makes the prosthesis seize up, she's coming to realize. Too much cold. Incompatible thaumaturgy. One of the two—she lacks the expertise to pinpoint which.

Lussadh catches up with her mid-corridor. "Your arm's bothering you."

"Was it so obvious?"

"You walked out before receiving any instructions as to your task. And—I can always tell." The general takes the crook of her flesh elbow. "Do you wish to see the chiurgeon?"

Not need but wish. That more than anything sways Nuawa. "Yes, I suppose I will have to."

"I did have this sudden urge to kiss your shoulder, to see if perhaps I could ease your discomfort, but likely the chiurgeon will offer a more scientific cure. And your shoulder's hidden beneath so much clothing, and this corridor is quite public."

She smiles faintly. "I'm sure the servants have seen worse. Why my shoulder, General?"

"The very geometry of your body delights me. The rounding of your hips, the swells of your collarbones. And your shoulders, they're a work of art. Finer than any statuary's. A hundred sculptors could be commanded to reproduce the shape of you and none of them would do the genuine article justice."

"You *are* tempting me to take off my uniform. But Doctor Bohyun is very prim and I don't want to explain teeth marks on my shoulder to them."

"Tell them it is from your spouse," Lussadh suggests. "Even Bohyun can't find teeth marks made within wedlock inappropriate."

Nuawa laughs, surprising herself that it sounds genuine—

that it feels genuine. Against all of this, it is easy to take shelter in the general, easy to seek comfort in those arms: so that she would be armored so that she would armor Lussadh in turn. She ought to loathe it and loathe her own weakness, but what is flesh if not weak. The more she resists that truth, the further it weakens her: denying the tides of her own body is pointless.

Bohyun receives them in the palace infirmary, a space of clean lines and airy windows, and two bedchambers sterilized within an inch of their lives and upholstered to be fit for royalty, who are in any case the intended patients. The chiurgeon brusquely tells Nuawa to remove her jacket and shirt, frowning when Lussadh stays in the room but passes no comment, either because the general is their liege-lord or because they consider it acceptable for Nuawa's spouse to see her exposed shoulders.

"There's some contraction of the material," the chiurgeon admits grudgingly, looking over the spot where prosthesis joins organic elbow. "I thought I'd already accounted for low temperatures, but I didn't account for *subzero* ones, as I should have. Considering. Do you want some painkillers, Lieutenant, before I take this off?"

She declines. The chiurgeon fits a key in the prosthesis' small lock—Nuawa has a copy—and turns. Pain strikes, immediate and acute, as the small prongs detach from the plating that covers her stump. She releases her breath in a single sharp whistle of air.

"No blood," Bohyun says, nodding as they remove the prosthesis. "Very good. You're a hardy one, Lieutenant. There's more bruising, usually, and higher risk of infection."

The absence of the prosthesis makes her feel naked; she's gotten so used to its weight, and she considers asking the general to leave. But Lussadh has already seen her bloodied and broken in the snow; what is a little more. Still, she keeps her eyes fixed on the walls or on Bohyun's equipment as the chiurgeon submerges the prosthesis in a sterilizing vat. The palace infirmary is sumptuously supplied: a steel cabinet where—she saw on her first visit here—forceps, scalpels, and needles abide like a gleaming bestiary. An oracular panel on the wall where images transmitted from a conduit, swallowed by the patient, displays all the body's mysteries and flaws. Bone fractures, a clogged artery, a bruised liver, or perforated lung. Bohyun has an extensive collection of engineered parasites, suspended in little tubes, that serve various restorative purposes: anti-toxin, elimination of curses and grudges, agents that speed the rebinding of muscles and ligaments. Nuawa has never received the service of a chiurgeon so well-equipped. It seems Bohyun would be able to produce anything from their cabinet, bottled miracles, and salves that could revive those a step from death's door.

Bohyun is meticulous as they clean Nuawa's arm, then coat it in pastes the shade of verdigris. They activate thaumaturgic mechanisms and soon those pastes are absorbed, disappearing into a surface that has been tailored to the exact hue of Nuawa's complexion. Bohyun tests the fingers, turns the wrist this way and that. It is an unsettling experience, seeing this limb treated like a mannequin's when it'll soon be reattached to her.

"There now," Bohyun says. "Let's put it back where it belongs. Be a good girl, give me your arm."

What is it about those in the medical field, Nuawa thinks, that compels them to infantilize their patients? Probably the state of the stricken and vulnerable—she was as helpless as an infant when Bohyun cut away her shattered wrist, kept cutting the dead flesh until they amputated her arm up to the elbow. She was not the queen's chosen then, a lieutenant who bore the hyacinth and a duelist who'd bested opponents in arenas and assassinated more in contracts. On the operating bed, she was a construction of failing meat. To chiurgeons, patients will never be full people: she wonders if torturers share this affliction.

The prosthesis is reattached, less painful than its removal. Nuawa takes a deep breath and when she exhales her will pours into the false limb. In a moment she can feel it, the intricate thaumaturgic strands that connect her volition to fingers and wrist that would otherwise be deadweight, inert matter. She makes the hand curl. "It feels much more supple."

"It very well should. Ought to function better when it's frigid, too. Come back if it doesn't."

The fingers close into a fist, open, close again. All nearly effortless. "Will it need this kind of regular maintenance, Doctor?"

Bohyun makes a noncommittal motion. "These things are individual, Lieutenant. Thaumaturgic prostheses are not like clockwork ones, those are predictable and this is not. The advantages are obvious--this looks and feels more natural, it's far less susceptible to wear and tear, and certainly, it does not rust. See how you adapt to it. If all goes well, you won't need a new one for a full decade, maybe more."

The thought that she'd be bound to such medical attention for the rest of her life—however long that entails—does not please her, and she'd need a specialist like Bohyun: this isn't a prescription for chronic pain or insomnia. She smooths that idea away from her face and thanks the chiurgeon. No payment to be made; to such services, she is entitled by virtue of her position. These days it feels like she never has to pay for anything and that money is ornamental, close to obsolete.

Away from the infirmary, Lussadh speaks of the disturbance in the city. "The task may sound like it's beneath you, but the queen understated it. You may recall Ytoba."

The Kemiraj assassin who promised her the queen's downfall if she cooperated with em by bearing Lussadh's child and resurrecting the al-Kattan line. In the end, she refused, choosing to forge her own path and capturing em to prove her worth to the general. She catches herself almost regretting that choice, of letting em and eir secrets to the queen's demise go. "Yes, ey was rather memorable."

"Ey used to lead the court assassins. It was part cult, part disciplined order. Most of them were orphans or disenfranchised children who belonged to the enamel-born—a Kemiraj minority that we've treated atrociously, the injustice of which I haven't been able to right overnight, for all that I've tried. I believed I'd removed all traces of the order, but Ulamat found remnants that've recently returned to the city." The general makes a small huffing laugh. "Highly unlikely that they've come back to celebrate me."

Nuawa glances down the hallway. In the distance, a servant scurries by bearing an armful of ghost cubes. Likely to fuel heating, or the kitchen, or lanterns. She wonders where the ghosts came from and how many were taxed from Sirapirat. A soul wanders forever until it's used up. "Am I to eliminate them?"

"No other answer is viable, unfortunately."

"Would you show me where at least? I'll need to be armed with information." And she wants to keep the general away from the Vahatma amalgam as much as she can for a reason she can't quite put her finger on yet. An intuition.

"Of course. I will have your back." A small smile. "Our first hunt together as a married pair."

FOUR

Lussadh reviews the notes Ulamat put together for her. The number of assassins. Their estimated ranks. Few achieved the mastery Ytoba did in shapeshifting, and she executed as many of those she could find; they should not have to deal with shapeshifters now, though there's no guarantee. Her aide's report suggests these were Ytoba's students who never rose past adept—dangerous in combat, but nowhere near the menace Ytoba used to be. As most, they might be versed in shadow and etheric manipulation.

"Were you going to just stand there and let me think I'm alone?" she asks without looking up. The door made no noise when Nuawa entered, and her wife—how odd to call anyone that, how new—can walk silently when she wants to. It reminds Lussadh that she first met Nuawa after the latter, back in Sirapirat, had most likely just assassinated someone.

"I enjoy watching you, and I didn't want you distracted."

She sets her pen aside and raises an eyebrow. "You're so fascinated by paperwork?"

"I'm fascinated by watching you at mundane work." Nuawa glances at one of the piles of wedding gifts and fishes out an emerald pendant. "This is a fantastic stone, the cut is excellent but the metalwork is terrible. How is it possible someone sent you craftsmanship so poor?"

"That's why it is in the discard pile. I'll sell them off and give the proceeds to Ulamat to distribute as he pleases. Do you want the stone, though? Keep it if you like, I'll have a jeweler deal with the setting."

"I do like the spark of it. Maybe I'll put it on my vanity just to look at." Nuawa absently pockets the piece then clears a stack of books from the guest's chair. Her mouth pulls, spasming into a grimace; she stretches her false arm, folding then unfolding it slowly. "I keep forgetting to do those little exercises. In any case, the idea of you doing anything mundane seems almost improbable. The people see you and think, there goes the lord-governor, astride the world, she must get things done by just glaring at them."

"If only. You should rest to give Bohyun's improvements the best chance to succeed. I wish you'd be gentler on yourself."

"You're one to talk," Nuawa says lightly. "I've only ever seen you working on something or another, General. If not with your hands then with your head. The great calculus. The abacus and logic machines that turn behind your eyes."

Lussadh holds out her hand. Nuawa accepts the gesture and lowers herself onto the arm of Lussadh's seat. "Not when I look at you. When I look at you I no longer calculate and compute." Though that is not true. Nevertheless, she pulls at her wife's shirt until she finds bare skin, parting and caressing until she captures a nipple beneath her thumb. "All I can think is, ah, I love her breasts."

A soft laugh. Nuawa wiggles so she straddles the armrest and leans some of her weight against Lussadh's side. "The real reason you married me."

"Hardly. I love other parts of you too." She doesn't try to unbuckle the belt; she leaves it on so that when she nips at Nuawa's stomach and plunges a finger down Nuawa's trousers there is a sense of the illicit, of stolen pleasure. That any moment someone would knock on the door and demand Lussadh's attention. The lieutenant holds precariously on her perch.

"It's ridiculous how quickly you do this to me. As though your very breath is wine, is aphrodisiac—" Nuawa stays her wrist. "Your curtains are open, and I see workers in the courtyard."

"Tinted windows from the outside. Very tinted. My ancestors were paranoid about sharpshooters. So am I, truth be told." She sucks on Nuawa's collarbone, at a spot she knows well; is rewarded by a small twitch of the hips.

"How important are these documents?"

"They will be fine on the floor."

Much as it would thrill Lussadh to sweep the contents of her work off in a grand gesture of passion, there is a good deal on her desk. Still, both of them move away enough to clear a narrow space on the lacquered, gold-veined wood.

Nuawa wastes no time in hoisting herself onto it, eyes bright, mouth quirked. She has buttoned up her shirt, smoothed it over until—from the waist up—she is covered, prim. "I want to see you bare, General, all of you in the sun so its gaze falls upon you and widens in jealousy. Even as it must submit to illuminating you, having no choice but to limn the architecture of your ribs, to alloy the topology of your musculature—to bow down in awe, and lavish your every contour with its gold."

"Now you're a court poet." Lussadh peels off the sleeves of her dress. Exposing one shoulder, then another. She unlaces the pearls that latch the bodice shut like a gate of paillette and zibeline. A languorous performance; on the desk Nuawa is avid, gaze like a knife, as though she imagines she could slice through the fabric with that alone, could hasten Lussadh's nakedness.

The dress falls to the floor, purring as it meets cold stone. Lussadh holds out her arms, steps out of the circle of skirt and bodice. "And next, my honey-tongued bride?"

"I want you," whispers Nuawa, "on your knees."

Lussadh obliges and loosens Nuawa's trousers, parting them

and parting the muscled thighs they sheathe. She slides the fabric off, down to Nuawa's calves, which she strokes; she grazes the back of one knee with her teeth, licking the tender skin there, the delicate ligament. She means to make it a measured seduction, but Nuawa has clasped the back of her skull, drawing her inward; the pace is set, and so she bends to it, to Nuawa. Who is already wet, who tastes of warm sea, the salt, and the sun: bright-sweet, a fast-rising tide. Lussadh suckles and laps at the nub of engorged nerves, wraps her lips around it, draws from it as she would from the world's last wellspring.

Nuawa presses herself into Lussadh's mouth, her panting loud and harsh, her heels digging into the base of Lussadh's spine. She clutches at Lussadh, heaving, shuddering. Release turns her rigid, soundless.

In its wake she slumps forward, her palms balmy with sweat on Lussadh's shoulders. Then, "Let me use my tongue —"

"I want to take your cunt. We'll anoint all this." She hefts Nuawa into her arms and pins her against the window: it squeaks against bare skin.

They fuck against the glass, Nuawa gasping at each deep stroke, the heat of her driving Lussadh on — it seems she can keep at this without end, wringing these urgent sounds out of Nuawa's lips, and they would suspend each other on this crest for eternity. She moves a little faster. Beneath her Nuawa shouts and begs and bucks, her feet kicking at the floor.

Lussadh bites down, almost without meaning to, on her wife's shoulder. She is able to hold them up a few seconds longer before she sways, and together they lurch in a controlled fall, entwined and slick. By luck, they collapse onto the pile of Lussadh's clothing. For a time there is no word and the only sound is of their breathing, loud as any beast's, in synchrony. She half-expects the window to have cracked from the strain of their passions. But it remains whole, sturdy.

Next to her Nuawa opens her eyes, blinking, bleary. She

shifts and wraps one leg around Lussadh's hip, stretching lazily. "Any time I touch myself, it'll be this I think about."

"It pleases me to inspire." She rubs the curve of Nuawa's haunch, feeling the hard muscles underneath skin striped by pale striae. "I could inspire you every day."

"Yes." Nuawa sighs, smiling. Her glance falls on the bound papers Lussadh has taken care not to sweep off the desk and she stiffens when she notices the contents. "You should be briefing me for my duty."

"I'm hardly sending you forthright this minute," Lussadh says. "Bohyun would have my fingers. This matter can wait a few days." By preference, she would've handled it herself—in all of Kemiraj she is best equipped to deal with court assassins. She, and a few officers she's retained through the change of administration.

"Nevertheless I need my instructions." The smallest pause. "I also suspect that if I take a few days off to rest while my arm adjusts, you'll take charge of this yourself. Alone."

"Not at all. I'd be covered by sharpshooters and thaumaturges. In fact, I've already sent some to seed wards in that area, discreetly." The assassins have holed up in their old temple, nothing if not predictable, coming back to the site of their worship and indoctrination. She has considered converting the place for administrative use, but all in Kemiraj know what it was for and none—not even soldiers—would breathe easily within it, and so it has stood, deserted.

"I can fight," her wife says, a little sharply.

"Of that there is no dispute. As I said, it doesn't need to be immediate. The queen commands, but she doesn't know this order as I do." Lussadh nods at Ulamat's report. "I'll leave you my aide's notes and an overview of the order's habits. In the meantime I've a few gifts to pick up for Imsou's and Guryin's betrothal—they were planning it for this week, but given everything they've postponed it to next month, circumstances willing. I'll be back by evening."

Nuawa searches her expression, likely knowing the ruse for what it is; there's no reason she cannot help Lussadh shop. But she merely takes Lussadh's hand, planting a kiss on the back. "Until I see you again, General."

A year ago this was not what she'd have expected of Nuawa, this slim blade of a woman, this living weapon whose integument is seamless as the finest armor. Little by little they've pierced each other, their substances mingling. She returns the kiss on her wife's brow.

Lussadh leaves the palace on foot. She still enjoys the pleasure of feeling its stone under her boots. Of watching something as simple as a bird alighting then taking flight from the shoulder of a statue, of watching a public park fill, of watching the sunlight illuminate the pale grass. What is here is not what she grew up with, that era of relentless heat and the dunes' ceaseless emanations. But it remains; Kemiraj endures. The city itself, the soul of what makes a city, the survival of its population.

She passes by teahouses: she stops and pays for rounds of alcohol, tea, lunches. She strolls through a street bazaar and takes care of purchases—a family's groceries for the week, celebratory baubles for familial or marital occasions: miniature qanuns, blunt decorative karambits, jewelry in brass and semi-precious stones and crystal. At an apothecary, she pays for medicine, tisanes, wheelchairs. She receives bows, curtsies, obeisance, though these are not the reason she makes such gestures. Ihsayn used to insist on it, making a great show of charity and casting coins in the streets. A king must be feared, and a king must be loved; the citizens should see, besides, that the taxes do not all go to the king's luxuries. Those processions used to be formal, scheduled. The citizens would scramble for the king's currency in the dust, fighting each other for a disc fresh from the royal mint.

She's done away with that practice, instead altering the taxation to be more equitable, easier on those with less and harder on those with more: a move that was not popular when the coup was new, but one that Kemiraj's gotten used to since—better to pay in money than to pay in souls, Kemiraj being the territory with the smallest mandatory tribute to the queen. The threat of the ghost-tithe is such that even her move to institute scholarships for the enamel-born was met with minimal resistance. But sometimes an impulse seizes her to give, to be generous, because it pleases her and because even now she believes the citizens' joy is one of her duties. Their thanks bleed into one another and she will not remember their individual faces or individual troubles, but she's done her part, and it soothes her.

By and by she finds an isolated place on this city-tier, a perch from which she can get a good look at the old assassins' temple. The Vultures, they used to be called, plain and unflattering but factual—their task was to pick the bones clean from the corpses left behind by Kemiraj expansion. Sometimes they facilitated such invasions; Kemiraj assassins were unparalleled shapeshifters, able to assume the form of an enemy ruler, their spouse, their closest confidante. An entire polity could be thrown into chaos, swiftly unmade from within. For centuries Kemiraj reigned supreme, uncontested either by neighbors or far-flung states.

The Vulture sanctum is modest in proportion, having always been built to look ascetic. A single hall for prayer and nothing else: the assassins used to live elsewhere, nearer the palace. Ytoba emself used to reside within the court, in a secret chamber that Lussadh has since dismantled. The area near the Vulture compound is empty for a wide radius. No business or residence. These days the tiers above have nearly obscured the temple's existence, parts of Kemiraj built over and around, burying this piece of ignoble history.

She steps away from the edge, eyeing the oracular lens that her thaumaturges have configured for her, a little cube of polished steel. It lets her monitor the temple's perimeter up close; there was some movement in the morning, but quiescent as of now. The seeded wards are visible to her through the lens and she verifies that they've been comprehensively placed.

Good enough. She deactivates the cube and puts it away.

A block from the Vulture temple, she gains a shadow. A skillful one—she doesn't catch sight of them when she stops before storefronts, and their footfalls blend into the noises of pedestrian traffic. She would glance backward and her shadow would be momentarily obscured by a rushing carriage. Whoever it is, they are nearly as good as one of Ytoba's, but not quite a match. She would not have noticed a Vulture at all.

Lussadh climbs up to a second-floor bistro, pays the proprietor for the exclusive use of the curtained balcony, and orders a serving of coffee. She settles at the balcony table, situating her back against the building's wall, trusting her protective charms to do the rest: she recently acquired one that would turn away projectiles. The coffee comes with a large helping of date pastries, cakes studded in sultanas, curls of well-stuffed zivas. A small bowl for her to wash her hands with. She pours a cup, watches the drink steam in the air, enjoying the view of this city level and the level below. The chiseled stone that makes and cantilevers platforms, supporting one another, an ingenious design that could never have arisen under King Ihsayn's rule—Ihsayn being too traditional, too hidebound. As her grandaunt would have it, Kemiraj would have remained a city of earth and dust rather than this towering grandeur, this unique metropolis.

A person drops onto the balcony from a roof adjacent. They do it without hurry: she has time to fill them with a bullet or five. Not especially tall, but elegantly made and elegantly dressed. They drop to their knees and bring the hem of her coat to their lips. "Might I petition for your time, Lord-Governor, as one of your loyal subjects?"

"Normally I must view anyone with suspicion who proclaims themselves loyal. But I have a lot of food here and no one to share it with. Do help yourself."

"It is as they say—the Lord-Governor's generosity is boundless. I am Ghazal." Ey rises, eir smile like the sun in sudden emergence. "I appreciate that you didn't strike me down as I gained this balcony."

Lussadh catches herself: her eyes are drawn to this stranger too quickly, too easily. The lines of eir chin and nose, the way light shifts across em as ey moves, even the delicacy of eir bare scalp. At her age, she is not given to such flights of impulse. "What would you like my time for, citizen?"

"In Kemiraj each subject has three chances in life where they may ask for and without question receive audience with the king. They may petition for justice, mercy, or unusual favors—they aren't guaranteed, but they may ask. I hear there was a tradition where a virgin may even beg the king or the prince to deflower them on their wedding night as a blessing."

Her blood rouses. Ridiculous—this stranger exerts almost a physical pull on her senses. The last time she felt anything like this at first sight was with Nuawa. "An old tradition," Lussadh says, "and not one that's practiced anymore. Nor do you appear to wear the accoutrements of a would-be bride."

"It's true, I'm no bride awaiting my wedding night. But I wanted to know if you'd recognize me."

A glass-bearer. Almost certainly. "Perhaps if you come closer."

Ghazal drops to eir knees once more, nearly crawls toward her. Ey tilts eir chin up, eyes bright, expectant. And then she, inevitably, sees. Within the pupils that look human enough abide twin starbursts, blue-white beacons within the black. It is a glimpse only, granted to her, quickly gone. Ghazal's eyes are ordinary once more, splendidly uptilted but as normal as anyone's.

"You," Lussadh whispers. "You're a part of the queen."

Ey grins broadly. The expression is nothing like the queen's, nor are any of eir other features. "The ice dolls that serve as her handmaids, those are like trained beasts or puppets, like the hound Tisui. I'm more autonomous, though she may see and hear through me, and her thoughts give compass to mine. But you already know that I think."

"You don't speak like her." Neither did the one who came before. The fragment of the queen that, Lussadh thought at the time, was a separate person, a human ambassador sent to Kemiraj to broker peace with King Ihsayn.

"Neither did my predecessor." Ghazal climbs into a chair, shaking eir head slightly as though ey is used to having hair. Which the queen does, while eir scalp is immaculately shaven. "That's rather the point, we exist as aspects of the queen, distinct from but oriented toward her. Let us say that she is like the earth, and I'm the moon in her orbit."

A city bird passes by, crowing. Evening approaches: soon the sky will gain the purity of desert night, livid indigo, unoxygenated arteries. "How much," she says slowly, "do you remember?"

Ghazal's eyelashes are voluminous, far more than the queen's, so that when they flutter they fringe eir eyes like lace. Another minor distinction. "Do you mean, do I remember being Crow, who was sent as envoy in your grandaunt's time and who inadvertently captured your eye? No. But by nature, I carry their memory, as I carry the queen's. It's like reading a book in a library, Lord-Governor Lussadh, a chronicle of your fame and deeds, a lover's journal of your grace and courtship. This is the first time we've met."

Her mouth is dry. She resists the urge to take out her callingglass, to demand answers directly from the ruler she serves. "Why are you here?" *Why were you made*, she refrains from adding.

"A number of things." Ey begins to eat a cake and does so with appetite. As though ey's never eaten before, which may well be the case. Eir creation can't have been longer than days ago. "The fulfillment of her wishes comes near. I'm a contingency. Beyond that, it's a way to have more time with you as she becomes more occupied, no? But I'll not plague you with my company if you don't want it, and I come only as a supplicant rather than in the queen's lieu. I have no authority over you, not one bit. How can I, when I'm so young and so new to the world's ways?"

"The queen experienced Crow's memories like her own." All those years ago she deflowered Crow under desert moonlight. "Yours too, by my guess. Doesn't she?"

"You've never asked her." Ey washes the cake down with Lussadh's coffee, swallows, and hums in the back of eir throat. "She keeps few secrets from you. She would have answered. Were you to ask her what happened to previous glass-bearers, she would have told you that most of them passed away in old age or in battle. She'd even tell you I've been spun out of souls and a single mirror-shard."

"I don't." Lussadh swallows. She looks away but then her gaze falls on one of the palace spires, a minaret full of the queen's likenesses. Banners fly above roofs that do likewise, reproducing the breadth of her, the height of her, the images of a merciless god. She commissioned most of them, perhaps because despite everything that is how she too sees the queen. "I could not have asked her about Crow." Crow, that first fragment of the queen who rode across the desert of Kemiraj and offered Lussadh their heart.

"But, Lord-Governor, that is how much she loves you. She would forgive you anything." Ghazal leans close, eir brocade whispering like petals falling. "She forgave you for killing Crow, great prince. She forgave you for killing her."

───

Nuawa does not quite steal toward the hall where the Vahatma cage is contained, but she does venture a few times in its direction. The second time Guryin catches her in the adjacent hallway and steers her away, saying, "It's *my* shift at the guard—well, mine and Imsou's—and for once we have to respect the division of labor. You wait until it's *your* turn if you want to be miserable so badly."

"I'm only checking to make sure you're fed and watered," Nuawa says mildly, holding up the small tray of desserts she's brought as an excuse.

Xe takes several hot, deep-fried pastries filled with sweet plum paste and pops them into xer mouth. "Mmm. I do appreciate it. Can I take the rest to Imsou?"

"Naturally. And the general's finding you gifts." Probing slightly, even though she knows that is not why Lussadh went into the city without her. "Do you want to look at the wardrobe I bought from some governor I've never heard of or spoken to? A lot of them seem more your taste than mine."

"I *love* gifts, and I love free new clothes. I'll come over to take a look soon." Guryin gestures with xer free hand. "For now it is drudgery. As you can see, it's not as if anyone's even going to attempt entry to that room."

No one other than Nuawa. She will not be assigned to guard the place—she already knows that. What strikes her as odd is that the queen would go to such trouble. To her, Nuawa should be no threat and the Heron is gone. But her tentative endeavors have borne fruit: while hovering about this part of the palace she's caught glimpses, again, of what the queen is calling. Tessellated radiance, far more defined and geometric than any ghost, bleeding through air and stone.

She doesn't return to her suite. What she means to attempt will be detectable to the queen by sheer instinct or etheric ripples; the Winter Queen is said to know and see all that goes in her domain, the entirety of winter territories. A few have even speculated her reach extends to the occident during the colder months there. Nuawa is more aware than most as to the bounds of her might. But for the moment, the queen is singularly focused on the god-engine and what she's bringing into shape.

Now is the time for Nuawa to take a risk.

She takes circumspect paths, checking once more the dead

drops she has hidden around the palace. Tiny chips that bear symbols associated with obscure Sirapirat poetry, ones that would have been part of the curriculum at the Sirapirat Academy of Innovation and Applied Theory, Penjarej's alma mater. It is possible the woman successfully avoided her mandatory literature classes, but in Nuawa's experience attendance is strictly required in Sirapirat higher education. For the past couple of days, she has left these chips of laminated wood, on which she's crudely painted archaic Ughali. Mehrut is the prevailing tongue in winter by dint of Kemiraj's position as the favored constituent. Ughali fluency is not common, let alone the formalized form used only in scripture and magisterial communication.

Fortunately, it looks like Penjarej did not skip poetry lectures. Nuawa finds one chip missing and replaced by a scrap of paper that contains a couplet. She unrolls it and finds it to her satisfaction.

She makes her way to the palace's deserted wing, the part that once belonged to King Ihsayn. Often she wonders why Lussadh hasn't had this area cleaned out, the grandaunt's mementos eradicated, but she's gathered the general has complicated emotions about the dead monarch. She's not pressed on what their relationship was like, though she gets the impression it was, at best, rocky. Opprobrious. When she told Lussadh the lie that Indrahi was Nuawa's austere, unloving guardian, the tale seemed to resonate.

Most doors are unlocked, past the main gate that separates this part from the other wings. She heads to the door of an old gallery, taking a start-stop route that puts her out of the range of oracular lenses. The gallery exudes the scent of fresh fruits and garlands, maintained by witching: nothing actually grows here, and no flowers decorate the hall. Nuawa understands Lussadh sold off a great many of its treasures, liquidating them into more practical assets or converting them into administrative funds. But a collection remains. War trophies behind glass cases mounted on plinths or secured to walls in place of murals or paintings. Severe, the way she imagines the old king was.

She waits behind the skeleton of an enormous tiger with front teeth the size of elephant tusks. It doesn't take long—about now is Penjarej's single designated hour of freedom where she's permitted to visit isolated quarters in the palace. As far as she knows, the professor has not been forced to wear scrying devices, but a thaumaturge may have been tasked to monitor her all the same, looking with her eyes. Not listening through her ears, however. Most practitioners can focus only on one sense at a time without the use of familiars, and there are none here. She's betting on Penjarej's monitor choosing sight, the default for most. Penjarej slips into the hall and circles the entrance, skittish.

"Keep your line of sight trained on the glaive trophy to your right," Nuawa says aloud. "This way any thaumaturge monitoring you will never see me. For verisimilitude, I suggest that you approach that plinth, the one with the Sirapirat crown. Very pretty, very historical, and it'd be reasonable for you to take an interest in it."

Without looking her way, Penjarej follows her directions. "You do think of everything."

Nuawa passes her hand over the smooth surface of the tiger's spine, kept the clean white of new bone by anti-decay wards. "I try, Professor. We don't have much time—I can't stay long either. I need you to tell me everything Indrahi told you about the queen, about the mirror."

"There's not enough time in a day to say all that, Lieutenant." For once Penjarej does not prevaricate, does not attempt to deny her association with Indrahi. "She never told me everything. A locked door, just like you. She raised you in her image perfectly."

It doesn't sound like a compliment. She watches Penjarej's back through gaps between tiger vertebrae. "My mirror shard's different. I know that much. What I don't know is what I can *do* with it." The Heron could access thaumaturgy similar to the queen's, drawing weapons out of cold and thin air; what she carries with her used to abide within him …

"Tafari was a practitioner."

Nuawa starts. She never—but then she doesn't *remember* her giving-mother Tafari, and Indrahi never said much about her. Too agonizing; too many memories. She could not make herself ask even if she burned to know, and there were no keepsakes, no convenient diaries for her to stumble upon. All was incinerated in the name of subterfuge, distancing Nuawa as much as possible from insurgents. "I thought she was a field chiurgeon."

"A single person can be many things. You know that better than anyone." Penjarej bends close to the Sirapirat headpiece, a fine and royal thing from the time Sirapirat had royalty: built high like a pagoda and topped likewise with a finial, gold and rubies and white sapphires. Gorgeous and antique, belonging to an era immemorial. "Tafari tested the glass shard—naturally. But she had to be careful not to trigger etheric resonance. So she worked around it, trying out wards and witchings, bending etheric matter. What she discovered was that if affected with the right etheric syntax, the shard could freeze things. Reshape water. Turn vapors into tiny statuettes, utensils, razors."

A lesser form of what the Heron could do. "How do I make use of that?"

"She didn't have you trained in thaumaturgy?" A small pause. "But no. Maybe that'd have drawn attention before you were ready. *She* would have kidnapped a child if she thought one bore her glass."

Nuawa imagines that—abducted as a child and raised in the queen's palace, with the snow-girls as her attendants and play-mates, educating her in the harmonics of frost and barren soil. What results would have been more wolf than human, and a hungry one? "Tell me what I should try."

Penjarej chokes out a little laugh. It sounds more like a death gasp than humor. "Even your mo—even she couldn't tell; neither of them could be sure. Their theory was that the glass protects its host from harm so that the piece can return to its progenitor, to the rest of the mirror. That's why they gave it to you in the kiln. So you coming under mortal harm might invoke its potency. Another way is—Tafari believed the glass exists in multiple dimensions. Physically embedded inside you and etherically embedded in your shadow."

She had learned shadow manipulation by the time she was twenty, in the specialist way particular to Sirapirat duelists: rudimentary and through tools, but functional. It never occurred to her that Indrahi encouraged her toward that profession for reasons other than to hone Nuawa for combat. A different kind of wolf, the thought occurs to her, but she quickly squashes it. "That gives me something to work with, at least. Thank you. What are you going to do?"

The older woman has moved nearly beyond her line of sight, examining a miniature fortress made of ceramic set into the shoulder of a bismuth crystal. Nuawa doesn't recognize the work —another artifact of conquest, a trophy belonging to some Kemiraj king since reduced to dust. "Did Indrahi ever speak of me?"

"She spoke of a friend from her university days," Nuawa says, carefully straddling the line between true and false. All identifiers were removed. Any information she knew could compromise her, lead to the trail that connected her to Indrahi's and Tafari's seditious ways. "I'm fairly sure she meant you, in hindsight. Obviously no names. She spoke fondly and said that if she ever ... became indisposed, she had a letter witched to reach this friend. To beg them—you—to take charge of me, for her sake."

The lines of Penjarej's body pull taut. "Well. She trusted me, if nothing else. And she mentioned no other matters?"

"Once while tending her greenhouse, she told me that she kept a rare orchid as keepsake for a woman she knew, whom she called as rare as a silver pearl, as excellent as mango blossoms." In fact, most of those things were said of Tafari, but she improvises. Penjarej was in love with Indrahi, she's almost certain. If she is to learn more out of Penjarej, she must offer something.

Penjarej's shoulders unwind. She draws a breath so deep it is audible from where Nuawa is. "I'm grateful. Do you know, I've lived in Kemiraj for so long but I've never been to this place? It was told to me by dear friends that you can behold Kemiraj's treasures here. Ill-gotten, to be sure. Stunning all the same—that cannot be denied. You were probably too young to remember it, Lieutenant Nuawa, but once Sirapirat was in dire straits. People could barely afford to eat or feed their children, there were so many dead, and the kilns were hungry—always hungry. Our tribute tax was punitive."

"It still is compared to Kemiraj's."

"Yes. You haven't forgotten that." The professor straightens. "I've always been a coward. You can tell. Have a good day, Lieutenant."

Nuawa lingers a while after Penjarej has left, back to the workshop-prison. She needs somewhere far from the palace; she wishes she'd rented a room out in the city, but even that may not be far enough, and doing such a thing would raise alarms. Ulamat would certainly report it to Lussadh—he regards her with wariness still. She tries not to think of the time he had her brother's body brought to Kemiraj as a test of her response. Back then she was too preoccupied; now she has the luxury of anger, and she has thought more than once of murdering him in cold blood. In battle, he's no match for her, prosthetic or not.

But she has a responsibility to see to, and such violence gratifies only in the shortest of terms.

In the end, she chooses a park on the palace's tier whose use is exclusive to senior administrators and military officers. She is both, in the most technical sense. The garden is walled from view by a high hedge, thick and bright with bromeliads. Paved stone paths, a pond softly gurgling with fountains. No child plays here, and no hound bounds. No one at all: bureaucrats and patrols alike are busy at work around these hours.

She ducks into a gazebo that overlooks the pond, finds a spot where her shadow falls straight and true. There is no preparing for it—asking Bohyun for numbing agents would have aroused suspicion. She lets her vision defocus. Everything transforms to a crystalline structure, to the fractal intricacy of glass. When she holds up her hand it is as if she's looking at a sculpture of clear quartz, translucent skin, and glistening bones, all the subsystems that make up and propel her turned to the queen's element. The Winter Queen was able to extract a large parasite out of her with ease, though not painlessly.

She runs a hand down her front, to where she can feel—barely—the hum of the glass shard. It reminds her of ghosts inside pipes or the vibration of engines, not something that resembles the human pulse. The queen's taunt: *you've changed too much inside, Lieutenant, your mortal essence has been diluted. My mirror transmutes its hosts, and you've been bearing it—activated—your entire life.*

More like the Heron, less like a human. An arc that bends toward the white-muzzled wolf, toward the teeth of ice unmelting. But even the Heron could defy the queen.

Nuawa moves until her shadow aligns correctly and she can see the core of this power reflected, this alien intrusion within her body: a blue-white pinpoint like the heart of a flame, like the starbursts in the queen's eyes. She draws her sword. Small but stationary target. She strikes.

She feels, more than hears, the sound of glass under stress. Pain radiates through her, but it is surprisingly distant. A roar in her ears as the point of her sword meets resistance, the blade shuddering, nearly bending.

Force slams into her, knocking her onto her back. Her skull narrowly avoids cracking against the gazebo. The sword clangs on mosaic tiles.

Her hands scrape along the floor as she gropes for purchase, trying to right herself. A dull ache throbs in her chest. She touches her shirt and is surprised to find it dry—no blood. Her vision has returned to normal. Her skin looks like skin again.

Where she has fallen, a layer of ice has budded. Her fingertips graze across: it is jagged, brittle. The flimsiest patina that would fracture at a breath. Experimentally she slides her hand across the edge of it and the patch spreads, following her.

The frost soon melts—too thin to last, even under the frigidity brought on by the queen's presence in the city. But she laughs, and for the first time in months she feels possibility; she feels the beginning of triumph.

FIVE

LUSSADH HAS NOT SET FOOT IN THE PALACE MUSEUM FOR A very long time. She does not have cause to and has left the place open to the viewing of high-ranking officials. Theft doesn't worry her—what relics remain here have been strongly warded to stay put, the only reason she hasn't sold them off. The ancient wards have fused to the palace's pulsing architecture and removing them would be like pulling teeth, a surgical operation as far as the palace-as-entity is concerned. She has elected not to: her coffers are full enough. The palace doesn't feel pain the way an animal does but she feels sentimental for it, for the pet-like loyalty it expresses toward her.

The museum is still fragrant, just like it was in her earliest years. Children in a different sort of family might have come here to play, but she and her cousins were too leery of provoking the king's disapproval; Ihsayn did not beat them but her coldness was punitive, and the prospect of being displaced loomed until they reached the age of majority. Lussadh was heir apparent from her adolescence, but even that could change. Not all al-Kattan children were guaranteed wealth, power, and security.

She looks over each display, but none of them yield answers. Reportedly Penjarej lingered over the Sirapirat crown for some time, yet that does not explain why she committed suicide this morning. The woman had no access to sharp things but there were enough components in the workshop she shared with Imsou that she cobbled together a primitive needle-gun and fired it into her skull. A conclusive demonstration of her engineering expertise.

Lussadh studies the crown, its complexity of gemstones, its whorled filigree. No. Nothing in this room caused the suicide; rather it catalyzed a decision Penjarej must have contemplated for some time. A reminder that a Kemiraj king defeated a Sirapirat monarch of old and thus Penjarej's homeland has been subjugated twice? It seems too ancient and abstract to prompt an act as final as this.

She backtracks to the room's entrance, where Ulamat is waiting for her, brows knitted and papers in hand. "There's nothing further from the autopsy, my lord," he says, frowning harder at the sheets as though he can will evidence of foul play from the ink. "None of the oracular lenses saw anyone passing through here except for Penjarej and her security detail."

Which doesn't rule out a second person, one who knows the scrying blind spots. The thaumaturge tasked with monitoring Penjarej also reported not having seen anyone, and apologized profusely for not having used a familiar or device to both watch and listen.

"Take care of the professor's funeral rites in three days," Lussadh says at length. "The monks at the Seven Spires should be able to perform the correct ones—she was of that faith, I recall—and I'll donate an appropriate remuneration."

"I'll attend to it at once." He tucks his folder under his arm. "Will her death disrupt anything, my lord?"

"Not exactly." Colonel Imsou is capable enough on their own, but Penjarej's absence may make maintaining Vahatma more time-consuming. Not a true impediment. "You may go, Ulamat. And keep all this quiet, for now." Not even Nuawa knows yet, and she intends to keep it that way for some time.

She stays behind. An intuition keeps her there, snagged into her like a sliver of wood under skin. For the second time, she walks the gallery, this time more deliberately, looking for something that might justify or dispel her misgiving.

A glint on the floor, trapped between tiles. Easily missed if she weren't looking for it. She drops to one knee and pries it out, and holds between her fingers a small emerald. The cut and size are unmistakable. Nuawa put that pendant in her jacket and it must've fallen out. A bare little item, of good cut and not much else, loosened from its setting.

Lussadh puts it away, tucking it safely into her shirt. There is no other trace and no other conclusion. Her wife was here, and something she said or did had goaded Penjarej to suicide. It could have been anything—Nuawa is callous toward the woman —but she also met the engineer in secret. Nimbly dodging the lenses, seeking the blind spots, staying out of the thaumaturge's line of sight. For her, it would have been easy.

She has the museum cordoned off: no one in and no one out until this is resolved. Or rather until she can pretend it is resolved.

None of this she allows to show on her expression when she passes Durgesh and Imsou at the entrance to Vahatma's hall, the former birthing chamber. She nods at Imsou, who keeps any complaints about Penjarej's absence to themselves, and at Durgesh, who sharply salutes her.

The queen is holding in her fist what Lussadh recognizes as the Heron's heart, a glittering organ that resembles an enormous diamond shot through with capillaries gone to the blue-black of deep ocean. "My treasure," the queen says, "you're just in time. I've been preparing. Can you see?"

"The heart, my queen?"

"No." She bends her great height and reaches inside the cage to stroke apparent empty air. "I was hoping you'd be able to. None of the glass-bearers can, not even Major Guryin, who you would think is entwined to the energies of such things … but xe is engaged to the shadows, to the elements quite distant from my own. A shame. Nevertheless, you'll be able to view it all shortly. The engineer's death is an irritation."

Lussadh does not bring up Nuawa. Instead, she says, "May I ask about Ghazal?"

The queen withdraws from the cage. She cups the Heron's heart the way most might cup a sleeping kitten. "You may ask me anything; you know that. I made em to act in my place when I cannot be away from this hall. Does ey not entertain you?"

"Will you be appointing em publicly, to act in an official capacity?"

A ringing laugh. "Why—should I introduce them to the palace as my cousin or my get, long kept secret and now unveiled in my hour of need? Is it believable that I might have sired or borne offspring? Perhaps if I insist, the subjective truth will bend to my liking well enough. But it's more useful that ey flits around, unseen and incognito. You may take em to bed if you wish, I cannot be with you as often as I prefer, especially not now when I must watch this place like a hawk watches its young. Ghazal will be most willing, indeed eager. Will it not be interesting to lie with a part of me that is more like you—more flesh, more blood? And when time permits, I shall bring Ghazal into our bedchamber. Ey and I will pleasure you from root to stem."

Against her better judgment—and her more intellectual parts—Lussadh lets that prospect take hold a little longer than it should. "I'm not sure even *I* possess the stamina to stand up against such an onslaught."

"Why not? We'll take care of you with such inventiveness, such attention. Not a single part of you will escape our mouths." The queen gazes at her, wry, through filigreed eyelashes. "Pleasure must wait. I will show you something. You alone are permitted to witness what I am made of."

The queen opens a frosted jar she's kept at her side, and from it ghosts pour like smoke: these are nearly solid, well-fed on offerings and incense and prayers. Luminous, though as ever they are the color of fog, of pearly haze. She draws the ghosts and spreads them across the Heron's heart like swaddling gossamer, and puts the whole into Vahatma's engine mouth.

"Souls," she says, "are the final currency. The coinage that moves the world and runs through the earth like precious veins. With enough of them, I may reshape the land, remake mountains, suppress the tides. And I may create an entryway into what is otherwise sealed to this world."

It happens quickly. Lussadh flinches from the bitter cold that grips the air—cold even for her, rime spreading across the floor tiles, quick-forming stalactites descending from above. The snap-crack of frost budding and pushing against itself. Her eyes sting.

The queen stands tall, shining with a serrated brilliance. Her eyes are shut. When they open again, the starbursts of her pupils have become enormous, eclipsing the black of her sclerae.

She might have spoken; she might have not. When she reaches out above Vahatma, a window to an otherwhere seems to have cut itself into the world. She pries this rift wide, this glimpse into a crystalline glade swept by noon, and plunges her arm in.

A howl carves through the hall. The queen holds on, striving against the force that fills the room with the fury of a hundred storms. Lussadh braces herself against the wall. Shadows burn black, geometric absences into the air: precise squares and isosceles triangles elegantly pointed blossoms.

On instinct, she draws her sword.

The dark shapes whirl toward her; she swings and cuts through as if they are taut paper. The black shreds coalesce into bipedal outlines: like paper cutout approximations of human bodies, lithe and nearly two-dimensional with razors for hands. She slices them apart as they near her, and as they scatter and reform she fires her swarm-gun. The snow-bees cling to the dark particles, bearing them down, engulfing them in white wings.

Soon all the black geometry turns still and spent, falling to the ground like mundane dust. The Winter Queen has wrenched out of the rift a seething angular mass. What veils it recedes, revealing a thing of biting edges, more crimson silhouette than solid shape: an impossibly long gash of a mouth, bristling with white fangs. The elongated eyes of a fox, not two or three but an array, some the size of pebbles, others as large as a hand—a dozen spread out across the creature's pointed face, the tessellated ribbon of its body.

The queen pins it in place—in material reality—with ice. Shards and spears and javelins, even needles and lancets.

"This," the queen says, her mouth feral, "is a god of Yatpun, a god of my birthplace. One of my makers. I've bound it to this world and soon I'll force it to manifest enough that it can be hurt. After so long, I will become what I was always meant to be."

When Nuawa passes through one of the wards around the Vulture temple, she feels the presence of it like an electric buzz; if she lets her eyes defocus she can glimpse the shivering haze that forms the ward's formula and grants it etheric integrity. While the wards last, no living being may pass in or out of the area that does not bear the queen's hyacinth. It is a peculiar specification and anyone who steals the hyacinth would be able to circumvent it, but she supposes the existence of the mirror shards is not divulged even to court practitioners.

All this—the wards being visible, thaumaturgy being palpable to her skin—is new. She's not yet experimented with the rest; better to bide her time.

She descends from one tier above, alighting on the roof. The place is awkwardly situated and she quickly sees why more destructive methods haven't been employed—demolition tools would damage several load-bearing points that hold up the next layer of city. Her calling-glass pulses and lets her know Major Guryin has reached the temple's other end, xer familiars hovering overhead. "Normally I'd make just the one, but this is a special occasion. I'll have one circling around to scout. Another will be with you. The general will have my head if you so much as break a fingernail, younger sibling."

"I'm not so fragile as that," she whispers back, well aware that Guryin would disagree. The actuality of her prosthesis, the fact she hasn't fought since losing the flesh hand. But she intends to prove that what she has—what she's adapted to—more than suffices.

According to reconnaissance reports, there are five assassins present; all have been trapped within the temple for half a week. By now they should be parched and hungry, feeble from the cold. The temple has received no renovation and boasts no ghost pipes or any insulation against the Winter Queen's climate. The assassins should be easy pickings.

Nuawa has dealt with their teacher and leader Ytoba personally and suspects it will be otherwise.

Lussadh is stationed not so far, also monitoring through an oracular lens, along with the sharpshooter team the general handpicked for the occasion. Nuawa is surprised the general is attending in person at all—Lussadh has seemed preoccupied the entire day, distant, deep within herself. Brusque, uncharacteristically so. She gave Nuawa thorough information on the temple but was short with everything else.

But Nuawa can't let that distract her, and in a way, she wants to show Lussadh—out of vanity more than anything—that she remains capable of combat; that she has not been reduced to a helpless shell. She moves across the roof, pleased that her balance is unimpaired and her feet are as light as ever. Not that she expects to go unnoticed. If these assassins are anything like Ytoba they will be more than a match for her, and much better at stealth besides. Famishment may not even slow them down. Ytoba was fed the thinnest gruel under Nuawa's watch—and had eir limbs removed—and ey could still muster the energy to shapeshift and taunt her before the end.

Guryin reports no sighting of assassins at the building's

perimeter. Nuawa, having been told what Ytoba could do, treads cautiously as she approaches spots where shadows gather. She watches the edges of them for shapes that are not quite right or where they pool a little too thick. On Lussadh's instruction, neither she nor the major are to enter the temple proper. Guryin's familiars flit in and out through narrow window slits.

"Shit." This from Guryin. "One of my familiars was taken out."

Nuawa takes up a spot beneath a window. "Can you generate another?"

"They're not paper cranes, Nuawa. Would that I could make dozens on demand! I'll drive other scryers out of business then."

She concedes the point: that Guryin can maintain multiple familiars at all shows exceptional craft, and for most practitioners creating even one takes a toll. Her hand passes lightly over the temple's stone exterior—it is rough, barely shaped enough to act as building blocks, slapdash like everything else about this place. Intentionally so, she expects. Likely this was only ever a synecdoche house of worship, for brief prayers and spiritual gatherings rather than residence.

A shadow close by blooms, the edges of its quivering like petals in strong wind. It lasts mere seconds but she knows the tell for what it is. Her blade whips clear of its sheath, the probability shadows spreading in simulacrum of wings—an echo of Guryin's familiar watching over her, deep cobalt, jagged feathers, and needle beaks.

She strikes true. The tremulous shadow turns from penumbra to bleeding flesh. A person of unremarkable features and build falls, untidily clawed open sternum to gut. Too much viscera, boundaries too muddled, to tell which is the entry and which the exit wound. Despite herself, adrenaline pumps and sings. This is the first person she's cut down since the Heron took her hand. To her, killing has never been special: it is a matter of achieving and honing technique so that she can fulfill the goal Indrahi gave her—the bounties and the arena were for practicing. She did not relish them beyond the simple fact that she could demonstrate herself through them, the methods by which she could exert herself upon the world. But this—this is confirmation that she has not dulled, that she has bent but not broken.

"One down," she says into the calling-glass.

"Don't challenge me," murmurs back Guryin, xer voice thrumming with good humor. "Wish I'd learned to scatter shadows, but that's neither here nor there. I'm seeing what you saw now, though. Race you to the next one!"

Xer familiar darts into one of the windows: there is a scream. It cuts short. Nuawa edges forward, fingering a bead in her pocket made of brittle crystal. She has been instructed against entering the building, but this should serve her well enough. And there are only three left, now, each much less durable than Ytoba.

No light source within the temple—it was never wired for artificial illumination; back in the day it must have all been lamps and witch-radiance, or even torches. The thin slits provide next to no entry for sunlight, despite the high noon.

Guryin is calling her urgently to retreat—"I can't see inside with my familiars"—and she's considering heeding xer when the shadows roil.

A voice whispers, almost right into her ear: "Where is the prince?"

She tosses the bead into the air and slashes. Her blade splits crystal.

Captured sunlight blazes. Three figures in tattered dun recoil. She lunges at the nearest. Her sword shears through fabric, cracks against the resistance of bone. Remains there: the assassin clings to the blade as though it is their lifeline. She lets go and levels her gun. One of the others barrels into her and she twists aside. The prosthetic chooses that moment to seize up and her grip on the gun slackens; it drops and clatters on the floor.

She's held down. Arms immobilized, legs likewise, the point

of a jambiya at her throat. Weapons are second nature to her and she's learned to identify more than most: this is the type particular to Kemiraj, nationalistic pride she thinks, even more urgently curved than a talwar—steel that curls nearly fetal into itself, demonstrating the smith's mastery of the forge, the tempering, thermodynamics, and structural integrity. Showing the smith gifted with an eye that can bore into the mystique of metal, that can strip away its integument and expose the secrets at its pith.

Nuawa tenses her legs and torso, maneuvering for the leverage she needs to throw them off. She can't quite. The prosthesis is twitching madly, no longer responsive to her will, an alien apparatus.

The weight abruptly lifts. The assassin who was pinning down her legs rolls away, thrashing in a seething mass of white. Snow-bees. She wastes no time in flicking out her sliver-knife and slashing open one of the hands holding her down. They jerk away—she follows through with another cut: this time beneath the chin, a neat quick gash.

She pulls to her feet, breathing heavily. The remnants of spilled sunlight illuminate the hall in weak stripes. Lussadh stands at the far end, holstering her swarm-gun.

"General," she says. "My thanks."

"Think nothing of it. You've saved me like this before. This should be the last of them."

"You're not going to chastise me for ignoring your recommendation?" Nuawa keeps her voice light, aware she took the fool's option, more embarrassed than she wants to admit. All this to show that she is as capable as before, only to fall short.

"Not precisely." Lussadh takes her hand as they close the distance to each other, then abruptly pulls her in for a kiss.

It is rough—all teeth. The general's grip on the back of her skull is firm, fingers digging into her nape, and she finds her panting shifts to something that has much less to do with exertion and killing, and much more to do with the fact of Lussadh's physicality. The hard planes of it, the unyielding frame, the insatiable appetite that hides behind the urbane mask.

"Here?" she says against Lussadh's mouth, for a split second almost yielding her good sense to her libido. The corpses around them will soon be unpleasant; she's already caught a whiff of foulness. Fecal. The indignity of death.

"No." The general's voice is thick. "Let's get out before I lose control of my wits."

After the temple's gloom, the noon is nearly blinding. The general delegates Guryin to handle the rest—recovering the bodies, performing the necessary autopsies, keeping an eye out for any other acolyte of the Vulture that might crop up. Xe complains but stays behind to attend the cleanup.

Once they're in a carriage together, the general seizes Nuawa again, resuming their kiss, raking fingers down her back. "I've never fucked you fresh from killing before," she says, fumbling with Nuawa's belt.

"We haven't had the chance, no." She reaches for the general's trousers. The carriage rumbles into motion. They have plenty of tiers to ascend—time enough. "I don't murder as often as I used to in the arena."

A laugh, foundry-hot against her skin. "The savage core of you, under all that efficiency. I can smell it in your sweat."

There's little space, the quarters too close, and taking Lussadh into her is almost painful—it is like accepting a spear. That soon changes as her own arousal mounts and she finds handholds on the general's shoulders. Her nails claw at fabric, which shall prove little protection; she knows she will find imprints on Lussadh's back later, reddening and purpling.

As they both approach the point of culmination, Lussadh nips at her earlobe. "Be mine, Nuawa."

"I already am." Her voice is harsh.

They separate halfway before they reach the palace. Nuawa rights the state of her trousers and buckles her belt, thinking already of what they'll do once they are back at the palace;

whether Lussadh will take her in a corridor that's not so far from public eyes. She breathes in the faint myrrh that the general wears.

Lussadh has her hands in her lap, prim, her own clothing already done back up. "Penjarej took her own life."

All thoughts of lust dissipate. "She—what? Why?"

The general's expression flickers—she was expecting a different reaction, Nuawa is certain. "Who can tell? Her absence won't interrupt anything, at any rate, but it was surprising. The palace guard who found her was quite rankled; a man of surprisingly weak nerves for someone selected for an important security detail. But I thought you'd like to know. I've arranged for her ceremony at the Seven Spires. Do you wish to attend?"

"No." Nuawa feigns indifference without effort—she is, by now, used to it. First her brother. Now Penjarej, a woman who pined for her mother; would have done much for Indrahi out of that love. "I rarely find myself drawn to spiritual cleansing, which is the function of funerals for strangers. It is a shame, but she's served her purpose."

"Pragmatic," Lussadh says. "When we get back, do you want to take a look at more wedding gifts? A new batch just arrived, most of them addressed to you. Originating from Sirapirat, in fact. From ex-lovers, perhaps?"

Something about this has been a test. She has not quite passed, yet. "What ex-lovers, General?" Her voice turns breezy. "In your arms, I've already forgotten all others. It is almost as though I came to you a virgin, or at any rate a clean slate."

It works, insofar that it makes her spouse chuckle. "My wife with the nectar from her lips. I might even believe it that I've branded you inside and out such that all other records have been expunged from your nerves, your muscles, your skin. But do take a look, all the same. You never know what might turn up in such a cornucopia of well wishes."

SIX

"A DELIVERY," GURYIN SAYS AS XE TRUNDLES INTO THE parlor, xer arms full of parcels. "Can you believe it? First, the general delegated the most boring tasks to me, now she wants me to be a courier."

Nuawa watches, amused, as xe carefully lays out each package. The general is elsewhere—cooped up in the hall with the queen and the machine-god again—and she's sure that one or more things in this pile will be another part of the test. One way or another Lussadh's suspicion has been tripped, likely due to Penjarej's demise. "You didn't have to, Major."

"I like unwrapping presents."

The spread is diverse and expensive. Nuawa didn't think she knew this many people—most of them are from mere acquaintances or, incredibly, some of her opponents back in the Sirapirat arenas. Jewelry of various quality and showiness dominates: sanded silver, topazes, sapphires. Numerous articles of clothing in gold with jasmine motifs. Boxes of preserved fruits and pressed amaranths.

"It's a lot." Guryin picks up an ivory mermaid with impossible proportions and waggles xer eyebrows. "You're popular, Lieutenant-Consort."

"More like they want access to the general and believe I can provide it." A rectangular box catches her eye: she opens it to find a note from Ziya Jiang wishing her a long and blissful marriage, and a gun. It is unusual, even for something procured by her old marksmanship tutor, coated in a substance bearing the complex, shifting sheen of bismuth. The grip is painted matte black and fits her hand as though it has been smelted just for her —which it has been, knowing Ziya. The holster is leather, dyed a deep cobra green.

The major whistles. "*That* is beyond beautiful. Custom made! One of a kind, I'll bet. What sort of ammunition does it take?"

"The usual ones." For Nuawa that includes bullets with etheric-scattering force, enough to sunder common wards. She hefts the gun: a little heavier than her current one and, Ziya's note promises, with a better rate of fire and smoother trigger. She will have to send him her thanks, a return gift, something for his dogs, and the guaranteed attention of Kemiraj's best smiths. He's always after new contacts, more for the thrill than the profit. "It's from a teacher of mine."

"Lucky," xe says with a little sigh. "All I ever get from *mine* are long letters about what a disappointment I've turned out to be. Well, not in so many words, of course, I've secured a fair position and they're back home comfortable ..."

"Back home?"

"One of my parents is from Johramu; the other is from Pamalidos, and that's what I consider home. Very beautiful, very warm. Visit one day—ask the general; she'll go wherever you like for vacation. I'll be your guide. You might fund the heat shocking."

That startles her. She assumed the major was native to winter; she assumed that of every glass-bearer, even though it isn't especially logical. Guryin speaks Mehrut without any trace of islander accent and xe looks like xe could have come from nearly any winter province—owing to the Johramu parent, she supposes. Perhaps that explains xer lack of conscience, lack of scruples; why resent the Winter Queen if one comes from a land free of her influence, untouched by her cold. A home to which Guryin can return any time, wealthy from xer service. "It doesn't bother you to spend so much time in winter?"

Xe shrugs. "I can go home when I want. My folks live quite well, considering ... ah, I won't bore you with the details."

"And you have living family." That too should not come as a surprise. She is biased by the peculiarities of herself and Lussadh both. But she supposes not every single glass-bearer is a self-made orphan.

"Sure. Aunts, uncles, and ... let's translate it as an auxiliary parent, that's the best Mehrut can do. Plus a sister, she's an apprentice pearl diver, and she's very ..." Guryin trails off then frowns, pricked by alarm. "I've never mentioned her?"

"This is the first I've heard of your family."

Xe laughs, but the sound is wooden. "Come now, I barely shut up about her. To Imsou, anyway. Well. Must've slipped my mind. I'll be sure to regale you endlessly with stories of Pamalidos too. It *is* a beautiful place."

A desperate note has crept into Guryin's voice as if xe is trying to reassure xerself. There is an odd absence, unnatural almost. She remembers something her mother said. "Major," she says, "what's your sister's name?"

Guryin stares at her, silent, for much longer than is comfortable. Xe opens xer mouth and quickly shuts it. Then xe gets up, abrupt, and says, "Excuse me."

It is beautiful at first, snow, until it erases and turns all you know into a copy of itself. Soon you no longer recall a time without. Soon, you remember only what it wants you to remember. Of winter, Indrahi said that. Nuawa used to think that meant merely the physical landscape, the shape and hue of the sky. But Indrahi knew more than she let on, Nuawa is certain now, had wrung intelligence from the Heron that she never wrote down in that letter from beyond the grave. And now the Heron, too, is dead and that river has run dry.

She returns to the gifts, simply because the physicality of them centers her: as a whole, they are meaningless now if ever they signified anything. Piece by piece she sets aside the trinkets, already determining that Ziya's gun is the only thing she will keep when her fingers brush across a plain case. Teak wood, unembellished, not even any carved patterns. By the material alone she would guess this is from Sirapirat.

Almost she laughs as she opens it: how blatant it is. The inside is lined in black-striped mulberry paper. It crackles as she examines the case's content, a wooden charm with ornamental witching that makes its painted river ripple and run prettily and a message claiming to be from Indrahi's associate. If she wishes to establish correspondence, she's to send a message to an address in Qingyuan. What an obvious trap. Her mother would never have associated with anyone who sends communiques in plain letters rather than code.

Nuawa's thoughts veer to Penjarej and she shakes that off with a pang. For now, she needs to be certain the mirror fragment hasn't made *her* forget the way it has made Guryin. "Tafari," she says under her breath. "Indrahi." The names of her mothers. She isn't the type to keep a journal and Indrahi gave her a spy's education. Nothing's to be written down, neither personal nor correspondence, unless absolutely necessary. Even cipher goes so far and all written codes can be broken. So she has never kept records of what she does, records of where she has been—those have always seemed unnecessary.

Part of her considers contacting some of her old acquaintances, what passed for friends, in Sirapirat. *Is there anything important you think I should remember but I've forgotten?* Except she kept herself close, was to most of them a tightly sealed book. She looks through the list of those who sent her things, who want to court her favor and therefore the general's. It fails to be informative. She recognizes the names, but by itself that doesn't mean much.

Very quickly she dresses. She clips her gun to her belt and, on second thought, also loads Ziya's gift and adds that. It's rare for her two carry two—their combined weight is unfamiliar—but considering everything she'd rather have two loaded guns than need to pause to reload.

Kemiraj has an excess of bookstores, most of them concentrated around the universities. She chooses one she patronizes every now and again, mostly to buy installments of Detective Sushmita's adventures and the occasional broadsheet. The respectable ones that report actual events, not the gossip sheets that speculate about her and the other glass-bearers—they are, she has learned, a particularly popular subject in Kemiraj, though the writers always steer clear of the queen.

"Lieutenant-Consort!" The proprietor curtsies to her and gestures at the shelf behind him: new arrivals. "I've got the new Sushmita, the thirty-seventh. I hear the author's trying to branch out with something new, but for now, tales of the great detective continue apace."

"I don't suppose you know who the writer is?" She scans the covers—garish illustrations, bold lines. Above her a small oracular lens glints. Though the store is commercial, they do stock a minor collection of scholarly texts, rare volumes, pricey enough to need surveillance.

"Somebody." He flicks his hand. "Writers are fanciful creatures, Lieutenant-Consort. Very difficult and not always pleasant. What'll you have today, sir?"

"*The Detective and the Snake-Headed Seeress,* certainly. And I'm looking for ..." Nuawa hesitates. "Books about me."

Without missing a beat, he leads her to a section full of precisely the broadsheets she avoids and a rack of titles that straddle the line between fiction and unauthorized biographies. She spots, on one of the broadsheets a headline interview with Yifen, one of her sometimes-lovers from Sirapirat. Who has profited, evidently, from claiming extensive intimacies with her and describing her as "Absolutely insatiable, a true beast in the sheets." On one of the novels' covers, a taller, fuller-breasted version of her—the character's name slightly changed—poses inexplicably before a giant, fire-breathing bird, sword in hand and half-naked. "I'm more thinking of compilations of Sirapirat duels," she says. "One of those yearly overviews. Factual." Her manager strove to ensure all their duelists performed well enough to appear in those.

"Ah, not the ones that suggest you were born from a strike of lightning then? Oddly enough I do have those annuals in stock, you've truly turned interest in Sirapirat duels around, sir. Given new life to some specialist presses. I must say I never did use to sell those, but now …"

"How do those get written so quickly, anyway?" She nods at the stack of *The Gladiator Bride: A Novel*. She tries not to look at the illustration but inevitably catches a glimpse of a figure with startling resemblance to her entwined with a figure with startling resemblance to the general. "I haven't worn the hyacinth for even one year and the wedding was just days ago."

"Writers, sir. Some are fanciful and profound and erudite. Some are … very good at riding the wave of public interest. When the queen grants her favor to a new officer, my trade becomes very brisk and I greet the occasion with supreme gratitude. I congratulate you once more, sir, on your connubial delight."

"I hope *that* keeps your trade brisk too," she says flatly.

She walks out with the Sushmita book, gratis, and volumes of commentary on Sirapirat arenas from the last five years. They're cheaply printed and not bound particularly well, serving a niche professional interest. Nuawa steps into a teahouse—not ideal, but it'll have to do. She asks for a secluded table and a pot of assam.

Paging through the annuals, she looks for the significant contests and tournaments. Winning those brought in not just good money but better contracts and bounties. To her relief, the events recounted line up with her recall, as do the names of her past managers, memorable opponents, colleagues. Hardly a scientific method to verify that her memory is unimpaired; better than nothing.

"I hear the general had to step in and rescue you, Lieutenant."

Nuawa nods, downward, to acknowledge the dog. "Fair morning, Tisui. In fine form as always." She shuts her copy of the most recent annual and pours herself tea, making no move to invite him to sit. "Is there anything I could help you with, Captain Durgesh?"

His expression hardly shifts when he draws his gun and puts the muzzle to her temple. The teahouse stirs around them. No one makes a move to assist her or to call for city security. The queen's favored cannot be gainsaid, even if they are about to kill one another in broad daylight.

"Captain," Nuawa says slowly. "This isn't what I had in mind when I asked if I could help you. I don't believe we've fostered between us such animosity that this is necessary." Theatrics, she thinks, even as she calculates how quickly she can draw. The arena again: it all returns to the lessons learned there.

"Tell me what you are, Nuawa Dasaret."

"An eccentric question. What I am everyone knows perfectly well, unless you're under orders from the queen or the general I don't know about?"

Around them the teahouse crowd has cleared, putting as much distance between them and the queen's soldiers as they can. Some have outright fled. Durgesh's voice lowers. "What is your intention?" The muzzle jerks. "Why did you let the general die, against the Heron?"

"Almost die," she corrects. Even the waiters have scampered out of sight—she imagines the proprietor has similarly made themselves scarce. "I did not let anything. There was a spear heading for her and I wasn't sufficiently in the way that it'd have gone through me instead. Our assailant had fine aim. Even Her Majesty was aware I couldn't have possibly done much about it and I would think you would be satisfied with her judgment."

The captain's grip tightens on his gun, but not on the trigger. The calm inside her hardens until it is as perfect as a mirror, reflecting a dark sky frilled by frostworks. She brushes a cup gently, tipping it over. It dashes to pieces on the floor in a spill of ceramic and tea and for an instant that distracts Durgesh.

In the same motion, she stands up and yanks on his wrist. His gun drops. She draws hers and slams him into the wall—a clatter as more utensils fall; she will have to compensate the teahouse later. The muzzle of the gun Ziya has so thoughtfully commissioned for her glints, bismuth shine against the fine umber of Durgesh's brow. She places it in the midpoint, such that it both occupies his vision and is frustratingly at the edge.

Tisui's teeth sink into her calf. The pain runs up along her spine, a line of white fire. She ignores it: she has learned that she can survive anything.

"Call your hound off, Captain," she says, her voice almost seamless. "I feel you've led an easier life than I have or you would never have given me an opening. But I can endure tremendous pain, and my hold on the trigger isn't going to waver."

Durgesh holds her gaze. "Her Majesty has told me that you attacked her. She forbade me from speaking of this to any other glass-bearer or to the general herself. But I know your true nature, Lieutenant, and she has tasked me to keep an eye on you."

"Has she, now." The hound or the man. In practical terms she can't get away with murdering Durgesh; Tisui would be another matter. She wishes she carries two guns. In a minute or two she'll no longer be able to stand. "Then I suppose I ought to behave."

His smile is grotesque. "How old were you when you went into the kiln?"

Her fingertips turn cold. The back of her mouth turns dry. "What did you say?"

"The woman who held you then, that was your mother, wasn't it? You were insurgent get, and inside the kiln you watched them die. That must have gone on for hours; the removal of the soul is a gradual process. Your mother and her compatriots withered one by one. Only you survived. And I think I know precisely—"

Nuawa strikes him with the grip of her gun. Cartilage crunches: blood spurts into the air. He reels back.

She swings the pistol down, shoots Tisui in the head almost without thinking or aiming. The shot resounds as she tears herself free of the hound's jaw—a burst of fresh agony—and ducks under the arc of Durgesh's club. Her thoughts turn smooth, running well-oiled, automatic. She fires into Durgesh's knee, and then she fires into his head.

It is over quickly. A fight between a club and a gun always does.

Nuawa is breathing hard as she straightens. Pain creaks inside her. A glance down tells her that Tisui took more out of her calf than she would like, the trouser leg shredded and drenched; a wonder at all that it let go. The hound whimpers at her feet—she missed the brain—and she feels a distant, remote sympathy. Captain Durgesh is not making any noise, so there at least she did not misjudge.

Her breath rattles. A good thing that Ziya's gun is capacious. She shoots Tisui again, more fatally this time. Still plenty of ammunition remaining.

She doesn't make it far from the teahouse. Gritting her teeth, she limps into an alleyway between the teahouse and a tenement home. Laundry snaps overhead in the wind—saris embroidered with gold thread, kurtas laden with paillette. Wealth is casual in this city, she thinks, but her mind slows when just a minute ago it was such a faultless thing. Tisui's bite was deep, its teeth long and sharp, and even the mirror shard's fortification of her body will not instantly close the wound.

It occurs to her too late that she doesn't carry medical supplies, not even painkillers. She's become complacent when she should treat Kemiraj the same as the wild lands of her adolescence, back when she hunted bears and wolves. First aid. Things with which to keep warm. Instead, she has come to regard Kemiraj as a home, albeit one in which she must walk on a knife's edge. A deranged laugh slips out of her throat. To hemorrhage to death here, in this absurdly spotless alleyway, when she has just regained her footing and wrung a measure of promise from her shard of glass.

By the mouth of the alleyway, a carriage has rolled to a stop. From it steps two matched snow-maids. They bow to her in unison, nearly dropping to their knees and then straightening back the way a sprung toy might—abrupt, with uncoiled force. Then they glide toward her.

———

Nuawa remains conscious as the snow-maids carry her into the palace. More appear to join them, descending from the ceiling. She can't see from where they came—a vent, a gap between ghost-pipes embedded into the palace's system: too small by far, either way, for creatures of this size to pass through. There is something fluid about them, unhuman rippling as they draw themselves to their full height and straighten their shoulders. Without sound, as if under their deep-sea pallor there are no bones at all.

Revulsion, sudden and absolute, arrows through Nuawa. The queen's handmaidens have never registered to her as a danger—strange and alien, but not that. She considers struggling, testing the limits of the snow-women: how durable they are, whether their substance can withstand the force of bullets. It is a fanciful thought, swift to dissolve. She's in no shape.

Through the palace they lead her, and if the sight of them makes servants or courtiers curious, all know to quickly avert their eyes and turn their attention elsewhere. Nuawa wonders if she looks like a prisoner being escorted to her execution and the idea startles her into laughter. Her earliest memory, walking into a ghost-kiln. She did not feel afraid then.

The snow-maids bring her to narrow, twisting stairs toward a part of the palace she has not seen before. Noises of governance and activity fade: the walls are red and bare, and there is dust on the floor, as though this area has been disused for years. Elsewhere the staff is meticulous, even the smallest, most remote corner is swept and polished, kept clear of vermin and detritus. There are dead insects, here, brittle and crackling when Nuawa crushes them underfoot. It is bitterly cold—this section is not connected to the heating, to ghost-pipes—and the only light comes from the snow-maids themselves, who glow like gentle lamps, or like anglerfish.

Double doors at the end of the stairs. The snow-maids push her in—lightly, hands on the small of her back, almost gallant. She stumbles and the agony in her leg flares.

This room was splendid in its days: the floor is tiled in semi-precious stones, the long window framed in cut glass and blue steel, and wall brackets spaced far apart. They might have held a collection once, of elegant spears and talwars, the most gorgeous scimitars Kemiraj's smiths can make. These, Nuawa realizes, were the king's chambers.

As if alert to the rhythm of her thoughts, the queen says, "She was executed here, King Ihsayn al-Kattan, in her own quarters. A statement, one might call it. Lussadh killed the rest of her dynasty elsewhere, but the king had to die here, her blood on these stones. They'll say I commanded this, but I will tell you that I never did. Ihsayn did not matter to me. Of course, I stood witness: that is the way of it." She is reclining in a complex structure, part seat, part torture contraption. Solid frost most of it, but the rest is vitreous, slow-moving and susurrating against itself. "She was led by sense, *that* is the way of her, rather than cruelty. But you, Nuawa. Are you hoping to provoke me so I might kill you in a fit of fury?"

"I'm sure I don't know what you mean."

The queen stands and motions. "Bind her."

She is forced into the strange structure, the handmaidens pushing her into the seat, a cradle. It rocks under her weight, the frost circling her wrists. She tenses, then makes herself loose, yielding. Of late she has known pain, a great deal of it, untellable agony. She can know it again and live. Or perhaps not. There's only so much that can be done before her body gives.

"No doubt you're eager to meet the limits of your mortality." The queen cups her chin, bending to meet her gaze. "You imagine it will be simple enough. Beyond a certain threshold, your flesh will part one final time and all the blood in you will vent. Your consciousness will bend and break long before then. All you need to do, until that point, is retreat into yourself."

"In recent times," Nuawa says, "I've become forthright in my intentions. You let me run free, great queen."

Ice numbs. She hardly feels it when it opens her like a scalpel, so sharp it is and so fine, more than any blade of metal could ever be. A red pearl on her cheek and perhaps a glimpse of bone. The queen touches a fingertip to that, tender, and flicks away the blood.

"Look," the queen whispers.

One of her maids has made a mirror of their stomach, and in the gleaming surface Nuawa sees that the cut is gone. Better than new, the skin of first youth. Then the queen's hand is inside her, has cleaved--in an instant--through muscles and fat, through the structures that shield the inside of a body from the world without. She feels it then, the pain greater than Tisui's bite. It is as though she is glass and now she shatters. Her mouth falls ajar and at once it is filled, a handmaiden's fingers slipping between her teeth, cushioning her bite and stoppering her voice.

The queen's expression is distant with concentration. "I can feel your heart. The drumbeat of it, like thunder you house deep within yourself. Flesh fails easily but while it holds, it is a marvelous apparatus, host to incredible complexity." Her fingers move, almost a caress, against something inside Nuawa: there is a wet noise, a pancreas or intestine. "You're a glass-bearer, Nuawa, and that means I have claim to you. The smallest piece of cartilage. The most minor ligament. The least to the greatest of your flesh is pliant to my hands."

The handmaiden and the queen withdraw. Nuawa gags and spits, saliva and frigid water streaming down her chin. Her uniform is torn but her belly is healed, though damp with red, with other fluids. Even her calf no longer throbs. Pain lingers in echoes, twitching through her nerves, under her skin. But the vastness of agony has left. Panting, she slumps back, limp in her restraints. All of her feels untethered, buoyant.

"I hold the key to the gates of your vitality." The queen crouches before her, one hand alighting on Nuawa's knee with the delicacy of sparrows. "Mine to lock or unlock as I choose."

Nuawa's forehead splits. Blood pours down, hot, blinding. The handmaidens hold her as she screams.

Gashes open as if she is clawed from the inside; welts flower as if she is gripped by plagues. Wounds like bullet holes, skin flayed in delicate strips, flesh gouged out in chunks. The distinction becomes meaningless: there is only sensation and the small respite as the queen restores her to wholeness. Each time it must be final—fatal at last, the queen cutting too close—yet each time it is not. Her voice breaks. Her consciousness gutters.

Time blurs. She blacks out, in the end.

She comes to on the gemstone tiles that have drunk the blood of a king: she lies in a puddle of meltwater, cold, her clothes tattered and stained. A stink of copper. She does not know whether she has soiled herself; can barely tell wet from dry or air from stone. Information arrives at a remove, her senses sluggish. Her eyes drift shut. Most likely she can move, can rise to her feet —all the damage must have been reversed. She'd hardly be alive otherwise. Despite everything she feels serene, cocooned in a peculiar peace.

A hand slides under her stomach. "Can you hear me?"

"I can always hear you, General." She is lifted up in arms

with a mountain's might. "You discover me like this too often. But this time I'm not wounded."

Lussadh says nothing as she carries Nuawa out of the room. The door is left ajar. Nuawa hears a roaring wind, though that may be in her own head. She slips under. Not for long. When she is fully alert again they are in the baths. The general asks, "I'm going to take off your clothes to clean you up. Is that all right?"

She nods, lets Lussadh tug and slide off what remains of her uniform. The water has been pre-heated; steam rises with the sweetness of jasmines, the tartness of tangerines. Still, she feels remote from her own skin, from the contact of it against cool wood, against the rich lather the general is working up along her back. "I do not want to be treated as though I'm breakable, General."

"You aren't. Your will is iron. Time and time again you've proven it."

Nuawa doesn't ask, *Why did you not stop her.* The general can no more contradict the queen than the tides may contradict the moon. She stares into the bathwater, into the fog. She lives. Living means continuing, and continuing means she can thwart the queen once more. And she will do that, over and over, until the queen no longer has a reason to keep her alive.

The general lowers her into the bath and finger-combs her hair, lock by lock, strand by strand. Cups a handful in her palm and brings it to her mouth. "My love for you is total, Nuawa. I set almost no conditions on it. For you, I would ruin entire kingdoms." She spreads soap lather on Nuawa's scalp, massaging it in. "And for the queen it is much the same."

Almost no conditions: Nuawa doesn't miss that qualifier, and it makes her wonder what conditions Lussadh has imposed on her devotion to the queen. What might drive a wedge, what might cleave it in two? But that is for another time. She lets herself relax into the water, into Lussadh's touch. The breadth of Lussadh's hand, the curvature of her wrist. She says against the general's thumb, "You're a love song, the sweetest of them all."

When she is clean and toweled off, Lussadh drapes a robe over her. She refuses it, instead draws the general with her to their bed. "Stay with me," she says, her lips against the general's palm.

And Lussadh does, skin to skin. Nuawa drifts toward deep, dreamless sleep, but before she can fall completely into her dreams she hears a voice. It rings from a distance, and as it grows closer she realizes it is her own, though the words are not.

We meet at last, child of glass. My thanks for keeping her occupied so I could sneak out and reach you. The voice is now close, in her ear. A breeze plays along the back of her neck. *I propose a pact. Belong to me and I will guide you to victory.*

SEVEN

GURYIN IS EXPRESSIONLESS WHEN LUSSADH SUMMONS XER. Asks, very cautiously, "How is she?"

They are away from the palace, on the second floor of a tenement that Lussadh owns but has leased under a pseudonym. It is a legacy of the distant days when she wanted a space of her own, away from Ihsayn's domain. She has not used it much for the last two decades, has thought of consolidating it under government use, this dusty second floor with its dusty office. A single window, smaller than her office's in the palace. Two bookshelves holding nothing of particular value, cabinets that contain blank papers and stationery—the ink long dry—and a few knickknacks that are at least half her age, bought and left here twenty years ago.

She did not anticipate wishing to remove herself from the palace, from the place that is now hers alone, without the threat of her grandaunt present—the king to whom all servants and soldiers reported, the one who controlled both the country and Lussadh's destiny. But the palace is, presently, not exclusively hers.

At one point she had dreams of being merely herself. At one time she had dreams of a life where she could wander as she wished and do as she pleased. They were vague, and she's discarded them before they could crystallize: even after Ihsayn's fall, such fantasies remained fantasies. There were new responsibilities, a new order, and a new Kemiraj, and she trusted no other to guide it.

"Nuawa is physically whole," she says, at length. "Her constitution is like a young god's."

"That's not an answer, General." The major leans against one of the shelves and grimaces. "Surely that was too harsh. She's never punished any of us, let alone like that. Nuawa could've just… been admonished the normal way. Judicially, legally."

"The queen had her reasons." None shared with Lussadh. *This is my wife,* she said to the queen, quiet, their voices reverberating in the place where Ihsayn fell. *And I am your queen,* came the answer the color of frazils.

"I don't think you're fine with this," Guryin says. "She's the only woman you've ever loved so much you asked for her hand."

"And the queen is my liege. Let us bend ourselves to more substantial matters."

Major Guryin thins xer lips. "You're not executing Nuawa. Are you?"

The thought alone pierces her like a javelin. With which she has had firsthand experience and a ready visceral comparison. "No, I'm not doing that, or anything close to that." Guryin certainly sounded as though xe expected she might. "But something has to be carried out publicly. Durgesh wasn't no one, and he served me very well."

"Tisui was a fine beast." A sigh. "Durgesh was popular in Jalsasskar. In the army, especially. A lot of the senior garrison commanders are not going to like this, and Nuawa had to go and murder him in a teahouse so there's no hope of coverup. Hell, Imsou's furious. The two of them were close in that academic rivals way, not that I could understand why."

Lussadh turns her head to the bookshelves, to the thin volumes white with dust. She can barely remember her tastes from that time, can barely remember being that young and that little in control. "I'll decide on her discipline." No more pain: the queen's done plenty. It will need to be formal, but more than that it must be publicly visible. Even the general of winter may not show her own wife so much nepotism as that.

"Fine." Guryin's voice is tense, a little angry.

"Would you mind looking after her for the day? I don't think she would like to see me just now."

"You think wrong." Xe exhales. "I'll keep an eye on her, General. Need to make sure Imsou doesn't go anywhere near her, at any rate. My betrothed is usually so calm, but this —well."

Xe takes xer leave. For a time Lussadh paces the office, knowing already what she must and will do, not yet ready to commit to the act. She's saved when her calling-glass pulses. Ulamat.

"There's a problem, my lord," he says, voice slightly indistinct. Wherever he is there is considerable commotion—the noises of a panicking crowd. Either trying to get away or reach something, a site of disaster. "I'm near the train station. A citizen from Qingyuan dropped dead right on the platform. Completely eviscerated as though someone's taken an ax to them, only finer somehow, but nobody could see anything. If it's thaumaturgy, it's one of an exceptional nature."

She starts moving, all of her alert, malaise forgotten. "Do you have a practitioner on hand?"

"Yes. Ey couldn't find anything. A more senior one has been sent for and should be coming soon."

By the time Lussadh arrives at the train station, soldiers have cleared out the platform. Ulamat stands by the corpse, expression pinched. There is no reek, as of yet. The cold stems that. But no amount of frigidity could have concealed the state of the body: this shredded mound, bones cut to fragments, torn ligaments, and punctured viscera. For all her experience with war, she's never seen anything like this. She searches the scene for any trace of glass or crystal—the Heron's methods are fresh in her memory—but there's nothing, just butchered meat.

She circles the area as Ulamat disappears to fetch the senior thaumaturge. Stops when she hears Ghazal coming, not because ey makes noise but because the air almost moves differently around em: the same as the queen, though much more muted, a lesser echo.

"The god bound by the Winter Queen," Ghazal says, conversational, "is a beast of tricks and storms, one of her makers. Its winds cut the flesh like threshing blades and, according to her, it delights in bloodletting—the more the better, a true lover of sheer quantity. Luring people to their deaths in the blizzard and all that. She believes it contributed a great deal of cruelty to her genesis."

Lussadh raises her head, looking into eir face and at eir impish smile. So unlike the queen in demeanor and comportment, even if ey is as much as part of the queen as a finger or a tongue. "If she's caged it, it shouldn't be able to act like this. Should it."

"Not exactly. Or rather it can act, a little here and there, but not to free itself. It could slaughter a hundred hapless people—this was a merchant, I think, the poor soul—and it wouldn't be able to harvest a single soul for its own uses. In all the ways that matter its hands, or forelimbs, at any rate, are tied. It's just lashing out." Ey lifts one shoulder. "Like a child throwing tantrums. It can't touch glass-bearers, though. You're safe, General."

She thinks of what she's seen in the Vahatma chamber. "Will it do this again?"

"In a week or so, it won't be able to anymore." Ey twirls eir fingers about eir neck, as though meaning to twirl hair that isn't there. "Are you angry with the queen?"

"You're the queen."

"I'm not," ey says amicably. "You're allowed to be angry with her. Resentful even. You do love Nuawa, that part's obvious. I think you love her the same way you loved Crow. The love for a wild and dangerous thing that you can't entirely know, whose inner workings are opaque to you—the fascination of a mysterious engine, the intricacies of its machinery. How such things invite one to disassemble them."

A pressure in her chest, and then relief. Ghazal is not Crow. As beautiful, yes, as much a fragment of the queen. But so distinct that there's no danger she might long to kiss that pale throat, long to crush that slender frame against a wall. This creature will not have her torn. "How many casualties from this god should I expect between now and then?"

"Much fewer than an average ghost tribute. Even compared to Kemiraj's small tribute." Ghazal chuckles and shakes emself a little. Eir brocade flutters and seems to glisten as though made of ice, but it is merely good fabric and metallic thread. "I'd like to walk with you. You may not believe it, but to me Kemiraj is fresh and strange, as are you. When we are created—when our consciousness begins—we are as new to the world as any child, except that we're more developed. Intellectually, physically. It'd hardly do for us to take entire decades to mature."

There's no mystery to solve here, and no point for her to remain except to be seen by the citizens that the Lord-Governor is in attendance, taking control of the incident. The illusion that she has a tight rein on the city and all its happenstances must be maintained. "Let me settle matters here first."

Ey has a knack for disappearing and by the time Ulamat comes with the senior thaumaturge Ghazal is gone. Like smoke or frost-haze. Lussadh does not try to quell the spread of what's happened here, though she bars entry to broadsheet writers for now. She dislikes their tendency to swarm like flies, their penchant for sensationalism. Back in the day, Ihsayn didn't tolerate broadsheets at all and it's one of the few policies Lussadh, in hindsight, agrees with.

Ghazal is there by her carriage; climbs in after her without being invited. "The queen and I are functionally different people," ey says, as though continuing a conversation. "I serve as a useful perspective—don't you ever wish you have another self, detached from the situation, to give you a second opinion? But if you've quarreled with her, it is not as though you've quarreled with me."

Lussadh brings the carriage into motion, taking a circumspect path. "Do you consider yourself human?"

"No. But I can be that if you'd like." Ghazal grins. "You can even kiss me. My mouth, unlike the queen's, is harmless and poses no threat to your glorious soul. Would you like to try it?"

"That you're beautiful you already know. But no." A missing element. She does not feel drawn, not to this. Whether this is proof the fragments of the queen are truly autonomous she cannot yet tell.

"I *don't* know that I am beautiful. I'm still waiting to be told so by someone who matters. And my mouth has plenty of uses, I could get on my knees right here ..." Ey laughs. "I see you're not to be persuaded and my charms are not sufficient. It's a shame. The queen's wrapped her mouth around your instrument so many times, to such fine result, and I've been wanting to see what that'd be like for myself. To worship you, to swallow ..."

"Enough." Lussadh finds her voice sharper than she meant it to. Did the queen make you so insolent, she wants to ask, the way the queen must have made Crow a perfect temptation for her—the courtship, the deliberate seduction. "I asked you before and you wouldn't give me clear reasons why you continue to put yourself in my path."

"I gave you information, didn't I? Surely that was helpful! I'm here to be of use."

"You mentioned you were a contingency plan." A thought strikes her. "The queen can use your body. Can't she."

"Possibly," Ghazal murmurs with a shrug. "I've told you, I'm not the queen. That means I cannot forecast her thoughts any more than you can. Whatever she wants, I can only glean after the fact. I just happen to have a more direct line than you do."

It is a futile discussion; she's not going to get them to divulge eir true nature, the specifics of how ey functions. "The trapped god—is there any logic to the way it attacks? Does the palace need evacuating?"

"I don't think it chooses victims by proximity." Ey leans back and frowns. "It used to favor travelers, back home, but that was the people likeliest to be out and about in bad weather. Mostly it left children alone. Does that help?"

"No," she says flatly. "Is there nothing else that can be done to contain it? More wards around the hall?"

Ghazal attempts, again, to touch hair that does not exist. Sighs. "The thaumaturgy of this world doesn't affect it. Your practitioners might as well try to hold it with a lattice of spun sugar. Something made of ghosts …" Ey stiffens and grimaces. "My apologies, great prince. Her diction takes mine over occasionally because I'm so new. Give me a year, I'll be much more distinct."

Lussadh tries to imagine what that would be like, to be a being of artificial soul and cognizant of it, and apparently content with this abstruse manner of maturation. "I'm sure that must feel difficult."

"It's actually rather comfortable. Might I get off here? It wouldn't do for me to be seen at the palace."

She lets Ghazal disembark but for a time stays to watch, peering through the window at eir receding figure. Ey never disappears or dissolves into snowdrifts and ice. As mortal as anyone, as human, just like Crow was.

Nuawa wakes up alone. This is not unusual but she somehow expected otherwise—that she would stir to solid warmth, to being held by the one who calls her *my wife*. But that is foolish: for most of her life she has woken up alone, and this has not given her pause or made her weak. Why change now.

When she looks out the window, one of the queen's hand-maidens is watching her.

It is as naked as she is, its stare unblinking, its smile slight. Its hand moves across the pane, leaving no smears. Its breath—if any—does not mist the glass. Her heart judders in her chest, a sharp hammering rhythm, but she meets the creature's gaze.

Between one blink and the next, the snow-maid departs. Now here, now gone.

For a time she's not sure whether she *has* woken up. Her rest was troubled by fragments of moon-white skies and an expanse of snow so infinite there was no division between above and below. She recalls feeling removed from it, similar to the way she felt when her sleep was invaded by oneiric craft. But she can hold onto little of it, now, save the impression that in the dream her footprints were curiously small. Like a child's. It does not hark back to her walk to the kiln--the sky was black then, seared by frostworks.

Her thoughts scuttle without direction until they veer to the voice in her skull. Absent, for the moment, leaving no evidence it's ever been there. But she remembers the words clearly. What she does not recall is whether she said yes.

A flash of red at the window catches her eye.

A handprint presses against the pane, the metallic red of tiger pelt, though a shade so vivid that she has never seen it on a true animal. The shape holds as though it's been frozen in place, glittering like zircons. Out of impulse, she reaches to touch it, spreading her fingers, finding that the handprint matches hers exactly.

On the window, her reflection cocks its head. Its eyes lighten to a muted amber and her chest tugs—the mirror shard, the fragment of the queen's power.

Mortals sleep so much, the thing says, conversationally. *In sleep the soul is at its most vulnerable.*

"The queen's handmaidens," she begins.

Those. They are less than dolls. The reflection shows her a mouth full of incisors. It enunciates differently than she does, as though it is trying words out, a new language. Borrowing how she pronounces Ughali and then reshaping them slightly, rounding out the edge, sanding off certain consonants. *I can veil myself from them any time and veil you the same. I'm a god.*

Nuawa can't quite help it—she barks out a laugh. "Certainly you are."

A flash of eyes shaped like thin slashes, now black, now brilliant candle-gleam. They run down her simulacrum's jaw, radiant fault-lines. *Do not disrespect me. I'm not even wholly in this world. That upstart snow-woman must balance a spider's line between drawing me here —which is what she needs—and keeping me from manifesting so much she can no longer hold me back. A delicate boundary, one she's failed to maintain in any case, or I wouldn't be speaking to you.*

She shrugs on a robe. When she tests her weight on the injured leg, she finds it entirely painless, and when she examines it she discovers no vestige of Tisui's teeth. All of her is whole, physically at least. The queen ensured that much. "What do I call you?"

The Blade-of-Winds, the Beast-of-Storms. The Sickle. The mountain's syllabary is sacred.

Another being of Yatpun who will not divulge a proper name. Nuawa remembers the queen's boast. *Why bring the fight to them when I can force them here?* This is the cumulation of the Winter Queen's long work, her ancient oath she called it. To summon the gods that made her and avenge herself upon them. "You need me to free you." Simply saying that restores her sense of control: she is not yet defeated—she has something to bargain with again.

An air current skims along her cheek. It is not quite the threat of a razor blade against skin. *Whereas you require me to overthrow your little tyrant. Shall we work together, or against one another?*

Through the course of her life she's received this offer many times. What strange allies working against the Winter Queen attracts. "For a god of foreign shores you sound almost human."

Winds are fluid things, child of glass. One thing is obvious: no cage may contain the storm.

"What will you do once you're freed?"

Another impression of those eyes and a sickle claw dragging slowly along the wall. It leaves no marks, nowhere near corporeal enough. *What will I do? Are you afraid, glass-bearer, that you'll unleash on your world something worse than the little tyrant? She couldn't bring me all the way across. What you hold is a mere fragment—be assured that you wouldn't be able to host the entirety of what I am. Nor do I wish to remain in or take your country.*

"How can I trust that a god of Yatpun wouldn't want to repeat the Winter Queen's despotism? You made her." Even as she says that she knows the name Yatpun is wrong, that the queen's homeland is called something else entirely. A name like a magnolia made of verglas and the first glaze of dawn, which in the mountains—those mountains of gods—is a deep, unique blue. Unbidden knowledge, shared by the Sickle's presence.

The god's voice deepens to a smoky contralto, the voice that she knows nearly as well as her own. That she has heard in amusement, in pain, in carnal ecstasy. Lussadh's. *Yours is a wretched world, glass-bearer. It is inhospitable to us. That the little runaway can survive there at all requires unbelievable expense in the dead.*

The real reason the queen's always taken such an excess of tithes. Not mindless greed but ravenous necessity. Nuawa ponders that, not that it improves her opinion of the queen any.

The door opens. She whips around, half-expecting the Winter Queen. Instead, it is the general.

"How are you holding up?" Lussadh's voice is careful. She takes off her coat, an affair of oxblood fabric and a lining of near-black threaded through with motifs in brass thread. It is an unnecessary layer since she doesn't feel the cold any more than Nuawa does.

"I'm not in any pain." Nuawa stops herself, barely, from glancing back at the window to check whether the Sickle is still there. It would not show itself to anyone else, and she suspects even if it did nobody would be able to see it.

"That's good."

Silence, for a time. Neither of them approaches the other. Nuawa does not need to look hard to know the general is armed —she always is, with a blade and the swarm-gun, however subtly the latter is holstered. Nuawa is unarmed entirely. Letting her hands fall she allows the robe to gape, give Lussadh a glimpse to recall their wedding night. It fulfills its intended purpose—the general's gaze follows that in an exact line, stopping at the tip of one revealed breast.

"Nuawa," the general says. "Will you tell me why you did it?"

"I didn't wake up that day with Captain Durgesh's death on my mind." Nuawa wonders how eyewitness accounts describe the event. Probably with little accuracy. "He asked me how I felt when I watched my mother die."

Lussadh's expression is still, no longer distractible by any offer of the flesh, any tempting suggestion. "That was provocation, yes."

A coin-toss between dissembling and partial honesty. She chooses the latter; as far as counter-interrogation tactics go half-truths are far more useful than outright lies. "You know whose child I am. Someone must've already told you. The captain must have."

"I know something of your family." Lussadh keeps her hands at her sides. No sudden movement, in the same way she wouldn't make any around a skittish animal.

"Then you know everything." Testing the general in turn: this is where Lussadh will admit how much or how little she is aware. If at all, but there's no possibility of complete ignorance, with what Ulamat did when he had her brother's corpse brought to Kemiraj, and now with the insinuations Durgesh made. Lussadh wouldn't know of Nuawa's attempt on the queen but all else might well be an open book.

The general says nothing. Waiting for Nuawa to go on and implicate herself, perhaps. Quiet is its own tool.

She obliges; she performs. "The queen bore witness to my execution of Indrahi Dasaret, the woman who raised me. You met Indrahi, I recall." Her hands clench in her robe—not entirely feigned. "I was raised a certain way, with discipline and precision, but I didn't grow up entirely miserable. The person who went into the kiln with me *was* my mother. Truth be told, I don't remember much about her. Maybe she loved me. Maybe she brought me into the kiln with her because she did not, or maybe she had no choice. It's not as if I could ask. And I don't remember my time inside the kiln, either. In any case, I am monster enough that it hasn't mattered all that much."

Lussadh draws closer, taking her hand, guiding her to the divan. "I would have forbidden Durgesh this, had I known what he meant to do. Your history is not to be toyed with."

"So the captain must've discussed some of that with you." Nuawa grips the fabric harder, reminding herself that she stands on the cusp. "You didn't say anything to me or question me."

"It wasn't Durgesh. I knew of it earlier. I've not brought it up—you can appreciate that my particular background predisposes me to view such things differently."

What she says next will be critical, even how she says it. So she yields, softening against the general's arm, looking down. "My past forged me—makes me as I am. But my present decides my actions, and what I want now is to be yours, General. For you to do with as you please."

The general kisses her brow. "About Durgesh. I'll need to take action, if only for show, to demonstrate that even my wife is not exempt from punishment. Other glass-bearers will need to see it, the officers who don't wear the hyacinth will need to see it. Durgesh was loved by the soldiers in Jalsasskar and feted in Qingyuan, his birth city."

"What have you decided on?" Flogging, Nuawa speculates, or hard labor—something degrading and utterly public.

"Something nominal. You're *my* wife." Lussadh cradles her chin in one hand. "Publicly I'll announce that I have banished you. I will send you to the very edge of winter's territory, a place in Johramu's outskirts where you'll need to lie low. Officially you'll be under house arrest. In practical terms, you'll live semi-anonymously. It will not be long. I will come to you as soon as I can."

Her shoulders tense. "And the length of my sentence?" From that distance she won't be able to hinder or stop the queen.

"Three years, because of who Durgesh was. But …" The general takes Nuawa's hand and presses it to her chest, lets Nuawa feel her heartbeat. "I'll discover some exonerating facts, a crime or treason unearthed from his recent activities. The captain served me as well as he could, he never did me ill and he was fine as a glass-bearer. Yet to have you with me again I will tarnish his memory if I must. For appearances, let's say that it will take me a few months to finesse this. Your banishment will be reduced or rescinded altogether. And even before that, I'll go stay with you. The place I have in mind is by the sea, a gracious house with its own staff—I do not mean to send you into squalor and misery."

"Who will be my chaperone?" There'd have to be one, to ensure her good behavior. Darkly she thinks it's as well her kin are gone; no one may be held hostage.

"No one. I know you'll wait for me. I have every trust in you."

She's passed the test, for now. Nuawa flattens her palm against the general's chest, stroking down, leaning close. "Then have me, General, and let me have you." She doesn't say, *For one last time*. Why tempt the vagaries of fate, hurry the turn of samsara.

"So you'll have something to remember me by." Lussadh pushes her down onto the divan.

For the first time what they do together is gentle, slow to the point that Nuawa is nearly impatient, used as she is to their mutual conflagration—to the roar and the flare—but she lets

Lussadh set the pace, allows herself to be held down. More tender than restraining, more longing than lust. She has never thought Lussadh capable of such, of this demonstration of sweetness.

Lussadh moves slowly inside her, agonizing, as though she means to trap Nuawa on the verge for eternity, the precipice from which she can't quite fall—held suspended, breathless, wanting.

But the fall comes, and even this is softer than it's ever been with Lussadh, a fall in which there's no great plummet or shattering. Instead, she lands lightly, feather on dandelion. Nuawa clings on, her breathing harsh, her need incandescent. When it ends she whispers the general's name, once.

EIGHT

In the carriage, Major Guryin sits opposite her. Nuawa expected snow-maids to escort her, but xe has volunteered to be her sole guard. Most of the ride has been quiet until now, as they ascend and draw near the train station. Guryin holds out a long, sable-trimmed coat. "This is in your wedding gift pile. Johramu's colder than here; I thought you might want something warmer than our uniform."

"Thank you, Major. That's thoughtful. I suspect I'll not be wearing the uniform much where I am going." She keeps her tone casual as if nothing has changed. "Did you get a chance to speak to your sister?"

Xer expression tightens. "Yes. She was … vexed with me. You didn't strike up conversation about my sister or Pamalidos out of nowhere. Did you? You'd never asked about any of that before."

"I only thought it small talk when you brought up your home." Nuawa picks her words with care; she can hardly say that her mother gave her an oblique warning. "The rest occurred to me as you spoke because details were missing. I didn't know that the … gift we all bear might affect the mind. Make things slip."

"You're sure."

"I am sure. Have you asked anyone else? If there's anything missing."

"I've been poking Imsou about it, they seem to have all in order, it's just ..." Guryin flutters xer hand as if trying to shake off a persistent fly. "This is hard to verify. But about Durgesh."

Nuawa checks her suitcases one more time, ensuring each lock is tight and in place. Funds will most likely not be a problem —she has enough assets in Sirapirat she can liquidate, if that is what it comes to, and her wages from the military will keep her going a good while yet. "What about him?"

"The general said you had cause to act as you did. It just doesn't seem like you."

"It was rash. Yes."

"Listen, Nuawa, I don't know what goes on in your mind, not exactly. You're a difficult person. But even with this ... issue we're talking of, even with you having to go away for a time, this is a good life."

"I suppose that it is, Major."

"It is. You have money, you have power, you can have nearly anything you want. And you have the general—the general! One of winter's greatest beauties and you're wedded to her. Many would kill to be in your place. Not just that. You and Lussadh are in love, you're glad to be waking up next to each other. What you have together is a supreme treasure and you can keep having this for years and years. Decades."

Nuawa folds the coat more compact so it will fit into her lap. A luxury of texture, passing through her fingers like a dark brook. "You're a true romantic."

"Yes. If anyone threatens what I have with Imsou, I'd hunt them down and their family too." Guryin leans forward. "I mean that. And I mean it too, about you and her; you can't lie to me that you are not helpless for her. This fortune you have seized, it's not going to come again and most never find its like. Don't risk this. Don't do anything to break Lussadh's heart."

All along, Guryin has known—has intuited, in the abstract if not in the specific, that Nuawa is not what she professes to be. And yet xe has never put her in jeopardy. Why not, she wonders. That sincere desire to see Lussadh happy. That weakness of the heart, the exposed nerve of tenderness: raw to the elements, easily wounded. In that way, Guryin may love Lussadh more than Nuawa possibly ever can.

"She has not annulled our marriage," Nuawa says, at length. "I remain hers. I'll endeavor to be worthy of that, to be worthy of her. To cherish her heart as I would cherish my own."

"See that you do. Though I don't know if you treat *your* heart all that well." Xe uncrosses xer legs. "Johramu's not so bad. Lussadh is putting you up in a little house she owns, rather nice, I recall. Think of it as a vacation. Live in slow time; no responsibilities."

They pull into the train station. The major takes her suitcases for her, and together they wend onto the platform, their uniform and hyacinth parting the crowd before them. Nuawa pays for a civilian's ticket—no one presses why she doesn't board the military carriage, where passage is free for a soldier of winter.

"I'll come visit you." Guryin hands her suitcases over. "Stay out of trouble."

"I'm proficient at that, Major. I will behave." Nuawa inclines her head slightly. "Older-sibling."

Xe stares at her, then blinks quickly as if to stem sudden tears. "Until we meet again, younger-sibling."

It feels like a short time ago since she arrived in Kemiraj. She follows the trail of steam in the distance, of a train departing for Qingyuan. Bearing pelts, crystallized cactus sweets, jewelry. And ghosts, always ghosts. The currency that outstrips gold, platinum, or the core of meteorites. No coin matches it in value.

She takes a private compartment, first-class, notes in passing that it is far less plush and comfortable than what is offered in the military carriage. A seat that pulls out into a bed, a luggage rack overhead with straps to hold it all down, several pamphlets that inform her of the dining car's menu and when food is served: for a first-class passenger, food can be had at nearly any hour.

Bohyun gave her medications against infection and against pain in case the prosthesis acts up; a charm to reconnect the prosthesis should its couplings loosen; a referral to a Johramu chiurgeon. Thorough. As she examines them, she considers whether the queen engineered this, revealing what she did to Durgesh with the knowledge that Durgesh would try to provoke Nuawa. Almost certainly. She rose to the bait, played right into the queen's hand. She wants Nuawa out of the way, but what is occluded is *why*. The queen could simply have ordered Nuawa to attend some busywork at the furthest end of winter. Unless the goal was to also drive a wedge between her and Lussadh.

No point brooding over it now: she doesn't intend to stay put in Johramu and is already planning how to steal back into Kemiraj. She waits for the Sickle to speak, but it's chosen silence. Perhaps once they're further away from Kemiraj, provided the physical distance between her and Vahatma's hall doesn't sever the connection entirely.

She is famished. It is unlikely she will be attacked here: Lussadh said that news of her disgrace will be delayed, publicized tomorrow at the earliest. Even if by chance Nuawa encounters a soldier or Qingyuan citizen who was a devoted enthusiast of all things Durgesh, they wouldn't know yet that she is the reason the captain is no longer around for them to adore. All the same, she keeps her arms on her.

The dining car is half-full. She takes an isolated table and orders herself steamed dumplings, one of the few items on the menu that aren't Kemiraj cuisine. At this moment, Kemiraj dishes make her think of meals with the general. Those intimate moments. Nuawa steers her mind away from the prospect of never regaining them.

Despite the hyacinth she wears prominently, she hears footsteps coming her way as she is halfway through her dumplings. She looks up into the face of the foreigner Ghazal.

"We keep running into each other," ey says in eir peculiar accent. "It must be fate. Could I join you? I can tell from your expression you'd rather be alone, but this is *such* a long journey. We'll be here for three whole days, according to my maps, and I needed someone to talk the new Sushmita with …"

Ey has put aside eir robes in favor of trousers and vest, practical and sharp, and thigh-high black boots. At eir waist hangs a blade of unusual length, the hilt charred black, the scabbard made of wood. A weapon that demands attention: too showy, Nuawa thinks, more suited to a duelist about to step into the arena. She can see no hint of others on Ghazal's person--no holster, no ammunition.

"You have a license to carry a blade?"

"I do. Honest." Ghazal draws a doeskin fold from eir vest, opens it, and pulls a laminated permit from one of its sleeves. Registered to eir name, it grants the use and bearing of weapons, excluding firearms. Authorized with the signature of the Johramu governor, acting in the Winter Queen's name. "May I sit with you now?"

Nuawa gestures. "By all means. You're right that it is a long journey." For all that she prefers solitude, thinking while alone has not solved any of her most pressing problems. What the queen wants. Why she has been sent away. A distraction may be what she needs. "Could you remind me what you do for a living again?"

"I never did tell you. Would you believe it if I say I'm a wandering poet?"

"Who pens verses with the tip of a sword? And who obtained an arms permit that takes quite a lot of bureaucratic navigation for foreigners?"

Ey laughs, holding up eir hands as ey sits. "I work as a translator for an occidental embassy in Johramu. My mother was from Qingyuan but became an occidental man's mistress, and I spent much of my childhood in those benighted lands—thus my Mehrut being substandard. But I do have the perk of the ambassador getting this permit for me, though as we speak I'm called home to mundane duties."

Nuawa puts one soup dumpling in her mouth. No use letting it go cold. "You're part occidental?" Ey doesn't look it.

"Oh, no. I was a baby when my mother became occidental property."

She wonders if she should offer condolences. It doesn't seem appropriate. Instead, she pushes the menu over to Ghazal. "My treat, traveler."

Conversation with this foreigner is easy. Ey speaks of eir time in the occident, regaling her with how much in the Detective Sushmita books is accurate and how much is not, adding, "Not that they *have* to be realistic, they're entertainment after all." If eir childhood was difficult, ey makes no mention of it beyond that the cuisines of eir childhood home were bland, and that Nuawa would likely find it utterly inedible.

"Is there anything to recommend the occidental countries?" Nuawa asks at one point.

"Largely suppressive theocracies." Ghazal ticks off eir fingers. "Women are kept in cages, essentially, and may own only so much property; your marriage would not be recognized as it is not between a man and a woman; the transport infrastructure is terrible. The food, as I've said, is fit for pigs and not much else. No, I can't think of any redeeming grace."

Other than the absence of ghost-kilns and the taxes paid in souls. "Would you prefer to settle in winter?"

"Oh, absolutely. It's why I got myself this posting. The result of a decade's worth of labor."

After the meal they part ways, Ghazal disappearing to the less expensive end of the train. She spends a few minutes guessing at eir angle: striving to curry favor with a winter officer, perhaps, in search of an advantage that'd secure eir stay in winter. For the moment she doesn't mind the company, and in any case, she no longer wields the influence to get em anything of the sort.

There is not much to do on a train and little room to move about; in the end, she returns to her compartment, reading some of the books she packed for the journey. Those become tedious after a time. She should've purchased more mindless entertainment, but even the Sushmita doesn't keep her attention for long.

The recesses of your mind are less dull than I expected. In fact very ordered, like exploring the inside of a beehive or a clock. Yours is such a computational soul, the result of melding with that mirror. Most unusual.

She glances up, finds once more the Sickle in the windowpane—she wonders if glass is a common affinity of Yatpun gods or whether all reflective surfaces serve. Again it's taken on her form, though it's chosen to make her lips fuller and redder, luminescent. Veins of vermillion light run, fluvial, beneath the Sickle's skin.

"I take it distance from Kemiraj won't hinder our communications."

The Sickle shows her its too-long teeth and its too-long tongue. *There's no exorcising me. I've put my hooks in you and in your shard of glass. That's what you agreed to, remember? Our little pact.*

Nuawa closes her book, returning it to her luggage. "What can you do if I'm that far away, in Johramu?"

Let me worry about that. First I want to extract from you a promise. Will you do anything if it means your enemy's downfall?

"Define *anything*."

In the pane, the Sickle has grown several mouths: thin slashes beneath its cheekbones, across its clavicles. *I'm very hungry. The upstart has starved me, thinking she can weaken me for the harvest. But we can come to mutual benefit. Reach toward me.*

She does, with caution. When she touches the glass, frost buds in the shape of petals: serrated geometry rapidly layering itself into angular roses and lilies. They crack and hiss as they form against the blur of the landscape rushing by. Pain throbs in her wrist as this happens, a direct line from her chest to fingertips. Unpleasant, but endurable.

You see. The spirit cranes its head toward her. *I can pluck at*

your piece of mirror—I helped make it—and allow you to wield it. In
exchange, I'll need you to feed me.

As the god takes shape, the size of it grows and grows until it fills
the room, dwarfing Vahatma's. A creature of chiseled angles and
hard edges like filigreed iron, and a lower half that flutters gently
in the air like a long banner of silk. The anatomy of it is impossible, and Lussadh tries not to look too hard at the point where the
upper body descends into the flat, two-dimensional part. Two
etiolated limbs extend from its torso, chitinous and taper-curved
like scimitars.

The queen has raised a throne for herself and she sits,
watching the solidifying god and drinking souls out of ceramic
cups. Her snow-maids sit at her feet, their gazes rapt upon the
god, unblinking.

"You've been ordering thaumaturges to weave wards around
this hall," the queen says, setting her black lacquered cup on a
handmaiden the way she would on a table or a tray. "Very many
of them. It must have been resource-intensive. Ghazal must have
told you? It'll not work on this thing."

"It seems worth trying." Lussadh briefly considers that the
queen speaks of Ghazal as a being of eir own volition. "I'd prefer
no further senseless death."

"Were there more casualties?"

"A few." No one important, at least. But after dethroning her
grandaunt, Lussadh has tried to adopt the creed that *unimportant*
does not apply; that all citizens of Kemiraj are hers to protect, so
long as they do not disrupt the administration or the law.

"It won't be long. Soon I will cut this god's heart out, bleed it,
harvest it—make what it has my own. Then I will force the next
one through."

She stiffens and glances at the god's multitude of eyes. "How many, my queen?" The prospect of this repeating, perhaps wilder and less predictable next time, is hardly thrilling.

"Ideally until my homeland is empty of these tyrants." But she laughs. "No, I can only do this to the least of them. Three, perhaps. How I long to break their might once and for all—but I must not get ahead of myself. When it's time for me to take this god, will you be here? I want you to see." The queen reaches for her, takes her hand, and kisses the back of it. "I'll distill their power into a miracle, and that miracle I'll turn into a gift for you. The greatest gift that can be granted any human."

For all her unease, the queen's touch still spears her, a frisson. The tenderness that is given to her alone. She bends to kiss her queen's head. "I'm used to your extravagance, but this seems exceptional even from you. To bend gods into a gift—what is it really, Your Majesty?"

The queen cranes her neck back to look up at Lussadh. "To make your soul a dark ocean, endless, the same way mine is. There is no point to my accomplishments if I cannot bring that about. When the time comes, you'll understand. But let us set that aside; are you aggrieved that you had to send Nuawa away?"

"I would have preferred not to."

"You didn't have to." The queen's voice thrums, amused, as she drains another cup. One of her handmaidens refills it, a liquid-shadow soul. It flutters like a caught bird as it sloshes into ceramic. "Some might have protested, but you could have ignored them. Still, I let you run things as you will; time apart might make your reunion more piquant. And I shouldn't keep you from your duties either."

She knows a dismissal when she hears it. "Summon me if I'm required, my queen."

Outside the hall the air is gravid from the sheer concentration of wards, a mesh so tightly constructed that no curse or hex may permeate it. The work of half a dozen thaumaturges in tandem, with rotating shifts. It may be superfluous in the end, but she dislikes not being able to do anything. Etheric force is etheric force: surely the Yatpun god must be subjected to constraints.

Returning to her office, to her mundane work, feels almost alienating. More so when she remembers what she did with Nuawa on her desk not so long ago. She goes through her papers, the things that require signing, the administrative appointments she'll need to confirm or postpone or cancel. But she finds she cannot concentrate. She paces in hope of clarity and is soon reminded that tonight she will be sleeping alone. It shouldn't bother her—she has slept alone often all her life, far more than she's slept with a bed companion.

In the end, she turns on a charm Guryin made for her, one that shifts her features slightly off true, enough not to be recognized save by those who know her intimately. Then she leaves the palace by one of the many exits only she can access—the architecture continues to be hers, as sensitive to her moods and wants as a devoted pet.

She is not sure, at first, where she is going until her feet lead her down the tiers. Kemiraj has several houses of pleasure, but she avoids the one where she might run into her own ministers and subordinates. And at such establishments Lussadh will need to reveal, at the very least, that she is an officer of winter to gain entry. Better to head to a place more agnostic to status that answers to the plainer scale of money.

The Pomegranate Orchard is one of the older establishments in the city and was often her choice when she was young in search of wilder fare than the palace courtesans. Ownership of the place has changed hands over the years, but a standard is kept. She's welcomed into an expansive tearoom, placid at this time of the day—too early for those who seek what the Orchard has to offer, this particular sport being more suited to evenings and late nights when the blooming of dusk roses begins and nocturnal birds make their emergence. A succession of staff serves her tea, delicate pastries, little plates of spiced plums.

After her obvious disinterest toward a male waiter, the rest that attends her are women or, like her, any of the four other genders particular to Kemiraj. The scythe, the chalice, the ziggurat, and the cornucopia. She always found it amusing, as she began orienting toward the full shape of herself, that hers is expressed in symbology as the scythe. King Ihsayn was chalice in her younger years and ziggurat later on—apposite in some ways, in others less so.

Midway through her tea, Lussadh half-expects Ghazal to appear—a diversion, a bit of entertainment; this time she might even sleep with em, should ey make that invitation. But ey never materializes.

Her eyes fall on an attendant who's just entered the room, beginning their shift, built not like a courtesan at all but a runner. They're clad in an austere coat and underneath that trousers and vest more suited to military service than to a brothel—at first, she thinks them another patron until they bring her a tiny portion of crystallized pineapples.

"Sit with me," she instructs.

The courtesan gives her a smile that goes through her like an arrowhead. At once she realizes who they resemble—the same build, and they must be from Sirapirat or Qingyuan, fair-skinned in the same way Nuawa is. Little alike in features except in the most passing of ways, the shape and angle of the nose, a part of the profile. Nevertheless, the resemblance—and much of that may be delusional on Lussadh's part, her eyes seeing Nuawa in everything—tips the balance of her mood. She could go to bed with them and have a perfectly satisfactory afternoon; anyone working here is bound to be skilled.

She makes conversation. In that, too, the courtesan is adept, and though the more they talk the less they resemble her wife, still she cannot unmake the association. She watches their hands move. She studies their lips. She thinks of Nuawa on the divan.

When her calling-glass chimes it comes as a relief, and she

leaves the Orchard roughly the same amount it would have taken to hire the courtesan for a couple hours.

Outside of the Orchard she activates the glass: Guryin.

"This is urgent," xe says, xer tone careful. "I'm at a barrack near the train station. Ulamat was just here to commandeer more practitioners, and … I don't have an easy way to put this."

"Out with it." Lussadh finds her tone more snappish than her wont, especially with the major.

"Can you head this way? It's … bad news. Very bad news."

There is only one thing that could make Guryin this reticent. And only glass-bearers, supposedly, enjoy any protection from the Yatpun divinity's fury.

Ulamat is no glass-bearer.

She reaches the barrack in no time—it is close enough, in walking distance. A captain, pale-faced, salutes her and nearly falls to his knees begging her pardon, as though he could possibly have prevented anything.

"Get up, Captain," Lussadh says, controlling herself as best she can. "Take me to the site of incident."

The site being the infirmary, where she is told Ulamat was consulting a barrack medic for their expertise on wounding thaumaturgy, on effigy sacrifice. Someone kept the window open.

Ulamat has been left where he fell. Torn apart like the others, in a pool of his own gore. She cannot look at it clinically as she's looked at all the others.

"I'm sorry," Major Guryin offers from behind her. "I gave him protective charms, but they just didn't do any good. Kept an eye on him even, because I knew you'd have wanted me to, and my familiar couldn't do a single thing when this happened. I couldn't even *see* what was going on."

"Leave me." Lussadh knows her lips must be a taut, pale line.

They make themselves scarce, Guryin and the captain both. Lussadh takes hold of Ulamat's head, one of the few intact parts. She holds it in her lap, heedless of the leaking fluids, the congealing crust of mortal matter.

The child she brought out of the dust and the mud, the companion who's been her most loyal, through the coup, through the regime change. "My old friend," she says softly, cradling the shred of spine that trails from his nape. But he does not answer —in life he would have been appalled to hear her address him as *friend* rather than her servant—and nor will he ever again.

NINE

Nuawa stirs. She does not remember dozing off. An afterimage lingers: the vision of a young woman, hair streaming like a black comet, sprinting across snow as though there's no weight to her, as though she's flying. She kneels. A body in the endless white, sinking with its own weight, ruptured. The girl cradles this carcass, and for a flash she thinks she sees that this girl has eyes like starbursts.

The vision dissipates. She blinks and looks out to gray, sluggish dawn. Hours have passed her by, twelve or sixteen. Her throat is parched. She takes a sip out of her flask—discovers to her surprise that it is chrysanthemum tea rather than plain water. A small card is attached. From Guryin: *Remember to take good care of yourself. That's not a request.*

She stares at the card for a time before tucking it into her jacket. What a small thing to make her heart seize. She can't remember the last time she was cared for this way.

Outside her compartment it is quiet, the other passengers enclosed in their own. By now they must be halfway to Johramu, bound for a stop in the middle to exchange disembarking passengers for new ones, to resupply the train and refuel the ghosts. That will be her opportunity, her break for freedom.

The air is kept comfortably warm and sometimes she thinks of what it would be like without the kilns: nothing else is quite as efficient, as convenient. There are citizens of winter who believe that to live without the ghosts is to live as savages. The heating, the trains, entire thaumaturgic systems refined and held together by the queen's machines.

She marches down the length of the car, loosening her stiff muscles. Good sense points her toward the dining car, where there is more space in which to stretch her legs. But ghosts are on her mind, and she chooses instead to head for the car reserved for the use of military officers and select civil servants, the governors, or their retinues. She takes out her hyacinth, presses it to the military car's lock; it falls open, disengaging.

No soldier bars her way. Odd. The car is too cold and she soon discovers a window open, the winds howling outside. From her window, the weather seemed calm.

She almost steps onto a corpse.

At first, she hardly recognizes it for the remains of a human —she is used to violence in all its forms, to what can be done to a body: the swift murders, the ostentatious duels, the sudden ending. Yet none of them produce a result quite like this, not even when she tortured the assassin Ytoba. What lies on the floor doesn't seem as though it ever cohered into a person. It looks more like the ground of an abattoir, the consequences of unrelenting engines that flense meat from bones, and turn that meat into fine strips. How one might prepare pork for a deep, flavorful marinade that would later be charred, sizzling, and fragrant on a plate lined with banana leaves.

Hunger plucks at Nuawa. She bends closer to the body, drawn not by the scent of viscera—the slashed intestines, the tattered mesentery—but by something else, a fragrance that reminds her of passionfruit, touched with the mild floral note of mangoes. Impossibly sweet, nothing like how gore should smell. She is voracious.

Her fingers slide into the wet, almost-liquid folds of disemboweled flesh. But this is not what she's looking for, the gross mortal material that soaks her fingertips in transient warmth, that is fast staining the floor. She inhales, and then she sees it, the wisps that hover above the devastated carcass. They are like steam, except when she puts her hand in them they are tangible, the texture of thin cotton. It flows into her palm and she cups it in her hands, bringing it close.

The soul flies into her mouth like a bird eager for its roost. She's never tasted anything like this. It is sugared egg floss; it is palm fruit and lychee at the perfect stage of ripe; it is jasmine water and red tea steeped to perfection. All things sweet and delectable. Her heart leaps and her arteries course with a rush more potent than that of any liquor, more immediate than any drug. Strength and possibility, the knowledge that anything she wants she can possess; that any obstacle in her path she can crush underfoot. Limitless might. The certainty that the horizon can be hers, if only she reaches for it.

Now you know what it is to consume souls.

She bolts to her feet, whipping around. There is no one. Of course, there is not. What speaks does so from within her. "When did you do this?" While she slept—while it put her to sleep.

You cannot contain the wind. A noise like heels clicking on wood. *I have prepared for you a feast. You only need to eat. Taste what it is like to have no fear. Taste what it is like to be your foe's equal.*

Nuawa raises her head. Realizes, now, that the entire car is dead. Perhaps a soldier opened the window for a brush of fresh air, or because they preferred the cold over the artificial warmth. A single mistake, a tiny gap between windowpane and frame. "Why this many?" Not that it stains her conscience. For all her life, her opinion of those wearing the winter military uniform— the same one cladding her now—has never been high.

Its eyes burn bright, brighter. *I got carried away. But we are both famished, you and I.*

She opens one compartment and finds, as she anticipated,

another corpse. Utterly eviscerated, draped on the seat in slim ribbons. Her vision adjusts and, now that she concentrates, the ghost is luminous. Raw and fresh, as yet untouched by the processes that make them compact and containable, by the prayers the queen teaches her priests. She thinks of reaching for it; stops, even as appetite sings and claws at her ribcage. Almost identical to real hunger. Nearly impossible to distinguish between this and want for a meal of rice and fish sauce, a craving for the sweetness that hides within the heart of a marzipan fruit. "The Heron ended up poorly from eating souls."

The Sickle does not ask her who or what the Heron is; either it knows or it has delved deep into her memories. *He didn't have a divinity within him to temper the effects. You are in safe hands, child of glass, the most potent thing that upstart snow-woman ever raised. She's tried so many times to foster mirror pieces to perfection, and now there's you.*

The ghosts flicker like candlelight, and not strong ones. Intuitively she knows that if she doesn't take them they will dissipate, flee toward the afterlife, or maybe nothing at all. Nullified like smoke. "What is it going to do to me?"

Grant you greater might than what I've shown you before, allow you to perform fantastical feats. Drawing ice out of the air will soon look unimpressive. You're hungry, aren't you?

She is, and she knows she could be gluttonous, devouring and devouring. It would feed this god within her. It would make her strong, such that she can challenge the queen; all this and more comes easily, as though she's been aware all along, the same way she is aware that the sun rises in the east and sinks in the west. But she knows better than to trust it. Too easy. Against her better judgment, she closes her fist around the soldier's shivering soul. As before it flows into her the way filings flow to a magnet. The rush, again. Less overwhelming but still intoxicating.

There is no point asking the creature to promise that it will not malinger to reproduce the queen's evils once she's freed it from the queen's cage. She has no means of extracting any pledge, enforcing any contract. She has only herself and the scalpel of her own will.

By now she's nearly at the end of the military car. The train is slowing to a stop: not derailing or crashing, that much is sheer good luck, because she doubts the driver has survived the Sickle's demonstration.

Another corpse. By the robes, she can tell that this is the queen's priest, assigned to govern and nurture the train's ghosts. She squats on the floor and breathes deeply. The soul of a priest versed in thaumaturgy, she soon discovers, does not resist any better than the layperson's. Neither does it taste different. In the end, the dead are simply the dead, and one ghost is like any other.

The Sickle's hand seems to be clasped to hers, its flesh red, its claws long and black. *You must have seen that upstart disappear from one place then reappear in quite another, materializing out of thin air. Let me tell you of the craft of folding distances.*

Lussadh returns to her room sodden in Ulamat's blood. For minutes she stands there, unmoving, her muscles locked in place. She must've given orders for the collection and preservation of his corpse, for the upcoming death rites. But she doesn't remember any of them, barely remembers coming home.

Absence is like a thorn. It does not escape her that she has few people she holds dear who remain with her, who remain alive. The long decades and most of them spent killing. Most of the courtiers and officers loyal to her during the coup are gone. The few cousins she loved. And now Ulamat, one of the last pieces of her life as the king-in-waiting, the life that she hardly misses but there's value in longevity—in reminders. The faithful retainer who always said he'd die for her.

Now he has. Incidentally, ignobly. Not even an intentional sacrifice; he died like a dog run over by a passing carriage.

She sheds her jacket, tosses it into the hamper; knows it will soon stink. The blood will soak the lining. She can't make herself care. Exhaustion sets in, bone-deep.

When she walks into the bedroom, she finds Nuawa waiting for her in bed.

Her wife is naked, the furs covering one breast and one thigh, leaving the rest bare. Asleep, cheek pillowed on one hand. Lussadh's heartbeat hitches. It is like looking at a new dawn after a terrible night.

She approaches, thinking, *Fuck Jalsasskar*. The garrison commanders of both that and Qingyuan may rage outside her very door for months over Durgesh's demise and it would not matter. She'll issue an official amnesty, impose only house arrest on Nuawa at the palace. How her wife returned she doesn't care — the lieutenant is resourceful. Penjarej's death — she no longer cares about that, either. All that matters is having Nuawa at her side.

Lussadh reaches for a bare, rounded shoulder. The instant she closes her grip she knows this is not Nuawa. Could never possibly have been.

She snatches her hand away, repulsed. "You are not my wife." A fragment like Ghazal, or …

When the construct opens its eyes, she knows it's even less than that. A snow-maid, created in Nuawa's shape — the mold and nothing more, outline without substance. Its eyes are dark and blank, its expression serene, nothing like her wife's brush-stroke features. Alike in suggestion but without the animating force, a blanched statue next to the real thing's vibrancy. Her lieutenant has never been a woman of mobile expression but next to this she is vital, real.

Why the queen has sent her this is obvious: it is such comfort as a glacier might extend. Fury beats through her. "I want to see the queen," she growls. "Bring her to me."

The handmaiden looks up at her with Nuawa's gaze, or a thin simulacrum of it. The idea of sleeping with this turns her stomach. It tilts its head and she resists the urge to strike it. That would be no different from lashing out at a hound. It possesses sufficient intelligence to get out of her sight. She stares at the indentations it left behind, seized with an impulse to burn the bedding down. A deep breath. She strips, casting off the bloodied garments like dead skin, thinking of ablutions: hot and thorough. Lussadh doesn't seek solace in pain but scalding water does not sound so terrible.

By the time the queen arrives, she's nude. The queen enters through the window, a haze that reforms on her side of the pane. Lussadh has never seen her do this before, but now must be the zenith of her power. All those imbibed ghosts.

"You sent for me." The queen is dressed in the thinnest of gossamer, shivering membranes of ice, her feet and throat bare.

She did not expect the queen to come. "My aide is dead." And her wife is on the way to the other end of the continent.

"That is true. I was under the impression he wasn't one of your lovers."

Lussadh stares, appalled. "No. Of course not." Even if she were attracted to men, she'd never have bedded someone she practically raised from childhood. "That's — how is that pertinent?"

The queen blinks, her eyelashes crackling quietly. Granules of frost speckle her cheeks like miniature stars, an astrologer's chart. "Is that not how your love runs, in a singular line, a sole direction? Like time's arrow. It does not bend or diverge. It does not go backward or sideways. For those you desire alone you rouse your passion, and for them alone you reserve your grief and a seat in the abode of your heart. Myself. Your wife. All humans love this way, picking a specific sort of love and remaining true to the category."

Her mouth opens and this nearly turns into a disbelieving laugh. What stands before her has never been human, but the queen has been in this land for so long—much longer than Lussadh has been alive. It never occurred to her that she has been misunderstood so completely; that the queen would believe her capable of love only when it is tied to carnal need, to mating drive. "You've seen human families."

"Yes. They devote themselves to their spouses or to their children, never to both. I've seen them rip their hearts up because an offspring died, without care for their marital partner; I've seen them tear themselves apart because their lover perished and did not keep themselves intact for any progeny they had. Human love is obsessive. They live for one line of affection, a predisposition set from birth or by circumstances. So the first human I ever met said, and so I've found it proven true."

Sheer incredulity lances her rage. "What did they actually say?"

"Why, as much as I have said. That the coefficient of human affection is a single-minded thing. She was a blacksmith, strong of body, honed like the weapons she created. You remind me of her—you always have. It was from her that I took my name, the actual name that I've given to you alone, not this translated title." The queen folds herself and kneels at Lussadh's feet, putting her head against Lussadh's thigh. "The only other human I've ever loved apart from you."

She is inert, then she cups the queen's head, her fingers sinking into a largesse of unbound hair and frazils. It calms her, this exquisite texture, the sensation that she could keep stroking and never find the end of it—a sea more than a river.

"Do you remember," she says, "that when I entered your service you pledged to me that you would never make certain demands? That you'd never do as King Ihsayn did—testing my loyalty by requiring the death of those I love." Twice Ihsayn made her execute her own lovers. First a girl from Shuriam. Then Crow. Revolt came easily, after that.

"I never forget, my treasure. Nor will I violate our pact. No matter what I'll never make you stain yourself. Your heart is my tenderest possession. I'd allow you to break mine first before I'll endanger yours." The queen raises her gaze to meet Lussadh's. "I want you to trust me in that, and in other ways. That I'll never harm you and that I mean to correct the flaw of my first fairytale. The blacksmith was mortal; by the time I met her, she was already dying. But you — I will make *you* eternal."

TEN

ONCE THE SICKLE HAS SHOWN HER HOW, THE ACT OF IT becomes simple.

Under normal circumstances, Nuawa would not have chosen to walk. She is strong, her stamina considerable, but walking from here to Kemiraj is a fool's proposition. Now the elements touch her even less than before, and the distance before her seems like a thing she may cup in her palm, fold like paper, twist into a shape of her liking. Briefly, she wonders if this is how the Winter Queen experiences the world.

Physical topology is an illusion, the Sickle whispers, back to the mimesis of her own voice. *The little runaway has made this land a reflection of her hunger and saturated it with ghosts. They never dissipate completely. In the earth, in the air. Seeds that grow from this continent's soil are steeped in half-wraiths, divided and subdivided, carried in their flowers, their fruits. That's how she cultivated you. The glass-bearers who by chance were born in places heavy with souls, ghosts that seeped into the material of wombs that bore them, iron or flesh. And thus you grew into fine hosts, receptacles through which she refined her stolen mirror.*

She feels she can run toward Kemiraj and her feet would hardly touch the ground. The train is already well behind, will soon be out of sight. "I don't suppose you could tell me her real plans."

The god continues as though she's said nothing, *Once you have grasped the thread of this land, you can manipulate it, bend it as you would bend clay. Spatial relations become moot. You can be here, or there, at a thought.*

Nuawa blinks and her sight switches over. The world redone as silicate structures, everything turned to glass. How everything might look from within a fractured mirror, she thinks, the world as seen through the Winter Queen's gaze. The world that she has reshaped and infiltrated.

She bends and takes a fistful of wet, cold soil in hand. It is as the beast-god has claimed—every grain glitters, polluted by the queen's ravening. She imagines what she would see, now, near the kilns: the air as thick as fog, brilliant with ghost-leavings. "Is there a way to cleanse the land of all this?"

The answer is a huffing laugh, the noise more like an animal's than a person's. The Sickle does not elaborate. Not that it would have any reason to offer her assistance even if the queen's influence can be purified—its sole interest lies in its survival, and it'll help her only that far, not a single step further.

She is looking for the point of fulcrum that the Sickle claims is there that once pressed upon will allow her to cross cities' breadths in mere steps when she hears Ghazal behind her. Nuawa straightens and turns to them with her sword drawn.

Ey approaches with eir hands up. "Come now. No need to be so hostile, Lieutenant."

"How did you follow me, traveler?" Her blade-shadows flare out, tiny writhing tendrils, deceptively diaphanous. Coated in the same patina of ghost-ether as the rest. She wonders if any practitioner has ever noticed that after the queen established her dominion their thaumaturgy changed—everything steeped with the dead. The fakirs and shamans at least must have sensed the difference. But by now the queen's arrival on this continent is nearly out of living memory. No one remembers what it was like to live on soil untouched by the kilns. In this way, the Winter Queen has erased what once was and replaced it with herself.

"I walked." Ghazal's voice is casual. "You left a track."

Nuawa did leave a track, but no human could have kept up with her; by her estimate, she's a day's walk from the train, she has moved that quickly, even as her body doesn't acknowledge it. No hint of fatigue or muscle ache. "What are you?" But already she can tell, discerning from the brilliance that abides within eir breast like a captured star. A fragment of a fragment, kin to what's inside her.

"I can see from your face that it is a rhetorical question." A flash of teeth, eir thin lips peeling back: gums like bleached corals. Eir blade clears eir sheath with more speed than it should, for something so long and for a scabbard so odd. She catches the strange sword on her own: Ghazal's weapon gleams a pure, striking white as though it has been crafted from snow—she thinks at once of the Heron's arms. She deflects. Ey springs back several steps.

"Your reflexes are very good. That is a sword of probability shadows, correct? One doesn't see many of them about. I've been wondering if it is a specialty of Sirapirat blacksmiths. Sirapirat, now that's a fascinating place. Its very sky holds its second golden self, I have heard, a thaumaturgic feat so potent as to be likened to the divine."

She does not intend to let em, whatever ey might be, stall her. The tip of her sword pierces eir guard, slicing open eir flank. It should have scraped along eir ribcage but ey is nimble and it is instead a glancing wound.

If it hurts, Ghazal doesn't show it. Ey sweeps eir blade wide, a duelist's theatrics. "What do you suppose I am? Don't you think I could be the queen's kin?"

"You're one of her handmaidens." A different glaze but a similar core.

"Oh no." Eir laugh chimes, glass against glass. "I'm both less and more. I'm the evidence of your senses, Lieutenant. Look closely. Breathe in my scent. Bear witness to what I am."

Abruptly Ghazal is gone.

Nuawa pivots. Eir long blade whistles past her ear, missing but only just—it could have skewered cartilage, torn off that ear, made a bloody ruin of her face. She thinks at first it is a variation on the probability strands that empower her weapon, a matter of illusions infused with possibility. But then she realizes Ghazal is very much solid, that there is only one of em.

The fulcrum that shifts the nature of physical topology. Not just to fold distances but also to slip sideways: now here, now there.

If the Sickle has commentary or advice to offer, it has chosen to save it for another time, or else it means to test whether she can arrive at the conclusion on her own. She does not try to gain distance from Ghazal—pointless—and when ey materializes again it is from the air, dropping on her.

She answers with a strike that would have cleaved through Ghazal's knees, amputated em cleanly. Ey vanishes but not before her blade-shadows have bitten into eir calf. Blood in the white earth when ey materializes again--ey may be able to manipulate much, but not the coefficient of gravity, of arterial pump and peristaltic flow.

When Ghazal performs eir trick next, she sees it: the ripple of etheric fabric, the interruption in the world's flow. It appears like a serration in thick fog, quickly gone.

Nuawa does not know how to do it, not precisely. She does not yet have the finesse to wield what she's accepted. It is like using a muscle long untried, a muscle she wasn't aware existed. Ghosts in her fingertips. She reaches out; she plucks.

Her blood roars. The world goes silent, then very loud. Agony jabs through her skull. It takes a moment to orient herself: she is indoor, a hostel room she thinks, cramped and strewn with someone's clothes. Luggage lies open at a bed's foot.

Candles burn in sconces—the place is too impoverished to afford ghost-lamps. She shakes herself, trying to get upright.

Well done. Though if I wasn't here to calibrate the distance and spatial relations, you may very well be embedded in a boulder or turned to paste.

"I thought physical topology was an illusion." She presses her palm to her face. The pain recedes little by little. She can't imagine doing this again—and from her surroundings she knows that this is nowhere near Kemiraj. Too grimy by far, not the right style of interior décor; it lacks the intricate capillaries of gold and jewel tones that would run through the wood. A narrow window shows her that she's in a small township or village, likely a traveler's stop than anyone's destination. Worn-looking passersby, bare streets and barer houses. She hasn't the least idea where she is.

The god's mouth, disembodied, is a gash in the dim room. It bleeds light and teeth. *The human mind is susceptible to illusion. You believe in your mortality, so if you find yourself entombed in stone you'll very quickly die. Best stay on your feet, glass-bearer. Your enemy pursues.*

Nuawa sucks in a mouthful of air through clenched teeth. "How do I kill that?"

The usual ways. Though it seems this offshoot creature believes in eir mortality somewhat less fervently than you believe in yours …

The angle at which Ghazal strikes is impossibly precise, as though ey has calculated where she would be and chosen to materialize exactly there. Eir blade would have skewered her through the heart if she'd stayed still. Instead, she wrenches herself sideways and kicks at eir midsection. This time it connects. The little room is too confined for em to warp space without hitting furniture. She presses the advantage, her blade-shadows spreading and filling the circumference of combat. Everywhere Ghazal turns there is a little etheric tendril, and ey flinches from them in a way that lets her know these hurt em far more than the steel.

She is close to cornering em when ey disappears. The floorboards shudder, resonating with the ghost-traces, the path

Ghazal has forged for eir egress. Her blade cleaves through empty air.

A respite. She lets her rhythms slow, back to resting calm or something close to it. Equilibrium came easily to her during all her years in the arena. It does not come easily now. "How many more times do I need to do it? Before I reach Kemiraj."

Your endurance flags. It is admonitive. *Two or three times more.*

It'd be a miracle if she can stand one more of this. She is starting to consider waiting another day when she catches the reek of burning. It rises and thickens fast—the entire building must be wood. She doesn't waste time looking for the source; Ghazal must be trying to smoke her out. "Take me somewhere small and close. A cave."

The Sickle doesn't respond. Covering her mouth and nose, she looks for that thread, the loose place in etheric matter that she can widen into a gateway for her own use. For long minutes she can't locate it, even as smoke begins to fill her lungs and draws a wracking cough out of her. Her throat parches.

She finds it, eventually. A touch. A twist. The world bends.

Nuawa falls to her knees, doubled over, gagging on saliva and smoke. But the air here is clear, clean. She gulps it in and wipes at her mouth. Her gut heaves; she tamps the nausea down.

The chamber is stone, and now she sees the familiar motifs: the black sun with its innumerable rays, the crest of the al-Kattan dynasty. Not Kemiraj yet but close. This is the inner sanctum of a temple, in a place that was once Kemiraj's constituent by force, now winter's. A temple that hasn't yet shed its trappings from the time when the al-Kattan was revered as the descendants of the sun.

She can almost hear Ghazal's passage, drumbeats from a great distance. The same rhythm as what heralds the Winter Queen—she wonders now if that imperial beat has etheric significance if all along the queen traverses her territories not by train or carriage but by this. Fresh agony rakes through her—the price of the Sickle's gift—as she attunes to the percussion of this, the shivering in the air.

Material reality spasms, the tendons and nerves of it in jagged contractions. Nuawa counts, calculating against mathematics whose formulae and rules she can only guess at, roughly approximate. She tenses. She strikes.

Her blade sinks into flesh. It goes through a thigh rather than, as she'd have preferred, through the chest or the throat. But the hemorrhage tells her she struck a femoral artery, and she wastes no time in pinning Ghazal to the wall. Whether ey is made of the same material as any human she is about to find out: she seizes eir head and slams it into the stone. Ey makes a short, choked noise. She does it again.

After the third, ey goes still. By now Nuawa is used to the impossible and so she props eir body against an old icon—some other representative of the al-Kattan right to rule, the divine mandate. It is her habit to keep her blade whetted, a hungry blue edge, and so the first cut into Ghazal's neck is an easy one: the test of steel on skin is typically one of foregone conclusions. It is further in that more force is required, that more resistance is put up by the ligaments, by the bones. She lacks the efficiency of a true executioner, the momentum of the swing, or the elegance of the guillotine answering to gravity. Now she must saw, and the act turns to the sort practiced in a slaughterhouse rather than a judicial court. The spectacle of hemorrhage, the sopping viscosity, the vitreous matters.

Finally, the head comes free. She separates it from the torso and flings it to the ground. Her breathing is labored. "I hope that is dead for good."

Eat it before the power that resides in this construct flees back to its source. Souls are mobile things, and very fast.

"What—" But she can see what the Sickle means at once, the harsh brilliance within Ghazal, the telltale blue-white. Colder and brighter than any of the ghosts in the train.

It goes down scraping her throat like grains of sand or glass milled to glittering dust.

All at once, she feels whole, more than she's ever felt in her life. As though this was the part of her missing since she went into that kiln, since Mother Tafari died. Her breathing turns smooth, her pulse calms, the deep aches left by accessing the mirror shard are gone. She is renewed.

What you call the Winter Queen, the Sickle whispers, *is now stretched at her thinnest. Containing my spirit on one hand. Reeling from the whiplash of losing that part of herself on the other. There's no time to wait, glass-bearer. Now is the moment to strike, and when you do I will be there. When she reaches for what is within you—and she shall, that is the point—-I will poison it, and then together we'll unmake her.*

———

The queen stays with Lussadh through the night. Morning arrives like a fruit of sun-bathed alabaster, and for a time she remains in the queen's arms, in this circle of cool comfort. Clear freshwater. Spring's thaw, she might think, except in the technical sense the queen is spring's opposite. Her own clothes remain on the floor, still steeped in Ulamat's blood; she hasn't let servants in to collect them.

"I don't think we've ever slept together before," she says. "In the literal sense."

The queen smiles down at her. "I've set all things aside for the day, and I aim to spend it with you. Shall we go to a tailor? I've not had the pleasure of picking out your wardrobe for months."

"Why this all of a sudden?"

"There was a time when we spent days upon days together. I got to adorn you, watch plays with you, see the places that you love. Why don't we do that for a single day, to break up this monotony? The god I've trapped will not strike again, not in this city. I can promise that much."

She tenses, then she relaxes. The queen's a creature of

whims, and this one is both easy and pleasant to accommodate. She too needs to indulge—a single day may let her forget. Grief will resume soon enough. And then, whatever anyone's objections, she will go ahead and recall Nuawa. "First let me dress. I may be Lord-Governor, but even so, I may not traipse about the streets naked."

A laugh, almost girlish. "What a vision you'd be. The entire city would drive itself to distraction and nobody will get a single thing accomplished."

The queen chooses what she wears for the day. She and Nuawa have separate wardrobes, as mingled as their belongings are otherwise—their styles are too different, with Lussadh tending toward oxbloods and reds and golds, more jewel tones, whereas Nuawa prefers shades subtler and more muted.

"We can't go anywhere too public, my queen," she says, "and we must look grave. It won't do to have the citizens think I'm frolicking while they're still fearing for their lives."

"To humans I always look solemn." The Winter Queen draws little pearls of frost from the air, attaching them to her hair. "I'll quadruple my gravity. All who look upon me shall know abject terror."

They visit private gardens and specialized greenhouses— Lussadh thinks with a pang that she never got a chance to show Nuawa these, the circumstances being what they are, always too many pressing matters. She would have liked to feed Nuawa rare fruits, the pomegranates and tangerines, the pomelos and rose apples; she would have asked her wife how they compare to Sirapirat harvests. At each place she asks for the provenance of the fruits. Many of them are from, as it turns out, Sirapirat itself. She recalls reading poetry describing that place in the old days, when Sirapirat's sky-reflection was gold, as a paradise of bounty. Fruits in sharp colors, leaves like warm brass, splendid elephants in the streets.

In a small exclusive theater, they attend a one-act play: the avant-garde brainchild of some rising academic star. An eccentric little love story where all parties end up disappointed but surprisingly alive. The Winter Queen says it reminds her of home, of the poets in Yatpun.

"Tell me what love is," the queen says as the play draws to an end.

Lussadh glances at her quickly. The audience box gives them complete privacy, but even so, this is not the kind of question that's ever come up between them. "Love is what we have," she says, easily because like any former royalty she has a courtier's tongue. "It is a constellation that joins me to you. Have I ever given you reason to doubt, Your Majesty?"

"Never. But I want to know what love is to you. Is it the grace of a sword tempered to perfection? The clarity of crystalline structures? What made you fall in love with me," the queen goes on, "when you met the part of myself called Crow and believed them—and me—human?"

"I've never needed you to be that." The real reason, it occurs to her, that the queen made Ghazal. Synecdoche human. Simulacrum mortality.

"No. You have not. I lack all the flaws of a transient thing, the wear and tear of having been subjected to the world's mercies."

Lussadh realizes she has missed the mark by not saying as much; by not comparing the queen to the immaculate edge of a blade, to the impeccable color of new snow. So much for her princely training. "I love you," she says simply. "I have only that earnest answer, my queen. Unadorned and true."

A furrow indents the queen's statuary brow. "But that's not your way. You're always ready with a singer's finesse."

I'll bring down the moon and drape every living star on your shoulders. I'll put upon you more treasury than the sun itself owns. That and more she said to Nuawa without effort: it is as the queen says, her habit is to indulge her lovers, to crown them in paeans. "I'm under the weather. And I'm—distracted."

"I'm sorry about your aide."

She nods absently, knowing the queen doesn't understand in any case. But what is love, then, Lussadh thinks. She has compared Nuawa to a blade, to sharp and lethal things, in exactly the queen's terms. But there's more than that: there is the way her wife's eyes soften when she sees Lussadh. There is the way she looks when asleep, there is the roundness of her bare shoulders, the seduction of her collarbones. The way Nuawa enjoys desserts from Sirapirat and licks them off her fingers. The way Nuawa looks in uniform or wedding finery, even the way she winces when her prosthetic arm pains her. Small ordinary things, and there's nothing small or ordinary about the queen.

Next, they turn to a tailor's boutique, where the queen selects new dresses for her: fabrics like hummingbird plumage, like monarch butterflies, dresses and jackets that sit on Lussadh like gemstones spun to clouds. She tries to smile, tries to enjoy herself. It is hollow—she is already thinking of Ulamat's funeral rites in the custom of the enamel, of how difficult it shall be to find an enamel shaman willing to officiate.

On the way out, the queen stops. All of her goes still, inert as bas-relief. Then she doubles over, one hand flung out; Lussadh takes it, holding on as the queen shudders and gasps.

"Ghazal is dead," the queen says as she straightens, still trembling. Her mouth is a rictus. "Nuawa is returning sooner after all."

For a few seconds she doesn't connect the two statements. "My queen, what—"

"Before you asked for her hand, Nuawa attacked me. Not that it came out of nowhere. She always meant to do that—she's been raised and forged for the task of assassinating me. Her life's work."

Every muscle in Lussadh seizes. "You didn't tell me," she says, her breath thick, her throat a pinhole. Penjarej's suicide. All the warnings Ulamat and Durgesh gave her, all the evidence of her own eyes that she ignored because she was blinded by affection. By infatuation.

The queen looks at her. "Because she made you happy. Because if I'd told you, then your hand would be forced, and the pact between you and me would be broken. Do you not understand? Your joy, and the causes of it, is my priority—more precious to me than any treasure vault. I reached an agreement with her so that she could continue to serve you. No doubt she didn't plan to be your bride precisely, she's not so wise as that. She remains perfidious, but I didn't think she would make a second attempt after I taught her a lesson."

All this time. The one secret both have kept from her: Nuawa an insurgent from the beginning, having infiltrated her way into winter's heart with grand success. Even the marriage—a sham, too, Nuawa accepting it, agreeing to be hers. "I cannot forgive this." She speaks without quite knowing whom she means: the queen or her wife. *Because she made you happy.* The definition of love, for the Winter Queen—any deception can be maintained as long as it means Lussadh's pleasure, however surface, however temporary.

"You'll be able to speak to her soon enough." The queen grips Lussadh's wrist. "I'll prepare to receive her. Will you trust me? That all I do shall be toward your good, toward the goal I've pursued—toward your deathlessness?"

Ulamat is gone. Her wife was always a poisoned seed. "Yes. I trust you, my queen." Because she is the only one Lussadh has left.

ELEVEN

THE SICKLE BRINGS NUAWA TO THE ROOM SHE SHARES WITH Lussadh.

A displacement of time: from the window she sees it is deep dusk, the day bruised, turning the shade of unoxygenated blood. It was late noon when she executed Ghazal.

"Lieutenant."

She turns and the general is there, seated on the divan, at ease. Abruptly she feels foolish, the weight of Ghazal's head under her arm absurd. She sets it down and, doing so, spots a discarded jacket browned with dried blood. "Is that yours, General?" Unable to resist asking, needing to know if Lussadh bled while she was away.

Lussadh stiffens. "No. That is Ulamat's. He's dead."

"You loved him," she says softly. "He was so loyal to you."

The general's expression flickers, then hardens. "More than you ever were, yes. How much of it was a lie?"

Her resolve turns to seafoam. The general could stand and approach and run her through, and she'd never have reacted in time. She'd have bled, and she'd have begged to perish in Lussadh's arms. She licks her mouth. "I didn't lie to you in most things. Becoming your wife, that was real." *I love you,* she wants to say, but that is hollow, and will only decimate the last of her nerves. She cannot afford that. The Sickle thrums inside her.

"My first lover was a girl from Shuriam, back then an enemy state to Kemiraj. She turned out to be a saboteur. King Ihsayn made me execute her." Lussadh's face, she thinks, is that of the prince. That long-ago façade crafted to shield herself at court. "I suppose we never did tell each other everything. I'm sworn to defend my queen, and she's waiting for you. Bring that—I don't want a disembodied head in my room."

My room, not ours. Lussadh's loyalty was never going to be suborned. She picks up Ghazal's head and follows.

The sky yawns wide above the palace courtyard. All is glittering ice: the minarets' shadows lay across the stone like a tiger's stripes. Glass-bearers have been summoned and the snow-maids have mustered on the high walls, both a mute audience. Guryin does not greet or call to Nuawa. It feels like a replay of the wedding ceremony. A procession of glass-bearers and then the Winter Queen, and herself as the object of spectacle.

General Lussadh strides to the queen's side. The Winter Queen smiles. The sight of her—this statuesque predator, this symbol of atrocity—reminds Nuawa she is here to see through the culmination of her mothers' work, the final act that will ensure Sirapirat's future.

She throws Ghazal's head onto the frozen ground. Her breath mists but she does not feel any exertion. Cold lightning burns in her veins; no more tenderness, no more soft places that can be pierced and cored.

"Your Majesty." Nuawa feels her voice bite into the air: it hums with borrowed power, with the same substance that charges the queen's muscles and arteries with puissance, that ancient ichor of the gods' mountains. "I challenge you to a duel."

Something lances through Lussadh then; she wonders if it is pain, if it is agony. Then it is gone. All that remains is a mask, unreadable and absolute. Despite everything, Nuawa finds herself stricken. She expected more. Remonstration at the last minute, demanding that she reconsider. More reaction than this, but then Lussadh was always the queen's heart, a bond that took root decades before Nuawa was ever a factor. The real reason the queen has been so confident. She never stood any risk of losing Lussadh.

The queen cants her head at her general. "If she wants trial by combat, Lussadh, I will give it to her. It is a custom even in my land, for in the end what proves righteousness if not might? The truth of that is permanent. It endures past ideology or faith or even love. Strength is the final word. It proves justice; it proves innocence. To have strength is to be without sin or fault." She opens her hand and a long lance coalesces, all white opaque frost. "What will it be? Perhaps a sword would suit you better."

"It's all the same to me."

"You seem intent," the queen says, "to break yourself upon me until you are dust."

"I killed Ghazal." Nuawa nudges the head with her foot, what remains of the bloodied, fractured skull.

"For which I will take payment out of your skin." The queen closes her hand and when she opens it the lance has turned into a pale sword, identical to the one Ghazal bore. Her expression remains calm. "I've kept you alive this long, Nuawa, and you will fulfill your purpose still. Even this is part of it, though you don't yet realize how."

Nuawa draws her blade and feels the shadows spread, immense, a hundred gnawing lashes. It occurs to her this may be the last time she unsheathes this weapon and wields these shadows. She meets the general's gaze but receives nothing in return: what she sees is the remoteness of statuary, of portraits painted long ago. It is not a look Lussadh has ever given her—even at that first meeting in Sirapirat there was more regard, more intrigued interest.

And then there is no more time to think of Lussadh, to contemplate the heart's weaknesses and how they might undo her more fatally than any bullet.

Nuawa has never seen the Winter Queen fight. She remembers the figure in armor, sword in hand, on the night she went into the kiln. But she has believed that ornamental, has never had a reason to think the queen would wield a weapon in such a way; what is the need when she wields winter itself, the climate, and the elements. Yet Ghazal was easy with a blade and now it is evident from whence that came, an inheritance that sprang from the original fount.

The queen strikes, pressing the advantage of her height and long limbs, each blow informed both by expertise and brute force. Any of them could have sundered Nuawa or knocked loose her footing if Nuawa has not taken the Sickle's gift within herself. But she has, and the blade shadows—never predictable before—respond to her as though they are her own limbs, her own hands: they unfold and multiply, biting into the queen's etheric reflection.

Listen to the wind, the Sickle whispers. *See how it moves. There's so little restraint upon me now, and this upstart shall learn her lesson …*

Air roars. It slashes and claws at the queen, who stands unyielding even as she is opened, bloodless wounds that glitter like the inside of a geode. She advances.

The white blade carves toward Nuawa—fast, too fast. She concentrates and then she's elsewhere, out of the sword's reach.

The queen whips around and charges at her.

Nuawa pulls at the weft of space and bends it, and brings herself overhead. The currents whisper and pluck at her midair, and she knows that when she falls it'll be aimed. Her blade leads as she plummets and she should have cleaved the queen open from forehead to groin.

Instead, she has barely glanced off the queen, who's now in fast retreat, a thin line open from her throat to her stomach. Still, she does not bleed, and a slow smile begins on her mouth.

Her hand lifts and she says, "Come to me, my general."

There is no questioning. Lussadh does not give pause as she strides toward the queen. Her monarch has called and she answers—it is as simple as that. Nuawa shifts her stance, readying herself to face two opponents. No doubt the queen thinks Lussadh will blunt her, make her falter.

The general's expression is almost serene when the queen slices her open from shoulder to hip.

Someone shouts—Guryin. At a gesture from the queen, the major goes still, rooted to the spot. The rest of the glass-bearers are paralyzed likewise, struggling against unseen constraints. Nuawa starts to run as the queen catches the general in her arms.

"No nearer, Nuawa." The queen cups Lussadh's face in her hand. Rime spreads from her touch. She exhales, gently, onto the enormous gash. "I've suspended her mortality, though that cannot be forever. A question. What do you suppose you are, Lieutenant? You who have gone into one of my harvesting kilns. What do you think it took out of you, back then?"

She stares and stares and yet words do not come to her. This is the second time she's seen the general bleeding like this and despite the glass shard blunting her heart, she is undone—all her thoughts concentrate into a single point, into this person that she should hate, the one who in the end chose the queen. "What are you getting at?" She doesn't ask, *Why would you do this?* One does not ask the blizzard; one does not ask the beast.

The inhuman face looks up. Its grin is grotesque. "You've kept one of the Heron's shards inside you for so long. Though he probably didn't intend it, it took root in you and flourished exceptionally, fusing into your existence. You're on the path to becoming something like he was—as close to what I am as a human can get."

"I—" Her breath quickens. The sharp place in her chest bristles, like fast-growing briars.

"You can save her, Nuawa. Give Lussadh your piece of glass and she will live. Not only that but she'll no longer be mortal. Forever she will rule this land. We'll never part."

This is love, she thinks, the love of a monster. All along this has been the Winter Queen's desire, perhaps even greater than her need to avenge herself on her makers. These ancient schemes bent toward this single goal: of making the general a creature more than human, a creature who can be at the queen's side for eternity. She wonders if the queen has ever questioned herself when one objective eclipsed the other; when she began to love Lussadh more than she loves power, more than she loves the justice that she plotted to enact on Yatpun's gods. The Sickle reduced to a mere stepstone rather than the final objective.

"I refuse," she says, knowing Guryin can hear her—they all can, even if there's nothing they can do about the fact. *This fortune you have seized, it's not going to come again and most never find its like. Don't risk this. Don't do anything to break Lussadh's heart.* "Your destruction means more to me than the general ever has."

The queen cradles Lussadh one-armed: the blood slows but the general's eyes are wide, glazed with pain and terror, teetering on the edge of consciousness. "But you won't destroy me, Nuawa. You're not even my old servant and your hands are new to winter's element. A thousand times you might sunder me and still I would reconstitute, and by and by I'll wear you down to gristle and tattered skin. In the end, your efforts will have amounted to nothing, and I'll restore my general regardless."

"And then try again to cultivate a piece of your mirror that will make Lussadh your equal."

"I have time." Frazils glint like little knives in the queen's hair, framing the severe mask of her face. "So does she. Her life-span is already greater than most, and I'll work at extending it further still."

Nuawa takes a deep breath. She lets her blade drop: its shadows recede. In the end, it comes down to this, to this common ground, this former prince whose glory has bound them both. The queen's heart and Nuawa's own. "When did you realize this would be possible? You must've experimented with your own shards before. There must have been a reason you didn't just give her one of them."

"When she found you." The queen's teeth flash, stark and flawless. "When she pointed to you as though you were true north and she the needle of a compass. I grew surer and surer that the piece of glass inside you and the one inside her were once the same fragment. That is why you were drawn to each other so well. It was not love or even desire but simple magnetism."

She takes one step forward. Then another. "Why not kill me and remove it from my corpse?"

"The Heron did that and it warped him, reducing him to madness. I wondered why it didn't empower him as much as it should have; why it left him a twisted husk. When I damaged him, he should have been able to restore himself much as I do, but he couldn't. He took the shards by force. These pieces of my mirror, they have certain tendencies. For them to pass from one host to another requires willing sacrifice. That's how you were able to host the shard *he* nurtured within himself because he gave it to your mothers of his own volition."

"How can I tell the general isn't already dead?"

"Come and touch her."

And when she does, with her sword on the ground and her fingers on the general's neck—where the pulse beats still, strong and vital—she nearly unravels. She wants more than anything to see the general stand and call her *my wife* once again.

Then she looks up into the queen's face and remembers what must be done. Inside her the Sickle howls and cackles, telling her of the intricate equations that went into the queen's making; the same ones that can, now, be scrambled to pick apart the seams of her, to loosen the knots that keep her whole. A contagion that the god has vested inside Nuawa, a flower of annihilation.

"I willingly give up my shard of your mirror," Nuawa whispers.

The queen's eyes are as vast as the sky, as encompassing as the universe. "Yes." She bends to kiss Nuawa.

It is brief, this time. She does not feel anything, shielded by the borrowed might or perhaps this is the final kiss — *Three to part*, the god whispers, and then the queen lays a hand on her breast and plunges inside. Past clothing, past skin and fat and muscle: she reaches deep into that place where the shard of glass nests, drumming its ruthless percussion like a second heart.

Nuawa feels the moment the queen's fingers close on it. It is agony. It is bliss.

The queen's expression changes.

She will always remember this, the phase-shift from triumph to terror — the first time she has ever seen this expression on this inhuman face, this petrified panic, this confrontation with the possibility that an elemental force incarnate may be destructible after all. Black capillaries run up the queen's hand, spreading over her wrist. Her forearm cracks, and cracks again, the sound of ice giving under stress.

Nuawa flings herself onto the queen.

They fall together, the queen toppling onto her back as the god's rot overtakes her: the bitter black rippling across her frame, lacerating her broad white shoulders, splitting her chest. She is like breaking marble now and still her hand is trapped in Nuawa, trapped by the shard that has been transmuted for her ruin.

The queen screams. The air itself draws tight and Nuawa cannot breathe: the wind is choked out of her, the cold has become near-solid, so sharp that it is like swallowing razors. She holds on, straddling the queen. One of her hands, grasping blindly, falls on the general: on fresh, hot blood. The wound whose letting should have slowed, the mortality that should be postponed —

"You're killing her," she shouts. "You're killing your general."

Beneath her, the monster's head twitches to the side. The starburst eyes alight on Lussadh and widen.

And then the storm stops. The air goes still; the cold relents.

By now the queen has withdrawn from Nuawa — they are no longer joined — but there is no stopping the rapid decay: it runs through the queen's body, ink in water, impossible to separate or expel.

Nuawa scrambles over, taking the general in her arms. Staring down stupidly: she has no more idea of how to save Lussadh than she knows how to overturn the sun.

"Heal her." The Winter Queen's voice is a cracked whisper. "You've seen me do it. Breathe onto her wound. The glass shard reacts to it."

She bends to the gash, to the smell of butchery too close for comfort, though she cannot think of Lussadh that way yet: this is yet a living person, *hers*. She exhales onto the cut: is certain, at first, that it will do nothing—that this will have been for vain, and the general will succumb after all.

The blood slows, then stops. The gash seals, smoothing out. What's left is raw, red skin—a terrible expanse, but the skin is whole.

"A long time ago," the queen whispers, "I was alone. Created to be an empty weapon, gaining a soul of my own by accident. When my sapience began all I knew was solitude. Later on, I knew my oath to avenge myself, to free my siblings, to destroy the gods who made us. Lussadh—" Her voice breaks. One of her hands lifts; it disintegrates to icicles and snowdrifts. "She was the second thing, the second person, I learned to love. I wanted to cherish her. I wanted to make her everlasting. I wanted to always, always be with her."

Nuawa gathers the general in her arms, holding her close. "She loves you, that should've been enough. She chose you over me. She was always going to."

The queen tries to draw herself up but falls back, that elemental strength shattered at last. Her hair billows like smoke, already losing substance. "You still don't understand. My existence is long. It might've continued forever, and I never loved easily. Before her there was another and she died. After Lussadh there might never have been anyone else." A rattling that is not quite a laugh. "Perhaps, depending on how winter's element finds it level within you, you will come to find that out for yourself."

She makes no answer, merely watches as more of the queen crumbles. Only ice, in the end. Only frozen water.

"Tell her." The queen tries to crawl toward the general but what remains of her lower body no longer moves: it is as immobile as hewn granite. "Tell her that I loved her, that even at the moment I wounded her—that I would have given up all I am if it meant she could continue. My treasure. My general. I wanted …"

The wind gusts. The queen's final words blow away with it, and soon there's nothing left at all. Only fractured frost and a patina of verglas.

The last time Lussadh woke from a grievous injury, it was to the queen at her side. This time it is otherwise, for all that she wakes in the same room, the one Bohyun reserves for royalty. Stone ceiling, distant window, bare furniture by the palace's standards.

Guryin is sitting by. When she sits up, the major almost leaps out of xer chair. "Every god be praised. You're alive—well, Bohyun said you were. But there was no telling, you'd lost so much blood."

Blood. Her own. How frequent a sight that has become, how sharply familiar the smell. Once she guarded it much better. Memory comes back in stages. It does not terminate at the point she fell, the incandescent frost scything across her. "How long?"

"It's been …" Xe heaves a sigh. "Two days."

She runs her fingers over the furs that mound on her bed. Her conscious persisted, back in the courtyard, far past the point it should have: she recalls what she saw, even if at the time she was past making sense of it, past coherence. Impressions of storm and fury that now she can piece together. "Her Majesty?"

She already knows. Yet someone must say it, speak the fact into being.

"Gone." Guryin closes xer fists in xer lap. "I'm sorry."

"We'll need to rearrange everything. Whatever else comes, governance must go on and statecraft does not wait. The continent's never liked a political vacuum. I will see to …" Lussadh draws in air; releases it as though she is releasing a fragile animal caught in a trap—delicately, lest it shreds and breaks in the moment of freedom. "I'll see to what requires seeing, as soon as I can. What do you intend to do?" The queen. She cannot think about the Winter Queen yet, if she can ever again. A thorn lodged in her breast, a wound that never heals.

"I'm staying. *You* were always the one who earned my loyalty, Lussadh. Not … her. And you still need to officiate my wedding to Imsou, isn't that right? You owe me that, plus a small mountain of wedding gifts."

"I owe you that. And—I need to see to Ulamat's rites."

"Way ahead of you. I've asked courtiers who belong to the enamel how to do that properly. I'll let you know once we've found a shaman and there's a date." The major says nothing for a while and busies xerself with pouring a cup of water. "Are you going to ask about her? About Nuawa?"

Her pulse thuds. "Yes, what of her? I wanted to speak to her."

"She left you a letter." Guryin swallows and holds the cup with terrible delicacy. "She did say to tell you, that Her Majesty … that you were all she thought of, even to her dying breath. *The queen wanted to be with her always; the queen wanted her forever.* That's what she passed along."

Not yet. Not yet. The queen is an absence. Her throat clogs: no question, now, whether it was the shard or if it was genuine feeling, genuine passion, that brought her to her queen's side. "The Winter Queen had a name, beyond her title. I used to wonder …" Lussadh shakes her head. "I need to be alone. And—give me that letter."

For a long time, she doesn't open it. The paper is plain, folded neatly. A gauzy sheen of ice clings to its edges like angular lace, unmelting.

Lussadh busies herself, drinking water, examining what's been left behind in the wound's aftermath. Very little: the diagonal that runs from her shoulder to her hip is a hairline, faint silver in the umber of her skin, nearly disappearing into it.

It is much later that she attends to the letter. The ice cracks when she opens it, more secure than any seal, more unique than any signature.

To General Lussadh al-Kattan, Lord-Governor of Kemiraj,

We have injured each other too much. I will not ask for forgiveness because each of us must heal, and you may never forgive me. Neither of us is a monk. We have not been steeped in the training of mercy.

She was a monster and she loved you only as a monster can. I recognize it because I'm monstrous in my own way, as I have amply proven. Glass and steel and cold, those were the things that ruled her and ruled me. In one matter she was right: I was as close to her as a human could get, whether because her mirror changed me or because I was always going to be a creature of knives and terrible goals.

Of course, I had treacherous intent from the beginning. Of course, I saw you as the means to an end. And, of course, I tumbled down the well of you, I fell and fell, and I never wanted to stop. Every part of me—I never had dreams of becoming anyone's bride, General. You changed everything; you changed me. My world became torn. I was no longer a simple weapon. I became in every sense yours. It was terrible. It was exquisite. You were my vast agony and you were my ferocious delight. Poets have words; I have only sword and bullets, and I was never any good at expressing affection with those.

I go now to fulfill the task for which I was forged—I owe my mothers and I owe those who fought before me, who made me possible. I trust you'll not impede me in this, for what has Sirapirat ever meant to anyone but those born to it? We are but a little city, our only jewels in the fruits that grow from the earth and in the dreams that blossom between monsoons. All I desire is to see its streets turn gold once more and for our mundane matters to spin on our own terms, according to a clock of our own making. I'm no patriot, but I have sentimentality, even if it doesn't run as deep as yours does for Kemiraj. Have you ever smelled jasmine that didn't grow in a greenhouse? I'm curious to know its fragrance, to see if I can tell the difference. I want to eat mangoes that come to ripeness in the sun, to pluck tamarinds that are nourished by water and summer rather than by ghost-pipes.

But if healing is possible, General, I would like to issue you a letter of challenge. Five years from this date, let us meet again where we first engaged in our long, strange duel: when we first pushed and pulled, and when the power that resides within us first recognized each other's. Where you found me. Return to that point so that we might begin again.

EPILOGUE

THERE IS A SPOT IN THE PALACE OF KEMIRAJ. LUSSADH thinks of it often, of the gravestone she's erected there, even though there is no body—there has never been. In the end, the Winter Queen was only ice. Each day she'd visit the site, leaving a blue hyacinth or a platter of dates and figs. Occasionally she would tell the stone what she's had for breakfast that day, even though she knows no one is there to listen. But she likes to think a fraction of the queen remains when the temperature plummets, that the Winter Queen has become a spirit of seasons rather than one constant, unchanging weather. Some part of her must have endured.

Lussadh shifts in her seat, peering down the carriage. The train is running late. Five years ago they never did, for all trains belonged to winter, a single uninterrupted continuity and thus managed under a single united schedule. Now some cities have their own and the lines aren't quite as efficient as they used to be, subject to the caprices of commerce rather than mandates handed down from a single state entity. Still, Lussadh thinks as her train pulls into the Sirapirat station, there's something to be said for competition and variety.

It has been a long time since she last visited Sirapirat. She has not been here since she granted it independence, though any granting was nominal: five years ago, Nuawa marched into Sirapirat and cast out the winter-appointed governor, upending the order of things overnight and wielding the queen's power to enforce the act. By all accounts, she disappeared afterward or at least kept a low profile—certainly, she did not move on to liberate any other territory, nor did she return to the arenas.

The city is much warmer than Lussadh recalls, though that is true for many territories now. Not a sudden breaking of winter itself but a minute, gradual change. The way Kemiraj used to get when the queen had not visited it for some time. A difference of degrees, but all the same that is felt on the skin, on the breath as air enters the lungs.

By the footpath, a child sells intricate garlands woven from jasmines and tasseled with roses. She buys one and wraps it around her wrist like a corsage. Occasionally she draws attention, for even now she is recognizable, but she is without either an escort or accoutrements of her office: the uniform is gone, and she keeps the hyacinth out of sight, tucked into her shirt. The one piece of jewelry she wears openly is a silver anthurium pendant. That she bears arms—the swarm-gun that still surprisingly functions, the sword—merely makes her look like a local duelist. The thought snags, amusing her briefly.

On foot, it takes her some ten minutes to reach Sirapirat's largest university. Teachers in staid colors, dark green and brown; students in navy blue and white. These days uniforms are much thinner and there are not so many scarves or hats. What they wear now must be much closer to what was common here before winter's advent. Still not exact—the continent will never be that warm again. Nor can it, without ruining the land twice over. She imagines her wife has kept that thought in mind. Her wife: strange to think when that might no longer be what Nuawa is. *You are hereby pronounced lord and consort ...*

The same reading room: the same oblong table, the same five chairs, the same window that looks out onto a lake. Only the time is different, and the view itself—the noon sun has set the waters ablaze, limning the elegant petals of magenta lotuses and the broad jade discs of their leaves. Too warm, now, for frost flowers and wintry pines.

"My wife," Lussadh says to the figure with its back turned to her. "You issued your challenge, and here I am."

The most minute movement of the head, as though Nuawa is not entirely sure whether she should turn around. "You've always been punctual, General. None can fault you on that." A fractional pause. "General—you've kept the title, haven't you?"

"Something must precede my name. It's a bad habit I can't quite break."

When Nuawa does turn, she is backlit by the midday brilliance and Lussadh thinks then, this is how she was meant to be: cloaked in warm gold, her birthright, not the silver and whites of the borrowed element. Her wife blinks slowly. "You're over fifty now. I watch the broadcasts, but I don't think you've changed even a little. Not a single new line in your face."

A smile tugs at Lussadh's mouth as she unwinds the jasmine garland and sets it on the table. "Nor in yours." Though that is obvious, for someone who carries the queen's might. "Guryin thinks—well, xe thinks you're maintaining what's left of the mirror. That as long as you have what you have, for glass-bearers things will continue much as they did before. An etheric truce. You should discuss it with Guryin, find the parameters, ascertain the limitations."

Another minute movement of the head. Shadow hides Nuawa's expression. "The major is well?"

"And married to Imsou, finally. Xe sent you an invitation, I remember."

"I sent a wedding gift." Said a little defensively.

"Which Guryin appreciated. Imsou was somewhat ambivalent, but I don't think you were ever close. How have you been?" It is not precisely what she means to say, this mundane question. But it is the safe choice, for now.

Nuawa holds her hand a few centimeters above the table. Frost skims across the surface, budding and crackling. "I returned to Mother Indrahi's old house where I grew up—I don't remember if I told you she wasn't actually my aunt, that was just our cover story. Once a week I pay a gardener to come in to do something about the greenhouse and I've been learning how to keep chicken coops. It's a pretty enough place. Occasionally I see a chiurgeon named Rakruthai to maintain my prosthetic arm; she says she'd like to meet Bohyun someday. As you can see, mine is a staid, private life." Her hand closes. The sheet of ice recedes. "As for this, it's still here, about as potent as it was five years past. I don't know if it will diminish and eventually leave me, or … You can appreciate I can't consult a practitioner, and I stopped hearing the Yatpun god long ago. I wonder what they're doing now, if anything. Keeping their mountains frozen, I suppose. Practicing their tyranny, but tyrants are everywhere."

Lussadh can't stop herself from saying, "You've been living on your own?"

"I've had no company." The slightest twitch of the mouth. "Either in residence or in bed."

"For five years?"

"General," Nuawa says gravely, "before I met you, I seldom took lovers. Only with you did I indulge in such a … feast of carnality. Being celibate for five years didn't bother me; I didn't want to explain the ice to courtesans either."

"I've thought of hiring bedmates these last few years." Lussadh touches the ice that Nuawa has created. "But after you, who could compare?"

"You don't need to flatter me." But she does smile. "Do you have business in Sirapirat?"

"I'm here to discuss trade agreements with the governing council."

"Ah. I'm incidental then."

"Of course not. You know that. I just want you to be there, in case you have input or recommendations. *They* are incidental, the trade agreements are incidental. Those are merely statecraft and papers. Come to me, Nuawa." Lussadh draws a deep breath. "Please."

There is a delay. Nuawa stiffens and for a moment it seems she will not yield. There is a brittle noise of ice breaking—on the floor perhaps, little stalagmites—and then Nuawa is closing the distance in quick, near-military strides. She stops a pace from Lussadh, face flushed for all that it was just a few steps: the length of the reading room, yet an enormous distance. "My letter—"

"I've kept it." The thin frost on it clinging to the paper, after all this time, in its secure metal box.

"Not what I mean." Nuawa raises her hand and then lets it fall on Lussadh's chest. "I must've sounded so confident in it, so absolute. It's easy to be brave on paper; much less so in person. At the time I didn't think I would see you again, except from afar. After what I did."

Lussadh says nothing as she takes Nuawa's hand into her own, lacing her fingers into those long, slender ones. As callused as they used to be, around the thumb. She has kept up with her marksmanship and swordsmanship, no doubt remains as honed as she was in the tribute tournament. A spectacle like kinetic poetry. When she thinks back on it, desire was always inevitable, glass shard or not, the queen or otherwise.

"Tell me why you came," Nuawa says softly.

"I did not come because I've forgiven you. The queen was what she was—she did as she was made to do—and for all that I loved her." Despite the blow, despite that act. "I cannot help but grieve her; I always will. For a long time it hurt me to think that you came to me looking to use me as a stepping stone toward your goal; I couldn't think of you—of our time side by side— without pain. But you must agree with her on one matter: love does not come easily, and what we had together is not something we may find again anywhere else. Five years I've spent without you, experiencing what it is to be apart, and I find I cannot bear it. So I've answered your challenge because I want to see if we can find our way back, gradually, a little at a time. Maybe it won't be the same. But it will *be*. If you wish; if you want to have that."

"I almost wish we'd dissolved our marriage when you exiled me." Her wife laughs then, the sound half-hitched. "So that I can ask you, this time, to be my spouse. That seems only fair."

"We could have another ceremony. Anything for my wife. Rings, necklaces, the world. I could conquer the occident for you."

"None of those. Your wife—that's all I want to be." Nuawa laughs again and then pulls her down, claiming Lussadh's lips.

They kiss for a long time, wrapped in each other's hunger, devouring and devoured. They run their fingers through each other's hair, trace the lines of each other's jaw and cheeks and throat. They rediscover each other's geography, as much as they can in this little room where they cannot yet do all they want.

When they finally part, the sun has begun to sink. Lussadh smiles down at her wife, at this woman who is her sky and her stars. "I cannot wait to spend the rest of my life with you."

"Yes. This life, as long as it lasts. Every morning and every evening. Every day and every night. That shall be our vow." Nuawa reaches to touch the anthurium she gave Lussadh all those years past. "Come, General. Let me show you my city and all its gold."

ACKNOWLEDGMENTS

Many thanks to my editors, Jason Sizemore and Lesley Conner, who've been very patient with how long *Shattersteel* took to write. It's been quite a journey; I'm grateful to everyone who's come along for the ride (most of all to readers who have had to wait so long for this conclusion). Lussadh and Nuawa are the characters I've probably spent the longest writing in real-world hours, and I hope their story delivers on the promise of their jagged, icy beginning. (You'll never know how close their trajectory came to tragedy.)

To Mara, Greta, Sasha, and Isa, who've been with me throughout the challenge of taking on a trilogy of a continuous story: my endless appreciation. For Joshua, who's been greatly supportive and analytical of these books' politics: it's finally finished!

ABOUT THE AUTHOR

Benjanun Sriduangkaew has been nominated for the British Science Fiction Association Award and the Campbell New Writer Award (since renamed Astounding Award for Best New Writer). Having lived in Jakarta, Hong Kong, and Bangkok, her worlds are informed by Southeast Asia and post-colonial lenses. She is the author of the fantasy *Her Pitiless Command* trilogy and the space opera *Machine Mandate* series.

For more information:
https://beekian.wordpress.com/

HER PITILESS COMMAND

Winterglass • *Mirrorstrike* • *Shattersteel*

—

AVAILABLE FROM APEX BOOKS

CPSIA information can be obtained
at www.ICGtesting.com
Printed in the USA
BVHW070940161121
621763BV00005B/68

Flash

CW01022907

100+ Little Queer Tales

FLASH DANCES

100+ Little Queer Tales

by

Members of the Gay Authors Workshop

Edited by

Stephanie Dickinson
Peter Scott-Presland

with a foreword by Tom Robinson

Cartoons by David Shenton

Paradise Press

First published in Great Britain in 2024 by

Paradise Press, BM Box 5700, London WC1N 3XX

www.paradisepress.org.uk

Selection copyright

© Stephanie Dickinson and Peter Scott-Presland, 2024

A CIP catalogue record for this book is available from the British Library.

ISBN 978-1-90-458598-5

10 9 8 7 6 5 4 3 2 1

Printed and bound by P2D Books Ltd, Westoning, Bedfordshire.

Cover design by Tom Burgering

Typeset by Homo Promos, assisted by Ross Burgess

Set in Georgia 11pt,

Headings in Aptos 24/14pt

Dedicated to:
Andrew Lumsden, 1941-2023
A founding father of the Gay Liberation Front
and of Gay News

Murray Melvin, 1932-2023
Trailblazing gay actor

Ros Dalgarno, 1946-2024
Life Partner

Bette Bourne 1939 – 2024
Bloolips founder and GLF activist

Gokhan

This book has been made possible by the generosity of
Southwark Council through its Pride Fund 2024.

We thank City of Westminster for its support in hosting our
workshop series.

Old Diorama Arts Centre, Regents Place, NW1 provided
rehearsal and meeting space.

We thank too our many crowdfunders: Alan Martin, Robert
Green, Roland Jeffery, Graham McKerrow, Stephen Miller,
David Semple, David Gee, Hastie Salih, Nigel Warner,
Tahnyet Faroqui, Ninesh Muthiah, David Viey, Danny Smith,
Thomas V O'Carroll, Alan Jackson, Stuart Bishop, Terry
Murphy, John Crossley, Elizabeth Fosler.

Cartoons by David Shenton

Attack dog — Prince

FOREWORD

Songs have much in common with short stories. You could argue in fact that songs actually are short stories. From playground rhymes about Jack and Jill to Bob Dylan's bombastic ballads, every stanza tells a story.

Back in the Swinging Sixties, however, queer kids like me living out in the sticks never recognised ourselves in any of those stories. The pop music of our teens always conveyed some variation on the unrelenting theme of Boy Meets Girl, which left us feeling more isolated than ever.

Then, as a new decade dawned, the arrival of David Bowie offered misfits everywhere a liberating glimpse of alternative narratives. I moved to London where the exploding world of sexual politics brought stories of Girl Meets Girl, Boy Meets Boy, Boy Is Girl and more. Stories all reflected in our fledgling fortnightly *Gay News*, and our new pop hero's intriguingly open-ended lyrics.

To a songwriter like myself, these adventures proved both an inspiration and a massive kick up the arse — to start making work grounded in my own genuine experiences. I quickly learned how hard it is to condense real life into the constraints of a three-minute pop song... Turns out it's less about which bits you put in, and more about which bits you can leave out without spoiling the story.

I did subsequently enjoy brief pop success with the modestly-named Tom Robinson band, thanks to a tune called *Sing If You're Glad To Be Gay*. And over the next dozen albums — I did my best to stay true to that shared LGBTQ+ sensibility in my songs. Two decades later, having shifted along the Queer alphabet from G to B, I made a record called *Having It Both Ways*. Not exactly subtle, but you get the picture.

All of which is why it is an absolute honour to introduce this collection of Little Queer Tales by young and emerging LGBTQ+ writers. How far we've come in the last half century! For me, the first and most extraordinary thing is sheer diversity of subject matter. Timeless themes of autobiography, passion, oppression and bigotry rub shoulders with horror, fantasy, sci-fi, satire and surrealism.

Flash Fiction — the writing of super-short stories — has a long history, traceable back through Somerset Maugham and Walt Whitman, all the way back to Aesop. Shortform writing is a great place for any aspiring author to start from. After all, to prepare for running a marathon, your first step, literally and metaphorically, is to put one foot in front of the other.

Writing can also be a solitary, even lonely activity. So the authors in these pages have had the luck to be surrounded by like-minded people in a positive environment, thanks to the mentoring of London's legendary Homo Promos Theatre Company with Gay Authors Workshop and Paradise Press.

Do please sample and relish these tiny gems, in all their glittering variety. Whatever your tastes, the great beauty of Flash Dances is that, if you don't like one story, there'll be another one along in just a moment.

Enjoy!

Tom Robinson

CONTENTS

LOVE AND ROMANCE

IT'S ONLY SEX

HISTORY FANTASY HORROR

Additional material by Howard Bradshaw,
Craig Binch, Stephanie Dickinson
and Peter Scott-Presland

INTRODUCTION

Anthologies should be like those Bumper Annuals of *Bunty* or *Beano* that you got in your Christmas stocking as a child, if you were lucky: a great big plum-pudding of a book stuffed slightly haphazardly with goodies tumbling over each other, and always the exciting possibility of coming across that lucky silver charm. If we managed in the process of getting to our Bumper Book to foster some new LGBT+ talent, so much the better.

When we said LGBT+ talent, we did not necessarily mean LGBT+ material. Queer writers have many fish to fry [even the vegans], and are interested in a world beyond their own sexuality. So in addition to the highs and lows of same sex relationships, we have history, fantasy, social observation, satire and politics. It is still Queer writing.

To express this was our ambition when we decided to publish an anthology of flash fiction. A key part of that idea was to encourage writers who might not have previously written flash fiction, or may not have written anything much before, and we soon realised that the best way to do this would be to hold a series of workshops that would give writers space to explore new ideas, share their work with others for positive feedback and criticism and then, hopefully, submit their work to the proposed anthology.

What is flash fiction? It is a genre of fiction, defined as a very short story. While there is no set word count that separates flash fiction from more traditional short stories, flash fiction stories can be as short as a few words and might be as long as 1000 words. Despite its brevity, flash fiction stories still need complexity and to be stories in their own right. Each word counts, so writing flash fiction is an excellent way to teach you the value of word choice and imagery, as well as shaping a story to come to a good resolution or punchline.

We set up workshops to practise these skills. A series of both face-to-face and zoom workshops soon showed that there are enthusiastic and talented writers who just needed a place to share their work and develop their confidence.

The idea of being a writer is attractive; the process of writing is intimidating. It brings out insecurities: lack of education, being the wrong class of person, not having important things to say. These can relate directly to other insecurities of identity or sexuality. Our mission was to break down these physical and psychological barriers, so that creative talents could flower. The joy of flash fiction is that, writing it, not so much of your personality is at stake. You can write 400 — 500 words in an afternoon, and if you're not satisfied with the result, you can chuck it and start another, and no harm done.

As an added incentive we decided to create a competition where writers could submit their work in the following categories: under 40 words, under 300 words, under 600 words and under 1000 words. We were fortunate in having VG Lee and Jake Arnott as our judges, both successful and critically-acclaimed authors. They diligently considered every submission and finally were able to come up with winners in each category. The process showed how high standards had become, and the choice was difficult.

The result that's in your hands now is a result of this concerted attempt to eliminate the barriers which prevent access to that middle-class merry-go-round which is called Culture.

Peter and Stephanie met through the Gay Authors Workshop, an organisation that has existed for over 40 years. It holds monthly workshop meetings, both face-to-face and through zoom, and writers will share work that they hope might be published in the future. Paradise Press is the publishing arm of GAW. Membership of GAW is open to anyone on the LGBTQ+ spectrum, or a straight ally, with an interest in writing now or in the future. Details are at the back of the book.

We hope you enjoy our stories as much as we have enjoyed writing them and sharing them. And for those of you who haven't written anything yet, but feel you want to, this might be an excellent way to start.

ABSTRACT

Jess Glaisher

The study discussed in this paper will attempt to determine the proportion of 'flash' (which the author identifies as 'welding', referring to the bright light emitted, and also 'flashiness', as shown by opulence and theatricality) and the proportion of 'dance' (which mainly, but not exclusively, consists of ballet, erotic dance, jazz dance and breakdance) in the movie 'Flashdance'. The purpose of this paper is to quantify the ideal ratio of 'flash' to 'dance' that makes the movie so iconic, and such a favourite among queers of all letter denominations. Suggestions that mathematics have no place in good storytelling are taken to be irrelevant for the purposes of this paper. The author will conclude that there is an optimum ratio, which can be used should another filmmaker wish to take heavy influence from 'Flashdance'. The author cannot condone the use of this research for remakes of the original source material; one cannot improve on Jennifer Beals.

FROM
THE
WORKSHOPS

The class was asked to write a story in half an hour incorporating the following elements: A garment; a like; a job/activity; a colour; a gesture.

ARRANGEMENT IN LILAC

Peter Scott-Presland

Frank adjusted his lilac cravat. It had to be just so. Previously Bunny would have arranged it before removing a fleck from his camelhair coat, kissing him on the cheek and propelling him from the house. Now Bunny was bound for Southampton and a liner to Brazil, twenty-four hours ahead of the police.

'Good luck to him,' thought Frank. 'Bless him.' It had been an exciting five years, picking the pockets of the rich and greedy. He had been very good at it. The secret was style. But now he was having to carry the can, thanks to the Wall Street Crash and some intercepted telegrams.

He moved into the tea room, waited to be seated by the waitress. He thanked her graciously as she showed him to a corner table.

'The usual, Sir Philip?'

He had chosen his *nom de crime* from the beautiful, melancholy queer Elizabethan, Sir Philip Sidney. Bunny looked a bit like him.

'The lapsang souchong?' asked the nippy.

'Not today, thank you. Stomach ... ' He patted his waistcoat and winced. She clucked sympathetically. 'I'll just have some hot water.'

The nippy dipped to him and disappeared. He unfolded his copy of the 'Daily Mail' at the racing pages and, after glancing round for any telltale signs of the C.I.D., hid behind it. On the page there was a mark in Indian ink against a horse in each race at Ascot. He had always liked Ascot for its association with royalty. He was convinced it was lucky, and put down one hundred pounds in a seven-way accumulator on seven races. The last fling, the last possible way out.

His hands shook as he remembered how, in the last race, Phrisky Phil had stumbled and fallen at Swinley Bottom for no apparent reason. He'd been a fool to listen to the tipster, a fool to fancy a jockey in lilac. He took out his Parker fountain pen. He coldly scored through each marked name, fury mounting, until in a rage he gashed and slashed Phrisky Phil to oblivion.

He recovered, smiled at the other diners.

'Your water, Sir Philip.'

'Thank you, my dear.'

As he took the cup, he saw Inspector Goff standing unobtrusively by a potted palm. He felt in his trouser pocket, and smiled. He still had sixpence to leave as a tip.

HEMINGWAY'S END

Philip Inglesant

A house in Idaho. The porch. A shotgun. An accident?

Another exercise was to create a story from an opening line. In this case, 'You're standing on my foot...'

CONSENT

Tania Gardner

E: You're standing on my foot.

S: What?

E: My foot!

S: You call that a foot?

E: Well, what would you call it?

S: Slime.

E: Oh, that's nice, isn't it! Here we are stuck in ... this, and all you can do is hurl insults at me.

S: Well I wouldn't have to if you would just accept our fate.

E: I'm not sure ... I'm having doubts.

S: Doubts about what? They have done this over a thousand times. Can't we just accept that today, now, is a good day, a good night to dance together ... flow towards a new world, a new life!

E: Do you think it will really be OK, Sperm?

S: Yes, Egg. I think it can only be amazing.

Egg and Sperm take hands.

PROUD PARENT

Barry came rushing to Aidan. He had just been feeding their surrogate child.

'Hurry!!' he said. 'Rylan's said his first word.'

'Wonderful! What was it?'

'You'll be so proud. He said *Gay*!'

We encouraged writers to draw on the situations around them. In this case, Stephanie got hopelessly lost in the multiple exits from Elephant and Castle station.

A LUCKY ESCAPE

Stephanie Dickinson

'Meet outside the exit of Elephant and Castle station', she said. 'I'll wear a purple scarf so you'll recognise me'.

She didn't say there were two exits. I stand on the platform looking at the Way-Out signs. One says 'University', the other 'Shopping Centre' and they are at opposite ends of the platform. I have no idea which one I need. I know she's a university lecturer but is that a good enough clue? She also said we could find a café and get to know more about each other over a coffee. I dither but decide maybe a shopping centre would have more coffee opportunities. I turn in that direction.

We've been chatting online for months now, determined not to rush things, so slowly learning random things about each other. We both like jazz, Alex likes rural action holidays while I prefer exploring European cities. We do both like sport, though, and she was pleased to hear I play tennis. 'I play hockey', she said. 'But I've never played tennis before. Maybe you can teach me'.

We're both single, me for three years now and she split up with her partner eight months ago. Another thing we have in common is that we're both ready for a new relationship. Is this it? Maybe it is. Maybe in years to come we'll be reminiscing about the day we met, in person, outside Elephant and Castle station. And we'll be a couple 'Julia and Alex' or maybe 'Alex and Julia'. I won't mind which.

The lift is delayed and I emerge in the ticket hall later than our agreed meeting time. Will she wait? How long for? I'd wait longer than 10 minutes so I hope she would too.

I can't see anyone remotely possible by the ticket barriers but she's probably outside. I peer round the exit. No-one is to the right but to the left is a woman wearing a dusky lilac scarf. Would that count as purple? She's very conservatively dressed and slightly overweight. She certainly doesn't look sporty. Is it her? My heart sinks. She doesn't look my type at all. I sidle out of the station obscured by a group of tourists and hover in a door way. I don't want the embarrassment of a meeting when I know it won't work out. I observe her covertly. No, she is definitely not someone I feel attracted to. She glances at her watch and walks away. So she didn't wait long. I turn back into the station. A wasted journey.

Alex steps out from behind a parked car, smoothing her vibrant purple scarf as the wind catches it.

'I wonder if that was her?' She thinks. 'Julia said she would be wearing a yellow jacket but I was expecting something more vibrant than pale lemon. And she was behaving very weirdly, hiding in the doorway and then creeping around that big group of tourists.'

Alex wonders whether to follow her and ask her but what would be the point. 'She doesn't look like someone I would have much in common with. A lucky escape maybe' she thinks. She walks away.

[We asked our writers to take some inspiration for a story from their immediate surroundings. The workshop room in Walworth Heritage Centre contained among other things a stuffed bear ...]

BEAR/BARE

Susan Miller

I said I would write about the bear
Poor bear in a glass cage
Then I thought about bear baiting and felt sad
And I couldn't bear to think about it at all
It made me feel total rage
So, then I thought about baring one's soul
And how that can make one feel rather bad
And then my mind skipped
To baring one's body on a beach
Being beach-ready it was called
And it used to leave me feeling appalled
But now I simply don't care
And while, don't worry, I won't go bare
That left me with a smile
I'm out of MY cage — at least for a while

One exercise was to write a character description of four characters, and then find a way to combine them all into a story. Here are two examples.

A RAY OF SUNSHINE

Craig Binch

In one hand Emmy clutched a homemade card decorated with pipe cleaners and sparkles, in the other a supersized strawberry milkshake, with extra sprinkles. She hummed to herself as she watched the world go by, thought of her mummy's face when she saw it. She and Daddy were going to surprise her because he said she had been sad lately. Maybe she needed a milkshake too.

It was then she saw the little old man out of the car window. He looked a bit like a grubby Santa Claus. She smiled, and he caught her eye smiling back a lopsided gummy smile. Too many sweets she thought, taking another slurp of her delicious milkshake.

Distracted by the little girl's innocent smile, the old man walked straight into the woman, Sam, rushing out of the gate. She screamed, startled, sending her suitcase flying. He reached out as she stumbled, and instinctively she stepped backwards into the road.

Mo slammed on the breaks of his Uber moped stopping with a screech an inch before her. He flipped like a graceful gymnast in an Uber green arc, into the oncoming car. The car swerved, the milkshake spilt, Mo hit the wind screen with a thud and shattered it into a thousand diamond shards that shattered and sparkled in the sunshine. Emmy's smile turned to fear as the car careered into the opposite pavement, hitting it at speed and ricocheting up into a perfect pirouette, spinning not once but twice. Her unruly red hair cushioned her head when it bounced off the window as she shook like a rag doll.

The old man stared, the mother looked on powerless to stop the wheels of motion, the world slowed down, as she spotted the red hair burning in the sun as it bounced inside her car.

Then there was silence as the upturned car rocked them gently to a final stop. Sam crumpled, as the world fell away beneath her. The whole tragic scenario was solely down to her, a sliding doors moment of disbelief. There were sirens and ambulance men, firemen and a red blanket — she remembered little else. The guilt wrapped round her like a vice; she saw her daughter twirling in the air, the smile, the sunlight, eternally punished for a moment of selfish madness. Ironically, she had wanted to leave them, but they had left her in a much more permanent way.

There was weak tea and sad faces, she sat on the corridor in the emergency department, on a trolley. People hurried by; someone was crying; was it her? A tap on the shoulder.

'Sam, I'm going to take you somewhere quiet. We need to speak about something important in private; then I can get the chaplain if you like.'

In a zombie state, with dry tear-streaked face and puffy eyes, she entered the relatives' room. A plastic plant, plastic chairs, polystyrene cups, and van Gough print on the wall, all lifeless like her.

'There was a man involved in the accident — the Uber driver.'

She vividly remembered the fear in his big brown eyes through his visor, helplessly looking at her as he rocketed into the air.

'He has some internal trauma and urgently needs a kidney. We've looked at the files and Emmy is a match'.

The realisation washed over her like damp fog; the nurse carried on talking but she didn't hear a word. A paper was signed, and the deal was done. Four hours later, the surgery was a success.

Would this right her wrong, provide penance, forgiveness, or just put seasoning on the purgatory?

Weeks later, their story made the front page of the newspaper: a tragic yet fortuitous tale, Mo smiling a familiar smile squinting in the sun. Everyone around him was smiling, and so was Sam for the first time since the accident.

MARY, QUEEN OF SCOTS

by her Executioner

She waur one tough lassie. Tawk me three trawes to off her heid.

And when I picketit up, a' I had in my hond waur her wig.

I tell ye, she waur having a vair' bad haire daye.

THE CULPRIT

Peter Scott-Presland

The smashing of the glass resonated round the echo chamber of the cloister, causing Brother Cuthbert to bound from the Abbey library. He sniffed the air in search of wrongdoing, eager to blame, and he saw Percy at the wall of the chapel, looking with dismay at the cricket ball at his feet.

'You. Boy! Percy!' he barked. Percy looked in terror and was about to run, but Cuthbert transfixed him with his voice. 'Stay!'

He approached like a dingo eyeing its prey. 'Is that your ball?'

'Yes, but — '

'Silence. Do you know how old that stained glass window was? Over 100 years old. Irreplaceable. So you know what's going to happen now?'

'Sir?'

'Up against the chapel door. Turn round, put your hands on the door. Now lower your trousers.'

The word 'trousers' made Mrs Clegg cock her ear as she was scrubbing the ornamental tiles in the vestry. Where Brother Cuthbert was concerned, it acted as a trigger warning. She went to the window where she could see the boy miserably lower his shorts. Cuthbert was unbuckling the heavy leather belt which circled his body over his cassock. She held her breath.

The Benedictine paused, gathered his strength and brought the belt down hard. 'I'll remember this, every bit of it,' thought Mrs. Clegg, as she filed it away in a gallery of incidents involving Cuthbert. The gallery filled her with disgust. Somehow, though, she could never bring herself to report it. She was only a cleaner.

Percy winced, but didn't cry out. His body shook with the effort of silence. The month drew his arm back again, a fierce look of glee on his face. There was no doubt he was enjoying the punishment. 'I'll teach you not to desecrate God's holy place.'

'I didn't, I didn't,' Percy protested. Almost despite himself, he crossed his legs, and could feel a viscous sticky substance there, he knew not what. He thought it was another punishment, this time from God. This time he started to cry.

Mrs Clegg, watching in the vestry, saw Brother Cuthbert put his left hand inside his cassock. Though she couldn't quite see it, she could have sworn he was playing with himself, the way his forearm was moving. He brought the belt down hard again. She could stand it no more. She opened the vestry door, but was stopped by the sight of Father Patrick coming out of the Parish Office.

He was in his fifties, and a ringer for Mr Pickwick: rotund, rosy-faced and tender-hearted. His voice rang out in contrast, harsh and undeniable: 'Desist, Dom Welch.' The formal surname was a surprise to Percy and Mrs. Clegg, who were both transfixed.

'I broke that window,' boomed Father Patrick. 'I saw young Percy had a bat and ball, and I asked him to let me have a go. I haven't played cricket in ages.' Percy was about to say something, but the priest silenced him with a gesture.

'Come,' said Father Patrick. 'I shall take my punishment like a man. Out of the way, Percy. Go and get your ball out of the chapel.'

He pulled his cassock up, tucking it in folds in his belt. He bent down, exposing a voluminous pair of drawers to the junior priest.

'Do you want me to take my panties down?'

'No — I — '

'That's what you did to young Percy. I deserve the same punishment. Worse, I'm an adult and a priest.'

He pulled down his underwear, exposing two large fleshy moons.

'Well, what are you waiting for?'

'How can I?'

'If you can't do it to me, how much less should you do it to one half your size. Suffer the little children ...?'

Furious, Brother Cuthbert threw down his belt and ran out of the quad. Percy returned with the ball. Father Patrick reached out for it, examined it closely.

'So that's the ball I hit through the window, is it? It's certainly seen better days. I think you'd better have a new one. Is it hurting badly, Percy?

'Not so much as it was.'

'I dare say Mrs Clegg can find some ointment for your poor bottom, and we'll say no more about it.' He produced something dark and squidgy out of his pocket.

'Have an After Eight Mint.'

THE WRONG MESSAGE

He smiled to himself as he sent the last nude picture to someone only 500m away. He waited for the response, groin stirring in anticipation. Suddenly he realised he'd sent it to his work WhatsApp group. Heart pounding, he stabbed at 'Delete'. But not before saw two blue ticks. A colleague had opened it. Who?

I got into the habit of bringing in cakes and sweets to workshops, as a bit of encouragement. One week I brought in a Tate & Lyle Sticky Pudding Cake. — Peter

STICKY

Peter Scott-Presland

It was the first week of the workshop, and several newcomers had joined those who'd stayed on, eager for writing success. As usual, I'd brought some cakes to welcome people — a Jamaican ginger and that most voluptuous of all cakes, McVitie's Tate & Lyle Sticky Pudding. 'Sticky' told no lies. It was the superglue of cakes, it stuck to the knife, the package, the desk, the fingers, the mouth.

The most striking newcomer was Olaf, a strapping Viking with flowing blond hair and beard. He fell on McVitie's like a hero from Valhalla, ripping off the plastic wrapper ['Try me with custard', the strapline exhorted], taking a great gobbet of cake and ramming it into his mouth.

Andrew Pong, a returnee, sat opposite him, agape. Andrew — his adopted Western name — was a designer. He was Olaf's polar opposite, dark-haired, short, wiry from years of Muay Thai, and with a dazzling smile. I could see that from the get-go he was set on Olaf, but big, extrovert Olaf was set on wowing the whole class.

As he talked and laughed with his mouth full, Andrew gazed at him painfully. You could see his thought processes. When Olaf flicked a morsel from his lips with his tongue, Andrew imagined the tongue licking his own lips, inside his mouth. He could see himself delicately nibbling crumbs from the blond beard.

He offered Olaf another slice of cake, showing him the slogan. 'Do you like custard?' he asked.

'Sure,' said Olaf casually, and carried on charming my co-tutor. Andrew looked disappointed.

The class passed without incident, and everyone promised to do their homework and be punctual the next week. When Andrew arrived the following Tuesday, he was wearing a new tight-fitting V-neck top which flaunted his athletic torso. On it was written, 'Try me with custard.'

ALONE

'Am I weird? Do people think I'm weird?' Caligula asked his horse, the Consul, Incitatus.

One day we arrived at class to find a condom on the floor. Unused, thankfully.

A CONDOM

Peter Scott-Presland

The room was booked from six. When we arrived, we could see through the porthole in the door there were three young men still in there. Two were skinheads, with tattoos which looked more designed to intimidate than to adorn. You sensed that anyone wanting to play with them would be playing with fire.

The other had short ginger hair, but his face by contrast seemed refined, sensitive and a freckled white; his eyelashes were almost albino, and his eyes the palest blue. Our eyes met and locked. It took an effort of will to suggest their time was up, but they went, reluctantly, leaving us to wonder what they had been doing. It was hard to imagine the play they had been rehearsing. It seemed more likely they'd been sharing some lines of coke — the office was hidden away.

Suddenly I spotted on the floor an unused condom on the floor. Had they been having sex? Hardly likely, I thought, with the porthole offering a view into the room. Who did it belong to? I decided it must be Ginger's — or was that wishful thinking?

Following that line, I picked the condom up and ran down the corridor, shouting after them. Ginger turned.

'I think you left this behind.'

'Finder's keepers,' he said with a smile.

'Won't you need it? Otherwise, why carry it?'

'No, you have it. I'm sure you get a lot more opportunities than I do.'

'I doubt it. No, it's yours. You take it.'

16

'Most people don't like ginger blokes. Matter of taste. Fact.'

'I do,' I said firmly. And looked him in the eye. 'Tell you what: couldn't we both have use of it?'

'I wonder how we could do that. Hmm ...' He rubbed his chin, and we both burst out laughing.

One week we had to write a story entirely in dialogue, with a thirty-minute deadline.

SIGNAL FAILURE

'We are being held at a faulty signal. Thameslink apologises for the delay.'

'How long have we been here?'

'Ten minutes?'

'Oh look! A fox!'

'Where?'

'By the track. Bold as brass.'

'Vermin. They should be exterminated. A fox killed my cat.'

'I'm sorry.'

'I got over it. I got another one.'

'A fox killed my cat too.'

'Did you get another one?'

'No, I got another fox.'

ONE FINAL PROJECT

David Lindley-Pilley

It had been a long time since I visited my parents' house, but my mother had kept everything as it was since my father died – including his notebook always neatly placed in the corner of his study. Moreover, there was a range of pens which he had kept right next to his most prized possession. He always liked to write the old-fashioned way.

However, I realised that everything didn't have to be left as it was. There were some stories which deserved to be told.

Therefore, I took it upon myself to scour the notepad for the story that he most wanted to be published - the story that would relieve him from the pain that he feared he would face, even after his death.

Even so, there was a degree of trepidation around me doing this, so that when I approached his oak-panelled writing desk, it didn't seem as good an idea as when I was travelling across the Severn Bridge to my childhood home.

With the result that I remembered what my father looked like the last time I had seen him, the lines of worry etched on his face as if by the most sensitive of sculptors. Therefore, I turned to the part of the notepad with the bookmark he said would be there. And then I read the title of the chapter: 'The Sins of the Father.'

Another exercise asked people to take an opening line as the basis of a story. In this case it was: 'Didn't you know? X is dead.' Two examples.

LOST AND FOUND

Craig Binch

'Didn't you know Pamela was dead?'

She said it so matter of fact like she was announcing a new train platform. The young woman leaned nonchalant on the door frame of the run-down council house; arms folded. He stood there stunned, each word hit him like a well-placed poisoned dart. This wasn't the fairy tale ending he had half imagined, the one where she opens the door, a moment of recognition as the tears come ad she pulls him into her arms, whispering 'I knew you would come'.

Now of course there was no hope of him meeting his real biological mum, he was too late. Not knowing why, he said 'thank you', to this stranger who had in one short sentence shattered his dream. He seemed to shrink as he turned and walked down the garden path, he dropped the bouquet of limp flowers in the wheelie bin. It had taken so much energy to get this far, a reason to carry on and for nothing.

Pamela peered out of the upstairs window through the net curtain and took a long drag of her cigarette, blowing out an angry cloud of smoke through her flared nose, the tendrils flicking her nicotine-stained hair. He'd gone, thank God for that she thought, the letter was in the wastepaper bin, nestled amongst the cigarette packets. She hadn't wanted him then and she certainly didn't want him now. The other one had come the year before and she had him sent packing, why couldn't they just leave her alone, leave the past in the past. She'd kept Julie regrettably, but the others where gone boys could fend for themselves.

'He's gone Mum' Julie called up the stairs. 'I told him what you said.'

'So, you're not completely stupid then!' she replied, wiping the smile off Julie's crestfallen face.

'Don't be so pleased with yourself' Pamela barked. Julie flinched, and a smile flickered on her mother's lips. 'You should be grateful you're still here. You could have been chucked in one of them kiddy-fiddling homes. Now get to the shops and pick up my cigarettes before I give you something to be scared about.'

Julie didn't look at her in in the eye she knew better than to argue, grabbed her coat and bowled through the door before the swipe came.

Martin sat staring into his cold, but still full, cup of coffee, in the window seat of the café. On the table was an envelope with his photocopied birth certificate and a grainy back and white photograph of a young woman in platform shoes; on the back it said 'Pamela Johnson (Mum)'.

Julie walked towards the parade of local shops, a single tear on her cheek, shoulders hunched, and hood pulled up. She saw him, sitting at the window, he looked broken somehow, like all the life had been drained form his body. She took in his messy blonde hair and blue eyes, just like hers. He looked a bit like their mother, she thought, but with more of a square jaw. Julie had never known her dad, and she wondered if this is what he would have looked like. She was transfixed by the familiar stranger.

She wanted to see him up close, study those features, find out if they matched and what he was like. Had he suffered like she had? Her mother would go crazy — the thought made her look back to their street, stomach sinking. But if she didn't do it now, she might never get the chance again. Her hand on the door, she took a deep breath and pushed it open with a bit too much vigour. The doorbell jingled loudly, and everyone looked up — including him, a trace of recognition flickering across his face.

She froze as their eyes met and turned to run. He stood quickly, upsetting his cold coffee, and followed her across the street and into the park.

'Hey, wait up are you ok? She crumpled and sat heavily on the swing. He sat beside her on the next one. Teary-eyed she looked up; he smiled matching tears in his identical eyes.

'I'm so sorry about before' she said, quietly looking into his eyes. She knew then that he was as broken as she was.

He put his hand out, 'I'm Martin.'

'I'm Julie and I think I'm your sister.' Not believing the words coming out of her mouth.

For the second time today, he was stunned into silence. They sat like that for eternity not letting go of each other's hand, gently swinging their legs in unison.

RETHINK

Henry wears a badge, 'I'm Gay, get over it.' He sees across the street a fiery Latino lesbian with cropped hair, high cheekbones and melting eyes.

He's disturbed to feel a stirring in his loins.

'Maybe I need a new badge,' he thinks.

EPITAPH

Peter Scott-Presland

'Didn't you know? Mrs Cross is dead,' said the school secretary. 'Died three weeks ago.'

'Hardly seems possible. I had no idea. After all these years.' The voice on the phone was trying to sound sorry. But Gerald Holding [of Holding's Holdings] was not a good liar — it was surprising he'd done so well in business. 'How many years was it?'

'Sixty-two. She still ruled the school with a rod of iron. Refused to retire. It was her life.'

'And her death, it seems,' said Gerald.

'Frankly, she should have given up long ago. But she'd inherited Willoughby's from her father, and was determined to carry on his work.'

'How did she die?'

'As she would have wished. Giving a pupil a good caning. Now what can I do for you?'

'I had wanted to enquire about a place for my daughter Geraldine. She's coming up to four next birthday.'

Like many parents, Gerald obliterated the memory of his own awful schooldays when it came to choosing a place for his children; he convinced himself that the horrors had done him a world of good, and would do likewise for his offspring.

'Everything's up in the air,' said the Secretary. 'We'll let you know when the funeral is.'

Kindergartens don't have alumni associations, but a week later former pupils received through the post black-edged cards giving the time and date. Unusually, it was a sunny day for a funeral, and the several dozen pupils who turned up at East Finchley cemetery looked hot and uncomfortable in their mourning. There was no family. Mrs Cross had been childless, having stood Mr Cross in the naughty corner at an early stage of their marriage. He retaliated by running off with an organ scholar to Oswestry. This was her unmentionable Secret Sorrow.

Gerald recognised several faces from forty years previously. One, hiding behind a military moustache he had not earned, sidled up to him.

'Bill Forsythe,' he introduced himself, just in case.

'Bill! I'd have known you anywhere.'

'Had to come, just to make sure the witch was really dead.'

'Come now, she wasn't that bad. Of her time.'

'Really? Why don't you come for a drink afterwards? The Bald-Faced Stag does a decent lunch. I've asked Elsie and Charles over there — and Freddie's here too.'

They picked up a few others from the class of '52, and half an hour later a dozen sat round a long table in the patio garden. A few pints later, tongues were loosened. People started talking about what they remembered, and the past came flooding back. Elsie had been forced to eat scrambled eggs every Thursday for tea, despite having an allergy, and been sick in the toilet afterwards. For three years. Frankie, whom everyone had forgotten, told how Mrs Cross had sent him, aged six, in his vest and shorts to run round Priory Park three times in the snow. He'd caught pneumonia, nearly died, still suffered from breathing difficulties. Frannie had been forcibly separated from her best friend Ivy, as they were 'a bad influence on each other', and forbidden to talk to or even smile at each other. She hastened to assure the party that this had not prevented her becoming a lesbian.

Bill showed the crooked finger on his hand where Mrs Cross had hit him with the sharp side of a metal ruler and fractured it. The injury went unrecorded, unrecognised and untreated, so now he was unable to wear a wedding ring.

Suddenly Gerald was very glad his daughter had been spared Willoughby's. They all contemplated their past hurts. Then Charles said thoughtfully, out of the blue, 'I noticed there wasn't any sign of a gravestone ...'

'That's not right,' said Frannie.

'I agree,' said Pauline.

They discussed how best to memorialise Mrs Cross for posterity, and some two weeks later, Gerald approached the school on behalf of a concerned group of former pupils, offering to fund a suitable stone for the grave. The school secretary, distracted by the business of winding up the school, nodded the proposal through.

A month after that, a minor suffragan bishop, another alumnus, removed the cover from a large marble headstone. It read:

Mrs. Charlotte Cross
Headmistress, Willoughby School
1905 — 1991
1/10 — could have tried much harder

FAMILY
AND
FRIENDS

MISS JASON

Craig Binch

The ghost of Miss Jason sat at the bar;
The drag sisters gathered to honour the star.
The old regulars and fans had joined the procession,
A sparkling goodbye to the Queen of the profession.
Not a dry eye in the house as her theme tune was sung.
When you tell me that you love me, a song from when
she was young.
Jokes where retold and stories remembered,
From the brave to the bold – they stoked the sad
embers.
The wigs and costumes carefully packed away.
'Such a shame she's gone, she was the best,' the
mourners say.
A framed portrait was hung and tributes were made
For a treasure of the scene, a high price was paid.
There'll never be another, but maybe one's enough.
Saying goodbye will always be rough.
Shine bright like a diamond, you beacon of drag;
Always remembered, now let down the rainbow flag.
One last toast to the new star in the sky:
This is adios, my friend, this is not goodbye.

ROSIE

David Flybury

Their fine lives impressed me. One thing, the way they sat each day waiting for something. She said the day he died, it was unexpected, but she woke at three, asked him if he'd like a cup of tea. No reply. 'He's gone; I knew immediately,' she said.

Shocked on so many levels, I said, 'Rosie, first of all, I'm sorry. Bill was a good guy.' Worked as a postman. In retirement he took it easy. Smoked on the balcony. Didn't mind me. Didn't mind anything. He just didn't mind, 'But. If you had woken me up at three in the morning and asked me if I wanted a cup of tea ... ? I'd have punched you. Well, been most annoyed. What made you do that?'

'Oh we always did. If I woke in the night I'd often make a cup and then go back to sleep. I'd make one for him as well.'

I could see the quietness of their well-worn intimacy.

'Ok. So what did you do next, call the ambulance I suppose? You had to report it.'

'No,' she said.

'I had a cup of tea,' she said. 'Then back to bed. Well, he was dead already. No point upsetting everybody.'

I laughed to hide my affection for her. Lying there next to her husband, his corpse still warmed by her own heat, gathering the covers and the sentiments by which they had cohabited for some seventy years, how sweet to live that lasting love in a few hours of shared stillness.

Rosie lived twenty years, quietly smaller and more quiet until she too went. I never knew a better person.

DISTANCE

Bodicea Iceni

This is a life not tied to yours
A life that exists in its own right
A life that chose to merge with you
A life that now exists alongside

A life you've tried to destroy
A life you've tried to hurt
A life that you wish to deny freedom
A life that you say you love
but connectivity is beyond you

My life is not your life.
It never has been it never will be.
I exist but not for you.
Never for you.

RISE

Rainer King

In the dank barn, two boxers stand poised at the brink. The walls are covered with posters of past events and marks from fighters flung to the edge by superior competitors. This is where legends are forged; where city drama meets brutal survival. The demand for underground fights fuels a steady stream of desperate contestants. The winner walks free, to do as she chooses.

The crowd jeers and shouts, their eyes riveted to the raised platform. They have ventured to the outskirts of the city where the silence is usually broken by the sound of crickets and tractors making their way home. Tonight the air is dense and damp; it's raining heavily.

Earlier that evening, Jai, standing in a dimly lit room, focused on a blot on the wall — an imagined spectre. Her bare feet moved back and forth on the cool concrete floor to the rhythm of her breathing, shadows flickering across the walls as if to keep time with her movements. Her thoughts drifted to Ary, her opponent, who moved like a ghost in the ring, untouchable and enigmatic. Jai trained for two years in the mud, rain, and heat. She feels ready to make her mark. She wants to move on.

When Ary enters the ring, head held high, she punches the air to the raucous sound of the impatient crowd. Banknotes are flung into the ring in jest. Jai stands silently, her presence commanding stillness.

The bell's clang slices through the tension. The boxers trade jabs like whispered secrets. It's chess with knuckles, each move a question, each block a response. The air is thick with anticipation, spectators leaning in, hungry for violence and a winning bet.

The boxers continue with the sharp, staccato rhythm of combat. Beneath the veneer of aggression, a different dialogue unfolds, a conversation spoken in jabs, in the give and take of two boxers, their eyes meeting.

'You move well,' Ary says, her voice almost lost beneath the cacophony, 'Like you're dancing to another beat.'

Jai's response, a half-smile, even as she parries a swift left hook. 'Dancing's about feeling free. Isn't fighting the same for you?'

Ary dodges, ducking low, her counter a beat skipped in the rising tension of their waltz. 'Freedom in the ring is earned,' she replies, her tone holding a note of respect that transcends the fight, 'Not like it is out there.'

'You know nothing about out there,' growls Jai, striking out, with Ary's block and counter punch sending her across the ring. She leaps up, darting left and right, swinging round to keep sight of Ary.

'You did not grow up when I did,' says Ary, 'yet, your dance is something to behold.'

'We are no longer in that time,' Jai counters, circling left and punching Ary in the stomach.

'Every punch I throw is for those whose voices are silenced.' Ary recoils, hits back, and connects with Jai's jaw.

'Then let's walk away and fight where it matters,' says Jai.

Round after round, they speak in the language of their bodies, each strike a word, every clinch a sentence. As the penultimate bell echoes, something unspoken passes between them — an acknowledgment of shared experience and a yearning for more than the validation of the ring.

Jai takes Ary's hand, the gesture bridging the gap between combat and camaraderie. They leave the ring, hands clasped in a silent vow of unity, the fight behind them and the world ahead. In the dance of life played out in countless rings, the crowds that say otherwise matter nothing to those fighting for freedom.

JOINING UP

Susan Miller

Stella looked through the glass doors to see if the kids were enjoying the new library. They certainly seemed to be working hard. They could use their laptops in here too.

But there was a problem. A number of the library users were rushing for the doors.

Something must have gone wrong. She strode to the doors. The wall of the library had disappeared.

But why were they running towards the street?

Then she realised. There was a large whale in the room. The waters were rising. The Thames was fighting back. Everybody was treading through deepening waters.

There was nothing for it. Stella thought. She turned the table into a raft and paddled slowly away.

AESTHETE

Bodicea Iceni

You were always hiding,
Hiding your light under a bushel –
Not deliberately, not completely
But just enough to remain
a little out of sight
So creative, so full of life
So warm, so generous
So talented, so loving
Finding out that you prefer
the company of men
Would never change our history
Or the love you've shown me
It doesn't change my love
My eternal love for you
My nurturer, my caretaker, my life-giver –
One of many, but special none the less
Drinking your desires away
Won't change who you are
Will never change
The object of your desires
The object of your affection

Will never change the fear,
the anxiety, the feelings of hopelessness;
The feelings of hopelessness I have
as you drink your life away

As I watch you
Watch you drink and smoke
Yourself into obscurity
Hell bent on self-destruction,
Annihilation.
Bringing death forever
Just a little bit closer
Love is the only
The only thing that matters –
Don't you know that?
Surely you know that
In the final analysis
A pure honest force for good –
Don't deny it,
Don't deprive yourself of it
Let it in, let love in.
Self-love is no sin
Acceptance is the only way,
The only way forward –
Acceptance is key
If only you'd see
That we all just care.
Care about you.

Love yourself. We all do.

A PLACE IN THE SUN

Simon Fletcher

'I've just seen the confirmation email ...'

'Yes?'

'To Alicante.'

'To Alicante...??'

'That's right, dear.'

'I thought it was Switzerland.'

'Well, since they changed the laws in Spain about assisted dying, they've started offering much cheaper options in Benidorm. You're not upset, are you?'

'No, no. Why should I care? It's just a little bit shocking when you see it written in Times New Roman in an EasyJet confirmation email ... one return and one single ... rubs it in, really.'

'It seemed a bit of a waste to book two returns.'

'I know I know ... what's the room like, does it have a nice view?'

She shakes her head.

'Too expensive, was it?' he says. 'It's like Cluedo: 'The nurse, with a candlestick, in a room overlooking the car park!' What method have you chosen? Gas, needle, lead pipe, dagger?'

'Dagger'

'Dagger?'

'I mean needle ...'

'And what am I doing while this is happening? Did you choose the Whale sounds or a video of waves lapping at my feet in the Maldives?'

'Those options were slightly out of our price range, I', afraid.'

'Oh. So what then? Watching Last of the Summer Wine? Test card?'

'Homes under the Hammer.'

'HOMES UNDER THE BLOODY HAMMER IS THE LAST THING I SEE?!? You're joking!'

'You always liked it.'

'Well, I do enjoy watching the reveal, the transformation at the end.'

'I don't think you'll make it to the reveal.'

'What?'

'You'll be gone in twenty minutes so ...'

'So I die in suspense, not knowing if they secured a profit or what they did with the dodgy lean-to.'

'They always turn a profit.'

'You PROMISED me something relaxing'

'I'm sorry dear, but those WERE out of our price range and I wanted to save some money ... '

'Save money! What for? My wake?'

'No, I'm going on a cruise ... with Carol ... from number 46.'

'Oh ... well I suppose we did talk about doing that together didn't we?'

*****

In Spain......

'I'm disappointed you couldn't get me a nice view of the car park.'

'Yes. I'm sorry about that, dear.'

'It must have cost a fortune anyway. What with the NURSE, with a needle, the room overlooking Playa ... ?'

'Playa Levante.'

She held his hand as he lay back.

Whale music began to play and a series of relaxing images came over a screen at the end of the bed.

'This isn't Homes under the Hammer, is it?'

'It isn't, is it? I'm going to complain.'

'And remember, give it three months and then ...'

'... then I can date whoever I want'

'Yes ... and you'll enjoy that cruise ... with Carol ...'

She smiled and held onto his hand until she felt he was no longer in the room.

She stood up and took the printed flight confirmation out of her pocket. She folded it and ripped it in half, repeating the process until it was too much trouble to do it further.

She placed it in the bin.

'Are you ready?' enquired the nurse.

She nodded.

She was led to the next room with a view of the car park and took her position lying on the bed.

Whale music started to play.

PLANNING THE FUTURE

'Rutter, I need to have a chat with you following your end of term report,'

'Yes, sir.'

'Don't look so worried. It's nothing bad. But your 'A' levels are coming up and we need a talk about what happens after that. Do you want to go on to college? If so, which university? What subject?'

'Of course, sir. But ...'

'What's the matter, Rutter?'

'Do you think we could get out of bed first, sir?'

LONDON I LIKE

David Flybury

Jamie looked down at his feet, then up at me, his lips closed into an unhappy and difficult smile.

'I am sick of London. If London were a person I'd be saying, I no longer love you, London!'

With his hands in the pockets of his jacket, he expressively punched an imagined target positioned somewhere inches from his chest.

'It's still a big deal,' he moaned. 'I can't believe it. It's still a big deal. How has this happened? Maaaaaaaaaaan. I thought … I thought, he was the one!'

Our walk through Lincoln's Inn Fields was the result of a misunderstanding: We both thought the whole gay gang would arrive - an armada of gays; we'd sail the oceans of the din-filled streets (catching eyes), and, public parks with quiet endless lawns, bedding plants, (and solitary men), and, inside the bright interiors of small shops selling mobile-phones, we'd browse and pick our favourites, persistently eyeing-up the cool techie staff - but it was just me and Jamie. The weather was inclement: Swirling, glowing orange clouds occupied the sky like Jupiter, trapped between the houses and above the wind-rushed trees, threatening rain. We walked along a path around the grass; around and round and round and round.

Still he was complaining, '… but when he did smile his eyes really did twinkle. They really did. I'm not making this up. I'm not. I swear. I'm telling the truth. Honestly. That's how it was for me; it was like really really really … you know … real. It was.'

'I know what you're thinking,' said Jamie, after a pause.

'What am I thinking?'

'You're thinking I'm mad.'

'I'll tell you what I'm thinking,' I said, 'I'm thinking about how, given time, you'll get over him. It's as simple as that. Think of it like this: He was a cunt.'

'I ca'an't,' he said.

'Yeh, well, you gotta try cos all of this crap isn't doing any good. 'Twinkling eyes'?! Fuck. That. YOU need to get 'real'. You need to get a grip.'

Jamie was silent at last. He walked on some time and then lifted his hands, still inside his jacket, and wiped his face. Now, he was crying.

'Oh for fucksake Jamie. Get over it.'

'I can't. I want to die.'

'We all want to die.'

'I hate London. I hate it. I hate the men. They use you and then ...'

'You wanna go where there ain't any men. See how you like it. Do without men, why don'cha!'

'I could.'

'You could try.'

'I could.'

'You could try, but you'd be even more miserable.'

'I could go back to Mum and Dad and get a wife!' he laughed, 'Guess not.'

'One day you'll meet someone ... and get a dog.'

'Will I? What about you?'

'What about me?'

'Will you?'

'Will I what?'

'Meet someone and get a dog?'

'Probably not a dog. A goldfish maybe. Or a geranium.'

Jamie was again looking down at his feet.

But I'd seen a man I liked, earlier on the tube. I had a seat. He hung from a strap: Square shoulders, narrow to his waist, legs tapered, crossed in sharp-toed shoes; he came to an elongated, bifurcated point, teeteringly vertical, off-centred, like the spindle of a swaying gyroscope. His long, cantilevered wrist supported a phone screen into which he stared; it cast a pale-blue glow on his face. He stared and stared at it, occasionally texting, biting his nails.

Then he grinned at it, pulling back kissable lips, showing off his neat, gardenia-coloured teeth, even and miniaturely curved like the frontages of a row of Regency seaside hotels, exposing gums like walls of dark coagulating, pinky-grey and purple coffee coloured brick. I stared at him, catching sight of his tiny, shiny, short, wet tongue, extended briefly in concentration. Then he looked up, I caught his eye, and, for part of a second, we saw each other. Then, as I looked away, his eyes returned to his phone, twinkling.

BAD NEWS/GOOD NEWS

The airmail letter from Australia had a black border.

The old lady's eyes filled with tears. She recognised her daughter-in-law's handwriting.

Her eight-year-old grandson's eyes shone with excitement. He recognised the new 'Black Swan' commemorative.

It would look great in his stamp album.

THE COAL MAN

Craig Binch

I hear the truck trundle up and my heart flutters. The coal truck has arrived, and there he is, a perfect smile enhanced by a layer of coal dust that settles like mascara on his lashes, a square jaw, strong arms swinging the heavy bags of coal like bags of feathers. He's tall, strong and handsome and doesn't know I exist. He jokes with his team mates and as he lifts, he exposes a toned midriff, sending a tingle down my spine.

I have my instructions to ask for an extra bag, but I can't find the words or the bravery. I whip off my school tie and flatten down my hair, looking at my teenage face in the hall mirror. My hand trembles as I swing the door, and come face to face with the object of my daydreams...

We collided as I bowled out of the door, my hero catching me in his strong arms.

'Steady on, lad,' he half-laughed half-boomed. I had no words as he held me in his arms, and his mouth less than a foot away from mine. I smiled a crooked smile, my cheeks flushed. He flipped me upright in one movement and steadied me with his hand.

'Thank you,' I said feebly.

'No worries, young 'un. Just kind where you going, more haste less speed.' He winked.

I blurted out, 'Can we have an extra bag?'

He nodded, smiled, and I ran inside, closed the door, a coal-stained hand print on my school shirt, my heart beating like a drum.

I grabbed a towel, ran to the bedroom, locked the door.

RUTH AND ANNIE

Alison Rice-Murphy

Ruth looked down at her pair of life-buoy ankles. On the left one there lay a crooked Chelsea smile scar, the same dusty satin of her areola, left from a long-healed ORIF ankle surgery. She had fallen down the landing stairs several years ago, breaking both the lateral and medial malleolus, which were actually leg bones, despite its being called an ankle fracture. Ruth's daughter insisted on calling the incident 'Mum's little slip.' After a year of toe-lift exercises and ice-packs the colour of blue powerade, the doctor had taken the soft fluid of the ankle in his probing fingertips, and announced his bewilderment at the mysterious pooling that wouldn't leave. Ruth, with no more insight than a medical professional, had taken to her armchair. The years had passed by like softly flowing water through an algae-topped pond. Eventually, through disuse, the right ankle had also adopted expansionary measures.

'I'm going out. Dinner's in the oven.' A slight pause. 'Love you'

At some point during those years, Ruth's capricious daughter Annie had moved back in. Ruth had never asked her to. The way Annie's whirlwind voice thundered up and down the stairs of Ruth's two-up, two-down terraced house shook slumbering giants from the ground. Nine pounds at birth, Annie had always squeezed herself into casings that couldn't quite hold her. Like a hermit crab that had found a particularly iridescent shell. Ruth reached for her walking frame the hospital had asked to be returned, pulling herself up with expulsion of air from her throat. Annie used to bring her dinner in, then started leaving it on the upstairs landing, and now it was always left in the oven. Ruth heard the smash of feet on the cardboard box stairs, but she didn't have time to sit down before Annie entered.

'It's hotpot. Have you done your exercises?'

Annie's interjections were always two-pronged.

'Yes, love.'

All Ruth had wanted for some time now was a peaceful death. No cancer, or stroke.

Just a gentle liquefying of the extremities, or a dip mid-tango from which a clement partner never hoists her back up. Ruth was not a smoker, so she simply had to wait. She sat back down, this time on a chaise lounge positioned by the window upon which she could admire her unwieldy ankles. She watched her daughter walk down the road, lit sporadically by the amber groan of street lamps. Annie, who had seemed destined to take lilting strides into the world, like an overgrown toddler giggling at the casual destruction underfoot, had become stuck, searching for meaning in her home cooked meals.

Ruth picked herself up from her seated position, wobbling slightly as she rose, cursing though no one was there. The bedroom-cum-living-room was painted a burgundy which had, thirty years ago, seemed like a sensuous choice; a choice that suggested the possibility of laughter and mistakes. Now, it felt more like she was living inside a fly-trap. But Ruth still had fun: although she no longer drank alcohol, she had found other methods. Before her ankle troubles, she had tried online dating, meeting habitually on the last Saturday of every month with whichever never married man sent her a message. Sometimes they would come home with Ruth; always to her port-coloured bedroom and never the man's house. Ruth didn't need to look at their bodies, or faces, during the act, and no space was left for gazing. This was one of the ways she had stayed happy. She channelled all her disappointment, built up over years of mothering, into the ritualistic disappointment of her body. However, one day, she was discovered. Annie had burst in on some finickity errand, paused long enough to burn the scene into her occipital lobe, then exited in a similarly rushed fashion. Ruth had blundered after her, dressing gown barely drawn about her waist. It was in this episode that the fall, and consequent ankle fracture, had occurred. When the ambulance had arrived, the evening gentleman had left, and Annie sat in a state of oppressive silence on the foot of the stairs.

So now, Ruth had to seek other methods. Wielding her hospital walking frame she ambled through the corridor, down the fateful stairs, and into the kitchen. The hotpot had begun to bubble in a voracious staccato, hot air building until it found escape through a browning gap in the layered potato top. Ruth turned the temperature knob of the oven up several large jumps, and returned to bed. She could picture the morning scene now. Annie, hands dancing over the scorching plastic handle, yelling her name. She would demand, 'Why didn't you take it out? I told you dinner was ready.' 'Oh dear, I must've forgotten,' Ruth would reply, the carbonated hotpot already becoming a household relic.

FOUR BLACK DRESSES

Craig Binch

Four black dresses hung in four very different wardrobes and one black suit nestled against the cold silk of a coffin. The owners of the dresses mostly strangers up until today.

Death unites those that loved you, blinded by grief the man often becomes a saint and a legend. Now gone just like that, how very unlike him no warning, no fond farewell, leaving nothing but frustration and heartache for those left behind.

Death and departure can also be a time of hidden truths rising to the surface, do we really know the ones we loved. Surely everyone has a secret, a skeleton in the closet or a little black dress.

The first black dress was wool and could be described as shapeless, it was a perfect fit for the voluptuous shape of its owner. Accent jewellery would lift it a little and distract from the expanded waste line. After her heart was broken, she turned to carbohydrates to soften the pain and plug the fresh hole. For good measure she would spray and extra spray Chanel *Mademoiselle*, she knew it was his favourite. The children refused to come on principle and warned her of making an ass of herself, mooning over a man who had given her nothing but misery. Despite all that he had been the love of her life. She would miss him.

The second dress was short of course. It was an old faithful — one of those she had used as tempting bait in the beginning, to turn his eyes away from his dull spouse and then again towards her next; the vintage tag read 'well used'. They had had some good times in the beginning, but she bored easily. Her thrill was in that initial chase, the novelty of that unknown. She knew her looks were fading, just as her mother had warned her. Oh, but in her heyday she had used every inch of it and the men would come in droves. He was the same, infatuated at the start, not able to understand how he had managed to punch so far above his weight. She didn't know what it was, but there something about him, an old-fashioned charm. She would miss him.

The third was a plain yet classic dress and would be paired with smart lace up brogues, that usually took her to the WI. Practical and comfortable yet almost stylish in her twilight years, she was the one he turned to in his hour of need when the tart left him. They moved together into a comfortable uncomplicated life as they glided into retirement. The funeral was pre-planned and pre-paid, everything organised and practically arranged. The service was simple — no religious faff and the cheapest package. Maybe they weren't in love, but it worked. This wasn't how they had planned it; they were supposed to move to the seaside and wait out their final days together overlooking the sea. Now she would be going alone and that sat heavily upon her. She would miss him.

The fourth black dress, which was by far the most glamorous, was his, hidden in the back of his wardrobe, a dark sequin gown that skimmed the floor, a split almost to the top of the leg. He had liked the way it shimmered and clung to his figure; he'd had it specially made. If you ignored the hairy chest and manly hands it was nothing but elegant. The finishing touches were the expensive silk stockings, kitten heels and the raven bouffant wig. He felt like his heroines of the bygone era, Jane Mansfield, Marilyn Monroe, nothing short of old school glamour. He was careful of course no one would ever know. He would miss her.

The undertaker had received a discreet note from the solicitor with one last request. He was prepared for the last moment on this planet with the most beautiful suspenders and stockings under his Sunday best suit. Hidden in plain sight, he went to his maker dressed to the nines, the undertaker smiling to himself as he clipped the last suspender belt into place. Sweet dreams, you kinky bugger.

VIOLENCE A TELLING

Bodicea Iceni

Deborah looked up from her chopping board as the instructor arrived. She couldn't quite make out his face as he walked past her towards the stove. He turned suddenly and she saw his face. Eyes swollen and puffy. Below the eyes she saw black and blue — bruising. She was stunned and felt a little giddy. What could have caused this? she asked herself.

'Head trauma,' he states as if reading her mind, 'From rugby.'

Deborah paused, looked at his face intently, from one eye to the next, and then allowed her gaze to drop just below the right eye to the bruise. She slowly closed her eyes willing him and his bruising to vanish. Too much pain, too much trauma. Can't think, can't process, can't cope. Feeling overwhelmed.

'When I open my eyes, please no longer be in front of me.'

She opens her eyes. He's still standing there. She looks straight at him, unable to speak, then slowly lowers her gaze back to the chopping board and continues preparing the vegetables in silence.

At home later that night she sits quietly on the sofa, reflecting. She is triggered by the bruising. Although she is feeling emotional and distressed, she is not absolutely certain why. She allows her mind to drift to an incident in her childhood. Recalling her aunt with a swollen face on one side.

'What is wrong?' her visiting grandfather asks.

'A football hit me in the park,' says my aunt.

When? Deborah thinks. I've been with you for the last three days. I don't remember going into a park, let alone a ball coming at us. When exactly did this happen?

'That looks like a fist,' my grandfather states. Silence. Deborah and her cousin both look at her uncle, her aunt's husband. Did he do this? He sits on the bed next to my aunt looking perplexed and somewhat sheepish.

Deborah pauses for a moment to absorb her memories. The library is silent. No background noise from the TV as she doesn't have one nor from the radio as she barely uses it since Covid. She allows herself to drift a little more and is transported back to her aunt's first flat in Clapham. Her aunt was always keen for Deborah to spend school holidays with her. Deborah couldn't stand going there for holidays, quite frankly, but her aunt always asked and she couldn't possibly say no.

Deborah's cousin Sophia was like many younger siblings and cousins – incredibly irritating. Always trying to get her attention.

Today is no different. Whilst Deborah tries to watch TV, Sophia's attention seeking behaviour continues to escalate until her aunt comes over to intervene.

Deborah's aunt seems to be telling Sophia off. Sophia has little to no interest in what is being said. Deborah notices the belt in her aunt's hands. She then raises her hand and brings the belt down violently. Her aunt continues to strike Sophia three, four, five times with rapid thrusts and hellish energy.

By the eighth strike Deborah wants her aunt to stop. This is my younger cousin she's hurting. I'm meant to look after her, protect her. Deborah's ten-year-old brain is overloading. How do I protect her from her mother? I can't. Feeling overwhelmed, tears well up but she doesn't cry. She somehow manages to restrain the tears.

The following day Deborah hears her aunt recounting the story to her brother, Deborah's uncle. Her aunt mentions Deborah's response and she laughs. Deborah overhearing the conversation cannot believe her aunt is taking pleasure from the event. Later on, processing the display of utter madness, Deborah realises her aunt is retelling the story because she is pleased that Deborah wanted to protect Sophia. How anyone could have found a positive in this nightmare event was beyond her but she thinks, Happy to have entertained you.

She is now back in her library. She acknowledges that she wanted to stop the beating, that it was torturous watching it but she couldn't protect Sophia from her mother. She was powerless to do so and was forced to be a bystander, now also a victim, to this horrific incident. An inescapable memory now with her always. She never allowed her ten-year-old self to cry, not during the event and certainly not after. But she could now decades later.

THE SURVIVOR

Hastie Salih

Every cell in her body was shaking, screaming to leave her contaminated body, but when the composed doctor squeezed her clammy hand, her tears shined like gold in the endless dusk.
'Your hair will grow back ... Mine did too.'

RURAL IDYLL

Stephanie Dickinson

The cat creeps through the long grass towards its goal. The fish is still there. Its body gleams as it circles the pond, silvery scales catching the rays of sun that filter through the reeds. Its body is plump. The cat settles by the water watching intently, its head moving imperceptibly as it tracks the fish's progress. The fish comes nearer and nearer to the bank where the cat sits. A shimmering heat haze and the silence of the remote rural setting adds a languid, hypnotic air to the moment. The cat's body stiffens as it judges the moment to pounce.

The boy's cry breaks the silence. He has seen the cat from the doorway of the cottage. It is orange like the fluffy stuffed toy that lies on his bed. He has a black and white one too. And a stripey one. He is entranced by cats. He climbs carefully down the steps into the garden and starts unsteadily towards the pond. Walking is a new skill for him and needs concentration. The garden lies in front of him, a forest of long grass and prickly brambles. The cat is still sitting by the water. It watches the boy curiously, the fish forgotten for a moment.

Sarah is folding clothes in the bedroom. It is really too hot to be doing anything and she needs a long, cool drink. Charlie will be awake soon. She will get their drinks and set up a picnic rug under the big tree that shades a corner of the lawn. She smiles to herself. 'Lawn' is rather an ambitious name for the tangle mass of green that makes up a large part of the garden. That is one of the unfulfilled projects she had set herself: to turn the wilderness into something that looks vaguely like a lawn. Something that Charlie will be able to play on now that he is walking. She moves towards the window to remind herself what a mess it is! The shrill cry alerts her before she sees what is happening. Charlie, crawling now, is heading doggedly down the narrow, flattened grass path that trails down the long garden.

Sarah watches idly. Her whole day is focused around Charlie, what he is doing when he is awake, what she can do when he is asleep. How can such a small being fill you with such a mixture of emotions: tenderness, frustration, helplessness. It isn't like that for Sam. Sam works in the city, catching the train from the next village at an impossibly early hour and returning home late from a world of excitement, of adult conversation, of new experiences, a world that she had once been part of.

They had moved to this impossibly remote rural cottage because Sam thought, well they both thought, that it would be a wonderful place to bring up children. And they both wanted children. Two was a good number. Sarah would look after the first baby and Sam take on the role as earner. After a couple of years the roles would be reversed. Sam would stay at home looking after a second baby and Sarah would step back into the world of work.

She cannot wait for that moment. She hadn't planned for the exhaustion she would feel looking after a small child, the isolation of living so far from any facilities that she has to use the car to get to them. And the car! Unreliable at best, it now lies in the drive inert and probably unrepairable while she and Sam debate whether they can afford to get it back on the road. She feels trapped. She has thought about moving back to Islington. Toddler groups, parks, cafes — everything within walking distance. Living there with a baby would be fine. She sighs. If Charlie weren't here, they would move back to London. Even Sam couldn't persuade her to stay in a house if a tragedy had happened there. A tragedy like what? Like Charlie falling in the deep water at the end of the garden ...

Another shriek, of excitement that his goal is nearly within his grasp, jolts Sarah from her thoughts. She looks out of the window again, now intently. The fear that grips her is palpable as she sees the tiny figure, upright again, stumbling through the wilderness towards the pond. So near the pond. So near his goal. The fluffy orange cat still motionless - and so near the water.

'Charlie!' she shouts out of the window. 'Come back.' No reaction.

'An ice cream,' she cajoles. 'I've got an ice cream for you'.

Pointless. Charlie shows no sign of hearing. She has to get to him before he gets near the water. It would only take a minute to drown and she is minutes away from him. Why has she hesitated? What has she been thinking? Charlie, with his baby-soft skin, his delighted chuckle when he sees his toys, especially the cats, his trusting look as she sticks a plaster on a scratch or kisses a bruise better. She can't bear to think of anything happening to him. She will endure life in her rural prison if only he is safe.

She rushes to the door.

SHADOW PLAY

Richard Thompson

I must've been about five, maybe six,
I couldn't quite reach the latch on the gate yet,
I was definitely still lick-l-bit.
My world so far always existed behind that gate,
I couldn't wait to graduate.

My world was the best, I'd strain to peer
up the street but couldn't quite hear,
through its orange ornate spindles,
just about making out
the many hustling shadows in my game.

Every day was a different day looking through the gaps,
you didn't need a calendar or clock,
Saturday was always on the map.
A hive of activity at the end of the street,
where people were out in their droves,
to restock on food, bits, bobs, clothes.

Sunday was solemn, quiet and calm,
simmering brown rice, Gungo peas, creamed coconut,
and a whiff of chives.
Thyme and garlic filled the air,
Steve Barnard blurting out his latest wares,
Reggae Time always landed gracefully,
with nothing else to compare.

The familiar smell of singed hair,
hot combing, and moaning sounds of victims' despair.
Dad always trying to infiltrate the vibe,
with a rock steady tune or Jim Reeves bribe.
He was always defeated with Barnard's latest riddim,
from the legendary DJ's record bag, by now was a given.

Another two seasons to go then I'd be able to reach,
to see what others see before they retreat.
Even though I feel a pull
towards the hustle and bustle at the end of the street,
I feel content, safe, complete.
I know if all goes wrong,
I'll always have somewhere to sleep.

I'd like to stay here forever, if possible but it's not,
I'm growing taller and taller every day,
And soon, I'll be walking towards the end of the street
joining the shadows at play.

I SPY

We had no idea what Dad did for a living until we saw his picture on the front page of the *Sunday Express*.

He'd turned up in Moscow.

DUST IF YOU MUST

Craig Binch

Doreen drove the floor buffer across the floor in a well-worn path. The nuclear plant deathly quiet, except for the whir of her machine. Forty years she'd polished this floor, she could do it with her eyes closed.

That was enough for tonight; she poured a cup of hot, sweet, milky tea slurping it through her dentures.

Something brushed her leg. A rat. Startled she jumped up from the chair, spilling her drink all over the control panel, which fizzed.

'Christ alive,' she shuddered, whipped the cloth from her pinafore pocket and began wiping the buttons and controls, in no particular order.

Out of the silence a booming announcement: 'Detonation activated'. Doreen's eyes opened wide, then she shrugged, discreetly packed her cleaning trolley and trundled out of the room, closing the door carefully behind her.

SHAKESPEARE FOR TODAY

The pale, mournful young man came forward and fixed the audience with an agonised stare:

'To be or not to be, that is the question ...'

Michelle Ackerley bounded forward, shaking her elaborately curled locks and grinning. She gushed:

'Yes, that's today's question. Should Hamlet Be or Not Be. If you think he should be, text 87728, if you think he should Not Be, text 87729. Lines close in 15 minutes. We'll be back with the results soon after.'

MISSING

Stephanie Dickinson

'Kyle. Kyle!' Maggie looks around impatiently. Keeping track of the children on an outing to a busy museum is her worst nightmare. Where's Kyle?

Little Emily, ever-helpful, says 'He's not here'.

Maggie's heart sinks. She looks carefully round the hall. He is nowhere to be scene. A horrible feeling spreads through her. This time he might not just be mislaid for a few minutes; he might actually be missing.

Can you spot Kyle?

56

Thoughts swirl through her mind. She'll have to tell his parents. No, the school first. Or the museum? Yes, the museum staff. She looks around for a warden. Of course, when she wants one there was no-one in sight. Earlier it had been different. One had watched the children in her group like a hawk. 'Don't let them climb on the dinosaurs, Miss', he'd warned every time a child had got too close to the almost-lifesize models. Kyle, of course, was the main culprit. Kyle!

A thought suddenly comes to her.

Kyle.

Climbing.

Dinosaurs.

She looks up the tall neck of the Brachiosaurus right next to her. Of course!

TOO HAPPY

Stephanie Dickinson

Another Pride March. Walking with friends, exhilarated to be there, finally over IT. But ... across the crowd YOU are there. Walking, arms wrapped around another. Looking happy when you've no right to be.

Looking much too happy.

GREENHOUSE

Frances Gapper

You are in the greenhouse with two lots of glass between us, the house glass and the special greenhouse glass, which I think is reinforced although a pane broke before it was put together by men who'd done this before and it was a nightmare, so we kept hurrying down the garden with cheery remarks or words of anxious praise or weather forecast updates and cups of tea and bacon sandwiches made using your mum's technique of incorporating all the grease and frizzled morsels by wiping the bread around the pan and it cost us a fortune in best quality organic bacon donated by pigs free to roam in clovery meadows, the greenhouse which you sometimes mistakenly call the conservatory other times the Dog & Trumpet because you like saying I'm just going down the Dog & Trumpet and it has a sign painted on a smooth grey stone, it has windows that open automatically when the sun gets too hot for the seedlings in their trays and tiny pots the grown-ons and the ready to plant out any day now, it has ants and paving stones and half-used bags of compost and my old wicker chair which you kept leaving out in the rain and I kept taking indoors, until the greenhouse arrived and you said it can live in there to protect it from the weather and I said bit late now but OK and you said if we weren't married I think we'd still be good friends and I wondered what you meant.

BATTLEFIELD

Bodicea Iceni

Did we all know
Know what it would mean
To lose you, to bury you

Fears I know
we all had them
But to lose a mother
Irreplaceable

The anchor
The architect
The matriarch

Could we possibly
Have anticipated
What this would mean
What was to come next

The void left
Filled by someone else
A woman garnering
Less respect and no love

Unloved by the majority
The home becoming
A place of tension
A battlefield

Guns always cocked
Knifes barely sheathed
Swords at the ready
Fists always tightly coiled

Eruptions there were a few
But in the end
too few to note

Who were the winners
Were there losers
I was a pawn
Played at strategic points

Unknowingly but painfully
Played nonetheless
A child stuck in the middle

And then she passed
A third wife for a time
And then he was gone
Game over

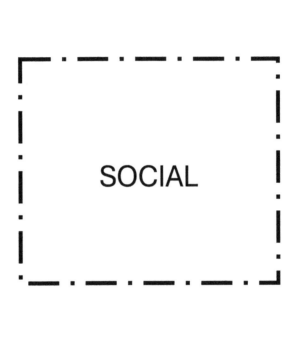

SOCIAL

NOT GAY, ACTUALLY

David Godolphin

Dennis wasn't gay but he liked having sex with men. It started at high school where boys experimented with each other as well as with girls. Dennis had his first girlfriend at fourteen, but he didn't have full-on sex ('*penetration*' — as the teachers called it in Aids-Awareness classes) until his third girlfriend, Juliette, when he was fifteen and a half. 'You're my Romeo,' Juliette told him, but he wasn't: she dumped him after five months for a nineteen-year-old waiter from a local Italian restaurant who was Spanish and marginally more qualified as a Romeo.

Dennis had sex with men in public lavatories and lay-bys on the county's A-roads. It was mostly wanking and blowjobs — still no 'penetration' — with Dennis always the receiver rather than the donor of oral sex. He was told he was well-hung and with his fly unzipped he was always quickly snapped up by men on the prowl.

One overweight middle-aged man in the woods beyond a lay-by expressed admiration for Dennis's bum: 'Very pert', he said; 'like a pair of peaches in a hammock'.

Dennis didn't understand how somebody's backside could be pert or peachy, but seemingly it was a blessing to have one that was. Already on his knees, the fat man made Dennis turn round and started licking his crack, which was gross but thrilling. He kept an eye out for this man's car, a BMW, on his drives around the county, and it was on their third encounter that Dennis learned that what this man liked to do was called 'rimming'. The man told him a joke about a posh punter who offered a prostitute an extra fee to rim him and then farted in her

62

face. When the tart called him a 'filthy bastard' the punter said: 'Young lady, I'll thank you to keep a civil tongue up my arse'.

'You can rim me if you like,' said the man who told Dennis this joke.

'No thanks, mate,' Dennis replied. 'I'm not gay, actually.'

'Oh, honey, I think you are,' the man said. 'Actually. We're all poofters here.' Dennis avoided him after this meeting, although he sometimes saw his car in lay-bys and wondered if his tongue was up somebody else's crack.

Dennis married Raquel, a petite brunette, when they were both nineteen and the first of their three children was on the way. Dennis had been a keen fisherman since boyhood; Raquel accompanied him on fishing trips, happy to read a paperback romance beside a river or a lake. Between spells of maternity leave she worked in various local shops. Dennis rose two rungs up the career ladder in the council offices.

He cruised the toilets and lay-bys more frequently as the years passed. After four pregnancies — there was a miscarriage between their second and third child — Raquel was not quite as petite and elasticity had moved from her vagina to her breasts. Dennis also suspected that his bum might no longer be pert or peachy; nobody else tried to rim him.

The age of Aids gave way to the age of the internet. Aids was still there, of course, but people weren't dying from it. With the internet came gay websites and chat-rooms. Online and on his smartphone, Dennis used a false name and a photograph of a great-uncle who'd died in his twenties during the D-Day landings in France and bore a superficial resemblance to 'Dirk', as Dennis was known in this global community.

'*Dirk, 26, bi-curious,*' is how he advertised himself, although he was twenty-eight the first time he posted this byline and he continued using it into his thirties. Through the internet he learned about cruising locations further afield and gay saunas in various cities. Fishing trips provided a useful smokescreen, now that his family longer accompanied him to lakes and rivers: the kids became quickly bored, which made their mother irritable.

One summer they went to a holiday camp on the Sussex coast; the children were teenagers now, lazy and impossible to please. Raquel read a Danielle Steel under a sunshade while the kids hung out with other surly teens. Dennis drove off with his fishing gear and visited a sauna in Brighton. In the steam-room he was cruised by a man younger and prettier than the men he usually met in lay-bys and toilets. Dennis suddenly — and disturbingly — discovered that he knew how somebody's bum could be pert, even peachy.

'Hi,' the young man said with a megawatt smile, 'I'm Dirk. From Amsterdam.'

Dennis abandoned his alias in front of a genuine Dirk. 'I'm Dennis,' he admitted. 'From Ashford. That's in Kent.'

'I came on Eurostar to Ashford,' the young man informed him. 'And from there on the diesel train to Brighton. Yesterday.'

In the course of the next forty-five minutes, on a scuzzy mattress in one of the cubicles, Dennis's inhibitions — his limitations — went the way of his alias. Dirk from Amsterdam was the first man Dennis kissed, the first he performed oral sex on and the first whom he rimmed — hesitantly at first but then with a degree of relish.

That evening's entertainment at the holiday camp was a Neil Diamond tribute act. Neil Diamond was Raquel's number-one favourite singer. The tribute looked and sounded nothing like him. Raquel drank too many piña coladas and raised a subject that she had long kept simmering below the surface.

'There's another woman, isn't there?' she said, loud enough to be heard by several nearby tables. 'These fishing trips — you don't go fishing. You're seeing some fancy woman.'

'No, I'm not,' said Dennis, surprising Raquel and their neighbours — and himself. 'I'm gay, actually. I'm a poofter.'

SEAGULLS

David Flybury

Two gulls fighting: evolved in dignity, clean expressive wings extended, threatening to stab each other's heads; warlike in beauty, though their squabble's subject was a piece of buttered bread — no, not the whole thing; just the crust.

COMING OUT, GOING HOME

Laurence Sullivan

An uneven clack shattered the stillness of the night. One heel had snapped off in the skirmish, leaving Lottie in an unstable state — now limping her way back home.

She found herself unconsciously clutching her arm, the feel of the officer's fingers still fresh in her mind. She had been near the back of the crowd, able to slip away almost unnoticed.

Yet he had clearly taken exception to her. Perhaps her height had marked her out immediately? Lottie had always considered The Stonewall Inn her second home, a place where appearances didn't matter. Yet to have been forced out so unceremoniously — to be bullied and harassed into silence — was to have that sense of self torn from her very soul ...

The lopsided steps which now defined her presence continued to resonate throughout the street. Yet she refused to let herself sob, to vocalise the void where she had supressed her inner pain. She had made enough concessions to the world tonight.

Finally, her hand came to rest on the front door of her home. The apartment block appeared only vaguely aware of her arrival, with scant few lights flickering to life.

None of her neighbours would listen if she decided to tell her story. They weren't the support that Stonewall had been, they barely acknowledged her existence.

This wasn't the home which affirmed her.

Stonewall was.

ANOTHER LIFE

Rainer King

The interior walls are pistachio, including the front of the house. I am painting the walls white. Or at least I think that's why I am in the house that overlooks the sea – which seems awfully close. I imagine that a high tide would wash away the house and it would float to another village, perhaps in another time.

The walls start to bubble and flake. The green is visible under the white. I touch the walls and the paint slips off, the pistachio colour remaining intact.

My mother pulls a brush from her hair, brandishing it like a magic wand. 'Watch and learn,' she declares, only for a glob of white paint to splatter on her left foot. She takes the rusty tin of paint and flings it at the wall. More paint tins appear and she throws them at the wall too. 'It needs to feel like home again,' she murmurs, almost to herself, her hands a blur as she covers the pistachio with desperate strokes of white.

I tug her arm, 'No one wants to live here. There's no one for miles. Please let's leave. The sea is rising.'

Her face becomes more determined as she moves on to another wall and slaps on the paint with her bare hands. My chest hursts; I know she won't leave. Her father is somewhere in this house and she will come back here. I don't want her to. How will I see her again? I try to reach her, my voice barely a whisper over the sudden roar of the waves, 'Mom, please!' But she's lost, her hands moving with a desperation.

I wake up disoriented by the sunlight coming through my window. It's 3pm on a Sunday, and the dream's vivid sounds and colours still cloud my thoughts, making the room around me feel irregular.

I've been having trouble sleeping, my unsettling dreams focus on shades of failure and nostalgia. The discomfort remains like I am still there, in the house – my chest aches. The pistachio walls in my dream are the exact colour of my grandfather's house in the depths of a small village by the ragged coast.

The last time I was there he asked me why my hair was short like his. I lied, told him I had been ill and had to cut it all off. I accompany him for his usual evening walk in the village. He strides ahead of me with his walking stick thumping the clay ground — dry, thankfully, now the monsoon has passed. People are chatting and milling by the street stalls and open market. He wants to get some rusk and milk bread for tea. He feels I need nourishment since I boarded a plane and came all the way to visit him. He worries the journey has depleted my strength. He lives alone these days. Most of his few friends have succumbed to different illnesses and those left hardly leave their houses. I worry about him but don't want to stay here and he won't leave – 'I will hardly know who I am if I live where you are,' he says.

He flips open his old black leather wallet like he is giving away state secrets instead of some money for bread. I remember the wallet from when he visited me when I was a child and he bought me a red pencil case. I was happy that day, just to see how pleased he was to be able to buy me something I wanted.

He takes out a crumpled note and pays for our teatime nourishment. As we head back, groups of young people just coming out of the local university stop and point. 'Boy or girl?' they say, and laugh. My grandfather tells me to ignore them.

'They know nothing,' he says irritably, 'Do what you want, don't listen to people, be who you want to be.'

As we walk, the taunts of the students linger in the air. My grandfather breaks open the seal of the bag of rusks and hands me one. He pats me on my shoulder and walks ahead leaning on his cane.

The memory lingers like a morsel of love. I flick on the kettle and watch my brown cat jump on the kitchen counter. My hair is long and unruly. These days I live in a place where most people don't look like me, sound like me, behave like me or think like me. I went to a queer gathering and one said 'Why don't you hang out with your own kind?' I thought I was.

I share a piece of rusk with my cat. 'I promise, this isn't a new diet,' I tell her as she nibbles the rusk with evident disdain. Her lack of enthusiasm makes me smile. She has no idea how easily her presence gives me temporary relief from my memories. I open my box of paints and find a slim brush. I sit cross-legged on the floor and start painting the white wall pink, red, orange, yellow, green, turquoise, indigo and violet.

ANSWER TO HEMINGWAY

Philip Inglesant

Wanted urgently: Baby shoes, preferably unworn.

A SEPTEMBER LETTER TO ROBERT

Leigh V Twersky

Thanks very much for your postcard
So glad you're enjoying the sea
I s'pose you've run off with the coastguard
And forgotten about poor old me

You've really no cause to worry
I just want to talk to you
I don't want to stew you in curry
Or pummel your chops black and blue

Thus starts an unusual epistle
Don't care if you read it out boozily
I won't make you sit on a thistle
Or sprinkle ground glass in your muesli

I'd feel incomparably better
If somehow, some time, some place
Instead of writing a letter
I could talk to you face to face

So, tracing the tracks of my biro
Go for a communicative bonus
When signing next for your giro
Lift the receiver and phone us

Call when you wake from your slumber
(Oh, why doth thy conscience prick so?)
But if you've forgotten my number
It's 413 5360

For frankness direct I'm appealing
I'm tired of ifs and maybes
We ought to discuss what we're feeling
Excuse the scratching — it's scabies

Are you cutting me out of your life?
Is that why your manner's so curt?
You couldn't wound more with a knife
But why should I have to be hurt?

I don't understand; I'm quite at a loss
Things haven't worked out as we planned
Do say if you're angry, speak up if you're cross
Cos I haven't a clue where I stand

'Twas almost as if we'd been violent
When everything suddenly changed
And though we could both remain silent
Let's not let ourselves get estranged

There's so much between us that's still left unspoken
My shoulders I could always shrug
So this poem's a prayer that not everything's broken
A smile and a long-distance hug

Though our dreams often crash and illusions will
shatter
Yet even a nightmare must end
And out of the blueness the thing that still matters
Is whether we both can be friends

Don't want gingivitis or dodgy infections
And I don't want to boil your cat
I don't want dejection, injections, rejections
But I do want to meet for a chat

By now you'll be booing and hissing
And shrieking, 'This poem's too much.'
But it's you (you great pudding) I'm missing
So please will you keep in touch?

Thus ends my plaintive epistle
Don't care if you read it out sober
Don't care if with ire you bristle
Just answer by fucking October

A SPANNER IN THE WORKS

Stephanie Dickinson

Funeral over, now reading the Will. Dad had two
children, me and Tim, a house, a car repair business
and some bonds. But ... two unknown names appear
next to ours. Trust Dad to put a spanner in the
works.

HEAVEN

Howard Bradshaw

I've never known anyone but you. You've always been the man for me. From the moment — what? — three years ago, when I saw you through the bars, I thought, 'Is this the one?' And then you took my face in your strong hands and blew up my nose, and, well, that was it. I've followed you ever since.

In the morning I know, I just know, that we're going for a walk together. OK, I don't like the harness much, but it's only till we get to the park and you take off the lead. I love the way you play with me, the way you swing back the ball-thrower and it goes high and ever so far and I run through the long grass, ignoring the other dog smells, and nose the ball out and bring it back in my mouth. Sometimes you pretend to throw it then don't, but that doesn't fool me, I know you will, eventually.

I'm really tired when we get back. So when you sit on the sofa, I lie with my head in your lap, and I'm so happy that you let me. I'm so happy I could lick my balls.

BEAUTIFUL PSYCHO

The judge passed sentence. Life. The hammer came down. She watched his expressionless face. How could this beautiful man have done the things they said? she would always love him. She blew him a tear-stained kiss, which he discreetly caught.

ONE-WORD STORY

Jess Glaisher

The stationery shop had stood at the corners of Neal Street and Velum Avenue for over a hundred years. Loyal patrons came each week for ink, for paper, to covet the marbled edges of the notebooks too fancy to write in, but too beautiful not to purchase, to display like hope on the shelf above your desk while you waited for inspiration to bring you the perfect story.

People moved around the shop like it was a church, all hushed voices and suppressed gasps: how beautiful, they breathed, and how magnificent, as they brushed their fingers carefully over the surface of the hand-printed papers, the leather-bound German notebooks, the chunky Japanese pencils with perfect pink erasers at the end.

It was a place for bumping into long forgotten acquaintances and bonding over pots of ink as you struggled to remember each other's names. A place for dreaming that one day you would pop in, on a random rainy Friday afternoon, and buy the pen or notebook or set of paints that would spark the idea that would make you famous. The one you would talk about in all the interviews as the Perfect Moment that turned your luck around.

Beside the pots of pens and pencils, the staff had set out pads of once-pristine cream-coloured paper, so soft it felt like freshly laundered cotton sheets under your hands. Each top page was now covered in a variety of inks and graphites, the eager markings of stationary-loving testers. Most had opted for squiggles, one or two for loops and swirls of colour. On one pad, someone had drawn a cartoon cat, chubby and smiling among the scribbles. On another, a person with beautiful handwriting had written 'Hello' to nobody and everyone, their ink, green, fresh and fragrant, ferns and forests wafting from the page. And on the pad next to the fountain pens, someone called Ainé had written their name in purple ink, a curling cursive script so distinctive that it stood out even on the 5pm, full day scribbled page. Above the name, that same fern-green script asked, 'Marry Me?', the question mark floating under the name like hope.

The pages beneath were covered in indentations from the too-hard press of the various writing implements. Tomorrow, though, or the next day, they should have been the top sheet, ready for their moment in the sunlight that streamed through the windows on fresh spring days.

Would have been except for the staff member who saw, as they tore off the ink-filled paper – a fresh start or the next morning – a mark on the next page down. They scrunched it, and the one beneath, and threw them in the bin. Without the context the mark meant nothing to them, just a waste of a sheet of paper. In purple ink, right in the centre of the page, the same hand that had written Ainé. A future contained in one small word:

Yes.

NOVITIATE

John Dixon

'He can be a bit difficult,' the supervisor said. 'He likes a walk to the shops, and a snack in one of the cafés. Point things out to him. Keeps his mind lively. It'll make a change for you too, from all the cooking and clearing up.'

I spent the first day getting the measure of the tasks required of me. The second day I felt the need to get out.

'Come on, Arnold. Wrap up.'

We walked slowly along the main road.

'Fancy a coffee? Will here do?'

There were empty tables on the forecourt. It was quite chilly, and inside was full. Perhaps, if, as was suggested, Arnold could at times be 'difficult', it might be best to sit outside and avoid other customers. I chose a corner table.

'How about a sandwich? Any preference for filling?' He didn't answer. I'd been told what he liked and disliked.

I kept an eye on him as I waited at the counter area. When I stepped outside with the tray he shouted, 'Here comes Percy.'

I shrugged and supposed he'd forgotten my name. Easily done. Should I prompt him? Say 'My name's John. I'm your carer.'

'Bang on time, Percy.'

And a pigeon flew down and landed on the next table.

'That's Percy. Percy the Pigeon. What have you got for him?'

I blinked and said, 'I bought *us* some sandwiches.'

'He'll like those.'

Arnold made a gesture as if throwing something down.

'Just teasing, Percy. Real thing in a minute. Hold your horses. Wait for me to finish. Oh, look, here comes another one. One of your friends, Percy?'

Arnold threw down a bit of his sandwich. 'They both like that. Lovely watching 'em fight, isn't it? Give 'em a bit of yours.'

I broke off a small piece of bread and threw it as far as possible. The two pigeons pecked at it, as if it were a football being dribbled forward. It lodged under Arnold's feet. He kicked it over to my feet.

And I kicked out at the pigeons. One flew to another table, the other to a chair opposite, where it did a poo.

Arnold nodded towards the poo. 'Clear it up.'

I sat back, surprised.

'Go on. That's your job. You clear mine up. And I do a lot more than that.'

Reluctantly, I leaned over and wiped the chair with a serviette. And as I did so, Arnold leaned over and threw my sandwich to the pigeons. I managed not to say anything or give my true feelings away.

A woman who had come to sit at a nearby table quickly got up. I think she gauged the situation. She didn't finish her cake.

Arnold called over politely, 'You're not wasting that bit of cake, are you?'

He pointed to me and said, 'My friend Percy here would like that.'

The woman smiled at us both, perhaps mistaking the cared-for for the carer.

MY MOTHER AND THE OPEN UNIVERSITY

Frances Gapper

Having gone to evening classes and to her astonishment got an A for English Literature, Mum enrolled with the Open University and began to work her way through illustrated booklets. She attended TV lectures at midnight or 5am. Watched men point at galaxies. Puzzled over poems about crickets and clocks, asked teenage poet me what I thought. Absorbed lives of the Great Philosophers (what they'd thought).

Attended a residential week at Durham University. 'Well! It was quite an eye-opener!' Bed-hopping, she whispered. Our phone kept ringing, but my mother said: 'Don't answer it.' She lifted the receiver but ended the call.

CONSOLATION

The tomato plants were ripped out, their roots dug up by paws eager to bury a bone.

Tucker looked up slavering, with big brown eyes and cocker tail wagging.

'Look what I've buried just for you,' he seemed to say. 'Aren't you proud of me?'

'You little bastard,' screamed Jason. 'Months I watered them.'

Delroy put his arms round his husband and whispered in his ear, 'I think I may be allergic to tomatoes ...'

THE SAMPLER

Peter Scott-Presland

Miss Emma was very reticent. She spoke rarely, and only to ask the single servant, Gladstone, if they might take tea in the withdrawing room.

While her four sisters had escaped into marriage with local worthies — the vicar, the squire's second son, the doctor, a retired colonel of dragoons — she was left to attend on her father. Papa had taken to his bed on hearing of the death of Prince Albert, and never went out of his room again. Emma washed him with blanket baths, turned him over to the hazard of her back, read the interminable works of various Poets Laureate to him, put liniment on his chest, lanced the boils on his neck, listened to his complaints. Rarely did she reply. No-one came to call, and they called on no-one.

The one pastime she had was sampler work. She sewed improving mottos such as 'Bless this House' and 'Virtue is its own Reward' in cross-stitch with thick tapestry needles. They proliferated over the twenty years of their joint interment.

When he died on August 16th, 1884 — paradoxically, the Feast Day of St Roch, the patron saint of invalids — Miss Emma stoically escorted him to the grave, then took to her own bed in turn and shortly expired.

When her chaste room was searched, it was discovered that she had been working on a tapestry all this time, now some thirty feet long. On it she had sewn:

AAAAAAAAAAAAAAARRRRRRRGGGGHHHH!

THE DATE

Kevin Crowe

When the waitress poured a small amount of wine in his glass, he swirled the liquid, placed it under his nose, took a sniff and then a taste. He put the glass down and said to the waitress: 'The wine's corked. It needs replacing.'

Ignoring the waitress as she took the bottle away, he turned to the woman sitting opposite and said: 'Just look at her! Dyed black hair, purple lips, a ring in her nose that makes her look like she's dripping snot and a face plastered with so much white slap it'd probably crack if she smiled. Shouldn't be allowed in a place like this.'

The woman said: 'I didn't know screw-top wine could be corked.' This brought a quick smile from the waitress who was at that moment depositing the replacement bottle on the table.

The man explained in great detail what being corked meant and what caused it. In such detail that she had finished her starter before he had even begun his. When the waitress asked if they were ready for the main course, he pointed to his starter and said: 'Does it look like it?' Then waving his hand at his still-full plate, said: 'Take it away. It's inedible anyway. I won't be paying for it.'

He smiled at his date. 'I've had better service at McDonald's — and more edible food.' He took a swig of his wine, then said: 'It was great meeting you again after all these years. Though how you can stand living in this godforsaken place, what with the rain and wind and midges, I don't know. A week is long enough for me.'

She began to answer, but she spoke no more than half a dozen words before he interrupted, changing the subject and talking about politics, music, literature, sport, work and himself. Mainly himself. Occasionally he asked her a question, but never allowed the time for her to answer.

She drank her share of the wine and ate, nodding or shaking her head as appropriate and rarely bothering with eye contact. At least not with him. He continued his criticism of the waitress, referring to her as looking like a zombie, saying: 'I feel like an extra in a Walking Dead film'.

His date's smile didn't reach her eyes.

After paying the bill, he leaned forward and, a leer on his face, asked: 'Do you fancy coming back to my hotel for a nightcap? Get to renew our acquaintance in more depth?'

She shook her head as she stood up. 'It's been an illuminating evening. Thanks, but no I won't be going for a nightcap. I have to see my daughter gets home safely now she's finished her shift.' The waitress had already put on her coat and the two women walked out of the restaurant together.

DISAPPOINTMENT

'Congratulations! It's a boy!' the doctor said to Dad.
　　'Not again ...' sighed Mum.

LITTLE WHITE DOG

Frances Gapper

Axel is only a little white dog racing around in the park. But in his imagination he's a Best of Breed winner at Crufts, going for Best in Show. Doing the obstacle course: leaping, crouching and swerving. I can hear the TV commentary and the claps. Talent scouts and judges stand in a ghostly horde under the bandstand.

'Stop it!' I hiss, but Axel takes no notice. Meanwhile other dogs are being obedience-trained, rewarded with praise — 'Good *girl*. Good *boy*' — and biscuits. Axel doesn't like biscuits, prefers to keep his figure trim. A so-called rescue dog, he taught himself house rules in five minutes.

Mortified, I go to sit on a bench. A passer-by compliments me: 'Lovely dog!'

'Thanks. He's not mine.' Competitive by nature, I always try to appear modest and self-effacing. Nobody likes a show-off. I've trained myself well. And now this.

FALLING IN LOVE WITH AN ASTRONAUT

Tania Gardner

Falling in love with an astronaut is hard
For they need a lot of space to be in the darkness
alone
And that you can condone.
But sometimes when you want to be there with them
They are far away
And find it hard to stay.
So letting them go is the best thing you can do
Even if it's painful.
It truly says I love you.

HAMPTON COURT

David Flybury

Yesterday we visited Hampton Court.

I think I have already been here twice. Once when I was very young, with Mum and Dad and my sister Cathy. Once before with my boyfriend Andrzej, when he and I walked romantically around the long lake with its distant views of the Wren facade.

I can remember the maze from my first visit, but this time we got quite lost through amazing fields of daffodils whilst trying to find the entrance, only to encounter a queue and an £8 fee to get in, so we didn't bother. History and storytelling have made it famous, but there are many other ways in life to get lost for less than eight quid, and most of them are preferable, and most of them I have tried. We returned to the daffodils, of which the Royal gardeners appear to have collected every single colour combination, size and trumpet iteration.

The palace and formal gardens are closed to the non-paying public (21 smackers per adult) so we looked at the rose garden (a bit dead without any roses in this season) and the restored kitchen garden (mostly bare earth awaiting the burgeoning of Spring). It was cold, and when the sunshine heated us for some moments in a sudden passing flood, it was still cold, because of the wind. This is the post-apocalyptic April we have now to come to expect.

A lot of people seemed happy to pay to enjoy the amenities of the palace and then to purchase its astoundingly silly souvenirs; these are the people, I assume, shelling out on cars, houses, and Amazon, sustaining the consumption-led recovery of post-2008

Britain; these are the people with kids, and kids to entertain, and Andrzej and I discussed later the incomprehensible absurdity of such a lifestyle. Where's the motivation? We drew a blank.

'enerytheeighth nicked Hampton Court off Cardinal Wolsey. Cardinal Wolsey was, like me, an Ipswich lad. He grew phenomenally wealthy in Henry's service, but his main job was as Henry's European diplomat, and when he failed to get Henry out of his first marriage Henry booted him out of Hampton Court and wasn't bothered what happened to him.

Wolsey remains the greatest historical figure Ipswich has produced, so far, though he has come perilously close to eclipse by Brian Eno (who wasn't born in Ipswich but lived nearby and went to school there – the same school as me, in fact, though we were never told) and Nick Kershaw (whose Mum taught me to sing, with no long-term effect, when I was about eight. I never met Nick Kershaw, though I'm pretty sure I did once sit opposite him, skinhead shorn of his 80s mop, on a tube train. We didn't speak.)

I was once a kid, and to entertain us my parents brought me and Cathy to Hampton Court. We went in the maze, for free, and into the formal gardens and the Oxbridge-like quadrangles of the palace itself. I don't know how much that cost. I vaguely remember the original Tudor building, typically brick, with gothic windows and a forest of barley-sugar twisted chimney stacks, as well as the ornate baroque galleries of Wren's perfectly balanced baroque extension – though I get confused with Wren's Greenwich Hospital which we also visited in those years.

On this occasion, yesterday, we did not go in, and I wondered if I ever would get to see the inside again, and I felt strangely sad at the thought that I would not. £21 seems such a lot to pay to be jostled and shouted around by a bunch of hyperactive children, preached at by a swarm of stupidly informative signage. But would I never pay to see that baroque interior and pace its gothic vaults? Rhetorical question. I looked at the looming edifice as the sun set upon it slow over the Thames, and felt as if my whole childhood were somehow and impossibly, forever and inaccessibly, trapped inside, twenty-one pounds distant, and a lifetime.

LAST WORDS

She's pulled the drips out of her own arms and dragged her cancer-ridden body into her old motheaten muskrat coat, and onto a bus. She wants to die at home.

She lies in the sagging bed she has shared with Fred for fifty-four years, though Fred is now sitting on a chair beside her, holding her hand. He leans into her and she whispers in his ear:

'You've been a terrible husband, but I forgive you.'

Thus ensuring he will never forgive himself.

TWICE A HALF-LIFE

Laurence Sullivan

Sleeping had become difficult for Keiko Ozeki over the years. She found herself getting up and down during the night, and so had taken to quietly preparing rice balls for the following day's lunch in the small hours of the morning. Her husband, Kaito, would feel the slow pull of the covers as his wife gently slipped out of bed, but he would always pretend to be asleep still. He knew it would break her heart to find out her subtle exits had secretly been disturbing him.

Tonight, though, none of that was an issue. Both Keiko and her husband were awake, the latter conversing on the phone whilst the television continued to hum away to itself in the background, providing details of the recent disaster to anyone within earshot. The screen was showing the area around the reactor in real-time — its corrupting contents continuing to spew out into the sea.

'Keiko-chan,' Kaito said softly, placing one hand over the receiver, 'will you turn that down for me, please?'

Keiko nodded and dutifully went to the television to lower the volume. After a few minutes more of conversation, Keiko spun around in her seat at the sound of her husband slamming the receiver down.

'They won't have us,' Kaito said, flatly.

Keiko's shoulders sank. 'They said no?'

'*They* didn't, the company did — the ones who run the plant.'

'They don't want us?'

'They think we're all senile!' Kaito threw his hands in the air. 'They think we don't know what we'd be signing ourselves up for.'

'But you were a nuclear technician.'

'That's what I said — I said that to them!' Kaito started thrusting his index finger wildly at the air in front of him. 'I told them I have a master's degree in nuclear chemistry, but they said that wouldn't make a difference to these people.'

'So what happens now?'

'They put us down on the list with the other seniors — there's apparently a few hundred of us. Better we liquidate the plant than the younger ones, we've so much less time to lose. They'll see that soon enough; they can't ignore our offer forever.'

'Well, that's good, makes me feel like we're doing something.' Keiko went quiet for a moment and turned her head towards the television, though it was clear from her face that her thoughts were elsewhere. 'Did you mention I used to be an auxiliary nurse?'

'Even my background didn't seem to interest them, dear. I didn't think it worth mentioning. I'm sorry.'

Keiko nodded softly to herself a few times but did not reply. For a moment her bottom lip seemed to tremble, but it soon stopped once she subtly tightened her hand and slowly released it again. Her gaze rose once more to watch the television, though the volume was far too low for her aged hearing to pick up any of it.

'We did that,' Keiko mumbled to herself.

Kaito turned to look at his wife, his brow furrowing. 'Sorry, dear?'

'Nuclear power, it was our idea.' Keiko sighed audibly. 'It was our generation that pushed it through, wasn't it? It just seemed such a good idea. Do you think it was mis-sold to us?'

'Misused, love.' Kaito ambled over unsteadily to join his wife, his hand reaching for support wherever he could find it. 'We didn't respect it enough.'

'I certainly do,' Keiko said softly, 'I know the damage it can cause.'

'Our cells divide slower; the radiation's effect will be lessened by that.' Kaito came down to rest next to Keiko before holding her hand gently in his own. 'Better us than the younger ones, with their whole lives ahead of them.'

'I know, I'm not afraid.' Keiko clutched her husband's hand tighter. 'My father was in Nagayo the day the second bomb dropped; he was one of the first to care for the people fleeing Nagasaki. If he was brave enough to help, we can too.'

'You never told me that.'

'It's not something he liked to talk about.' Keiko paused for a moment, her face etched with sadness as she turned to look out of the window. 'I suppose that reluctance has rubbed off on me a little.'

'I can only imagine ...'

'Unimaginable.' When she turned back to her husband, Keiko's smile had returned. 'Still, things have moved on, haven't they? They'll have things to protect us now, won't they?'

'They will, suits and such — they'll keep the radiation at bay whilst we help with the clean-up.'

'You've always reminded me of my father, from the moment we first met. Brave and knowledgeable, just like him.'

'I only wish we could have met.'

'He'd have loved you, I'm sure. Mother certainly did, didn't she?'

'Like mother, like daughter.'

Kaito leaned in towards his wife and kissed her lightly — she giggled a little as he did — feeling like the beaming young woman gazing back at her in their wedding photo on the wall. Her husband looked so different now, time had been unkind to him, weakening his skin in places until it was thinner than *washi* paper — stained blue and black with bruises that spread out like ink blots. She had fared better, though the peach-like softness of her skin was all but a distant memory. As she gazed into Kaito's eyes, though, she saw that they still shone as brightly as they ever had, like burning beacons keeping eternal vigil over their love.

'Whatever damage has been done when we get there, we'll face it together.'

The pair fell silent as they watched the images of destruction flicker before them, each imagining a seemingly infinite, invisible ocean of atoms ebbing and flowing throughout the air — threatening to contaminate anyone who came too close. Their hands still tightly entwined — love and warmth radiating between them — husband and wife wondered, if by their sacrifice, they might give another couple tomorrow a chance at the lifetime of happiness they had shared together today ...

Q. & A.

The girl's hand went up uncertainly.

'Mr. Hemingway, you said once that a writer had to write with his balls.'

Ernest nodded emphatically.

'Well, what I want to know is – how do you get them into the inkwell?'

Elsa Wallace was one of the founder members of the Gay Authors' Workshop, going back to the late 1970s. She was a committed disability activist and the life partner of the G.A.W. Secretary, Kathryn Bell. We include her work to acknowledge the great literary continuity embodied in G.A.W. This story appeared in a South African magazine of the 1960s.

HASTE TO THE WEDDING

Elsa Wallace

Blanche put down her tea cup. 'I've fixed on cream, Mum. Suits my colouring better than white. Cream with auburn hair is gorgeous, and then I can wear great-aunt's veil too. I want the dress sort of old-fashioned, with a suggestion of bustle I think, long sleeves, high collar.'

'I don't think wedding gowns have collars,' said Mummy, swallowing a butter cake.

'This one will, high creamy lace collar, Edwardian, lovely, show off my long neck. My hair's going to be in one of these Edwardian styles, a sort of roll all around, sort of heavy and shiny and gorgeous. I've started growing it now so it will be long enough by then. I think I'll have the bridesmaids in cream, too. Or palest green.'

'Whether it suits them or not,' said Mummy.

'If it doesn't suit them, they must slosh on lots of foundation cream,' snapped Blanche. 'I'm having Freda for chief bridesmaid. If she can't come of course I'll have to have Alison but Freda would be better, same height as myself and good figure. For the other bridesmaids I want Margaret and Celia, or just Margaret and someone from his side, but I'm not having any of these little shorties, she's got to be five feet seven or she's out, I won't be made to look like a damn fool giant. Melanie can be flower girl, she's the best behaved. I'm not having any little beast from his side for flower girl. Melanie will look too sweet in a replica of my dress. I'll get Mrs Clarke to do the sewing, haven't booked her yet of course, plenty of time.'

'Shouldn't the other girls have Edwardian dresses too? They'll look silly in modern frocks.'

'Well, I can fix that later. I expect there'll be a big fat row about the style. I know the material I want anyway; you'll love it when you see it, Deirdre is ordering it for me, thinks it's for an evening dress. I can get the stuff for taffeta underskirts and so on here. This heavy cream lace is too gorgeous. Mummy, you *are* going to wear lilac?'

'I'd thought of blue actually.'

'No! You can't have that. With the bridesmaids in green! Besides lilac is *your* colour, you know that. His mother can be in a deep pink or green or apricot.'

'Anything you say, darling, after all, it's *your* day. When's it to be, have you picked a day?'

'Well, if everything works out as it should, the formal engagement will be on your wedding anniversary and then we'll get married on your engagement anniversary.'

'What a *sweet* idea. Your father will be thrilled. What have you chosen in the way of flowers?'

'White clove carnations, plenty of scent about them. Nothing but white carnations. Except on the wedding table — there I'm having an exact copy of your wedding bouquet. Oh, you mean my bouquet? I'm not having flowers at all, I'll just carry some delicate trails of greenery — pale, pale green, in a tiny silver holder.'

'I don't much like the sound of that. Even a single flower would be better. And you *liked* Doreen's bouquet, you raved about it, don't you remember, I thought you'd choose something like that.'

'And have her telling the town how I copied her? Oh, I remember everything about her wedding, don't you worry. I'm making sure I'm not having her rotten photographer; she'd think I really meant what I said about her photos, she'd go around saying, 'Blanche was *so* impressed by *my* photos that she's getting Maurice to do hers, poor thing, I suppose she *hopes* somehow that she'll come out looking like something.' No, I'm having Silver Studios. And I'm having a proper dressing-table portrait, not like Phoebe's. There she was grinning into the mirror, the tabletop a mess of tissues and make-up, you could even read the brand names, and two drawers pulled out with stockings and rubbish hanging out. The swan-on-lake atmosphere lost completely. No, I'm going into your room for that photo. The dressing-table must be absolutely bare except for a tiny delicate flower-arrangement. Or a piece of china. Your shepherdess would be sweet. Or maybe I'll have a photo taken of me looking into the cheval glass.'

'Shame to be so nasty about Phoebe, she was a bit flustered that day.'

'Yes, and we all know why. I'm having a proper backcloth to the wedding table too, an *ironed* cloth with flower sprays pinned on it. Mostly you get a ghastly bit of wall with cracks in it, or even light fixtures showing. *I'm* not having that.'

'The reception's definitely at the Laguna? That means about two hundred guests?'

'Yes, we'll take half-half.'

'We know what that means,' grinned Mummy. 'Seventy for them, a hundred and thirty for us. Just as well. I've already got a hundred and nine on my list and I haven't even mentioned it to your father yet. A lot of his business people have to come, and his old cronies. Still, never mind that. Have you decided yet who you're having, darling? Plenty of time of course.'

'Who I'm *having*? Oh, I see what you mean! Wondered what on earth you were talking about. No, I haven't settled on anyone yet. I've crossed off Peter though.'

'So I gathered. What about Patrick? Now he's nice.'

'You mean you get on with his mother. No, I'm not having him, his surname doesn't go nicely with Blanche.'

'What about Dennis, then?'

'No, his eye colour isn't good, wishy-washy grey, you don't want grandchildren with eyes like fish, do you? No, Paul is better, Siamese cat-blue eyes. His surname is nice too, I've always fancied myself with a French surname. I'm going out with him again this week so I'll soon see if he's worth working on. What do you think of 'Blanche Dubois'? Do you like it?'

'Very romantic,' said Mummy, taking another cake.

DEDICATION

The Great Man hesitated, as his fountain pen hovered over the page. 'My Life in Words' — sixty years of writing about families, men and women. His publishers wanted a dedication.

No-one had ever known. He'd been discreet. Was it time now ... ?

He decided. It was time.

In a firm hand he wrote, 'To Brian Apsley 1898 - 1962, my life partner.'

A NEIGHBOURLY ARRANGEMENT

David Lindley-Pilley

'Oh, for fuck's sake!' said Janine.

'What?' said Terry.

'He's looking over the hedge again.'

Terry leaned forward and squinted as the sun rays came down in their droves. Sure enough, the white-brimmed hat of Mr Sully crested the rose bush which encircled his family's residence.

In this heat, Terry wanted to conserve his energy to open one of the cans of Stella that had been unceremoniously dumped on the floor following his wife's latest haul at Asda. He was already ten cans down and it was expected that he could make way for at least five more. Perhaps, in milder times, he would have gone down to the gate and given Mr Sully a piece of his mind. He didn't even trust swear words to come out of his mouth in anything more than a garbled mess – though his barometer for coherence was calibrated differently to others. Years of taking every non-prescribed tablet that his boys in Kent could fix for him, and fights when they didn't square up, would do that to you. For now, reclining in his manure-flecked deckchair seemed like the best option.

'Fuckin' cunts. Got nothing better to do with their lives than lodge complaints to the planning authority. All we wanna do is just build more of a home for ourselves.'

'Damn right, Tel,' said Janine.

She leant over to the BBQ conveniently placed within arm's reach of their festering summer encampment, plucking a slightly charred piece of bacon from the grill. It was already starting to attract the flies, but they'd both had far worse. She threw it to their two Dobermans to see which one would rise to the occasion first. The breed's allegiance to hunting was little in doubt as they both tore the strip of meat cleanly in half and wolfed their respective slices down with intimidating adroitness. The glints in their eyes showed they were far from satiated.

'When are the guys coming round to fit in them CCTV cameras?' said Janine. 'I saw one of 'em councillors walkin' their dog the other day. Think he's in on it with the Sullys. We got nothin' to hide, but I still wanna do someone in for lookin' where they shouldn't be.'

'Got another two days yet,' said Terry.

'Fuckin' cunts,' Janine retorted.

There was a circularity to the life of the Barnetts that offered no resolution, or indeed respite from swearing and disparaging comments to others. Round and round they went on their merry-go-round of bitterness, cracked on all sides through the passage of time and a cold shoulder from the local council.

Janine sighed in a way that only someone with a massive chip on their shoulder knows how to. Her last bout of employment ended with a showdown with her boss; she won points for the inventive use for a stapler during a team meeting, but came undone for woefully inappropriate workplace conduct. She'd taken the stapler back home with her as lugging the office computer would have been a struggle – even with her kleptomania. There were still remnants of her boss's blood on the stapler, serving as a worthy reminder to anyone of what she was capable of. Luckily her boss had decided not to press charges as he was a lackadaisical sort who ran for the hills whenever conflict started brewing. Janine was fired with immediate effect by the HR Director instead — the boss would say he was delegating, Janine would call it cowardice.

As the Barnetts and their Dobermans continued to languish in the heat, two shrieking voices could be heard, making their way slowly down pothole-ridden Potter's Lane. It was the Sully children — 10-year-old Clara on rollerblades and 7-year-old Mark following closely behind on a glistening new scooter. Their endless after-school activities and play dates with friends, honourably supported by their parents with all the car ferrying, would almost certainly lead to a car face-off between the Sullys and Barnetts. The steep and narrow country lane leading to both families' houses would be an exercise in reversing for even the most seasoned of drivers. The Sully's Audi was always fair game for the imposing Land Rover of the Barnetts. This alongside the Barnett's impressive arsenal of swear words didn't make much of a contest.

The Dobermans' heads swivelled away from the BBQ to Potter's Lane, ears prickling like radio antennae catching their first sound waves. They gracefully rose from the dirt of the Barnett's encampment, not even registering the hiss of yet another can of Stella opened by Terry.

As the Dobermans pelted down the hill, Janine turned to Terry and asked, 'Did you lock the gate?'

MARGINALIA

Jess Glaisher

She spotted the cookbook in the window of a second-hand bookshop, one rainy Sunday afternoon when spring had tucked itself back in bed and the winter cold bit at her nose. Her partner said she had too many cookery books, but she tended to think that second-hand ones didn't count. And besides, she'd been looking for this one since it went out of print.

She flicked through its pages for pure joy, noting pages she'd come back to: pictures of feasts she longed to cook for friends, dishes for her mum's birthday, delicious treats for herself on nights when her partner was away for work.

She could have just bought it, as she knew she would, without looking through. But Sunday afternoons were made for poring over pages of books in cosy little shops, and she was in no hurry.

Besides, if she hadn't flicked, she wouldn't have found the book's greatest treasure. In the bottom left corner of page one-fifty, was a small pencil note, the handwriting so like her grandmother's it made her breath catch, and the person behind the counter look up for a second from their paperback. Next to a recipe for a plum cake, it read:

August 19. Made w/boys w/glut of plums (7kg) found by accident in the garden. Loved it! Hot w/ice cream. Like a clafoutis but less eggy. Walnuts helped! Very wet even when cooked properly.

She had started near the back of the book and now searched greedily for more pencil notes, more information about the person who had made the cake, the boys, the accidental plums. But this was the only note. She was left to wonder what had become of them. Had this book only yielded that one recipe and, having copied it out, it had been donated? Had the person died and the book had been donated when their house was cleared, no-one noticing or caring about the walnuts, or how good it tasted, hot, with ice cream?

She wrote in her books too. The date she first tried something, or additional ingredients added on the first try despite the received wisdom that the first time you make a recipe, you should follow the instructions to the letter. She wondered who would care about her scribbling when she was gone, if the books she treasured now would someday be set upon with an eraser, dumped wholesale at a charity shop without a second glance, as if her careful archive had never existed.

She closed the book, her finger lingering on page one fifty just a moment longer, keeping her warm skin away from the pencil in case it should smudge. She took it up to the counter, handed over £5, and walked out of the shop, clutching the book to her chest, as the winter wind whipped up once again to bite at her nose.

A REPETITIVE HAIKU

'Can we start again?'
You say, so we start again.
Then *you* start again.

A HATCHET JOB

Peter Scott-Presland

Dan and Brian were an ideal gay couple, not only wedded but welded. Brian, 57, greying hair still thick and curly; Dan 28, blonde and straight — the hair, that is. They regularly worked out together in an industrially-named gym, so Brian retained the body of a thirty-year-old.

The gym was four doors from their shop, a delicatessen famous for its bespoke sausages — rabbit and rhubarb, sweetbreads and swede, anything alliterative. It was called 'Gang Bangers', a pretty retro shop all white tiles and mirrors. The shop uniform was a slim-fit muscle vest accentuating abs and biceps; on Brian it seemed like a come-on, but any customer who lingered hoping for a bit extra lingered in vain, risking a furious row with Dan.

Their one difference? Dan became a vegetarian at 15, a vegan at 18, and professed an allergy to blood. Once, early in their relationship, the sight of Brian eating a rare steak with pink juices flowing sent Dan rushing for the bathroom. A distinct disadvantage for a butcher. [He also experienced severe migraines, for which he took occasional beta blockers.]

They resolved the impasse by division of labour. Dan concentrated on Management — ordering, despatching etc. – and staying away from the shop. Brian employed two assistants as easy on the eye as the bangers were on the tongue.

The business suffered, like most, during lockdown, but Brian started home deliveries. When Dan contracted Covid, the shop survived.

One night, a man was walking his dog down an alley between the gym and the shop. The dog stopped to sniff a shapeless mound surrounded by what in the crepuscule looked like black treacle. He pulled the mutt away and phoned 999. Beside the headless body, police found a meat cleaver, and a gym bag.

It took time to identify the corpse, but a gym attendant, visibly queasy, recognised its chest hair. He'd also seen the man earlier in the shop, alone with Brian. He'd been at the gym, but wasn't a member, and he'd given a false address. He'd left the gym at 9. The time of death was 9.15 — 9.30.

So much the officer-in-charge, D.I. Hastings, told his sergeant as the two stood outside the door leading to the flat over Gang Bangers.

When tackled by Hastings and Sergeant Parker, Brian was quite frank. He'd had a fling with this Euan, as he was called, before he'd met Dan. Then by chance Euan had seen the shop and Brian. When Brian rejected him, Euan tried to blackmail him, threatening to tell Dan. Brian panicked, stuffed a fistful of notes from the till into Euan's gym bag. He pushed him out of the door, locked up, and went upstairs to watch the World Cup semi-final.

Meantime, Dan had been entrusting a parcel to a courier on the street. He'd come back by the side door and gone upstairs to lie down with a migraine.

'They have separate rooms,' observed Parker, who had questioned him — 'Don't shout!' pleaded Dan, lying in the dark.

Dan gave Brian a complete alibi. He swore the TV was on all evening, as the match went to extra time.

'If Brian went out, Dan must have heard him, the bedroom door creaks like a gothic horror. They never got round to fixing it — I checked it.' He paused. 'Of course, we've only got Dan's word for this.'

'The loyal husband?' asked Hastings. 'No, there's more. Brian's chum watched the match at home too. They sent each other messages in What'sApp when anything exciting happened. 7.45 to 10 p.m. As an alibi it's solid.'

'Dan using the phone instead?' Parker suggested.

'Accomplice? Not likely. Dan's no football fan, what would he say? In addition, he's got a severe migraine. We know he's on medication. No, the murderer has to be Brian. There's no-one else. Only he knew Euan. They were alone in the shop. It was Brian's meat cleaver. Poor Brian. A happy marriage, a successful business, suddenly threatened by a nasty Ex. I think the judge will let him off lightly.'

The judge was indeed lenient. Dan was sentenced to a mere five years.

'How'd you realise it was Dan, not Brian?' asked Parker in a café later.

'Do you read detective stories? As the Blessed Sherlock says to Dr Watson: 'When you have eliminated the impossible, whatever remains, *however improbable*, must be the truth.' We were so busy looking at Brian's alibi we didn't check Dan's.

'Consider this: 1. Dan's quick temper. 2. What he could see through the window from outside. The shop's full of mirrors. Whispering, money changing hands — what's he to make of it?'

'But he's a vegan,' objected Parker, 'He pukes at blood, it's a powerful phobia, he gets migraines.'

'I was coming to that. 3. In the dark alley, blood didn't look like blood. Anyway – 4. He'd had Covid, he couldn't smell anything.

'And finally,' Hastings said triumphantly, '5. Dan took beta blockers. They're also used in the treatment of phobias. They take effect in about an hour. Put it all together ...

'Dan comes through the side entrance while they're still arguing in the shop. He collects the cleaver from the cold storage before Brian locks up, and whizzes upstairs; he takes his beta blockers. Now he's ready. Later he goes out quietly — he could hear Brian's door, but Brian couldn't hear his, because of the TV.'

'But how did he know where to find Euan?' asked Parker.

'Where else would Euan go with a gym bag? Dan just had to watch the gym ... It's strange, isn't it, how in a relationship between an older and a younger man, so often it's the younger man who is insecure ...'

'I wonder what happened to the head ...' mused Hastings.

Meanwhile Gang Bangers displayed a limited special offer on a new line of sausages: Brawn and Broccoli.

GREETINGS

Kim looked up at the alien. From the monstrous jaws dripped sulphuric bile, while the razor claws lashed out indiscriminately.

Kim held up a hand brightly.

'Hi,' Kim said. 'My pronouns are They and Them ...'

THE FRIDGE MAGNET

Stephanie Dickinson

The fridge magnet covering that scratch on the fridge door. A souvenir from a daytrip to Brighton. A day of sun and sea. No sand but it didn't matter. Candy floss on the pier, fairground rides and tacky souvenirs. Walking on the bumpy pebbles, holding on to each other and laughing. Sharing ideas for the future.

The wedding of a lifetime. Expensive but worth it. Too expensive so the honeymoon in Brighton instead of a tropical island paradise compensated. Plans. Making plans. Sharing plans for the future.

Finally, a house, a front door of our own. Not shared. And a fridge door of our own to keep our fridge magnets safe. Our collection growing, expanding, detailing our lives together.

Our lives! Unravelling, disintegrating, splitting. The house sold. Our possessions squabbled over, debated — and finally divided.

Except for the fridge magnet.

Symbol of when we had hope.

No-one wanted that.

A CHICAGO HAIKU

What a nice surprise,
Mr. Capone! Didn't know
You played the violin ...

FIRST & ONLY

(A TRUE STORY)

Leigh V Twersky

The ptarmigan if you didn't know
Exchanges its summer feathers
For camouflage in Highland snow
All white in wintry weather.

A happy year was '89
I'd gone to Inverness
A ptarmigan I'd hoped to spy
The reason for my quest.

I'd had a row with my old friend
He said I was the barmy one
I countered he was round the bend
'A petty-minded ptarmigan.'

From that day on I was obsessed
With sighting this weird bird
And so began my mighty quest
That some would dub absurd.

Up the Cairngorms trekked I then
But ptarmigans spied I none
Not in the hills nor in the glens
Yet still I had much fun.

The owner of the B & B
(I stayed in Aviemore)
Found out what I had hoped to see
And said, 'A treat's in store.'

She led me down into a room
I deemed it best to please her
I didn't want to meet my doom.
She opened up her freezer ...

'I got it from the farmer's son
With duty-free French fags.'
She pointed to her ptarmigan
In plastic Tesco bags.

'We'll have that for our dinner
This year on Christmas Day.'
At least I got a glimmer
Before I went away.

FRAGMENT

'You have the most amazing eyes.'

'Me? Really?'

'Yes, really. What colour is that? Is it hazel? I thought so. If I look deep into them, I can see yellow and green.'

'Really?'

'You have the most beautiful eyelashes too. So long, so silky ... I could look into them all day.'

'You'd better not. There's a queue building up.'

'Sorry. Cod and chips, please. And a large gherkin.'

'Do you want the gherkin now or later?'

They both smiled.

THE CURTAIN TWITCHER

Richard Thompson

She's just been delivered. Asda? Tesco? No, it's —
Waitrose! She's gone up in the world.

A full crate this week. Personally, I think it's a waste.
Well, it's only her and the twin, when she decides to pop
in, and when she does, she's half-cut. Every week she
pushes that trolley, packed with empties, swaying from
left to right, step by step down from the first floor.

Tweedle Dum, her twin, lives directly above my head.
She's no ballerina, she's the original Nelly the Elephant.

Every Friday evening, six-thirty, Tweedle Dee, that's
what I call her, brings in the takeaway. Fish 'n' chips,
from the posh Fish House at Lauriston — the best for
miles.

It's a twenty-minute walk there and twenty back, but
Tweedle Dee's only got short lallies. It takes her an hour.
The Fish House has those quality white bags and
matching cardboard boxes. Not the cheap plastic carriers
and newsprint the Turks around the corner scrve up.

It could be worse. You could be wrapped in one of
yesterday's tabloids. Your chips could have an imprint of
Myra Hindley or Fred West's face glaring at you, and let's
face it, who wants to see those two Dolly Eeks just as
you're about to bite into a battered sausage.

It's busy in the neighbourhood this evening. It's been
busy all day. That's the tenth blue light I've seen fly past
and in so many hours. Four ambulances and six Old Bill.

It wasn't like this in the eighties. No, it was worse!

It's all 'hipster' round here now. Gentrification, I
think they call it. 'Vintage' them hipsters call it when they
sell their tat on Feistybook. I call it second hand.

I wouldn't put it past her upstairs to tell her sister to pop into the takeaway round the corner en route to the posh house. Their battered fish is battered alright - it was clubbed to death. But Tweedle Dum would tell her to buy a sav. and two wollies[1], then ponce a handful of posh bags for the 'catwalk' back 'ere through Market Street. By the time she gets back the fish will need mouth to mouth.

She must have one of those new-fangled air fryers dumpy Alison Hammond keeps banging on about.

I saw dear Joyce from across the road in Dinmont House bent over like a washerwoman, dragging one into the new year. Santa wasn't good to her at Christmas. Hold on a minute — Tweedle Dum can't have one. I would've seen it on its way in, boxed with a massive picture on the side with writing underneath it, 'Air Fryer'!

Tweedle Dee, must be four-foot-nothing. They're identicals, you know. Tweedle Dum and Tweedle Dee. Ruth and Linda, that's their real name.

They keep themselves to themselves. You might get a 'hello' from Ruth now and again. More again than now. Linda is a different story. She avoids eye contact and always looks like she's chewing a wasp.

It wasn't that long ago Linda carried her shopping home from Lidl on Well Street. She hid it in two Bags for Life from Marks & Spencer. Who's she trying to kid? I swear on our Queen Consort, dear Camilla's, life that the contents of those bags were one hundred per cent Lidl, value range. Cheap Garibaldis and own brand tea bags, makes me shudder just thinking about it.

She's been on benefits for years. I'm just saying. How do I know? Well, every now and then, when the

---

[1] South London slang for pickled gherkins

postman's nursing a hangover from the night before, his door numbers get a bit blurred. I got Linda's letters once. One was brown. It reeked of benefit.

She's booked an earlier Waitrose slot. She thinks she's clever, timed it so her neighbours just arrive home in time to trip over her veg box. In time for all to see that she's a Waitrose woman now, not an Iceland pound-a-packet-of-ten-fish-fingers girl.

It's all keeping up appearances if you ask me. Who gives a toss what they graze on? As if I haven't got anything better to do.

'Can you buzz me in please, I've got a Domino's Pizza delivery for No.6?'

I told him, for the umpteenth time, I wasn't the concierge, I've never been the concierge and never will be. It's been a thorn in my backside having to answer every buzz on that intercom when nine times out of ten it ain't for me. It could be Amazon, the man who reads the gas meter, a Prêt à Manger breakfast for her at No. 7, Domino's Pizza, or the postman who can't get in. I don't mind letting him in. Abdul's his name. He's what some would call 'easy on the eye'!

So they're having another takeaway at No.6. That's the fourth this week. I'm not one to keep a tally, but I'd be very careful if I was them. Truth be known, they've both been getting broader since Christmas. A bit stout. Period. They must be having a competition to see who can pop their reinforced seams first.

I wouldn't mind but, according to him at No. 5, who's got his nose in everyone's business, they've recently had a ten-grand kitchen fitted. By the look of their *Just Eat* traffic, it's still got the plastic wrapping on.

Tweedle Dum gets a food delivery from Waitrose now. I reckon she's already been onto Fortnum & Mason, pleaded for a delivery and offered to pay for petrol. If they said yes, which they wouldn't, might I add, I swear she'd drop her Waitrose Bags for Life like a brick!

(There's a second buzz on the intercom.)

Turkish — "Bay Harvey'ye balık ve cips teslimatı" (Fish and chips delivery for Mr Harvey.)

(Allegro) Flustered, Harvey hastily buzzes the caller in, opens his front door, snatches his regular fish and chips order from the local Turkish takeaway, then quietly shuts it before his neighbours see!

OIL AND WATER

Talim Arab

Sumudra hands Abba a brochure.

— *Sunnyville Acres.*

Sumudra buries her head in her palms. Her father puts an arm around her.

— Water and oil never combine except in our tears. Our body's phenomenon.

In Abba's eyes, Sumudra sees galaxies, stars, and herself on the cusp of heartbreak and a miracle.

POWER RECLAIMED

Thai O'Reilly

Red sky in the morning, shepherd take warning. Twenty-eight degrees. A warm summer's day, the air is light and fresh like a bakery. Sunlight trickles in through the window, illuminating the room. So silent and peaceful, Carrie is in the foetal position, curled up so tight, nothing can penetrate her.

Suddenly, the silence evaporates. Buzz buzz: Carrie's phone is shouting with each ring and vibrates with aggression. A minute or so passes. Her zombie-like body, sore, wriggles side to side, disgruntled, she grabs her mobile quickly, forcefully; in those few seconds Carrie contemplates throwing it at the wall: 'Wouldn't that be nice? An escape from this world.'

Carrie sighs with relief; her bed is empty. It's the only time she can truly relax. Buzz: a text from him. Her stomach knots at impending doom while on a 100mph rollercoaster. The text reads: 'Home late. Make sure dinner is ready ... B'.

Carrie's mind, temporarily frozen, flashes back to when his texts were friendly, flirty and loving: Oh how times have changed. Time to get ready for work, she thinks; something long-sleeved is best.

'The next train to arrive is the 8:05 to Liverpool Street'. The train is engulfed with bodies of all different shapes and sizes. We're flying through the city like we're riding a dragon, such power. For a moment, Carrie is lost, she ponders the idea of being able to fly wherever she wants. Carrie's eye lights up like the Fourth of July at the idea – the things she could do, the places she could see. 'Oh, the freedom,' she murmurs. Eyes burn into her churning brain. 'I beg your pardon!' exclaims a passenger, as if Carrie is mentally unwell. Carrie escapes the flying vehicle.

'Medical Research in Toxicology' reads a shiny sign on the tall metallic building; security dotted all around.

'Morning, Dr Carrie! How was your weekend?' asks her lab partner, Fiona.

'Er — ok,' responds Carrie, unconfidently. They discuss the weekend and their work lab results.

'Interesting stuff, and dangerous in the wrong hands,' says Carrie.

'And how's Brody?' Fiona asks inquisitively. 'Is he still treating you like shit?'

Carrie is silent, which Fiona knows all too well. Fiona discovered the bruising on her arm, which Carrie tried to hide with her sleeves.

'Right, that's it I'm calling the police.'

'No,' protests Carrie. 'I'm working on it, ok?'

'I'm worried about you, boss.' Fiona's eye roll so far back that her head begins to ache.

The sky is beaming, smirking even. Red sky at night, shepherd's delight. Carrie's eyes wonder, transfixed. She grins for the first time in what seems five years.

A few weeks later ...

'Dinner is served, honey, I made your favourite'.

Brody's face is heavy from his long day working. 'This tastes like shit ... you changed the meat?'

'No just a different recipe.'

Brody is hungry, so he wolfs it all. The silence between them is loud and tense. 'My shirts, have you ironed them?'

'No.' Carrie's response is swift.

'I beg your pardon?' Brody snaps back.

113

He grabs Carrie's face in both hands and yells, 'You're a weak, pathetic excuse for a woman,' his six-foot-four frame towering over her five-foot-six body. Carrie stares helplessly up at him. Shivering with fear. His eyes laser-locked with hers. 'Nothing to say ...?'

He leans in further, the musk of his sweat, alcohol and anger smothering her. No reply. 'Ha! Didn't think so'. His footsteps pound the ground as he marches towards the door. SLAM! The room fills with darkness as the light fades away. Carrie is isolated with her thoughts. Tears roll down uncontrollably. 'Please someone save me'.

Sometime after, there are muffled screams. Inaudible sounds echoing, until Carrie makes out, 'You bitch!' Carrie grins like a cheshire cat. 'What's happening!?' cries Brody in pain, blood splattering all over the snow-white carpet. 'Strychnine (Stry-Che-Nine), aka rat poison. It's a perk from work. It attacks your glycine receptors.'

She decides to rub his nose in it.

'In other words, those twitches will now become violent convulsions as your nervous system stops. Toxicologists will decide you've had a heart attack.' Brody's body uncontrollably arches upwards, arms stiff, fists clenched and head resting on the ground. Brody's life flashes by in a heartbeat. Dead.

Halfway across town, the sky is now dark, opaque, but clear enough for anyone to observe the stars lit like fire. 'I'll take the train,' declares Carrie, now confident, certain. Her vision of flying anywhere is now a reality.

SECOND THOUGHTS

Howard Bradshaw

What a bastard you are. Four wasted years. Taken advantage of at every turn. Exploited, humiliated, cheated on every time you turned your deep blue eyes on some leering Adonis on the opposite side of the bar.

Sure, you were good in bed, the best, but what's that to the pain of betrayal? You were faithless, untrustworthy, devious, parasitic — eventually I had to use the Thesaurus.

I never want to see you again, you can pack your bags, take your annoying Trip Hop CDs and your pathetic Richard and Judy Book Club recommendations. I want you out of this house as soon as you get this. And don't try to turn that Little Boy Lost Look on me again.

I'm going to save this under the title 'Cunt'. Just to remind me what a toerag you were. I'm going to print it and shove it under the door of your room — locked as usual these days. I want you to feel my rage in your hands. There!

What? Paper jam? Printer fault?

I'm so glad.

CHANGE

Craig Binch

Love is odd. Yesterday I looked at your picture and smiled. Today I looked at your picture and cried.

115

DON'T THINK ABOUT MARTIN AMIS

Frances Gapper

As you lie in the dentist's chair, try not to think about Martin Amis, his tobacco-stained and crooked teeth replaced by shining implants. Or Lucy Partington's mother asking him please not to write about his cousin, one of Fred West's victims. To whom Amis subsequently devoted a chapter of his well-received memoir. For while having his teeth pulled under anaesthetic, he'd often think of Lucy in the cellar.

Or Amis loftily telling Lucy's brother as they drove along: Your sister was just terribly unlucky. As if the poor guy didn't already know that.

Don't recall the time your own brother, driving you through New York, failed to respond to your comment, which he must subconsciously have laid claim to, because five minutes later he repeated it (You know, I've often thought ...) Don't seethe as you try to put the incident out of your mind. Forget all that stuff. Does it really matter in the scheme of things.

Don't think of your mum at her birthday meal in a vegetarian restaurant: Look at the lovely flowers James gave me! The ones you'd given her. But who cares who did, so long as they gave her pleasure. And at least you behaved marginally better than your sister, with her objections to everything on the menu.

Don't feel guilty for having written about your own family, imagining your brother dead and storifying your what-ifs, or using your tiny megaphone to broadcast

116

secrets and forbidden topics. Where else will you get material? Remember the wise saying: If people didn't want you to write about them, they should have behaved better. But don't laugh, you're in the dentist's chair.

Don't let your mind drift to Frances McDormand in Three Billboards, who had every reason to distrust her local practitioner (whereas you have none). Or imagine yourself seizing the drill, overpowering him and drilling a hole in his cheek. Or Laurence Olivier as a sadistic dentist in Marathon Man, a film you've never seen and don't want to.

As he turns to select an instrument, just say sorry, I'm feeling unwell. And tell reception of course you'll pay for the cancelled-at-short-notice appointment, and when does Mrs Kumar get back from holiday?

TWO SUICIDE STORIES

A FINAL HAIKU

Suicide note: When
You said, 'I wish you were dead,'
I thought you meant it.

CHOICES

Craig Binch

The pill bottle was empty. He made a choice and placed his fingers down his throat. Maybe there was another way.

AS I LAY TALKING TO MYSELF

Shaf Ullah

'Wake up!' I shouted at me.

The Sun is out and the dust fairies are dancing.

The gecko on the wall is laughing at the drool on your cheeks, TIK TIK TIK.

Pick up your soiled clothes from last night, they hide so many secrets, wash them.

Who were you with, why and how did you end up in his car at 3am? Drunk.

By the way aren't you meant to be in college today? You called in sick? For what?

Your thighs are bruised, nuances of purple or blue? The bottle of champagne empty by your bed?

An entire bottle of bubbles, hiding troubles?

Your pillow is smothered with makeup from last night — oooh, that foundation is too dark for you.

Did you wear red lipstick too?

Why is your kitchen tap singing? Tap tap tippity tap. Get it fixed.

Click clock ting ting ding dong, get up now. The bed smells of yesterday.

Wash the covers, it'll hide the marks from last night.

Is that my painting on the wall? Crimson roses, garish orange hues, purple irises, reminds me of my friend Iris.

She died last year; loss of her lover had completely devoured her.

Is the Sun baking me now, trickles of sweat beading on my forehead?

Should I use the blanket to dab my clammy face?

Why are my hands so rotten dark, nasty, smells of testicles?

Is that my wig on the floor? The burgundy, so luscious, it's calling me again.

Cmon get up, get ready and hit the road.

To be picked up tonight, yet again.

THIS ISN'T ME

David Lindley-Pilley

'Two minutes till curtain call!'

The stage manager's timorous voice barely cuts through my cocoon of anxiety.

As I make my way through the dressing room to the stage door, the cast give me the standard pat on the back and reassuring smile, most likely sympathy at the fact that I'm the first on.

One of the leads entertains with an anecdote about a misplaced codpiece on stage, but the punchline is irretrievably lost in my heightened state. I have nothing to come back with, apart from the lines that I've diligently rehearsed for this production.

I breathe in the musty smells of the wardrobe, a congealed mass of deodorant and perspiration clinging to the fabrics. Each piece promises the chance to be someone else entirely, to feel so energised, so completely in control.

I feel the stage manager's now frantic energy matching the pounding of blood in my head, my hands, my face.

I have one shot to set the tone, to be the threshold that my castmates can reach, or surpass. It's time.

My feet tread lightly on the planks encircling the stage.

The shaking of my muscles getting picked up by the floorboards, which started to vibrate in response. I have to be certain that I'm in control.

I'm given nothing more than a perfunctory 'good luck' from the stage manager. I don't know how to respond, I never do.

An awkwardness is shared between us, which I hope will not be part of any post-production debrief. To me, the only thing that matters is what happens on stage.

The lights dim and an expectant hush falls on the audience. One shot to set the tone, to get this right.

I step onto the boards and the words that come out of my mouth are fire, my movements fluid, my emotional core rooted.

This isn't me, but the audience doesn't care.

DEPARTURE LOUNGE

Craig Binch

He found himself in a waiting room. It was full of a strange mix of people, some in night clothes, some in nothing at all! Was he dreaming? He wandered through the crowd to a lady dressed in white sitting at a white desk in the white room. She slid her glasses to the end of her nose as she looked up, clearly inconvenienced by his presence.

'Welcome to the recently deceased departure lounge. Please confirm your name and religion.'

He stammered, 'What do you mean? this must be a joke'

'Do I look like I'm joking?'

'But I'm not dead, I was just out walking the dog!'

'And I suppose none of these other poor buggers are dead either?' She signalled to the crowd of sorry souls. 'And I'm the queen of Sheeba, take it a ticket and find a seat if you can.'

We've got quite a backlog. Gaza ... Ukraine ...

PILLS

I laid out the pills as usual. Different sizes, different colours from different dispensers. I'd never remember them otherwise.

Twenty-three of them.

There's a new one today. Green. To counter the side effects of Number Twenty-Two.

Dear God! Won't they ever find a cure?

LOVE

AND

ROMANCE

AMAZING

A LOVE STORY WRITTEN ON VALENTINE'S DAY

David Flybury

'When I think of how we met,' said Joe, 'I'm amazed it came to anything; and now, of course, like so many gay couples, I'm ashamed to admit we met in a sauna.'

Joe and Michel had met in one of the worst saunas Hamburg had to offer. Sex had involved the participation of five or six others; Joe recalled their hairy opulence, and the way Michel and he had to, without destroying the rhythm of the orgy, maintain a kind of specialness between the two of them — a link that spanned the limbs and writhing bodies, the mouths and other orifices and, of course, the flipping uncountable penises jabbing at everything.

Michel recalled, privately, a fear that Joe, the only one he fancied, might extricate himself and disappear whilst Michel had (so to speak) his hands full with another. Joe, conscious of the demands of so many groping hands, nevertheless felt Michel's attention penetrate (if you'll forgive me) the intertwining nest of men, until their joint frustration forced a cut to this Gordian knot when, somehow communicating, the two of them heaved out of the pile in which they were involved and left the steamy den — accompanied by sauna disco pounding its porn track all around.

Partially deaf, priapically combined, Joe and Michel left to find a mouldy carpeted nook in which to consummate themselves; a stairwell not designed, explicitly, for sex. Unwipeable.

Then, showered, re-dressed, and, full of bewilderment, they stepped into the dependable afternoon sunshine amazed that, having left this incubating shrine, this nest, they never would go back.

MONOGAMY

'I'll always love you, and only you,' said the earthworm to the other earthworm.

Down came the sharp edge of the spade.

'How do you feel about a ménage à trois?'

SHOELACE

Tania Gardner

SCENE 1

Bus Stop. Summer's Day. Swansea.

SARA (13, a shirt pixie cut, a 'they/them' badge) is sitting at the bus stop, school uniform, school bag. BILLY (14, trans boy) is standing a little further away. Pause, awkward.

SARA. Do you want a shoelace?

BILLY. A what?

Sara pulls out sweets.

SARA. A strawberry shoelace?

BILLY. No, I'm fine.

SARA. Oh ... ok.

BILLY. Actually, yeah, could I?

SARA. Yeah.

BILLY. Ta.

BILLY. You going straight home?

SARA. No, I'm going to visit my friend Ellie, she's just had a baby

BILLY. Banging.

SARA. It is, yeah it is ...

Pause.

BILLY. Are you still getting the same bus as me?

SARA. No, I'm getting a number 69.

Billy sniggers.

SARA. What funny?

BILLY. Nothing

SARA/BILLY. Why didn't you/what are you ...?

BILLY. You go?

SARA. Why didn't you come to my party?

BILLY. I wanted to, I did.

126

SARA. But you didn't.

BILLY. No.

SARA. Why?

BILLY. *[Pause]* Can I lie?

SARA. Just this once.

BILLY. Visiting my Gran.

SARA. That's a rubbish lie. You could have at least of thought of something interesting, like aliens came and kidnapped you but you were hungry so they took you to Ice Mania for ice cream but you tricked them and they all died 'cause they can't eat lactose –

BILLY. Well I can't eat ice cream, I get a rash ... on my arms.

SARA. You missed a smashing party, I was wearing 3-inch heels and fishnets. I'd have been taller than you.

BILLY. Don't be daft.

SARA. I would have.

BILLY. Do you know how small you are?

SARA. You're not about to make a midget joke, are you? You know I don't like it.

Billy comes over, giving back the strawberry laces.

SARA. The party wasn't that good in the end. Only eight people turned up and they were already pissed. My mam sent them away after half an hour, it was embarrassing. Really, why couldn't you make it?

BILLY. I ... don't know ... I didn't know if you'd want me there since, me changing,

SARA. What are you talking about, you are my best friend whatever gender you want to be, right?

BILLY. But I — ugh!

SARA. What?

BILLY. You look ... really ... umm, like every day at school you look really tidy.

SARA. What? Clean?

BILLY. No!

SARA. Scruffy then?

BILLY. No!! Pretty. You are pretty, stunning in fact.

SARA. You're being sweet, stop it.

BILLY. Well - I got a present for you.

SARA. Really?

BILLY. Yeah. I was going to give it to you on your birthday but I think today is better. Close your eyes.

Sara closes eyes, puts her arms out in front of her.

BILLY. Actually, can you put your arms behind you but keep your eyes closed?

SARA. OK.

BILLY. Ok... don't peek!

SARA. I'm not.

BILLY. Ok, just shut up!

SARA. Now you're telling me to shut up, you know I'm now a teenager so I can technically tell you off whenever you say anything like that, especially swearing cause my mam says 'the world is filthy enough already without my mouth adding to it', but I just give her the finger, not that I would give you the finger, I just mean ...

BILLY. Just ... *(A kiss, moves away.)* Happy Birthday.

SARA eyes open.

BILLY. Oh fuck, I'm sorry.

SARA. What for? For kissing me?

BILLY. No ... yes, no, I don't know.

SARA. I'm not complaining,

BILLY. No?

SARA. What do you take me for?

BILLY. I thought I'd done it wrong.

SARA. How can you kiss wrong?!

BILLY. Well the boys at school said I should try and get you to —(*Does a wanking motion with their hand*)

128

you know ... you know, jerk me off, but I told them to fuck off, sorry - swearing - then they started calling me a Fanny — shit no, I'm sorry, anyway I said no I'm not going to do that because I like her more than that, and if we're going out I want to take things slow, and then they all started chanting 'Fanny' and saying I was a girl which is just fucking ironic.

SARA. What did you just say?

BILLY. Oh shit, I said fucking again, didn't I?

SARA. I don't care, the other bit you said ...? About us going out?

BILLY. Is that what we're doing?

SARA. Are we?

BILLY. I don't know.

Pause

I hope my bus has air conditioning I am boiling.

SARA moves closer to BILLY who is looking out for the bus.

SARA. Billy ...

BILLY turns to face SARA; she gives them a kiss but misses and pokes her finger into their eye.

BILLY. Argh! What was that?

SARA. Fuck, shit sorry!

BILLY. What you playing at?!

SARA. I was trying to kiss you!

BILLY. You got me on the eye.

SARA. I know. Well, I've got bad hand-eye co-ordination, my mam says I've got that word I can never spell wrong with me – dyspraxia I think ...

BILLY. You mean dyslexia?

SARA. Think so ... Is your eye ok?

BILLY. Yes.

Pause, they stare at each other, a bus arrives.

SARA. That's my bus.

Sara gets her bags and goes to leave.
BILLY. Will I see you tomorrow after school?
SARA. Umm, Yeah ...
Sara exits and then comes back in.
SARA. Are we going out then?

REMEMBRANCE

I've always loved older men, but they didn't seem to like me. I wasn't particularly handsome, I had what they called an old face, and I didn't give them the sense of energy they seek in the young.

So I counted myself lucky when at the age of 26 I met Philip, a retired architect who commuted between Guildford and the island of Skyros. We had five brilliant years before his health started going. I nursed him through a long and painful illness, before he died, as he would have wanted, on the sun-soaked terrace of his villa. Then I began to realise how little I knew about Philip, his old life, his friends. All I had was the address of his sister. I told her about his death and invited her for the funeral.

By the time she arrived the authorities had insisted we buried him. There was no refrigerated morgue on the island, he would have been a health hazard. So I organised that, and the activity took the edge off the numbness I was feeling.

Her name was Violet. I settled her into the villa, and took her to the grave. There was no cemetery, so we buried him among the olive groves near Rupert Brooke. She looked at the stone — just name and dates — for a long time.

'You've spelt his name wrong,' she said.

THE FIRST TIME

Kevin Crowe

He had wanted this for so long and now it seemed it was about to happen.

A 4x4 vehicle complete with bull bars pulled up at the agreed lay-by near Ullapool, the passenger door opened and Peter got in, his shorts exposing his muscular thighs, a bulge already visible beneath the denim.

He looked at the driver. Surprisingly his internet profile had been honest — long curly brown hair, tall and slim and looking in his mid-thirties. His eyes rested on Peter's crotch, then, after a quick flick of his wet lips with his tongue, he smiled, saying 'I'm Andy' and stroked Peter's thigh before returning both hands to the wheel.

As the car headed north into the Highland County of Sutherland and past the iconic peak of Suilven, Andy began talking. 'Your profile said you're a virgin, right?'

Peter nodded, unable to speak because of the lump in his throat. Andy smiled. 'Good,' he said, 'That's just what's required.'

Peter cleared his throat. 'I'm — I'm nervous. D'you think it'll hurt the first time?'

Andy shrugged. 'It may do, but not for long — and then you'll be fine, I promise.'

'How far are we going?' Peter asked. He had never been this far north before, had never seen the hills, lochs and burns of Sutherland before. Normally he loved being among mountains, but he was so wound up he couldn't enjoy the scenery.

'Just north of Kylesku — and then all the way!'

Peter giggled at the pun.

'You find that funny?' Andy asked.

'Well, all the way — that's what I want.'

'And that's what you'll get.' He patted Peter's knee. 'Don't worry, it'll soon be over.'

'Oh,' Peter said, disappointment in his voice.

Andy laughed. 'As I said: it'll soon be over, and then – it'll just go on and on.'

Peter wasn't sure what he meant.

Andy's voice pulled him out of his reverie.

'I asked if you believed in God.'

Peter was puzzled: what did that have to do with anything? 'I'm not sure. We did religion at school, but apart from weddings and funerals, I've not been in a church for years. Why're you asking?' They were approaching Kylesku Bridge.

'There's no hope for me: I'm a sinner — I'm heading for Hell no matter what. I can't control my ... my urges. God knows, I've tried, but you — you have yet to sin, you have not yet committed the sin that is an abomination in the eyes of the Lord. Your body is pure. You can be saved for Jesus. I'm already condemned, but at least I can save you from yourself. Pray with me.'

As he recited the Lord's Prayer and Peter screamed 'No!', Andy pushed the accelerator to the floor, driving the car through the bridge's barriers into the cold waters of the loch below.

OUZO, WINE AND OLIVE OIL

Katerina Mimikou

I was begging you, begging you to stand up and play some music. That night, late in August in Athens. After all the begging, I convinced you. You played a song, the song that you taught me the first day we met. The tavern was full, people sitting everywhere, inside and outside. It was a very warm night. Everywhere smelled of ouzo, wine and olive oil. I stood up and came next to you, next to the stage, next to the microphone, but opposite you, so I could see you. You were feeling so shy. And when you started playing, I started dancing for you. Only for you. There was nothing else there for me. You, the song, and me, the belly dancer.

Hours later you drove me home. The image of your lips still comes to my mind so often. And that moment. The moment. It lasted centuries, everything moving slow, in fullness. Kiss. Everything is soft. The hug. Tight. My hands on your back, nails diving deeper and deeper in your skin. Hands, fingers, nails. The metal. We stopped. And then, we started again. You hold my back, you pull my hair. The hair on the back of my neck.

Tulle. Silk.

Your hug is a whole world.

Our kiss, a whole galaxy.

I kiss your neck. Your neck is water. And right then, when I did that, it was a one-way trip for me.

Soft. Black fabric, metal. Time stopped, sounds silenced, the car disappeared.

I fall inside your hug.

I see your shirt. I touch it.
Do you like it?
Very much.

Months later, I left Athens. Yesterday night, I dreamt of you.

I was in the tube, listening to that first song that you taught me. I was going to work. People. Strangers. Others. Noise. I closed my eyes and I saw you, right there, giving me your shirt. Your warmth. The night that you taught me that song. Tears run down my face, burning. Like a verse from that song when I was dancing for you. Like a thought in my head when I left you and I cried. Because I cried. I told you that I didn't want us to break up. I told you that it took me a really long time to move on. I told you that I wanted you in my life. I told you that it wasn't right. I told you that ... There were many things I didn't tell you.

You told me that you missed me.

I miss you too. Yesterday night, I dreamt of you.

GARDENING

The garden centre staff were all stud-muffins. Hank was served by Gabriel, lean, tanned, lantern-jawed, five-day stubble.

'I wanna get some phlox,' said Hank.

'Pardon me?' said Gabriel

'Phlox.'

'Was that with or without an 'l'?

'Could be either,' said Hank, eyes twinkling.

The two turned out to be hardy perennials.

A WALK IN CYPRUS

David Flybury

Finally we found a bench and sat down next to each other to admire the 'stupendous' view - a steep valley filled with pine and a sheer rock face climbing opposite. To our right the valley opened into a distant plain, sun-flooded and golden. I could see a small white town; it looked like a pile of salt. Brown paths crisscrossed the cradling earth. To our left it rose to a peak, tip caught in clouds. Birds of prey wheeled in the sky above and below us. The sounds of the forest echoed around. Flies and bees vibrated the air.

When a sharp ray of sunlight broke through and entered the trees behind our heads it landed on his bare hands as they rested on his legs, naked where his shorts had ridden up. I was distracted by the sight of his pale tanned skin, the backs of his hands and the small nails on each finger. I became aware of his neatly folded cuticles, the pale half-moon shapes at the base of each nail, the smooth surfaces of barely-reflective pink which led to the perfect white crescents at each tip. They weren't moving; they were frozen, as though aware. Like a bird stands frozen.

The sunlight faded.

'Wonderful view, isn't it?' – I was surprised to hear him speak, his voice caught in the whistling breeze of pines. Lost in dreams, I glanced at his face. He was looking at the mountains. His bronze profile ate into the blue solid sky like a hero.

'Majestic,' I said.

He laughed. 'Wow, see that eagle!' he pointed to the birds floating in front of us.

'Is it an eagle?' I said, hardly caring enough to drag my eyes away from him.

'What is it then? With that wingspan ... it's 'absolutely' 'majestic',' he said, reusing my words.

My arms seemed almost to be moving without my will: I hooked them over the back of the bench willing him to fold himself into me. He jumped up.

'C'mon. Mist's coming in,' he said, facing me. I pulled my eyes away.

'Lead the way,' I said, relishing the opportunity to stare at his back, his pretty rotating behind pulling at the fabric of his shorts, his brown calves.

As we walked further, I felt an overwhelming urge to kiss him, to put my arm round his waist and crush myself into him – stiff in my pants, deliciously uncomfortable to walk – when off to our left, in the valley, a partridge took off with the noise of a running horse, thundering, and then gliding back into the undergrowth. We were distracted.

'I know what you're thinking,' he said.

'What am I thinking?'

'You're thinking what you're always thinking.'

'Well, what's the point of a boyfriend who's not thinking about sex? What were you thinking about?'

'I was thinking about house prices.'

'That's the opposite of sex. The mathematical inverse of sex.'

'I know it is,' he said, 'but they are skyrocketing, and I think you know how that feels.'

We lay, later, in the bright bright sun.

'Shut your eyes,' he said. 'Shut them. Stop looking at me, just this once.'

I did as he said, and we lay, staring at the inside of our eyes, an infinite expanse of clouds flickering glowing

136

red, for what seemed like an infinity of time during which I pictured his face, like a memory.

After a while he said, 'You know, you cannot photograph the inside of your eyelids.'

KNOWING

'Sapphic love? Fiddlesticks, Mr Labouchère!' said Queen Victoria. 'No woman would know of such things. Delete it from the Bill.'

The portly bearded gentleman, about to protest, thought better of it. He bowed and exited, backwards.

She had never liked him. Republican. Atheist.

But when he left, she smiled to herself. When he had mentioned Sapphic love, she knew *exactly* what he was talking of.

MISS CUED

Allison Fradkin

The first time we kiss, we are wearing playbill-patterned pyjamas, blaring the soundtrack to *Starlight Express*, and swearing off guys, all of whom we've never cast an eyeball at in the first place.

We've been too busy making eyes at each other: root beer float-brown gazing at gumball-green. Except now we're looking at each other just enough but not too much, like actresses cheating out to deliver dialogue. Only we've both gone up on our lines. Or maybe we just haven't learned them yet.

Eventually, we pick up our LGBT-cues and the distance between us starts to dwindle, until your sugared grapefruit scent and piggybank-pink pucker are kissably close — closer than a checker on a square.

I just can't wait to be kinged. So I don't. I lean in and latch on. When it comes to kissing you, there's no business like slow business. Everything about it is appealing: the overture that relevés into the opening number, with its thoroughly modern melody; the up-tempo standard that grapevines into the introspective piece, rendered with restrained longing. And when the power ballad pivots into the emotional climax, with its harmonically-held high notes, one singularly sensational kick line starts inside my heart.

From the stereo, the cast launches into 'A Lotta Locomotion,' and even though it's not *the* locomotion, we are definitely doing a brand-new dance now: experiencing something wonderful, loverly, and truly scrumptious.

Afterward, we huddle in a cuddle of ingénue giggles, stage whispers, and bass clef-style smiles. We share the lyrical sentiments that inspired our introductory intimacy: *I'm the bravest individual I have ever met,* Sweet Charity contributed; *I'd be surprisingly good for you*, evoked Evita; *I think I'm gonna like it here*, Annie averred.

'We're gay and thespian,' you remind me, threading your fuchsia-frosted fingers through my theatre-curtain-coloured ones. 'So what she really warbled was: I think I'm gonna like it queer.' I try to reply, but the inter-mission between our first kiss and our second kiss has ended on a high note. The skate-shod *Starlight* singers may be on a roll, but this lip-locked lesbian is in a role: your leading lady.

REPLY TO LEIGH V TWERSKY

Peter Scott-Presland

The ptarmigan is ptruly ptasty
I just can't ptake enough;
Though delipterious to your pteeth
And pterribly pterribly ptough.

139

THE MARK OF A LOVER

David Lindley-Pilley

For the past hour, the ticking of the clock hands had punctuated every second of Elizabeth's insomnia. There were seven hours to go until the alarm emitted its piercing call to arms.

She turned to the right-hand side of the bed in the hope that a new position might be exactly what she needed. She stopped suddenly. The slight depression in the mattress left by Mark's supine figure just served to remind her of why she was truly awake.

It was only yesterday that she had said farewell to Mark at the train station.

Memories of their previous night came flooding back to her, replacing the inexorable ticking of the alarm clock; both jockeying for the highest place in her anxiety, like two Ritalin-charged children on a seesaw.

As soon as Mark had walked through the door that night, he embraced her tenderly. His stubble grazed her cheek, triggering ripples of pleasure through her body.

They locked lips, tongues darted back and forth with the reckless abandon of young love. Hands traced every contour on their respective bodies, wishing to leave their mark in a world where even the kindest of people can feel short-changed by love.

There was something in Mark's eyes that night as their lips parted; a moment of realisation for both him and her. And then it was gone; only to be replaced by the same ardour as when he came through the door.

Clothes hit the floor one by one, leaving morsels of gossip that the neighbours in their sedate enclave in Iver would no doubt hoover up.

They lay down in bed together, searching, feeling, and savouring. That night, the ticking of the alarm clock was subsumed by their ecstasy.

Elizabeth traced her fingers along the imprint that Mark had left. With her heart hammering with such ferocity, she had no choice but to climb out of bed. She needed to gather her thoughts once more, and she had a feeling that she'd be more successful doing that than reaching for the evasive veil of sleep.

Elizabeth walked down the stairs to find the folder, with all the documentation she needed, precariously balanced on the baby's crib they had bought together.

She braced herself for the wave of anger that was going to hit her as soon as she opened it: the abusive messages, the discrimination, the letter terminating Mark's employment at one of the highest profile Magic Circle law firms in the city. Elizabeth was resolute in saying that Mark never deserved any of that – no one did. He'd been diagnosed with young-onset Parkinson's a couple of months prior. Soon after that, the assignments kept drying up, whilst the mountain of abuse increased.

As reports came in yesterday of the delayed 6:20 train from Iver to London Paddington, Elizabeth was standing by the kitchen window, tears in the cold winter crystalising the grief she felt.

She had to move on. She closed the folder, fingers tracing the biro indentations as she waited to leave for the 06:20 train from Iver to London Paddington.

GOING WEST

Howard Bradshaw

The Kid was a lean, mean hunk of a man, six feet three in his stockinged feet. Not that anyone had ever seen him in his stockinged feet, he slept with his boots on. His eyes narrowed as he watched Mae sashay across the bar towards him. Hers was a generous figure, and she was used to giving herself for a generous figure too.

As she crossed the bar, the men parted in front of her like the Red Sea. Her body seemed to be on springs, all operating independently. She rolled her eyes, and other parts of her anatomy.

'Hello there, big boy,' she purred. 'Is that a gun in your pocket, or are you pleased to see me?'

A shot rang out. She clutched her pearls, a surprised look in her eyes, as she slid to the ground.

'Does that answer your question?' asked the Kid, re-holstering his Colt and turning back to Daisy. Not for nothing was he called a cow-poke.

THRICE

Jess Glaisher

It took three meet-cutes for me to notice her.

The first time, the darkness of the only lesbian bar left in town was my excuse. The noise of the speakers thumped in my ribs, her voice invisible. I could see her lips, though, smiling a half smile. She caught me, eyes flicking upwards as if she knew I was watching her. At least my jaw hadn't dropped. I think. She came over, told me she liked my shirt, biting the straw in her drink. I thought she was just being nice.

Walking back to my table in the corner, I realised: 'Fuck!'. But of course, I couldn't find her amongst the sea of denim and leather.

The second time, was a concert raising money for that same lesbian bar, now under threat of closure. Everyone was there, which in my small town meant she had to be too. I couldn't see her on my first pass of the dance floor. I'd probably got it wrong: she wasn't queer, I'd made her up. She was just a tourist.

But there she was, by the raffle table, counting out rattling change from a butter-yellow wallet. I walked over, heart pounding, reaching into my pocket for a couple of pound coins.

'Two strips.'

She turned, not surprised, eyes meeting mine. Raised an eyebrow, holding that eye contact just a second longer than necessary. I took my raffle tickets, turned, cheeks hot, and walked back to my friends.

She won a free haircut in the raffle; I won the booby prize: a plaster cast of the bar-owner's breast. She clapped as I went up to collect it. That night, I didn't buy her a drink.

The third time, I opened the door to the barber's, my hair an unruly nest after three months without a cut. She was in the chair, laughing as the clippers tickled her neck. I reached around the back of my head, embarrassed at the fluff, considered leaving.

She lifted her head to compare the image in the large mirror with the small hand-held behind her. She caught me staring, asked the barber for a pen and held out her hand to me.

On my sweaty palm she wrote her number and sauntered out of the door with a backwards look over her shoulder. Above the number she'd written 'Cam – third time's the charm'.

Those were the first three times I met my wife.

MEMORIES

It was Alan's smile that most attracted him — radiant, white, even teeth — he never tired of it.

Now, fifty years later, he still adored it. As he looked at it nestling in the Steradent in the glass by their bed.

144

Ian was a long-standing member of G.A.W. who died earlier this year. Despite illness he kept writing almost to the end. Our condolences to his partner, Sidney.

SEA-SIDE DREAM

Ian Everton

I was walking on the beach,
Saw him, he didn't see me.
We thought we were alone.
The shortest trunks in the hottest sun.

I kept away in privacy.
The sand, a sea for one,
And wandered by a rock
Where I would lie

Not naked, I was not alone.
Closed my eyes. His face was clear,
Body smooth and lean
As he walked the other way.

And I knew – like an animal does —
Someone was there.
Opened my eyes and looked up.
It was only him looking down at me.

We hardly talked at all.
He sat by me and then lay,
Both looking into the sea,
Hands clasped behind our heads.

Energy came between us
Of all coincidences;
He said no one would come
As far apart as we had been.

I felt him stroke my hair
And instantly smiled;
Stroked his, turned to him
As his arm came round me.

Eyes met, lips met.
The longest kiss as time
Was our friend,
Embraced in our nakedness.

The afternoon was evening
Before it grew cold.
We ran bare into the sea
Washing off passion fluids

And again when we returned
To where our trunks were placed
We clung to one another
Like time had never been.

Again we made love
With the tenderness of finality.
How lucky I was,
And an evening breeze came across the sand.

The tide was coming in.

He had to go right, I left.
We shivered as we passed.

Light enough to get back home.

These micro-flashes by Craig Binch are inter-related into a greater story. Some people can write a whole novella from a series of 20-word micros.

REVELATION

He picked up the phone. 'We've been having an affair for the last six months, I thought you should know.'

CURSE

Strand of her hair, a rose thorn, a curse on parchment; he spat, screwed up the lid and dropped it in her bag, 'Bitch!'

THE EARL'S WAISTCOAT

Elsa Wallace

The Earl of Hell's waistcoat wasn't to hand one morning. His modest apartments were searched, to no avail.

'But it was right here. You saw me put it with your other things last night,' said his valet.

The earl nodded but he had noticed no such thing, the disposing of his garments being of no interest to him.

As a democrat, he hadn't desired a valet in the first place. This aide or lieutenant had gradually adapted himself, unasked, to the role. When the earl had cast off his wings and robes and kicked the halo into the river for a young otter to play with, he had opted for a simple tunic and boots, and this valet-to-be had emulated him and so bound himself closer. The earl was well aware of his own vanity and when the three-piece suit arrived, though it came from inventive and despised humankind, he found it so flattering to his neat figure that with minor alterations in cut he had worn one ever since, a new outfit each year, elegant black of course, hence the saying 'Black as the Earl of Hell's waistcoat.'

Helping him on with his coat (unnecessarily) as usual the valet murmured that another waistcoat would be ready and waiting for him in the morning if this one were not found.

Again the earl nodded and departed to his study where he could be alone for the day. He was fully cognisant of the erotic implications in the valet's assiduous care of him, after all they had been present for millennia. No sex this side of the divide, my cloven foot, he thought.

Not that it affected him. A workaholic, he applied himself to the monumental task of his memoirs. A third of the angelic host had defected to him. A lot of history there. He had his diaries of course but wished he had kept more detailed notes. He must get as much done as he could in this breathing space while hell was closed — there being hell on earth at present, there was no point in being open.

His pen moved methodically for long hours. As stygian darkness fell, he repaired to his bedchamber where the valet awaited him, garment in hand.

'Not too Liberace for you, I hope,' he said. 'It's a temporary measure.'

It was black but with a thin silver stripe and silver buttons.

'It will suffice, thank you,' said the earl.

The valet smiled and bowed himself out. His quarters were adjacent. Before he put on his own night attire he snuggled himself into the purloined waistcoat, soft against his bare skin. He caressed its satin panels and jet buttons. Losing himself into a happy sleep he mused: 'Nearer my Lord to thee.'

REALITY CHECK

Mutton wishes to sell lamb's clothing, after buying a mirror.

DRAGON MONOLOGUE

Tania Gardner

Ugh ... This is the first time I have sat down all day. You know, free advice from a doctor, and unless you start going private all advice from a doctor should be free.

I tell you – tequila and wine, is not a good combination especially if you want to be functioning the next day, without a roaring headache and tummy rumblings ... I was absolutely twatted.

See it wasn't even meant to be a heavy night, considering it's the first I've had off for months and will be till well into the New Year. I never go out, a 12-hour shift and overtime will guarantee every spare hour is spent sleeping.

Though this was different, my Mentor/Registrar Mike - the big boss with his scruffy uniform, dark beard, and large personality, offered to take me for a drink, ahead of my London placement interview.

So even if I was tired after a string of night shifts & just having witnessed a woman discharging from both ends what can only be described in the best way as a strawberry chocolate coloured bath bomb from Lush called 'Strawberry Chocolate Fountain of Dreams' – with essential oils – I will go for that drink, I don't care how tired I am.

It was all going well until Mike started bluntly prepping me for the contrast that London will be to Swansea.

MIKE: London's a shithole ...

He blurted it out as he gulped back more wine.

I didn't think it was, so I said so, but he just looked at me like I'd farted.

MIKE. Have you ever been to London?

AMY. Yeah, of course I have … (aside: I've been once, when I was a kid) *I've been loads of times, me.*

I can tell he doesn't believe me, but he takes a deep breath and then comes; the speech:

MIKE. You need to be more assertive Amy. If you need a crash team, get one. Shout. Shout the roof off. Don't always rely on getting a Registrar or Consultant, trust your gut. Try using that sassy Welsh attitude to get what you want; there's a reason the Welsh flag is a red dragon, it says it all 'feisty as fuck'. Show me more of that dragon. And don't drink the water, it's shit, tastes like piss.

About now is when half a dozen surgeons enter after a gruelling shift and Mike gruffly hails them over. After the now two, no, three, glasses of wine that I have already drunk due to nerves, my nerves peak when the flipping gorgeous surgeon Trish I have been smiling at for weeks – comes into the pub! And she buys a round of tequila shots – for the whole table!

She touches my arm as she asks me:

TRISH. You want one, love?

I don't know what to say. I just stare at her keeping hold of her hand as I realise she is looking at me funny as I haven't said anything in at least 30 seconds … *(breathe)*

AMY. Yeah. Go on then.

TRISH. Amy, isn't it?

AMY. (surprised) (Aside: she knows my name!) *Yeah, it is!*

And I see a smile form across her face as she says

TRISH. It's so nice to meet you properly.

I can't stop smiling as I try to answer.

AMY. (high pitched) Yeah. (aside: lower your voice, low, low) *(still high pitched) Likewise.* (aside: fuck) *Trish, isn't it?*

And she nods her head, handing me a shot of tequila as our hands brush past each other I feel an electric pulse go through me.

Oh she has glowing skin and the way she moves her glasses is so cute. She has not quite straight teeth but she has a confident air about her and the way her eyes light up when she talks about her patient's bowel movement make my knees buckle.

Three shots later and I'm dancing with everyone on the dance floor when the music slows down and Trish takes my hand and asks would I like to dance, you know just me and her together and just as I'm about to say 'yes', I nod my head and suddenly PUKE all over her shoes.

Thus ending my night off.

RELIEF

When I came out to my father, he had two responses. First, 'Don't tell your mother'. I'm sure if I'd told her, she would have said 'Don't tell your father.' Either way, the secret remained a secret, and it was back to square one.

Second, he warned me of the dire consequences. 'None of your aunts will kiss you,' he said.

I pondered this later. What an incentive! I was surprised that my entire generation of cousins hadn't turned out Queer.

ONE LAST SONG

Craig Binch

He'd put on a smart shirt, found tucked at the back of the wardrobe, a squirt of Paco Robane and headed into the city. The lights, music, and whiff of MDMA greeted him before he arrived on rainbow road.

Somehow the queens were younger and the fashion changed. Everyone wore trainers, everything was casual or extreme, he was conscious that he stuck out like a sore thumb. An iridescent rainbow jacket, a tiara worn as a choker, another one in a skirt, probably one of those metrosexuals. And quite a few bears thank goodness.

Some of it hadn't change so much as he made his way through a team of hen party goers dressed all in white, heels in their hand and flip flops dug out of bags singing or screeching some Beyoncé number. Had it really been so long, it took him a moment to get his bearings.

He found the old door down a side road, manned by a drag queen who was sucking hard on a menthol cigarette. Ill-fitting dress and wig that had seen better days, she clocked him and smiled a lipstick's smile, welcome to paradise that'll be £10 but you get a free drink, have a good night daddy she winked.

He made his way down the stairs into the belly of the beast, the music thumping getting louder with each step. It was packed and everything and Anything goes.

At the bar he ordered a whisky chaser, took the paper from the DJ booth, and wrote 'When you tell me that you love me and looked around at the patrons, Greg would love all this, the camp the glitter.

He waited for his turn among the swaying crowd lightly sozzled and enchanted by the sparkling drag

153

queen and the latest karaoke victim. He'd sang well, which made Peter more nervous. He took a deep breath and ordered other drink,' Greg, I hope you're bloody enjoying this torment, but a promise is a promise.'

The music slowed; applause. and then over the crowd's hum he heard his name. The onlookers parted as he gingerly made his way to the stage, all sweat at the base of his spine; 'Fuck it,' he thought. 'This is for you!'

He could almost see him leaving on the bar, a cheeky smile as if to say 'I dare you!' The crowd took a disinterested look and when back to their vodka red bull. The drag queen compare flashed her painted smile, adjusted her bra and held out a manicured hand with a giant sparkly gem! He took it and stood nervously next to the Amazonian host, what the fuck was he doing?

'So who have we got here, hope you didn't pass a red light on your mobility scooter!' The Audience laughed and he flushed smiling awkwardly. 'Well try not to put your hip out, we don't have insurance!'. The spotlight shone and the words lit up on the stage screen, inviting.

He sang, not well but he sang from the heart, for all the good times, the love, and the laughter. He sang to him standing next to the bar, likely with tears in his eyes.

He sang for the twenty years of companionship, always being by his side, he sang with his whole heart.

The song went down better than expected, the crowd silenced and swayed, joining in with the chorus.

The drag queen host half surprised began a rapturous round of applause, which rang out for a lifetime.

He took a modest bow, smiled and exited stage-left, heading out into the night.

WAITING

Howard Bradshaw

The news on the radio was dreadful. A multiple pile-up on the M5, caused by a lorry and an oil spill. Thank goodness Suzie and her girlfriend had decided to come by train, instead of on that machine. It looked terribly dangerous. She was glad it was off the road. She looked at her watch, they shouldn't be long.

Suzie went to collect her motorbike from the garage. She admired its new, and newly oiled, drive chain. She rang Molly on her mobile. 'Get your leathers on, doll,' she said. This command was part-joke, part-turn-on. She looked great in leathers, and she knew it. Molly looked great too. She checked the time on her phone. They should beat the Bristol train by an hour with any luck. Her mother would be surprised.

She switched off the radio. It was all too depressing. Disturbing and depressing. She looked forward to Molly and Suzie cheering her up, they always did.

She felt under the tea cosy. The tea was getting cold. She started to feel concerned.

TRIGGER WARNING

Tracy opened the book. Inside the cover, the words: 'This book contains words, images and discriminatory language which you may find distressing.'

She turned to the front page and started to read: 'In the beginning was the Word ...'

MOVING ON

John Dixon

His passing
split the double-bed in two.
I didn't feel to sleep his side.

For a time
I was tempted
by irksome thoughts:
things I conned myself
he'd never let me do.
Free. Defiant. New.
And all untrue.
No-one was ever invited back.

Should I have rented out the upper floors?
The thought of others living here
while I still was …
… was more than I could stomach.
Up went the For Sale notice.

Tonight's the Farewell Party.
Buffet in the kitchen.
Barbecue in the garden.
That was how we'd entertained
when we first moved in,
a gesture to calm the neighbours' fears
and let work colleagues see
how civil partners really lived.
We made lots of friends,

perhaps too many,
one half didn't get on with the other.
We had to invite them round in separate groups.
They all turned up for his funeral.

And here they are once more,
some with new-found partners.
I watch them spill into the garden
and take the evening air.
One's just claimed he's seen a bat flit past.

Would I want a Warming Party
in my newly-purchased flat?
Does one celebrate a downsize?

UP CLOSE AND PERSONAL

Rod Cross had been a heartthrob a long time, playing strong men of action in tough situations. I'd watched him romancing the likes of Angelina Jolie, and thought 'What a waste!' Though I'd never met him, I disliked him intensely.

When I went to interview him, I was surprised how short he was.

And I was sure his secretary was more than a secretary.

But I still disliked him.

THE RIGHT TIME

Hastie Salih

Jenny glanced at Charlie, sitting next to her on the plane to New York. The long eyelashes, stretching up like reeds on troubled waters, the mournful brown eyes, the soft, kissable lips ... Her reverie was interrupted when a slender stewardess stopped at their seats and asked,

'Tea or coffee?' Charlie shook her head, barely able to smile, the past events had taken their toll on her.

Jenny fidgeted in her seat and asked for water. Her lips were parched from the long flight. Charlie and she had been friends for many years, and Jenny had consoled Charlie during her acrimonious divorce a few weeks ago. As if that hadn't been enough to break Charlie's tenacity. Then came the dreadful news that Charlie's mother in New York was suffering from terminal pancreatic cancer. That's when Jenny decided to accompany Charlie on a trip to the mother who had abandoned her as a child.

Jenny took a deep breath. Would this be the right time to convey her deep feelings for Charlie? Geez! Emotions were exhausting. And yet, a brave chat might lighten the emotional burden Charlie was currently having to deal with. Jenny cleared her throat, preparing her speech. Would this lead to the end of their friendship? Her heart was pounding. It was time to brace herself.

A jolt pushed their seats forward. Charlie turned her head towards Jenny, eyes dilated with fear.

'Brace, brace,' the stewardess shrieked as they plummeted towards the white cumulus clouds, innocent in the unfolding drama of turbulences and their dangers.

Jenny squeezed Charlie's clammy hand and leaned in to kiss her cheek, but Charlie turned her face to meet Jenny's quivering lips. They locked eyes, leaned towards each other and trembled as they dived into the unknown abyss of the infinite sky.

THE TEA IN MY FLASK IS STILL WARM

Stephanie Dickinson

Time stretches reluctantly
slowly meandering
around the afternoon.
Sporadic thoughts
scatter and disperse,
somnolence
spreading like waves.
Doodles drift
across the page.
Time passes ...
months, years, aeons?

And yet
the tea in my flask is still warm.

LIEBESTOD

Peter Scott-Presland

I knew today was the day. I could feel the pheromones. She was calling me. It's impossible to describe if you haven't felt it, but it's a kind of thrumming: in the air, in the ground, in your body. Suddenly the whole world is brighter, the colours more vivid, and every one of your eight eyes sees more clearly, the side ones detecting the slightest motion.

Then there's the pull she exerted. It felt like a magnetic force, drawing me out from under the boardwalk alongside the bungalow. Once in the sunlight, I was blinded and felt my way along the edge and round the corner to the rear of the building. There, out of the sun, I could smell her, and the overpowering scent of sex.

It was a large web, because she was a good size. She must have been at least two years old. Her huge round abdomen, shiny black with its gash of orange, drove me crazy. A warning bell sounded in my brain, she was ten times as big as I was, she could have crushed me soon as look at me. I inched delicately forward, feeling my way with my front legs. All the time my palps were swollen and heavy with stored sperm. This was going to be one hell of a congregation!

I pushed one of my palps into one of her sperm sacs. God that felt good. I wanted to just lie there and wallow in the exquisite swoon of it, but I knew I had to press on. The other sac had to be filled, and I had the other palp to empty. Oooh. If you've never had a double orgasm from both palps, you haven't lived.

Then something strange happened, all of its own accord. I gave a big jump, somersaulted over that vast

160

belly, and found myself staring upside down at the enormous hungry eyes which burned into me with desire. I could feel her mouth parts sink into my abdomen and rip my guts. The pain was exquisite, and combined with the hard pumping from my palps, I thought I would explode. She bit my flesh, my heart, but still I went on, I couldn't stop. I —

Colin's fellow spiderlings, who had shared a web with him for several weeks, had also been drawn towards the female redback. They listened in awe to the steady crunching of what was once their brother.

'Poor Colin,' said Trevor.

'Don't grieve,' replied Alex. 'It's the way he would have wanted to go.'

THE WEDDING

Shaf Ullah

1781, Halda, Himachal Pradesh, India. The powerful
Bose family had arranged to be united with the Chandol
family in matrimony. Gokul, the only son of the Bose
empire, was to be wed with Ashwin, the youngest son of
the Chandols, and the last of the son-marriers. In this
way both clans kept control of hundreds of hectares of
lush green paddy, jute and mustard fields.

Ashwin at 13, stood little more than a metre and half,
with locks of deep burgundy and tiny feet which had been
bound for many years to prevent them growing too man-
like. His glossy skin, massaged twice a day with the
purest mustard oil, radiated a glow so golden that his
grandmother called him 'Shona', which means 'gold' in
Bengali. He was fed honey from bees that fed on mustard
blossoms too which made his voice velvety and sweet.
Ashwin was forbidden to speak in front of men; many
older eyes coveted him.

His mother tied gold bells on his delicate ankles;
every time he walked through the Shish Mahal 'Glass
Court' halls, they shook the exquisite crystal flowers
adorning the chandelier. No one was allowed to see
Ashwin and his world was limited to the Andar Mahal, or
inner courtyard, of the Gulmohar Palace.

He had been promised to Gokul from birth. The bride
price was a hundred elephants, fifty of the finest horses
from Uzbekistan, and the finest muslin from West
Bengal. He was home-schooled, trained by a vocalist
from Hyderabad who would often visit the shrines of
many a prophetic figure. There all the drunk and high
poets dwelt; he would buy the best poems from them to

bring to Ashwin, to teach him how to sing with notes of melancholy, death and poisonous love.

Their lessons were conducted in the presence of Ashwin's grandmother, a blind woman of 102 who sat between Ashwin and his teacher by a muslin dividing screen. At the end of each session the old woman would cover Ashwin's face with a gold-embroidered veil. Only then was he allowed to walk back to his part of the Mahal, where he would set his thousand pet pigeons free for their evening flight. Like Ashwin, they had their wings clipped, so their longed-for journey was just flapping of wings to the lowest tower of the palace, and then back to the slippery, marbled courtyard. For Ashwin, this was the high point of his dull day. To others, a thousand pigeons jumping up and frantically falling down, was a hideous spectacle.

Gokul loved horse riding. Four massive slaves from Haryana carried him in a jewel-encrusted palanquin to the mount, and laid him tenderly in the saddle. Likewise they conveyed him to the pond inside the palace grounds, where he loved to swim, thrusting his deep chest forward, pulling himself through the water with his muscular arms and shoulders.

He was the youngest of five brothers and was raised to marry the son of the richest local landlord, when he was of age. He was unloved as a child and grew up in the company of his horses, in the green pastures where mango blossoms heavily incensed the monsoon winds. His brothers had long gone away to occupy their own lands and create their dynasties, but he remained, waiting for Ashwin to be ready. His parents, now aged, wanted someone to care for him when they could not, and to feed his neglected soul.

The morning of the dynastic wedding, Gokul's mother had adorned a hundred ox-chariots with marigolds so orange that the Sun itself looked mundane. The palace was lit with silk wicks dunked in fine ghee, and the marriage bed was a garden itself, blooming with garlands of jasmine and tuberose. A thousand butterflies fluttered in his stomach as he dreamt of Ashwin entering his magnificent mahal with humble, nimble steps. The temple gong woke him from his reverie, the slaves carried him in his palanquin to his mother's mansion, to be generously rubbed with turmeric paste and bathed in fresh milk. His muscles gleamed gold and resplendent, and virgin cheeks blushed in awe as he was led to the temple.

A tiny hut had been erected by the Madurai Temple, which stood sixteen storeys high in homage to Shiva. The god's statue welcomed the thousand guests who had come to bless the couple. Ashwin was lost in a sea of faces around the blazing fire under the September sun and in the shower of crushed rose petals. He was lost in the spectacle; it felt like the feverish festivities had ended even before they began. He remembered feeling Gokul's soft palms as he rubbed vermillion on his sweat-beaded forehead and a rush of warmth tingled through his spine. He had never been touched by a man before.

Ashwin's parents looked turned away as they gave up their exquisite son. The priests bound the grooms with the sacred red thread: bound in life, bound till death. Gokul's mother and father accompanied the tiny groom in the ox-cart, and the celebrations disappeared in the glittery dust of dusk. It was almost midnight when they arrived at Gokul's part of the palace.

The wind, damp with desire, faded to silence. The grooms were welcomed over trills and ululations and

Ashwin's tiny feet washed in coconut water. Suddenly, everyone was gone, leaving the new couple amidst the piercing screeches of crickets and fireflies. Ashwin with his deep, kohl-lined eyes tightly shut, now felt a sympathetic touch on his intricately-hennaed hands. He looked up amidst giant tiger lilies now flaccid from the day's heat. At this auspicious moment he bent down to touch his husband's feet and get the blessings of his master, the man who would set fire to his funeral pyre on his final journey.

But there were no feet. Gokul had no legs, no feet.

THRUPPLE

Craig Binch

Was he excited by the concept or weirdly fascinated? In his brain, socially-groomed for forty-five years, the very idea was odd. Three people in a relationship – how did it work? What were the dynamics?

Severino and Wanderlay had been his friends for five years. A beautiful couple, one Spanish one Brazilian, and clearly in love. Always kind and considerate, they coexisted in the most tranquil alliance.

It was always an open relationship, but this was on another level that he couldn't quite get his head around. Of course he was happy for them and he would go with the flow, but already he didn't like Number Three. They'd never met, but Severino was gushing about the final piece in their thrupple, enamoured, life now complete.

His spider senses were telling him that Severino seemed keener than Wanderlay. He imagined himself in that space; where do you put your jealousy? There could be favourites and imbalance, it could break up their happy home.

Not sure when he'd become quite so old-fashioned — this was the modern world. How many gay couples really were monogamous? The Grindr survey said nil.

What would their mother think? What would the neighbours say? But then again, what did it matter?

He debated with his inner voice: whatever, these were his good friends and he had to trust their choices, even if he didn't get it.

Of course on principle he didn't like Number Three.

But a quadruple ... Why not ... ?

IT'S ONLY SEX

AN ENCOUNTER

('TIS FORTY YEARS SINCE)

Ross Burgess

A perfect day. Only a few clouds in the sky, the sea very blue, a couple of sailing yachts out on the bay which curved round to the Old Harry rocks in the distance. After my swim, I walked back to the little hollow in the sand dunes where Andrew was improving his all-over tan and guarding our clothes and car keys. A perfect day, except for the lack of men. On previous days it seemed as if almost every hollow in the dunes had been occupied by a man or a couple, many of them ready and willing for some fun. There had even been a rumour of someone tied to a tree, encouraging all-comers to take advantage of him, but maybe this was just a rumour. Today only a few die-hards were left, hardly anyone interesting, and the few that were, were not interested. Still, I always enjoyed walking naked around the little hills and valleys of the dunes, my body caressed by the light breeze, and sometimes by the long grass, occasionally seeing a lizard scuttling out of the way

I stretched out on the towel, feeling very relaxed, at one with the sun on my back, the world turning beneath me, and the skylark singing somewhere above. Andrew renewed the sunblock on my back and then went for his last walk around, but was not gone very long. 'Nothing doing,' he said on his return. It was of course a Tuesday after the bank holiday, and it occurred to us that most of those who'd been around on previous days would now be back at work. Anyway by this time the heat had gone out of the sun, so we went for a meal and a drink in a pub near The Triangle, and then back to the guesthouse.

We turned in quite early, but we weren't ready to sleep. Since our last visit the fire regulations had enforced automatic closing doors, but John, the proprietor, had thoughtfully provided doorstops so that those who wished could leave their doors ajar to encourage visitors. We propped our door open; but no-one came. 'I need a pee,' I said, 'and maybe I'll see if anyone else is awake.' None of the rooms at St Michael's Guesthouse had en-suite facilities, which gave an excuse for men (at least those who didn't like to pee in their washbasin) to prowl round the building during the night.

I went to the loo, and then explored both floors, but there was no sign of life. Eventually however I found a door that was propped open, and looked in. The guy in the bed looked quite acceptable by the light of his bedside lamp. 'Hello,' he said, 'Do you want to come in?'

'I've got a better idea,' I replied. 'My boyfriend is waiting for me in our room. Would you like to join us?'

He seemed quite happy with this. I led him back to our room, and we got in bed either side of Andrew and cuddled up. None of us seemed in too much of a hurry to get down to business, and I was still feeling a bit cold after my naked tour of the guesthouse, so we chatted while gently warming up and starting to explore each other's bodies. The visitor told us his name was Philip. He and his new boyfriend had been in Bournemouth for a CHE conference: the boyfriend had gone home after the weekend, but Philip had another week off work and decided to stay on a bit longer. 'That's interesting,' I said, 'We've been to some of those events. Do we know your boyfriend?'

'You might do,' he said. 'His name's David Walters.' This came as a shock: immediately the erotic charge of the situation seemed to evaporate.

'Oh,' said Andrew. 'Yes, we know him very well. He'd not told us he'd got a new boyfriend.' David Walters led the CHE group in a neighbouring borough and we'd got to know him very well over the years. It somehow struck me that for us to have sex with his partner in his absence would be a betrayal of friendship, something between adultery and incest. Without a word being said it was clear that Andrew had come to the same conclusion. We shifted our hands to less erogenous zones.

Philip seemed to get the message, so by mutual consent we all three gave up on any idea of sex, and chatted a bit further, until he got up and went back to his own room. 'See you at breakfast,' he said.

WOBBLE

Sometimes even the best of us wobbles, it starts off with a stubbed toe, or unexpectedly rancid milk and rollercoasters into a spiral of annoyances.

It happens to us all, none of us are immune. Sometimes you are the target, the world is against you and that's a fact.

Mother Nature plots with fate and Lady Luck to spice up your day with unnecessary and insignificant drama, purely to test your metal and provide maximum inconvenience. Just because.

Well Mother Nature, Ms. Fate and Lady Luck, you can all piss off. I will dance in the stumble, and take my coffee black, for none of it truly matters. And today is going to be a good day.

LETTING GO

Rainer King

In the city, where night is more brazen than the day, Aristide found their escape.

Neon lights pulsed awakening sluggish hearts, and the air was thick with the scent of sweat and sweet decay. It was here, in this cathedral of chaos, that Aristide sought redemption, a chance to rise from a life too ordinary.

'Dancing is like fighting with the rhythm as your opponent,' he mused, recalling a line from a forgotten book as he pushed through the crowd. The club was a furnace, and the dancers its flames, each moving in their own despair and delight.

Aristide wasn't there for the transient touch of strangers. He sought the alchemy of movement, the release that came when foot stepped to beat, and the body moved so the world crumbled. He craved the metamorphosis, to emerge from the cocoon of his own skin and become something else.

The DJ, a maestro of madness, dropped the bass like a hammer on anvil, and Aristide felt the call, surrendering to the rhythm, his body an instrument of their will, his personal response to the limitations of the day.

But tonight unlike the others was different. Tonight, the dance floor was a battleground, and Aristide was not alone in his quest. His eyes met another's, a mirror reflection of his own suppressions. Saul, as he later learned, danced not to find himself but to lose everything. Where Aristide sought clarity in the chaos, Saul sought oblivion.

The night wore on, sweat turned to steam, and the crowd thinned, but Aristide and Saul remained, locked in their dance. With each step something shifted. The music became a language, speaking truths he had never dared to acknowledge. The music told the truth of his experience, his life and his body contorted to reflect it.

With the first light of dawn, the music slowed, and so did they. Breathing hard, staring into the abyss of each other's eyes, they knew. They had found what they sought, but it was not what they expected. It was their connection that had transformed them – the recognition of another.

Aristide stumbled out into the cold air, alone. Saul was a ghost, a figment of the night, gone as though he had never been. But the change was real. Aristide felt it, a shift in the very fabric of his being, he had found his truth in a mirror, a reflection of his solitary contemplation in the form of another – Saul. He walked home, feet aching, a smile playing on his lips. He had gone to dance his way into a new self but found instead the shared rhythm of the human condition. And somewhere, in a place not marked on any map, Saul danced on, a reminder that we never truly dance alone.

TO-DO LIST

1. Ring clap clinic for appointment
2. Uninstall Grindr

WAITING FOR A LIFT

David Flybury

Waiting for a lift today, I noticed the buttocks of the guy standing in front of me filled out his workwear nicely, but though his trousers were tight, they hung loose elsewhere. It reminded me of my somewhat derided theory that if you have a great physique, it doesn't matter what you wear, you'll look great; ill-fitting, generically-designed clothing can only serve to emphasise your assets, but if you are out of shape then you can't do much about it with couture. I guess I've never understood fashion, in reality.

Nevertheless here was a gorgeous bloke who could definitely wear anything and draw the attention around him of anyone with blood. We were joined in the queue by a lady in a tracksuit – now that clothing never flatters! She had a highly decorative pet dog. It was like a very small spaniel, or a large chihuahua. Its coat was quite long, white with brown patches. It had a flouncy tail which it held up so that the well-groomed hair waved about like a silky palm.

Then we were joined by another lady, and at that point the lift arrived and we all piled in. The lift was only big enough for four, and the cute guy had a short, folded ladder — he was glamorously real — so the squeeze was quite snug. The little dog was sniffing everything and the second lady said hello to the dog as it jumped up at her legs. She lived just beneath the lady who owned the dog, it turned out ('I often hear barking ...') and they got talking.

The second lady called the dog a 'her' —

'Isn't SHE pretty!' — and the owner corrected, 'He's a boy, you know!'

The doggy wagged its flouncy tail with the confused enthusiasm that such dogs often exhibit.

'Ahh,' said the second lady, 'I was misled, you see, by all the hair. It always looks like a skirt to me, so he looks like a little girl dog! But you're not a little girl dog, are you?' she said to the dog. She had the dog's full and somewhat manic attention. 'It must be so difficult being a pretty boy!' she continued.

'Tell me about it,' I said, accepting my cue with a practiced air as, at the precise same moment, the cute guy said, 'Oh, it's a BIG problem!'

Everybody laughed (except the dog, which seemed to be on the edge of panic, the way such dogs often are), and my eyes met with the cute guy's across the top rung of his short ladder. We shared mirthful glances and I saw that he had a beauty that was indeed one it must have delighted him to find burdensome ... and I remembered a time when it might not have been entirely fanciful to imagine myself the prettiest boy in the shaft. Alas.

He got out at the next stop — we were still laughing — then the second lady — and then I was left with the lady in a tracksuit, and her dog — it sensibly avoided my legs. The lady congratulated me on my timing, 'You said it first!' she said as she proffered a palm for me to hi-five in celebration. I smacked it incompetently; I don't naturally hi-five, and, in any case, it felt like an inadequate consolation for a contest I'd obviously lost.

CHRISTMAS CRABS

Craig Binch

I didn't really get off the starting blocks in my new gay world at twenty-one. I stumbled out of the closet, moved to London enticed by the bright pink lights, and met a handsome exotic Sicilian after three months. That went sour when he decided to open the relationship but forget to tell me.

So with a band aid on my freshly broken heart, I found a new freedom and dived into the hedonism. I was back on the market and quite frankly would have shagged anything that moved. The harsh reality is that not everything that moved wanted to shag me and the market was largely high end. I did by chance catch the eye of a student at university, he wasn't one to take home to mum, but he did have a nice bum. It was Christmas time and my housemates and I were hosting a party and my student was on the guest list, just in case nothing better turned up.

The morning of the party I felt an itch ... down below, followed by a distinctive pinprick sensation. In the privacy of the bathroom, I stripped off for further inspection. I spotted the tell-tale little black dot and ... it moved.

As realisation kicked in, I was mortified. This was definitely not on my Christmas list. Instinctively I grabbed the nail scissors and began hacking away at the jungle of pubic hair. Once I could see through the undergrowth, I went in militantly with a pair of tweezers. Like Atilla the Hun, I savagely decapitated heads and amputated legs from the little beasts until there nothing but a pubic graveyard of corpses. For good

175

measure, in the last steps of my cleansing I boiled the leftovers in a boiling hot bath with TCP.

In the bathroom cabinet, between the Savlon and the Lynx for Men, a bottle of Derbac cream sat like a little soldier called to battle. I poured the cool and foul-smelling contents all over my recently cropped thatch and waited for the magic to happen.

I was half angry, half amused when I thought about announcing my discovery to the greasy-haired student who had been my only recent bed fellow. I hadn't expected monogamy, but cleanliness and absence of unwelcome STI wasn't much to ask. I prepared for the confrontation.

Treatment complete, I dusted off my pride and went to load the buffet table, although I had quite lost my appetite. The guests began to arrive, including Mr Christmas Crabs. I played the game kissed both cheeks with some hesitant resistance and handed him a drink. He scratched his balls!

'Can I have a quiet word?' Like a puppy he followed me into the kitchen and smiled at me, probably expecting a pre-party fumble.

'Is there anything you want to tell me?' He looked perplexed, the cogs in his addled brain whirring.

'Put it this way, I've brought you a Christmas present.'

'What ...? I ... don't ...' The penny suddenly dropped as he scratched his groin.

I handed him a Derbac-shaped package wrapped in Christmas paper with a pretty pink ribbon. Then I shoved him towards the front door. As I opened it for him, I said, 'Use it twice a day. Happy Christmas.'

HISTORY
FANTASY
HORROR

Cannibalism proved a popular theme at workshops. Here are two examples.

EAT YOUR MEAT

Bodicea Iceni

A: Mum, I've already told you, I'm now a vegetarian.

B: Really, sweetie. No one in this house is a vegetarian unless I say so. More to the point no one can become a vegetarian unless I agree to it. I haven't agreed to it. So please eat your supper. I've worked hard to prepare it. I'm working full time as you know. I've shopped for the items in my lunch break, then come home, prepared and cooked the meal, and I won't be finished for the day until the dishes are cleared, washed, dried and put away. I can't be dealing with this. Not today, not tonight, not after the day I've had. Barely got two ha'pennies to rub together but I'm here still putting food on the table. Now eat.

Λ: Mum where'd this meat come from?

B: Where'd you want it to come from?

A: Is it organic? Is it from a small holding? Is it battery farmed?

B: Well I don't bleeding well know love. It's meat, let's eat.

A: Mum, please tell me more about this meat.

B: What do you want to know?

A: Is it chicken, beef, lamb?

B: No, dearie, it's not.

A: Venison, ostrich, kangaroo? Grouse?

B: Well it bleeding well ain't grouse, is it? You know full well it's not Grouse season.

A: So mum — please, what is it?

B: It's meat. Please tuck in. Eat, it's getting cold.

A: Where is Mr Carpenter tonight? The lodger? I haven't seen him in days now.

B: He left dear, left in a hurry. A call from his dear departed wife.

A: Sorry mum what did you say? Mum? Did you say departed? How could she be calling him? Mum, his room is still full of his things. He's not left. Where is he?

B: Okay now that's enough. No more questions. No more talking. Eat.

A: Mum, what meat is this?

B: Eat. Just bloody well eat, will yah?

A: Mum? Is this Mr Carpenter? Are we eating Mr Carpenter? Have you cooked and served us up our lodger?

B: What would you say if I said yes? Yes, it's Mr Carpenter. I fell a bit short this week and ...

A: Okay mum. Thanks for telling me. Thanks for being honest. Tomorrow we both go vegetarian. Now pass the salt.

`

FLASH FICTION: HOMAGE TO SAKI

'What do you think of that, young master?' said the boot boy, lowering his trousers.

Theodore screwed his monocle into his eye, and inspected the object disdainfully.

'Well, I would have said it was a penis,' he drawled, 'but it's far too small.'

LAST-MINUTE PREPARATIONS

David Lindley-Pilley

Five minutes till the guests arrive. So much to do.

I glance at the arrangement of cutlery placed as per Mr Shadwell's requirements. Everything spick and span ... until I see the remnants from last week's gathering on the dessert spoon. I had specifically requested to Ms. White that everything must be spick and span.

My mind feels like it has been clamped down by a vice; an all-too-common sensation when preparing for these arrangements. My tremulous hand picks up the spoon. I will have to take matters into my own hands and Ms. White will bear the consequences at a later date. Everything must go according to plan.

I prowl the banqueting table looking for any imperfections which could derail the evening. Not once, but twice. Everything must go to plan.

I descend the rickety stairs to the kitchen of the Shadwell residence. Only two weeks past, one of the young servants had fallen down the stairs and broken her leg. An unfortunate incident, the price of inexperience.

I approach the sink, full to the brim with soap water. I submerge my hand into the hot water and feel grateful for the momentary respite from my mind. I start buffing the spoon with a level of industriousness that only thirty years of service for the esteemed Shadwell dynasty can provide.

I place the spoon down and I am immediately confronted by the chef who requires my advice on the most suitable infusions for tonight. Is there anyone with experience in this house? They will soon learn.

I thrust the now-clean spoon to Ms. White and task her with delivering it upstairs; the tone in my voice not belying the admonishment that she will receive when the evening has concluded, though there never really seems to be an end to these things. Not really.

I find the source of the chef's consternation – a pile of lemons – stacked neatly by the main dish in a way which made me think that the chef had not even tried to fulfil his responsibility. They will learn.

I plunge one of the lemons deep into the cavity, the juices flowing inside as I do so. My mouth quivers, anticipating the melange of smells to come out of the oven.

The clacking of the door knocker reverberates around the kitchen, waking the staff from their reverie – or whatever it was which was causing them to be so absent-minded.

They are here. Everything must go according to plan.

I hear Ms. White open the door to the guests at the same time as Mr Shadwell descends the marble staircase.

I wait for the bell to usher in my involvement in the proceedings upstairs. All the guests must be seated before that happens.

The sounds of knives slamming against chopping boards, taps running, and the oven kicking into life combine and allow me to feel part of a tight operation. Emphasis on feel, of course. They will learn.

I can hear the bell ringing upstairs through the cacophony down in the kitchen. My ears are finely tuned.

I smooth down my white apron and inspect for any irregularities. Not once, not twice, but three times. Everything must go to plan.

As I ascend the stairs, I hear the clink of glasses and laughter. I steel myself outside the door to the banquet room. Despite all the years of doing this, my mind is never quite at peace. But I have memorised the menu. Everything must go according to plan.

I enter the room; an immediate hush descends. I do not know whether it is respect for Mr Shadwell, but I take my moment and reel off the menu to expectant faces:

'For the starter, we have a lightly braised Charles Picklethwaite: one year old. The main, a lemon-infused Roger Picklethwaite: 26 years old. And followed by dessert, a sugar glazed Mary Picklethwaite: 22 years old.'

THE GIVEWAY

Mrs Widdecombe was giving that talk which every mother has to give her daughter when she reaches a certain age. She was drawing to a conclusion, a rousing peroration which she hoped the girl would never forget.

'Promise me,' she pleaded. 'Whatever you do, whatever other girls tell you to do, you'll never, never, ever touch yourself there. If you do, you'll go deaf. Promise me? Promise?'

'Pardon?' said Ann.

Kathryn Bell is a founder member of G.A.W. She recently celebrated her ninetieth birthday.

TRAVELLING HOPEFULLY

Kathryn Bell

She bent to pick up her shopping bags. It had been a mistake to put them down to ease the weight for a minute; it only made it harder to pick them up again. Their handles bit her fingers and their weight made her shoulders ache, but these were the least of her pains. Her back and legs hurt, permanent aches intensified by cold and tiredness.

Never mind, she was at the corner of her road. Not far to go now. Two hundred yards perhaps, two fifty? Something like that. It was only about six o'clock, but dark as midnight. Normal for the time of year, as was the icy wind from the east — it always seemed to be from the east, sending the rain horizontally into her face, giving her a headache. An ice-cream headache without the ice-cream, she thought glumly.

There was a blister on one heel; her shoe rubbed it painfully with each step. And both shoes were letting in water. The rain turned the day's snowfall to dirty slush.

But soon she would be home. There would be warmth, and light. She wouldn't unpack her shopping at once, she would have a little rest first. There was a comfortable old armchair where she would sit with a hot cup of tea, letting the tiredness drain from her body and limbs into the chair, then to the floor, then down, down to the absorbent earth. Soon she would be warm and dry, and then her back wouldn't ache so much. And there was a soft fluffy rug in front of the chair, to sink her sore feet in when she'd kicked off these blasted shoes.

She crossed the road, no traffic to hinder her. It was always a quiet road, and she realised that since she'd turned the corner, she had seen no one; no cars, no bicycles, nobody walking. She had the dark silent road to herself. Everybody was home, putting on their radios and televisions, starting to prepare their evening meals, as she would be soon.

And now she'd arrived. Here was the short garden path, and she could see light behind the glass pane in the door. She put her bags down to get her key out of her pocket. She touched the key to the keyhole, and the world exploded in a flash of white light.

When she could see again, she was back at the corner, her bags on the ground beside her, and in an instant of horrible clarity she remembered. This had happened before, thousands of times before, and would happen again, millions, billions, infinite number of times, because this was Hell, constantly renewing itself, for ever and ever.

The lucid moment passed. She picked up her bags, thinking she should never have put them down, and plodded on, the freezing wind driving needles of rain into her face, and everything hurt, and she was deathly tired. Never mind, nearly home, not long to go now.

PERSPECTIVE

I'm gonna live forever,' sang the mayfly, dancing in the setting sun.

THE VISITOR

Stephanie Dickinson

'Expect me' and a smiley face. Jo glances idly at the message. No name, just the sender's number. Irritating. She texts back: 'Who are you?' No reply. DELETE.

Same time, a week later 'Expect me.' The face accompanying this message is not smiling, more neutral, and still there is no name. The phone number looks different but she can't be sure.

'Who ARE you?'. This time there is a reply, 'It is me. Expect me soon'.

'Who is ME?" she types back.

'Someone.'

The face with the message looks benign, then shimmers slowly into something more … ghostly.

The ages speed up. She dreads looking at her phone but can't resist. The phone seems to compel her. It looks the same but it doesn't FEEL the same. It's hot. Too hot — and something else. Something she can't describe, She doesn't want to hold it. Doesn't want to feel the malevolence that exudes from it burning into her hand. She watches the blisters creep across her skin. The itching is unbearable. She tries to throw the phone across the room. She can't.

The face is swirling, again.

'Who. Are. You?' she screams. And the scream is silenced as she stares in horror at the screen. A countdown clock appears. One minute … 59 seconds …

As each second passes the face morphs into something endlessly menacing. And grows. It's larger than the phone now and spreading into the room. Reaching out. To her …

AFTERMATH

Howard Bradshaw

It was a strange feeling, lying in the road. The gravel should have been digging into my back, but it wasn't. I felt I was floating. The medics were rushing here and there, checking pulses in wrists and necks. Stretcher bearers were carrying patients off to the waiting ambulances. Or, more ominously, closing eyes and covering faces and bodies with blankets. Police were cordoning off areas, taking statements from people who'd seen the explosion but miraculously escaped.

The scene was chaotic. People were shouting at each other and beckoning. But to me it seemed like a silent movie. I could see mouths moving, but hear nothing. I realised I was in a state of shock. Or maybe the blast had damaged my eardrums.

A paramedic was going past me. I tried to grab his leg but couldn't. I called out: 'I'm injured. Help.'

It was like I hadn't spoken. I shouted louder, but people ignored me.

After five minutes, two auxiliaries bent over me. 'At last!' I said.

One of the women looked at the other and shook her head. Next thing I knew, I was shrouded in darkness by a blanket.

SPARE

Victor desperately needed a helping hand. So he contacted his local body snatchers.

186

FORAGER'S DELIGHT

Bodicea Iceni

A lifelong relationship started with my uncle that goes back almost as far as I can remember. My uncle/brother was for a long time one of my primary carers after my grandmother died. He ensured I got up, was washed, dressed and ready for school most days. A neighbour's daughter would ensure I actually got there but it always felt as though he had a presence.

During what felt like long, hot, dusty summers we would go foraging for apples, plums, pears and blackberries. This always felt like a special time. Food from nowhere special somehow felt extraordinary, but the berries. Those are my fondest memories. Big fat juicy blackberries so ripe that I could barely touch them without squeezing them into non-existence.

The flavours were complex. Sweet, tart, bitter, floral, at times with a hint of sourness. This was my introduction to foraging and a tradition that I passed onto many younger relatives.

As an adult I came back to foraging when I was introduced to nettle, its uses, its benefits its nutritional profile. From here I then went onto wild garlic, garlic mustard, lovage, fool's parsley and hemlock. Hemlock.

Poison has always been termed a woman's weapon and has been used throughout history to terminate the lives of a number of less than savoury characters. Frenemies, mother in laws, abusive husbands, dependant relatives that were a drain on household resources.

The discovery of this plant gave me new powers and ideas that I could not have possibly entertained before. Turning it from a plant into a potion I could use wasn't difficult and my next step was to develop a usable recipe and test it.

But on whom?

CREEPY

Philip Inglesant

Hands shaking, he turned the key; the door creaked open. The space was dark and silent but not empty.

DEVIL MAY CARE

Craig Binch

Anthony ran through woods, thorns ripping viciously at his exposed legs, his lungs tight and ready to burst and his red face covered in angry tears. He fucking hated them all, he could never go back to school, not after this. Humiliated in front of the whole year, a naked photo was doing the rounds on Snapchat, and he was the unexpected model. The older boys had taken it in the changing room for a laugh, within moments it was viral, everyone laughing, the joke was on him again. Insult to injury, he looked like he was full mast in the unfortunately captured angle.

He ran out of steam coming to a breathless halt and leaned against an old oak tree. He sobbed heavily and he screamed up to the gods a soulful sound which reverberated through the canopy of trees, startling nesting birds.

The crack of a branch, a movement in the shadows, suddenly he was alert. The tears immediately stopped and he squeezed his eyes to see into the gloom; he knew he was not alone. A tall, slender, handsome man, ageless, came into the clearing; he stood proudly leaning on a stick. Anthony was transfixed by his charming, sinister smile.

'I heard you crying, boy. Are you well?'

The accent was familiar but foreign at the same time, well-spoken, his words clipped. A long slender finger with a sharp nail tenderly wiped a tear away. He was fixed to the spot, the air had gone cold.

'Now what could have happened to such a fine young man to have him in such a state?'

189

Anthony was frozen in fear, all his previous worries now gone as he was presented with this familiar stranger.

'Cat got your tongue Anthony?'. The man smiled mischievously, toying with him.

The boy's initial silence found a small bravery: 'How do you know my name?'

'I know many things, I am the past, the future, the wind, the rain and the air you breathe, my boy. I am magic and mayhem. Desire is truth, but alas I do not exist, so you have nothing to fear.'

He waved his hand and a mirror appeared; he turned it to the boy, who instantly recoiled in shame at the sight of the haunting naked image of himself.

'I can help you. I can make your real desires come true. You want to make them pay, don't you, boy?'

A flash of a small smile and then a bashful lowering of his head; the man smiled fiendishly.

'Just say the word, boy, and I can make it happen. All I need is your wish.'

'What do you mean?' he stuttered. 'What could you do? '

'I can make the photo disappear; I can make them never hurt you again; isn't that what you want?'

'But how?'

'I have many ways, but they are secret. Are you in or not? I don't have all day. '

'You won't hurt them? I mean not really?'

'Well now, you can't spoil all my fun. Besides, what do you care?'

'What do you want in return?'

'I desire nothing but Devilment.' He smiled widely, enjoying the game.

Anthony's phone buzzed, instinctively he glanced at the screen, another snap chat view count was at 200. He raged ...

'I wish it,' he said quietly. He looked up but the man was gone. He was alone in the woods, left with nothing but the sensation of a cold fading kiss on his tearstained cheek.

It was now dark. He got his bearings and ran all the way home without stopping, the image of the man burned in his mind and haunting all his thoughts. Straight upstairs, he slammed the bedroom door, locked it and dived into his bed. The Reel of Shame and Embarrassment on an endless repeat in his mind.

He woke to the sound of sirens. His plan was to fake illness, to buy him some time, maybe he would run away. With an Oscar-worthy performance, he walked into the breakfast room. His mum looked up from her phone. 'Speak of the Devil,' she said.

'Mum, I can't go to school today, I'm not well.' His most pathetic voice. She lifted an eyebrow,

'Well it's your lucky day, Anthony, no-one's going to school today. There's been an incident ...'

DINNER TIME

'I hope she goes and gets some food soon, I'm absolutely ravenous,' said the tapeworm. 'And I hope she remembers she's eating for two.'

HORROR STORY

Stephanie Dickinson

Horror happens only in films. You need a dark night, a thunderstorm maybe, an attic with creaky floors. Or a cellar. And definitely weird noises.

I'm at home. It's a beautiful summer's day. I should be safe. But I know I'm not. The feeling overwhelms me.

A vague change in the atmosphere. The dust motes floating in the air start to move together until there is a definite shape. Of what? Not a person but all the same of something that is alive. In some way. The shape undulates towards me slowly.

My cat darts under the chair. Fur bristling, its eyes are wide staring at the shape. Its horror is palpable. I know as soon as the shape moves nearer to me the cat will make its escape. And she won't come back. I hope she will be OK.

Its murmuring thought bore into my brain. Its intentions are clear. But the split second I recognise what it is saying I forget. I'm left with the knowledge that something horrible is happening — but what? It wants me. It whispers 'I want your shell'. It creeps ever nearer.

Soon I know I will not be me ... Not ... be

HOUSING SHORTAGE

Exchange: Tenant 2-bed council flat second floor, no lift, will exchange for 1-bed bungalow or ground floor flat. Pref. near hospital.

A DRAGON LOVE STORY

Thai O'Reilly

Long ago the Earth was inhabited by an intelligent and dominant race. We were powerful and feared by all other life, for we were known as the dragon race.

One dragon in particular, of fire, forged into flesh, was known as the great Belias. A fire-breathing, tremendous-sized dragon, of enormous strength and ridiculous height, razor-sharp teeth as long as swords, high soaring wings, coated in brilliant silver, red, crimson scales, engulfed in powerful red-orange flames. This dragon came from a royal bloodline dynasty, born to rule and reign. But Belias was not like the others. It had its own pain; it was lost without its lover. It explained:

'We, as dragons, have this tendency to be associated with war and destruction, blood and rage, but that is not all who we are. Let me inspire you, take you higher, let me ignite the spark that was lit up in me.

'Let me introduce you to my love; Piscerea, of water, solidified beauty like the vast ocean, deep, intense, complex. A petite, smaller water dragon, with royal blue eyes, so blue in fact you could swim in them. Golden wings, amplified by the sun's presence, so elegant and mesmerising. Long serpentine body, long neck, long tail.

'It's been a long time since the elements have mixed'.

Piscerea blushed electric blue. Body to body, pulsing. Scales to scales, colliding. Together, scratching. 'You itch my frills with your tail. Grab me, hold me. I twitch. A lot. Hot and bothered, I erupt with pleasure, and I explode with excitement. You wither and you dither, go weak at your little limbs, before you leak and evaporate.

'Like an inviting hug, your presence embraced me, suffocated me in the best way possible, with an intense force of passion that I had never witnessed before. Stunned, your energy lifted me off the ground, transported me far from here to another universe. I remember when our souls danced together in perfect harmony, the strength of your love, our love, magnetic, pulled me in. Your affection grounds me, betters me, frees me.

You are the rain, the calmness and solitude to my flame burning hell. You represent the moon, the element of change. You push and you pull like the tides of the ocean. And you flow like a river, meander, so graceful with every movement. Your beauty is what captured me, love at first flight. I remember when our vertical slit eyes met, locked in place. For a moment we were surrendered in time. My thoughts bled orange with curiosity at the peace I could have with you.

'What is love?' It's this indestructible force. My inferno and your tsunami interconnected, locked in this moment. Nothing could penetrate our force field of love.

My past echoes for I am born from the sun, like a phoenix, I am life, and I am death. Now, I am reborn in your image. I am the element of power, lust, and more. Others crave the status that I possess, but you, you, balance me, for I am fire, and you are water.

ON THE OTHER SIDE OF THE GRAMOPHONE

Shaf Ullah

The horned ikon sat on his amethyst throne and sighed. The forest mortals now turned into crystal ballerinas stood in silence, scattered under the frozen canopy of the once lush emerald forests.

London sirens now ringing in his ears, Iliad sat up trying to remember how he wanted to write this story in the first place. He stared at the rusty, copper gramophone that he had received for his 40th birthday from his husband and realized that the more he looked into the lily-shaped depths, the heavier his eyelids began to feel. Iliad now recalled how he had sat down with his comforting mug of stewed morning coffee in his tiny office space, in their cramped London art-deco-style flat; he had written three insignificant lines and kept pondering the words 'crystal' and 'frozen'.

His eyes felt as if heavy rocks had descended on them; as he pushed his body forward and pulled his limbs towards the typewriter to punch out more words, a force greater than his will had pulled him backwards into the warmth of the silk cushion and everything around him basked in a dimming candlelight.

The gramophone had pulled him into its depths and he suddenly found himself spiralling down a copper stairway. Everything around him had gone cold as metal. He pinched himself once, twice; no, he wasn't dreaming. He heard a clang and as he sank further into nowhere, he noticed a blue velvet French bulldog on a ravishing pearl-encrusted cushion talking to itself. This was strange;

195

Iliad had seen this dog before, but he could not say where. His descent, which was never ending, came to a halt when the dog looked over and said:

'Welcome to the land of Blooming Darkness, my name is Pluto'. He jumped off his cushion and trotted off, looking back at Iliad as if summoning him with a blue gaze.

More stairs ... darkness unveiled more darkness, and Iliad could only hear trotting feet. He saw the mouth of the gramophone now looking like the eye of a needle. Suddenly he hit a wall, little blue marmosets hanging on orchid vines scattered everywhere as he tried to keep his balance and his heart started beating fast. Marmosets! Little wise men of the underworld, he must remember this for his book.

... trot ... trot ... trot. He was on Pluto's heels:

'Enter the vines, it's time, follow me, now'.

Iliad brushed his fingers, now frozen to heavy tentacles, against the brittle petal faces and watched as the flowers opened their eyes and gazed at him, ushering him into a blue corridor. Iliad had only walked a few steps when Pluto told him to watch out for the pendulum. A heavy blow hit him on his forehead; he found himself flying into the dark air as the clock donged three times ... it must be 3 a.m. – or p.m.?

Was he inside a grandfather clock guarded by orchids and marmosets?

Iliad fell with a surreal thud at the bottom of his table and Tennor, his French bulldog, peeked in quietly to see if his Master was alright ...

As Iliad came to his senses, he felt a damp metallic smell in the air. Blood, bright blue, was trickling down his face and he felt the sizzling sharpness of the cut on his head. It was not a blow simply from dozing off and losing your balance on the table. It was a blow, a cruel blow from the smoky blue underworld that had pierced his scalp out of the dense gloom.

PERSONAL AD

Howard Bradshaw

Jewish hippy, 28, traveller living in all-male commune, seeks similar younger-brother type. I am surrounded by men, but none of them qualify as that special Dearly Beloved. Are you the chosen one?

I am tall, slim, attractively bearded, and very well hung — or will be soon. I'm told I have very nice eyes. I keep fit by throwing people out of the Temple and water sports. Interests include philosophy and mysticism, disputing with elders and public speaking. I am currently on a successful stand-up tour of the Galilee area. Excellent cook and wine buff, also impressive array of magic tricks.

You will be a good hugger and kisser, enjoy placing your head in my lap, and the laying on of hands. Sturdy ass a bonus.

Will be passing through Hebron in August to process some wheat. Look me up at the Grinder.

LEFTOVERS

Laurence Sullivan

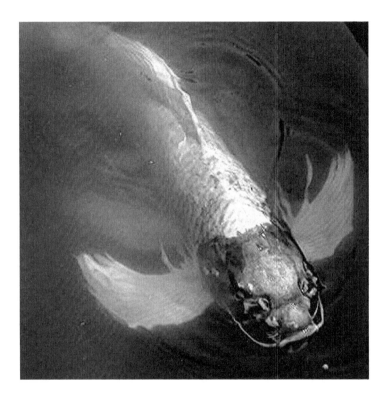

The pond's rising temperature could mean only one thing — the school had survived another night. As the morning wore on, slithers of sunlight would broaden out into big beams which were certain to draw in the crowds. That's when the koi would receive their reward for surviving.

Old Tsubasa was the one most park-goers came to see. Now in his fiftieth year, the rest of the school relied on the ancient koi for their security. When he was a sprat, he remembered how herons would swoop down like ninja in the dead of night — scooping up his friends and relatives alike. He was the last of his generation now, but large enough to defend the next.

Sure enough, shortly after the sun had risen high into the sky, the park started teeming with people. As they thronged around the pond — desperate to feed the fish — the koi swam into position, each mouth gasping gormlessly at the water's surface.

Old Tsubasa's impassive eye watched as a little girl emptied out a bag of feed she had brought, before letting go of the bag itself — shattering the pond's glassy surface as it fell with an audible plop. He knew that bag would eventually break down into a thousand ephemeral wisps — each destined for the digestive tract of one of his unfortunate fellow fish. He had seen it all before, and the slow, inevitable decline of his friends that came with it. During the feeding frenzy, anything floating was fair game, and in the scrum to scoop up the best bits, the little pieces of plastic would be swallowed along with them.

Old Tsubasa could thrash against the herons who came to feast at night, but — try as he might — he could never defend his friends from this most insidious of threats...

OPPORTUNIST

When Steven Spielberg was assassinated, his last words were, 'Buy the film rights'.

CENTRE STAGE

Susan Miller

Marjorie walked to the centre of the stage. There was a microphone set up, there was going to be one hell of a show later on. She tapped the mic as she'd seen people do on the telly and smiled.

'Hellooo London,' she whispered.

In her head the lights went on — back, right and left — a medley of lights. On her! All for her!

She twirled around, the audience was going mad. She was the Shania Twain of Lambeth.

But she knew in her heart that she wasn't a performer, she couldn't make it into the shops without blushing. She smiled again. There had been a younger Marjorie. 'Marj' they'd called her. 'Marj' was still in there, lusting after the spotlight.

'Have you cleaned backstage, Mrs Medlar?' The voice boomed through the empty theatre.

'Yes, all done,' she smiled in the direction of the voice. It was the Director Tony De Vere, a name straight out of an Agatha Christie.

Just then a shot rang out. It must be a silly props gun, she thought.

It made her jump though. What was Tony playing at? She walked towards where the voice had come from...

Later Mrs Medlar stared at the TV screen.

There she was ... on camera. Lights, jostling journalists, all concentrated on her. Numbly she watched herself.

'No, there didn't seem to be any reason for him to shoot himself' she was saying.

'No, he seemed ever so happy and the show was going really well.' Sitting on her sofa she pulled a blanket tighter around her shoulders.

Her face on the flickering screen looked so pale. And so old. She grimaced and turned the channel over.

She would definitely need a make-over if the news people came back.

Inside 'Marj' grinned — and twirled for the cameras.

REGRETS

The Holy Father was dying. He lay in the high-canopy bed with brocade hangings, breathing heavily. Two burnished tousle-haired cherubs fanned him, while in the distance the Vatican choir was chanting. The Papal Confessor was on hand.

"Do you wish to confess?" he asked. The Pontifex Maximus feebly shook his head. He had confessed enough, he had not the strength. "But surely after such a long life, you must still have regrets. Everyone has regrets.'

The Pope struggled to raise himself. The confessor leaned into him to hear his dying words. He could just make out in a faint, coarse whisper,

'I wish I'd had more sex.'

I MET MYSELF

David Flybury

I met myself the other day, my 26-year-old self, walking along the Caledonian Road. I recognised me by my long hair, my home-made clothes, and my shoes which I had once machine embroidered.

It was a surprise and, I must confess I was unsure whether or not to speak. I knew I wouldn't want ... to ... Oh hold on! I didn't know. I didn't know how this other me would react, but suddenly, seized by fear, I crossed the road and looked through the traffic at 'me', walking self-consciously, the broken embroidery on my shoes flipping inconveniently. I was afraid.

This other me, awkwardly dressed in shirts he'd made out of found cloth and shorts made out of cut-down jeans and patched and re-patched into a kind of afterlife oblivion ... his hair was overgrown and flicked into his eyes. I know how he felt: He felt ridiculous. Would it help to tell him that, in 30 years he would still feel ridiculous, but for different reasons? Knowing me, I know I'd suspect any older man making conversation.

How would I start?

'I am you, young man ...'?

That's not a good start.

I matched his steps, on the other side of the road. He was in his decade and I was in mine. When we got to the lights, down by Kings Cross, we waited, they changed, and he crossed, trundling straight towards me. I held my ground, waiting for a collision, but, not looking up, he steered around me so narrowly I could smell him – he didn't wash; now that I DO remember: He swam to wash and then, if he didn't swim, he didn't wash. Something else that didn't change, I could tell him, and also, come to think of it, I could say (because I remember this embarrassment), 'Always pull the chain, and always check and pull again if necessary. Just check.'

My God. I have nothing to say to this young man.

Nothing.

He passed, and as he passed, I suddenly felt a pulse of need and grabbed him; I knew where the shirt was weak and held it where it was firm.

'Are you?' I said, 'Alright?'

He looked at me and I found myself looking into the eyes of a stranger; someone who knew as much as I, but different things. He was confused and pulled his hair aside, behind an ear, and grabbed his shirt near where I had grabbed it, aware of its shortcomings structurally. I smiled; I hoped that would help.

'Do you recognise me?' I said, tears at my face.

He didn't speak, but stared.

He grabbed my hand and pulled at the fingers to release their grip; finally muttered, 'Let go of me, and, No; who are you?'

'Look at my face.'

He looked at my face.

'I am looking at your face.'

'I am you,' I said, stupidly.

'Oh. Right. Okay. Fine. Can you let go?'

'Do you want me to let go?' I said.

'Yes,' he said. 'I do. I want you, to LET GO!'

A TESTAMENT TO RESTORE FAITH

CJ Cass-Horne

In the small town of Catfish-Paradise Arizona, lived a kind-hearted middle-aged man named Timo Bumblethorpe. Timo was passionate about making a difference in the lives of those less fortunate. He had a particular soft spot for the elderly, believing that they deserved all the love and care in the world.

Timo was strolling through Catfish-Paradise, he stumbled upon a flyer advertising a care come. Intrigued, he decided to pay it a visit. Upon entering, Timo noticed the weary expressions on the residents' faces. They seemed lonely and neglected, and Timo's heart ached for them. He decided then and there that he would do whatever it took to improve their lives.

Driven by empathy and a burning desire to right the wrongs, Timo hatched a plan. He would go undercover and move into the care home to experience firsthand the neglect endured by the elderly residents. And so, Timo transformed himself into a new resident named 'Niko'.

As Niko settled into the care home, he quickly made friends with Clive, a charming gentleman in Room 23. Clive had been living in the Care Home for 20 years after his partner died. He had seen the steady decline in the quality of care. He shared heartbreaking stories of inadequate staff, negligence, and indifference of the current owners, Homeways Connect.

Motivated by his newfound ally's plight, Timo's determination grew stronger. He couldn't stand by and let the residents suffer. Timo decided to make a bold move. He would buy the Care Home.

Timo reached out to his wealthy lesbian aunt, who had always supported his noble endeavours. Aunt Layana wasn't convinced at first, but Timo's passion and dedication won her over. With her financial backing, they set out on a mission to turn the care home around.

Together, they confronted the owners of Homeways Connect, demanding that they sell the care home to Timo unless they'd rather be exposed to the press. The owners agreed, realizing they had no alternative.

Timo and Aunt Layana set to work transforming the Care Home. They hired compassionate staff, improved the living conditions, and organized activities that brought joy and laughter back into the residents' lives.

As their efforts bore fruit, Timo and Clive's friendship blossomed into something more. They became long-life partners, standing side by side, ensuring that the elderly residents were given the love and care they deserved.

News of the remarkable transformation at Catfish-Paradise Care Home spread like wildfire. Families from all over America started choosing the Care Home for their loved ones. Timo and Clive's home was a place where their elderly relatives would thrive. As the years went by, the Care Home became the epitome of love, laughter, and gay pride. A testament to the power of one man's empathy and a community's unwavering support.

Their legacy lived on in the hearts of those they had touched, reminding everyone that love knows no age, and that everyone deserves to be treated with compassion and dignity. And in the small town of Catfish-Paradise, the story of Timo and Clive became a symbol of hope and resilience for elderly gay couples everywhere.

[Peter: I wanted to see if I could write a detective story which played fair with the clues for the reader, but in the smallest possible space. Solution on p.210]

CHEATING AT EXAMS: THE PROBLEM

Peter Scott-Presland

Respected Professor,

Please review this paper, 'Sunrise Memories', from student A, which has been submitted for the Creative Writing course, Advanced Module 2. A perusal of the style and content leads me to believe there has been some unauthorised and illegal assistance. I will appreciate your second opinion. I need to convey your decision in this respect to the student by the end of the week. Please oblige. I attach the work in question.

Attachment

As the sun showered its golden shafts athwart the radiant meadows, Seth breathed in deeply, stretching his deep chest to soak up the spicy air. His biceps expanded; twelve-hour days on the scythe had brought his chest, shoulders and arms to a peak of perfection. He smiled a half-smile as he thought of the next eight hours in company with his life companion, Enoch, side by side swinging in perfect rhythm as the sheaves of corn fell beneath their eager blades. Suddenly he viewed the sturdy stockier figure of Enoch crest the hill. The light fell on his fair hair, which gleamed in its rays ...

A CHIP OFF THE OLD BLOCK

David Lindley-Pilley

'Is everything alright, dear? You've been rather ... out of sorts lately.'

'I'm fine.'

'Really? I feel like we haven't spoken properly in ages. Every day you come home from work and just seem so deflated. I'd hate for you to think that you can't be open.'

'I'm sorry. Just quite a busy day ahead. Pretty much got no sleep last night hearing all those carriages thundering along the road. People will do anything to get the best seats for today.'

'Yes, I heard. Apparently, people are coming from as far as Reading to see it. Mistress White for one told me she'll be wearing her finest garb. To be frank, I'm not sure that's entirely wise, with the blood splashing.'

'Talking of which my love, any luck with getting those stains out? The elements are the only things which should be pelting me from above, not bloody shit!'

'I'm trying dear. But I don't see why they can't supply you with a new uniform, there's enough money there.'

'I think there are other priorities.'

'And don't get me started on your work bag. The absolute state of it! How long have you had that for now? Coming up to 10 years?'

'Good god, has it really been that long? Enough to make me consider changing my career ...'

'Changing your career?!' You're so good at it though. The local butcher always says how much of a professional you are. You haven't botched a job in all these years!'

'Never say never. Don't you feel it's time for a new direction - especially with the baby on the way?'

'But what on earth would you do? You've a well-paid job with access to the cream of the crop in this country. My bell ringing isn't going to keep us afloat for God's sake - even though I've been hard at it all these years, with all His marriages and supporting YOUR work.'

'Let's talk about this when I get back. And by the way, you put too much clover in the tea this morning.'

'If you say so dear. Oh, don't forget your axe ... And send my regards to the King and whoever's on the chopping block this time – Anne something or other, isn't it? It must be so lonely up on those boards.'

THE WRITER'S SECRET

Stephanie Dickinson

'This is so impressive. Historically accurate. Critically acclaimed. You must have done so much research.' Debbie flourished the book in question.

Robin looked at the floor modestly. 'Well, of course, I researched the era. It's important to get the mundane domestic details and contemporary language correct.'

Debbie smiled at him. 'You're not giving yourself enough credit. You've written a Victorian novel from a young maid's point of view when you're a middle-aged man. What skill to achieve such an authentic voice!'

'People seem to like it,' Robin said self-deprecatingly. 'And there's the mystery. I use my real name, Robin Bishop, but readers seem to assume I'm a woman. That's why I don't do interviews. Must keep the mystery going.'

'I love the opening line,' Debbie went on. '"Today I started work as a maid in the big house." So simple. So direct.'

Robin shrugged. 'It just came to me,' he said.

Debbie stood up and grabbed her coat. 'Well,' she said as she turned towards the door. 'You've got a masterpiece here. I'm really looking forward to the next book. I hope there IS one?' She glanced back at him.

'Oh yes.' Robin smiled. 'I've even got the first line. I wanted something simple again so it's going to be "Today is my seventeenth birthday …" I've got sequels planned and I'm going to develop my protagonist's personality and interests as she gets older. And tie in her growing political beliefs with events of the time. She'll be a suffragette.'

'Perfect. Can't wait.' Debbie closed the door behind her and Robin sat back in his chair and breathed a sigh of relief. He opened the drawer of his desk and took out the pile of tattered notebooks. He looked at the first one. *My Diary by Florence Bishop* it announced on the front cover in careful Victorian handwriting. He turned the page and read that so familiar opening line: 'Today I started work as a maid … '

He didn't need this volume any more, he thought, as he placed it back in the drawer. But the second book … He took out his great-great grandmother's second diary and checked the opening line again.

CHEATING AT EXAMS: THE SOLUTION

Dear Colleague

Your suspicions are correct. The most obvious telltale sign is in the phrase 'the sheaves of corn fell beneath their eager blades'. Sheaves are not created until after the corn has been cut. This is clearly a logical impossibility averred by someone with little knowledge of agricultural procedures. Other phrases suggest an emotional overheating unattributable to current generations of AI copy content generators.

This candidate is disqualified because it has had assistance from a human brain.

THE END

Peter Scott-Presland

There can be many points of tension in a relationship. Russell made it a rule never to try to teach a partner to drive or to play bridge. His lovely other half Claudio went to a driving instructor, and doesn't play cards, so they seemed fair set to last.

The only bone of contention was films. Russell had been a dedicated cinema buff ever since he joined the National Film Theatre. Claudio would tag along as long as there was plenty of action and a few cute guys in the movie. When Russell proposed a film, Claudio would ask, 'Who's in it?' When Claudio suggested something, Russell always wanted to know who directed it. On this occasion, Russell had dragged Claudio to the re-release of Orson Welles' *Chimes at Midnight*, assuring him there was a spectacular battle, a lot of laughs, and Jeanne Moreau, whom he'd heard of.

However, the film was Shakespeare, a tough ask without subtitles for someone with English as a second language. Claudio started to fidget and look at his Apple watch. Russell was lost in the images, the language and the performances. Claudio began to think longingly of the nearest pub or wine bar. It's not a particularly long film but to him it seemed endless.

When the action is over, the camera pans over the wintry countryside with Falstaff's coffin pushed laboriously through the snow by his entourage; Ralph Richardson intones something from Holinshed's *Chronicles*. Claudio gathered his things with unseemly haste and made to leave. Russell grabbed his arm.

'Sit down,' he whispered. 'It's not finished yet.'

211

'It finished ages ago,' retorted Claudio.

'But I've got to see the credits,' protested Russell. He always stayed to the bitter end, through Second Unit Director, Gaffer and caterers. Besides, he liked the music of Angelo Francesco Lavignino, whom he'd discovered through a couple of Italian beefcake movies.

'The pub will be closed.'

'Only five minutes ...'

'For this shit?'

'Don't knock what you don't understand.'

'Don't patronise me.'

And so it went on, hissed, until Claudio clattered out regardless. He stood on the edge of Greenwich Park, breathing heavily in the dark. He took his phone off flight mode and dialled a much-used number.

'Hello, Duggie. Can I see you tonight? Yes, he's at it again. Always belittling me. Can I stay over? ... I don't care what he thinks. He can stick his *Sight and Sound* up his arse. Probably give him more satisfaction than I can these days ...'

Russell calmed his own breathing as the credits rolled up, seemingly endlessly, first for the original film then for the restoration, then for the distribution company.

He sat on, motionless, contemplating the screen, and the future. It faded to black with the words ...

... THE END

THE AUTHORS

Talim Arab:

Talim is an award-winning novelist, author of *Sexual Mathematics* and *The Square-Shaped Tear*. He was born in London and grew up in Queensland, Australia, which he revisits often. He has a passion for pianos, ballet, opera and good coffee. He is a Fellow of the Royal Society of Arts.

Kathryn Bell:

Kathryn is from Glasgow originally, and now lives in East London. She writes short stories, some of which appeared in the anthologies Queer Haunts and A Boxful of Ideas, and would like to write a novel, but lacks the stamina. She enjoys folk music, chocolate and arguing.

Craig Binch:

Craig is a 45-year-old nurse by profession and has had an interest in writing since childhood. He joined the writing workshops earlier this year and enjoyed the experience. He says, 'Exploring Flash gave me the opportunity to flex my creative writing skills and challenge myself in different ways. It has been a springboard, and I won't stop.'

Howard Bradshaw:

Howard made his film debut in 'Three Men in a Boat' (1956) feeding a bun to an elephant. He would have been in the world premiere recording of Benjamin Britten's *War Requiem*, but his voice broke. He made a career of writing 'fillers' for various newspapers and continuity for ATV. He has never kissed Peter Tatchell, but not for want of trying. His rendition of *You're a Pink Toothbrush* is a favourite of the Pensioners' Clubs.

Ross Burgess:

Ross lives in Scotland with his husband, Peter, sharing an elegant flat in Edinburgh and a 17th-century house in Falkland, Fife. They were an item in their 20s, never lost touch, and came together again in their 70s. Since retiring from IT Ross concentrates on writing and editing, mainly for the Falkland Society. He has designed and typeset several GAW publications. He shares with Peter an enthusiasm for conserving ancient buildings. www.peterandross.uk.

CJ Cass-Horne:

C.J. Cass-Horne is based in London. He has written a poetry collection *Dandelion Tea* and the short story anthology *Tulip Tears and Other Short Stories*, both of which were acclaimed. With years of writing experience under his belt, he is now preparing a memoir that promises to share an engaging narrative about his family. He does not share photographs.

Kevin Crowe:

Has had fiction, non-fiction and poetry in many outlets, print and online. Author of short story collection *No Home In This World*. Ex-editor of the Highland LGBT+ magazine *UnDividingLines*. Has worked in factories, social care, as HIV/AIDS worker and was bookshop and restaurant owner. Has been a volunteer for trade unions, homeless groups, LGBT+ groups and his local foodbank. He lives in the Highlands with his husband.

Stephanie Dickinson:

Stephanie trained as a primary school teacher in her thirties, which took all her time and energy! Once retired, she had the time and opportunity to develop a range of diverse interests, with a particular focus on writing, especially poems and short stories. She has co-edited *We Want to Tell you How...*, an anthology of poetry and prose celebrating women's loves, lives and landmarks.

John Dixon:

John Dixon has published two volumes of short stories, *The Carrier Bag* and *Whispering Campaigns*, and two poetry collections — *Seeking, Finding, Losing* and *Fancy That*. In preparation he has a novel, *Push Harder, Mummy, I Want to Come Out*, and a selection of diary entries.

Ian Everton:

Ian was a pioneer, coming out at school aged 14 and founding Sheffield CHE [Campaign for Homosexual Equality] in 1971. His novel, *Alienation*, was published by GMP [Gay Men's Press] in 1982. In December 2022 he married Syd, his partner of 50 years. He fought failing health and social workers with equal ferocity, and died in May 2024. He is greatly missed.

Christian Fletcher:

Christian was raised in the north in a large family. He has lived in London for more than half his life. He is a keen observer on life and spends much of his time travelling, often off the beaten track. In other lives he does crosswords, works in I.T. [sometimes] and frequents Wetherspoons. Recently he has been in Brazil — and Brazilians.

Allison Fradkin:

Allison Fradkin (she/her) has a gay old time creating poetry, prose, and plays that (sur)pass the Bechdel Test. She has contributed to *The MockingOwl Roost*, *Eggplant Emoji*, *The Queer Gaze*, *Vita & the Woolf*, *Snowflake Magazine*, and *Gnashing Teeth*; as well as the collections *Frozen Women/Flowing Thoughts* (Palmetto Press) and *Sapphic Eclectic* (Butterworth Books).

David Flybury:

David Flybury was born in Suffolk in 1963, moved to London in 1984, worked various jobs, met his husband in 1997, married in 2021 and lives now occupied by the normalities of domestic tranquillity, plus the internet. His novel *The Dalliance*, and short stories *Fragmentarium*, deal with growing up, coming out, relationships and death, travel, Art, and history ... and a few other things. Oh, and sex.

Frances Gapper:

Frances Gapper lives in the UK's Black Country with her partner Deryn and next door's cat. A retired subeditor of trade and business journals, her flashes have been published in four Best Microfiction anthologies and online in lit mags including Splonk, Wigleaf, Gooseberry Pie, Forge and Literary Namjooning.

Tania Gardner:

Tania Gardner (she/they) a queer writer/actor who hopes to keep being a storyteller for a long time to come. Represented by Lark Management. Work includes: *Deep Six* (Shortlisted for BAFTA Rocliffe TV), *Doctor Who: The War Master, The City of the Sick* (Big Finish Audio Drama), *Fly Girl* (BBC Radio). Theatre credits inc. *Whose Crime* (Arcola Theatre), *Blood Orange* (Old Red Lion).

Jess Glaisher:

Jess is a queer, disabled writer, performer, and drag king. Their debut novel *Dear Lina* appeared in 2020, 'A queer dystopia for our troubled times'. Her story *Hairless* won second place in the Dinesh Allirajah Prize 2024, and her play *Dyke Drama* was longlisted for BOLD Playwrights 2024. Their work has appeared online, and in print. They are currently working on a horror short collection and a second novel.

David Godolphin:

David Godolphin (who also writes as David Gee) has worked in telecommunications and journalism in London and the Persian Gulf. He has published five novels, including The Paradise Press, 2014) and, most recently, *Soap-Stud & Blue-Movie Girl* (as David Godolphin, Conrad Press, 2022). He lives near Brighton. His website/blog: www.davidgeebooks.com

Bodicea Iceni:

Bodicea the cycling poet was born and raised in London. She started writing at a women's writing circle in 2023. Her first story (p.185) was influenced by her reconnection with foraging during lockdown. A practitioner of vipassana meditation, she employs eastern philosophies to inform her world view and her writing. She now lives in south London and writes poems and short stories.

Philip Inglesant:

Philip Inglesant has been making up stories in his head for over 50 years but only put fingers to keyboard with the prompting of GAW's workshops. He loves short stories, especially those of Tennessee Williams, and aspires to write as well as this. Maybe with enough practice and GAW's help he might stand in TW's shadow.

Rainer King:

Rainer King is a queer writer of colour with a passion for creativity and storytelling. When they aren't exploring nature, reading or expressing themselves through writing and painting, they can be found relaxing with their two beloved cats, Bailey and Kit.

David Lindley-Pilley:

David has dipped his toes back into the creative writing pool after an almost 14-year hiatus,. He's loved to explore a range of genres through the 'Flash Fiction' workshops and hopes what he's written there will be the springboard to writing something a little longer in the near future. His work and his other passion is acting, so perhaps something dramatic is in the offing?

Susan Miller:

Susan Miller is a long-standing GAW member who lives with her wife and little black cat in Brixton, London. She really enjoyed the chance to create Flash Fiction. She's addicted to cosy crimes, and is keen to try writing one. A sub-editor of news, sports and business stories who loves the fun of creative writing.

Katerina Mimikou:

Born in 1997 in Athens, Katerina Mimikou studied Fine Art at the University of the Arts London and works as an artist and writer. She has published a poetry collection (*T'Agriohorta*, 2024), a self-published short story (*The White Pillowcase*, 2021) and a play-essay (*The Maenads*, 2021). Her work has appeared in *Soanyway Magazine*, *In Between Knots* and *Recipes for Resistance*, among others. She has taken part in book fairs and art festivals in Wales.

Thai O'Reilly:

Thai writes: 'Before joining the workshops I'd only written the odd poem, nothing 'official'. I didn't think I'd have any of my work included in an anthology like this (so soon!), so it's very inspiring to share something with the world. It was a challenge that I enjoyed, and I allowed myself to escape by drawing on my passions for the spoken word and creative writing/poems. Hope you enjoy. x' Thai works as a support worker for Stonewall Housing.

Alison Rice-Murphy:

Alison Rice-Murphy is a bisexual writer/translator living in Exmouth, UK. Her poetry has been published in the magazine *She Speaks* (2021), online journal *The Lickety~Split* (2023), and the anthology *Desire* (2024) She has performed her poetry on The Globe stage as part of Shakespeare and Race: Spoken Word(s) (2022) and on Crossword Lyric's show on Voices Radio (2024). She translates Chinese poetry and prose.

Hastie Salih:

Hastie published her debut romantic thriller *Dahlia and Carys* in 2023 and has had short stories and poems published in anthologies. She worked as a GP and GP trainer and currently lives in East London. She is a member of the RCGP, the BMA, Exiled Writers Ink, the Royal Society of Literature, Paradise Press and GLADD. Her hobbies are reading and writing, walking in nature, Zumba and playing with Misty the cat. www.hastie-salih.com.

Peter Scott-Presland:

Peter has been a writer/director/performer for over 50 years. He worked for *Capital Gay* and other LGBT+ papers and magazines. Of his plays, *Sir Herbert Macrae: A Tribute* and *Woody Shavings* won a Fringe First, and *Here It Comes* was nominated for Best Musical in the Evening Standards awards 1974. *Dorothy's Travels (1992)* and *La Ronde (2010)* were similarly nominated in Toronto and London.

Laurence Sullivan:

Laurence Sullivan's work has appeared in over seventy publications, such as 'Londonist', 'The List' and 'NHK World-Japan'. He became inspired to start writing at university [Kent, Utrecht, and Birmingham] after being immersed in all forms of global literature. In 2023, he completed his PhD at Northumbria University, analysing literary portrayals of women's domestic medical practice during the eighteenth century.

Richard Mark Thompson:

Richard Mark Thompson, is a multifaceted creative. An accomplished fabric designer, also he has credits as a performer, a vocalist, songwriter and musician. Richard has worked with many artists including vocalist Ruby Turner, and actors Kate Williams and Anna Karen; penned the lyrics for BBC-1's *South Of The Border*, and performed at the Theatre Royal, Stratford East. His semi-autobiographical book *The Black Closet* will be published in spring 2025.

Leigh V Twersky:

Leigh was born in London, where he lives. His stories have appeared in *Chroma*, *A Boxful of Ideas* and *Lost Places* (both Paradise Press) and *A Coup of Owls*. His dystopian debut novel, *Olympia Heights*, is also published by Paradise Press. He is delighted to have two poems in Flash Dances. For more information see: leighvtwersky.co.uk/

Shaf Ullah:

Shaf says, 'I am a conjurer. I bring tales from India and my imagination into conversations with the paper. My stories are full of dreams and colour, and remind me of when I was in the 3rd grade watching out the window, travelling across the veins of the jackfruit tree leaves while the teacher sang her dictation. The class would end, but my mind would be buzzing with stories of fairies that lived in that tree, standing proud in the school yard.' He is also a lecturer at the Fashion Retail Academy.

Elsa Wallace:

Elsa Wallace (1939-2018) lived in Africa until she was thirty, moving to East London in 1969. She joined Gay Authors Workshop in 1978 and published a novel, *Merle*, a novella; *A Short History of Lord Hyaena*, and three short story collections — *The Monkey Mirror, Ghosts and Gargoyles,* and *Kissyface.* Her favourite authors were Ivy Compton-Burnett and Charles Dickens.

SOURCES OF ILLUSTRATIONS

STORY	PAGE	SUBJECT	CREDIT
Contents	vii	Tolstoy	Caricature by'Snapp', Vanity Fair, 1901
Bear/Bare	7	Trophy Black Bear	Shot in N. India, 1885. A.A.A.Kinloch, 1838-1919
Sticky	14	Wrapper	Peter Scott-Presland
Four Black Dresses	44	Illustration	**David Shenton**
Missing	56	Illustration	**David Shenton**
Little White Dog	82	Illustration	**David Shenton**
First and Only	105	Ptarmigan	George Edwards, Yale Centre for British Art
As I Lay Talking...	118	Cartoon	'After The Carnival', F. Opper Library of Congress
This isn't me	120	Cartoon	'Mr Sothern and Yorick's Skull', Carlo de Fornaro, The Critic, 1903
Monogamy	125	Illustration	**David Shenton**
Going West	142	Cowboy	Frontispiece of 'Arizona Argonauts' [1924]. Artist unknown
Liebestod	160	Black Widow spider (female)	James Gathany for US Centre for Disease Control
The Wedding	162	Indian wedding	Marriage Procession in a Bazaar, Mandi, 1645. Arrival of the groom. Metropolitan Museum of Art
Perspective	184	Mayfly	Davide 125 https://commons.wikimedia.org/ wiki/File:Ephemeroptera01.jpg
Forager's Delight	187	Illustration	**David Shenton**
Leftovers	198	Koi Carp	Joe Mabel, 2007. Washington Park Arboretum, Seattle
A Chip off the Old Block	207	Illustration	**David Shenton**

All images apart from those by David Shenton are taken from Wikimedia Commons, and have been licensed.

Homo Promos ...

... is London's oldest LGBTQ+ theatre group, founded in 1987, although its predecessor, *Consenting Adults in Public*, goes back to 1980. It has been committed to running workshops since its inception, and to collaborative working with cabaret performers, other queer companies, and the London Gay Symphony Orchestra. This project is a continuation of that tradition. It has a particular interest in music theatre, and its last piece, *Home Fires*, about Ivor Novello's imprisonment, was banned by the Home Office.

It won the 2021 International Lesbian and Gay Cultural Network Award for its continuous series of 66 Zoom performances during the COVID crisis.

Explore https://homopromos.org

Edinburgh 1981

PARADISE PRESS ...

... is the publishing arm of the Gay Authors Workshop. It was founded in 1999 and has since specialised in anthologies of new queer writing, though it also publishes individual members of G.A.W., and offers editorial support.

Most recent publications are:

We Want to Tell You How... [2018]
Lost Places [2023]
A Boxful of Ideas [2016]
Olympia Heights [2024] by Leigh V Twersky

Explore the catalogue at www.paradisepress.org.uk

GAY AUTHORS WORKSHOP ...

... was founded in 1978, and is a co-operative of LGBTQ+ writers of poetry, drama, fiction and non-fiction. It organises meetings, both online and in person, to read, discuss and develop work in progress; it also sends out a regular newsletter and welcomes members' contributions to that, including reviews of other books and articles/essays.

There is a small annual subscription.

THE GAY AUTHORS WORKSHOP/
HOMO PROMOS WRITING WORKSHOPS

G.A.W./H.P. jointly ran a series of workshops in Spring/Summer 2024, from which much of the material in *Flash Dances* was derived. Six of the writers here testify as to the beneficial galvanising effect of these sessions on their work.

Bodicea Iceni:
I enjoyed the camaraderie of the group, really fun and supportive, in a range of tasks that stimulated, challenged and extended our skills as writers. My writing has moved on in leaps and bounds.

Shaf Ullah:
I loved the collaborative effort that went into creating these brilliant stories. The moderators Peter and Stephanie helped guide each of us to achieve something we'd always wished for and give us that gentle push. I looked forward to meeting up once a week. It was a privilege being part of such a dynamic group!

Philip Inglesant:
The workshops gave me the push I needed to start writing. Also very enjoyable and great to meet so many like-minded people!

Craig Binch:
I have dreamed of writing for a long time, the workshop has given me a window into the art of flash fiction and allowed me to flex and challenge my own imagination. I have the bug and now I can't stop!

Thai O'Reilly:

It was a new experience for me. The workshops made me feel comfortable and at ease to explore my writing without feeling judged. For a newbie, I felt right at home, they enabled an environment where I had a sense of creative freedom! More please.

Susan Miller:

I rediscovered my love of writing at the workshops. They were well run, fun and challenging all at the same time.

Gay Authors Workshop always welcomes new members and hopes to continue the workshop process. If you are interested in joining the group, or coming along to future workshops, email:

info@gayauthorsworkshop.uk